# THE
# BURNED SPY

## K. A. KRANTZ

## AN IMMORTAL SPY NOVEL

*The Burned Spy; The Immortal Spy: Book 1*
Copyright © 2017 by Kristine A. Krantz All rights reserved.
First Print Edition: January 2018

Cover and Formatting: Gene Mollica Studios, LLC

Published 2018 by K.A. Krantz

www.KAKrantz.com

Print ISBN-13: 978-0-9862537-3-7
Ebook ISBN-13: 978-0-9862537-2-0

Printed in the United States of America

*For Lexi*
*&*
*The Disastrophy*

# CHAPTER 1

The antidote burned worse than the toxin. Bix threw her head back and swore. Heat oozed through every cell, from the tips of her tangled teal hair to her broken, grimy toenails. Jörmungandr, ageless and accursed Norse serpent god, retracted his fangs from her forearm. His forked tongue laved the holes he'd caused, holes that finally broke the runic tracking spells embedded in her scars.

"Why did you summon me back from exile, Jör?" Bix muttered, enduring revulsion's crawl for the relief of his cure. Devolving past filthy and bedraggled in the ether was bad enough, but to be in such a state before a god whose personal fastidiousness bordered on compulsive made her criminal status all the more humiliating.

"Orders." He leaned back in the padded conference room chair and poured himself a glass of something that looked like water but smelled of vodka. His strong thighs kept her penned.

"Orders?" She turned her head away from his unflinching regard as he swished his drink in his mouth. She stared out the wall of windows overlooking the vast dark glaciers of Helheim illuminated by the aurora of the dead. "From whom this time? The judges at my trial? Did they rope you into being their sheriff again?"

"Don't be mad at me for doing my job," he chided. "The

only way to exile a woman who can cross Worlds wherever she wants, whenever she wants is to make sure she doesn't want to go anywhere. Turning you into a plague carrier guaranteed you stayed out of the Mid Worlds."

"You damned me to the ether between Worlds. No World would have me, no one would help me, no god would feed me." She met his glittering golden gaze. "You made me starve, Jör. You promised you never would, yet you did."

"Let me atone for my sins." He unbuttoned his crisp white shirt. "Let me feed you now."

"No." She shook her head. "Never again. You ruined what little trust was between us."

Large glass doors slammed against the conference room's tinted walls. Blasts of frigid air marked the arrival of Hel, goddess of the Norse Under World and current boss of the entire pantheon. Hel slapped a stack of glossy pages against her studded leather hip and arched a white brow.

"Jörmungandr, I said cured and dressed," Hel admonished. "That means cleaning her up too."

"Just getting to the fun part, sister dear." The serpent god snapped his fingers.

The funk of surviving in the ether slid from Bix like a serpent's molt. Her hair detangled as her locks twisted and twirled into a style. 1940s victory rolls, by the feel. Simple magic trimmed, buffed, and painted her nails dark iridescent green. Jör puckered his lips and tilted his head. He tapped the air, and clothes made of the basic building blocks of all Worlds whirled into being. A dress with a daring sweetheart neckline and long sleeves fitted to her form. He even deigned to make it in her preferred shade of burned-spy black.

She didn't need to see her undergarments to know they conformed to Jör's favorite style. There had been a time when the two of them had been so intimate that she knew his predilections almost as well as he knew her weaknesses.

"Shoes," Bix prompted, wiggling her newly pedicured feet.

"Oh, but of course. Who is Bix the Gatekeeper without her garish and impractical shoes?" Jör pointed at the ground. Block-heel pumps with zombie mice patterns appeared.

Snake humor. Not actually funny.

"It's not like I ever run anywhere now, is it?" Bix steadied herself on the long conference table as her legs reacclimated to shoes, walking, and gravity. "I didn't even run from you."

"You've never really wanted to." Jör watched Bix without blinking as she put distance between them.

Bix couldn't kill the mighty guardian of the Mid Worlds. It wasn't for a lack of desire; that she'd harbored for years while he'd acted simultaneously as her benefactor and tormentor. Gods simply didn't die. At worst, they were neutralized, drained of their powers, and left adrift in the ether. Once she figured out how to relieve Jör of his mojo, she'd skin him. The smarmy snake would make a couple thousand mighty fine handbags in any World.

Snakeskin never went out of style.

"Are you two done playing house yet?" Hel demanded.

"My sentence was one hundred and eighty years, Hel." Bix adjusted her corset, wincing as Jör's antidote seeped through her system. "It's only been ten years, seven months, three weeks, four days, and eight hours. What could possibly make you go against the ruling of the Consortium by summoning me?"

The four most powerful magical races—gods, Fates, dragons, and angels—oversaw the protection, population, and very existence of the hundreds of Mid Worlds. This collaborative, representative governing body was known as the Consortium.

Bix despised every single member.

"Think of this as a chance for early parole." Hel slung a page at Bix's feet. "A great transgression has been committed against my pantheon."

Bix glanced at the photo and grimaced. "A living sacrifice? That's bad for public relations."

"That's not a sacrifice. It's a trip through a meat grinder." Hel tossed another photo at her, then another and another.

3

"You have armies of minions possessing any number of magics. Why me?" Bix rolled her shoulders. For the first time in years, her insides didn't writhe with a billion magical bacteria feasting on her.

"Take a closer look at what you see." Hel chucked the final picture at her.

A small metal gargoyle with raised claws and curved horns lay amid a pile of shredded organs and muscles. She recognized that gargoyle. It was a pendant. A unique one crafted especially for her. A gift she'd given a girlfriend not long after they'd started dating. A girlfriend she hadn't seen since she'd been arrested.

Bix's hand trembled as she retrieved the final photo. Vomit burned her throat. She swallowed five times before words made it past her lips.

"Explain to me why I am looking at eviscerated remains containing the pendant I gave one of your goddesses." Bix gripped the picture in both quivering hands, burning away Hel's frost coating the glossy page. "What did you let happen to Mirri?"

"Don't you dare question me, creature." Hel flicked her wrist.

The tiny gesture slammed Bix against a wall more solid than stone. The husks of millions of souls sucked at flesh and fabric. Those desperate souls had the strength to hold any denizen of any World in place for a god's tortures, but their strength relied on proximity to their prey for success. As a gatekeeper with a specialty in creating passages from anywhere to anywhere, proximity was wholly under Bix's control.

With one thought, she opened a gate between her and the desiccated dead. A second thought opened a gate in the middle of the discarded photographs. One tiny step relocated her across the conference room.

Distance on demand. Easy-peasy. And infuriating as all get-out to the gods.

Bix smoothed her skirt and smiled to annoy Hel. Never mind that her back throbbed. It felt good to remind the gods their powers had limitations. Sure, gods could go wherever they wished;

however, what and who they could take with them had all kinds of restrictions. Some political. Some magical.

A gatekeeper of Bix's caliber was limited only by her ability to control the size of the gateways. Nose piercing. City block. Anything in between. Smaller was harder because it required more attention to details. Larger was riskier because it threatened the stability of the Worlds involved in the relocation.

"After your trial, Mirri assumed her place as our pantheon's ambassador to the Mid Worlds." Hel glared at the ceiling. "The others thought a goddess of healing would be best suited to smooth over certain troubles. She was protected by an elite team of Chwedlonol."

"Chwedlonol? The hodgepodge of magical beings in the Mids? You entrusted her life to Chwedlonol?" Bix choked on incredulity. "Not even I would have trusted Chweds to protect a goddess."

Hel sauntered toward her. "Are you calling me a fool?"

Bix repressed a shiver. Hel was every bit the daughter of a chaos god and a giantess. Pale eyes filled with the unabridged wisdom and knowledge of an incalculably long life bored into Bix's. Bix held her ground and the goddess's gaze.

Give a god a flinch and they'd own you.

"Chwed elite teams are part of the Cross-World Intelligence Guild." Bix tapped her own chest. "I was a member of the CWIG's elite. Again, I say, not even I would have trusted them to protect a goddess."

"Precisely. Now, do you still need me to explain why I've released you?" Hel angled her head until her lips hovered a breath away from Bix's.

"I'm more than happy to take on the guild that disavowed me, but I'm not going to stop there." Bix deliberately let her lips graze the goddess's. Raw energy singed her skin, awakening her hunger. She hadn't fed since the night before she'd been arrested. Exile had taught her the cruel lesson that she couldn't die of starvation. During the early days of famine, she'd prayed to anything listening that death would free her from the agonies of feeling her body devouring itself. When that had failed, she'd clung to the fraying threads of sanity by focusing on the pain of the infection Jör had given her. Eventually, her body had gone numb to everything. Eventually, her mind had learned to move past internal desperation to focus on the dangers around her.

Mere minutes in Hel's presence, and all that training vanished. Her stomach scrabbled for sustenance, and she was helpless to resist. Shuddering, she closed her eyes and sucked in the potent magic rolling off the goddess.

"The other pantheons have been alerted to your release, as have the Fates." Hel stroked her cheek as Bix drew in another dose of divinity. "I will notify the dragons and the angels after you and I are done here. It's been one day in the time of the Mid Worlds since Mirri was forced to flee her mortal body."

"Where is Mirri now?" Bix tried to focus on the conversation as her insides unknotted, unclenched, and begged for more. "Is she here in Helheim?"

"Frejya answered Mirri's cry." Hel pulled away. "It is she who confirmed the remains belonged to Mirri. She took her niece to Asgard."

Bix whimpered. She was nowhere near sated. If anything, she idled in the reawakened throes of desperate hunger. Damn it all. Still, she wouldn't beg either god in the room. Hunger would not be the trap they used to ensnare her. Jör stared at her through his heavy-lidded gaze with his knowing smirk firmly in place. She would repeat the long torment of starvation before she fed from him again. His sister watched her with equal smugness.

Bix forced her feet to take two steps back from Hel.

"Great." Bix cleared her throat. "I'll start there."

Mirri had collected artists' renderings of Asgard, and the only thing Bix needed to complete a gateway was a mental image of her destination. She could easily bypass the gods tasked with keeping her out of Asgard if she knew precisely where in that Upper World Frejya was hiding Mirri.

Frejya probably had the Valkyries protecting her niece. All Bix had to do was find a Valkyrie. Good thing she knew their favorite haunts in the Mids.

"Frejya put Mirri into stasis to save her." Hel quirked her lips. "Whatever happened completely shattered the goddess within the girl. Even if you could get near Mirri, she couldn't tell you anything. Her mind is nothing more than slivers."

Something moved beneath Bix's flesh, wriggling along her back from hip to nape. She kept perfectly still, unwilling to show any fear in front of these gods. But so help her, if Jör hadn't really cured her, she'd open gateways from the ether into every blasted World and start a thousand wars.

"I see hate in your face, creature," Hel cautioned. The air between her fingers sparked, and the temperature in the room dropped. "Be mindful in your choices, or I will be swift in my actions."

Bix took a deep, steadying breath. There was a time to be a dervish and a time to be deliberate.

Interrogating a fragile immortal goddess would be like hunting a dust mote through a house of mirrors, each turn reflecting a distorted memory overlaid by fear and tinted with a nightmare. Mirri couldn't help find the sicko who had hacked up her mortal body. Rationally, Bix knew that.

Rationally.

"Where are the souls, Hel?" Bix asked. "I know neither of you let Mirri's protective detail live."

"The souls of Mirri's detail have already been drained to husks," Hel said dismissively. "Jörmungandr questioned them before he devoured the lives they'd led."

"Mirri's protective detail never saw the attack. They were surprised to be dead." Jör flopped an effeminate hand over his chest, restoring his gleefully disdainful persona.

A persona she'd once found irresistible.

"Did you think to ask what they noticed just before they died, Jör? Five minutes before? An hour? A day? Did you look at their memories to see if Mirri had been acting oddly? Did she have any unusual visitors? Visit any shady destinations? Did you attempt anything remotely resembling a proper interrogation of witnesses? Or did your limitless ego end interrogations early?" Bix toed the remaining photos around each other until their backgrounds formed a complete image of the setting of the crime. This wasn't about a person. This wasn't about someone she knew, someone with whom she'd enjoyed spending time.

This was about a job. She had to be impersonal in order to be successful.

She'd been freed to exact a price for the heinous mauling of a Norse goddess. No more. No less.

"If the answers were obvious, you wouldn't be here." Hel perched on the edge of the conference table. "The slaughter of Mirri's mortal body in the Mid Worlds goes against the conventions of peaceful shared rule to which all members of the Consortium agreed. Such a violation is an act of war, but the pantheons are divided in their support of such an undertaking."

"Gods unable to agree on something other than my exile? Shocking." Bix walked a slow circle around the puzzle of pictures, studying every nuance. The torn edge of a weed. The sheared fork of a branch. The stains of blood.

The spatter on the ground was wrong. Way wrong. There were no voids where an assailant should have stood. The remains were piled on a huge tree stump, but no hack marks appeared on the stump.

The scene had either been tampered with after the attack or staged before it. That gave her a place to start the investigation.

"Politics within the Consortium is what it is. I will worry about that." Hel opened her hand. Glacial fire leapt from her palm and engulfed the hateful pictures strewn around the floor. The picture in Bix's hands remained untouched. "Sadly, said politics makes a factual inquest into Mirri's passing impossible for even the most determined among us."

"It led us to think of you." Jörmungandr tugged the French

cuffs of his tailored shirt. "Who better to hunt Mirri's assailant than the lover who abandoned her?"

Bix bit her tongue.

Fucking. Handbag.

"Your relationships in the Mid Worlds make you the ideal candidate to find the guilty party on behalf of the Norse pantheon." Hel clenched her fist, extinguishing cold flames. "Bring the soul to me for punishment. I don't care what you do to or with the body."

Bix inclined her head. "What if the soul is contracted to another god in another pantheon?"

"Bring. It. To. Me." Hel leaned forward and curled a lip. "Mirri is of my pantheon. I take her mauling exceedingly personally."

Bix studied the assortment of harried minions darting between cubicles beyond the conference room. Pantheons had evolved from Other World frat houses into multi-World corporations, feeding off the souls who dared believe in them. As communications traversed physical borders, so too did the myriad faiths and religions. The living's quest for knowledge beyond their singular World had unleashed an era of unmitigated godly greed.

She had no intention of being absorbed into the rapacious expansions directed by eternally power-hungry and morally ambivalent gods. Contracts were key to maintaining one's independence.

"If I'm to be your assassin, Hel, there is a price."

"Freedom and vengeance aren't enough?" Jör shook his curls from his face. "Greedy, creature."

"You need me because I am the only *creature* not beholden to the Consortium. The same thing that damned me now makes me useful." Bix pressed the picture of the pendant to her chest. The pain in her back concentrated between her shoulder blades like sporks scraping at her spine. "My independence makes me politically unpopular while making me a backroom darling. I am not an idiot."

"But you are careless, or you would never have been caught," Jör taunted.

"Enough," Hel barked. "Name your price, creature."

"Let's start with the obvious, my sentence commuted. The remaining hundred and seventy years your peers really want me to serve? I don't. No tracking devices. No parole officers. No check-ins, check-ups, or random inspections. No conditions of any sort, just pure unadulterated freedom from the moment I deliver the soul to you."

"They'll insist on some sort of leash," Hel countered.

"Free and clear or not at all," Bix insisted.

Hel inclined her head. "What else do you want?"

"Twice I have dragged myself out of the ether. This little meeting being the second. The first time was thirty years ago, when I had no concept of who or what I am. I barely knew enough to breathe and to flee. Slowly, I cobbled together a life in the Mids that required no memories, just abilities." Bix rubbed the bite marks on her arm. "Then your brother came along and told me I had a history, a long glorious history of which he possessed parts from my perspective, but if I wanted to learn any of it, I had to become his pet."

"Not quite the terms of our deal." Jör tutted.

"My memories, Hel," Bix said, ignoring him. "Jör will give me back my memories. All of them. Unmodified. Unedited."

Then she could be free of the handbag once and for all. Then she could finally know whether she was a freak or a member of a race from far beyond the ether. Maybe she had a family; after all, she had to be someone's daughter. It was horrifying to think that she might even have a daughter of her own who was right now wondering why her mother had abandoned her. Even if all her family had died, surely she had had friends.

Someone somewhere had to be missing her, didn't they?

Thirty years of memories might be normal for a short-lived human, but she wasn't human. That she hadn't aged in thirty years said she was long-lived, possibly even immortal. The long-lived accrued enemies far faster than they accrued wrinkles. She needed her memories back so she would know the faces of those who meant her harm.

As it stood, her lack of memories left her vulnerable and scrambling to protect herself.

"To appropriately apply a phrase, 'Oh, Hel, no,'" Jör scoffed. "You don't want to start in the middle of the story."

"Creature, you divided your memories among seven keepers in seven pantheons because you could not stand the pain of owning them." Hel braced her hands on her knees and peered at Bix through narrowed eyes. "Jörmungandr possesses only a fragment. A fragment without the whole is infinitely more dangerous than not having memories at all."

"I *chose* to forfeit my memories?" Bix rubbed her temple. Why would she have done that? What sort of insanity had driven her to do something so stupid? Had she—like Mirri—survived some sort of horrific ordeal only to seek a fool's solace in emptiness? Had there been no one left who cared enough about her to stop her from being so rash? "Who else has my memories?"

"I cannot divulge such things without jeopardizing the Norse. Discretion is part of the contract you made with the assorted pantheons when you were divested of your past." Hel smirked and shrugged. "I can only trade the possessions under my purview."

"Only if I agree, which I don't," Jör objected.

"Then you shouldn't have dangled them as bait to keep her coming back to feed from you, dear brother," Hel noted dryly, keeping her attention on Bix.

At some point in her life, Bix had wielded enough influence to sit at a table with all the Very Important Players of the pantheons. She hadn't been a mere gatekeeper. She'd been something more. She'd been someone multiple pantheons had wanted to *help*. What could possibly have their united positive regard? The concept alone was absurd.

Yet here she was with one of the most powerful gods asking her for assistance.

"Fine." Bix lifted her chin. "My freedom plus all my memories that Jör possesses in exchange for the soul of the fiend who assaulted Mirri. Some memories are better than none."

"Not for you," Jör muttered.

Hel held up her hand to silence her brother. "If you fail to deliver on this contract, creature, you will return to the ether to serve out the rest of your sentence. There will be no second chance of parole."

"I understand." Bix nodded.

"Then we have a deal." Hel smiled with a hint of cruelty. "Your time is finite. You have seven days in the time of the Mids before I go to Mirri herself and rip the answers from her."

Bix locked down her emotions before they betrayed her. "If she is so fragile she had to be put into stasis, forcibly taking those answers from her will completely destroy her. There will be nothing recognizable left of her."

"Tick-tock, then," Jör goaded.

A parchment sizzled into existence and unrolled along the conference table.

Bix gave Jör a wide berth as she approached the table. She took the paper made of souls and scanned the fine print.

Gods. Always ready to screw you.

"I will follow the investigation wherever it leads." Bix sliced her polished nail through the objectionable paragraph and slid the amended scroll over to Hel. "That includes direct interaction with the prosecutors and key witnesses from my trial. If anyone gets in my way, I will remove them—regardless of their membership in the Consortium. Managing all escalations is on you. Politics is your bailiwick."

Hel slid the contract to her brother. "If that's your only amendment, I'll accept it."

Jör's head tipped and his lips pursed. Hel stared him down. Ice spread in a crackling web across the floor and up his boots. A few moments of frosty protracted silence passed between the siblings, yet something in the standoff appeased his ego. He finally initialed the amendment and gave the contract back to his sister. Hel pressed her hand into the document, and Bix laid hers next to Hel's. Souls sucked at their palms, creating a binding imprint in the document. Bix shuddered and wiped her hand on her skirt.

"The fine print, Bix?" Hel snared Bix's chin with the edge of her sharp fingernail. "You are no longer a Dark Operations agent for the CWIG. I am your boss for the duration of this contract. Your actions reflect on me. If you start a war among the Consortium, then I will drain you past the point of remembering how to breathe and leave your husk to drift in a place far worse than the ether."

"Hel, the very fine print?" Bix closed her eyes and envisioned the crime scene. "If you serve me up to the Consortium for any reason, gnomes will turn your brother into a line of designer accessories."

It required only a memory of an image to open gates between Worlds.

The siblings' mocking laughter faded along with the rest of Hel's domain.

# CHAPTER 2

The stink of sulfur hit first. Cracked earth oozed white smoke and gasses from the coal fires raging in the old mines running below the abandoned city. Those fires had enough fuel from natural anthracite stores to burn for another two or three hundred years. Autumn foliage trapped the late morning haze, reducing visibility. In the distance, gold crosses gleamed against blue-green spires of a Catholic church. The church overlooked a pristine cemetery and graffitied sinkhole-laden roads long ago closed off with barricades of earth. Weeds battled ash for the plots of bulldozed homes. Fissures remapped the old mining town into an apocalyptic warning zone.

Centralia, Pennsylvania. Primary Mid World.

Bix knew it well. As an agent-in-training with the CWIG, she'd played war games here with her academy class. Seasoned agents had run the games, selecting their new team members based on performances. The town was already so wrecked that no one had paid any attention to the mayhem of magical maneuvers. The church used in a lot of modern horror films was where she'd been tapped to join clandestine services.

Good times.

But the location of the games changed every year, so what had Mirri been doing here?

Hundreds of Worlds comprised the Mids. This World, this earth, had been chosen by the Consortium to be the seat of collaborative governance due to the abundance of humans. Humans, for the most part, possessed no magic of their own; instead they grounded the native magic of the Mid Worlds and stabilized the flow of diverse magic wielded by other races.

The Consortium had set their capital amid the wetlands that had eventually become Washington, DC. Humans had been unconsciously drawn to the area by the higher concentration of magic. These days, the shared locale made it easier to blend with the indigenous humans, who couldn't handle their own interracial diversity much less coexisting with arguably superior races. Plus, the dense human population of the DC metro area effectively neutralized the surges in magic whenever tempers flared within the Consortium, which happened often.

Gods, fates, dragons, and angels all had ambassadors and their extensive support staffs residing in and around Washington, DC. Centralia was a little over three hours away by vehicle. The nearest preprogrammed cross-World gateway was an hour away. As for other gatekeepers, well, they had a habit of being assassinated. As far as Bix knew, she was the only one once again traipsing the Mids.

Mirri—a goddess locked inside a mortal body—had had to use Mid World transportation to get anywhere. She would have broken a dozen contracts had she abandoned that body to move around the Mids as an Other World goddess. Broken contracts would have rendered her useless as an ambassador. Besides, Mirri had been very, very fond of her shapely, petite mortal body.

So, some sort of vehicle as the method of transportation won out as the most viable.

Unfortunately, Centralia wasn't exactly wired, humanly or magically. No security cameras, no dryads, no flower fae, no nothing. The anthracite fires and fumes prevented squatters from lingering. Figuring out which car had brought Mirri to her attacker was a rabbit hole that would take more than seven days for Bix's team of one.

The question then became whether Mirri had been abducted by her attacker or had come by choice, then been attacked. The former required planning. The latter could have been a crime of opportunity.

In what had Mirri been involved that had pissed off someone badly enough to risk the wrath of the Norse pantheon? The culprit was either too stupid to fathom the repercussions of what they'd done, or they were geniuses applying pressure to just the right spots for a cross-World war.

Stupid would be easier to catch, but Hel wouldn't have freed her for stupid.

Bix tucked the picture of Mirri's pendant into her corset and hiked through the haze toward the sounds of activity. A sea of orange incident markers dotted five acres at the top of a modest hill. Yellow crime scene tape flapped in the chilling breeze. Generators on jacks whirred and droned beyond the tape. Low-hung string broke the hilltop into grids around the huge bull's-eye stump. Dozens of field techs wearing big white hazmat suits with CWIG stamped across their backs worked the outer grids, gathering samples and snapping photos.

Joy.

The Cross-World Intelligence Guild was still here. A day after the incident. That couldn't be good.

A parade of CWIG techs marched to and from an unmarked eighteen-wheeler idling on the cracked pavement. There was no mistaking all the stainless steel and tempered glass inside as anything but a portable lab.

More CWIG personnel in unbranded black camo prowled the base of the hill. Some carried automatic guns; others carried swords of different metals. Not every Chwedlonol was susceptible to steel or gunpowder in a copper casing. Each of the CWIG goons carried a full belt of black pouches containing assorted powders and potions for those Chwedlonol with impenetrable hides.

A decade had passed while she'd been exiled, yet basic op gear hadn't changed any more than Centralia had. Dead and dying trees covered the crime scene.

Bix opened a pair of gates and stepped from the perimeter through to the stump hosting Mirri's remains, neatly avoiding the crime-scene obstacle course created by the CWIG.

It was a fist in the gut seeing those remains. Mirri had come to the Mids to study the mental health benefits to gods of coexisting among a multitude of races. A champion of benevolence toward and respect for Chweds and humans, Mirri would spend days watching barn gnomes tending to bats or marveling at the way knockers overcame language barriers to help human miners locate minerals in dark shafts. When Mirri had discovered that human children could see beyond the glamours employed by Chweds, she'd volunteered at learning centers, trying to figure out the what, why, and how. All kinds of life in the Mids had fascinated Mirri, causing her to bubble over with infectious wonder and joy. Mirri was unlike any god Bix had known. Her guileless curiosity had ensnared Bix.

Unfortunately, that same curiosity might well have led to Mirri's horrific assault.

Bix had studied the pictures. She'd known what to expect of the crime scene, but the browning decay of Mirri's mortal body, still untouched… Bix inhaled slowly. Mirri—and what was left of her mind—was in Asgard, not rotting in Pennsyltucky. Rational thoughts. Rational, logical, impersonal thoughts.

Back to the trees. Start with safe observations of the damn trees.

The trees closest to the remains sprouted new vegetation that didn't belong in the woods of Pennsylvania, unless African wormwood and Num-Num had packed up and switched continents. Scraps of stained fabric fluttered from the highest branches of five trees near but not nearest the stump. The trees nearest had been burned.

"Only you would have the balls to surface at my crime scene looking like some Goth version of a Pearl Frush pinup poster."

Sometimes the Fates couldn't resist adding to chaos.

"Vidya Asariri," Bix said, turning around slowly. "When did HQ let analysts have guns?"

A lithe mocha-skinned woman in black camo sauntered up the hill, putting her gun back in her hip holster. Tattoos of moons in various phases peeked at the edges of her collar and sleeves. Vidya was an Oracle, and those moons depicted the successes and failures in trials set by the Fates to gauge her worthiness to join their ranks. Vidya claiming this crime scene as hers had better not turn out to be of those damn trials. Not when it involved gods. That way lay pandemonium.

Two tech wonks trailed behind the Oracle, likely loading notes into whatever latest gizmo they clutched. At the perimeter, goons trained their big guns so the little red dots peppered Bix's bosom.

"Special Agent in Investigative Services now, and don't be cute with me, Bix." Vidya winced as she neared the stump then retreated three steps. "What the hell are you doing back in the Mids? *How* the hell are you back in the Mids?"

"Tell your team to stand down, or I'll grant all of you express passes to the convergence of the Under Worlds." Bix slid a finger along her brows, straightening her bangs. "That'll be fun, for me at least."

"Any agent who knows you by reputation would try to subdue you right now," Vidya fumed. "They'd be calling in every support element they could."

"I've been terribly lonely for a very long time." Bix pouted. "I'd love a party, especially in my honor."

Vidya clenched her fists and screamed through pursed lips.

"Agent Asariri?" A disdainful guard presented Vidya with a pair of iron manacles engraved with arcane spells. "Do you need these?"

"Those aren't going to work." Vidya waved off her security guy. "She's atypical Chwed. The last known gatekeeper, in fact. Only the angels have succeeded in taking her prisoner."

The guard holding the manacles reached for a black magic bag.

"You'll contaminate evidence if you use that here." Bix tutted.

"Yeah, only slightly worse than you are," Vidya derided. "Since you're a convicted felon, I *should* arrest you on the spot."

"Do try." Bix thrust out her arms. "Let's see if I can break my personal record. Three milliseconds, wasn't it?"

"Bix…" Vidya scowled.

"No? Not going to try to arrest me? Not going to play the game, huh?" Bix wagged her wrists. "Look around. Everybody is expecting you to do *something*."

"Call the director," Vidya said to her tech minions. "Let him know we have an escaped convict on scene. Tell him it's Bix. He'll recognize the name. Ask him to advise."

"Killjoy," Bix muttered.

"The moment any of us gets too close, you'll pop to another spot, then another, and another, and another." Vidya drummed her fingers on her holster. "It's a joke to you, but there's nothing funny about what we're doing here."

"Then, in all seriousness, tell me why in the five minutes I've been standing next to this lovely pile of gore, not one of your techs has entered the inner grid." Bix pointed at the remains still on the stump. "I was never a special investigator, but I'm pretty sure body parts are supposed to be the first things collected at the crime scene. My guess is that none of you mid- or lower-caste Chweds can get near it. Where are the upper castes that are supposed to keep an eye on you?"

"They can't get near it either." Vidya signaled her men to stand down. "I've never encountered remains that repelled any caste, so it has to be whatever they're on."

"If you get me a baggie or a tray or whatever the wonks use, I can do you a solid." Bix puckered her lips and poked at the dots on her top as they lessened until three remained.

"Don't waste your bullets," Vidya hollered over her shoulder, snapping the thumb strap on her holster. "You'll end up shooting the guys from forensics."

The nearest guy in a white hazmat suit abruptly veered toward the semi. The final red dots vanished.

"Damn it, Bix, get out of there." Vidya motioned her out like she was a toddler.

So Bix acted like one.

"Make me." Bix turned her back on Vidya before she could succumb to the temptation to drop the former analyst into a very particular spot in a very particular Under World. Instead, Bix scanned the remains for the pendant. She pulled the photo from her corset and compared the image with the real thing. Absolutely every clump and cluster was the same, except for one detail.

The pendant was missing.

Bix swore. "Who tampered with the scene, Vidya? Who got closer to this stump than the lackeys laying the grid lines?"

"Up yours," Vidya spat. "Who the hell do you think you are, riding high and mighty over a location that's been secured from the moment…"

Bix glanced behind her at the sudden silence. Vidya's jade eyes changed to white. Her mouth froze in a soft pout.

Freaking Oracles. They spaced out at the most unpredictable moments, which made them unreliable in a pinch and a liability for a team in the field. Sure, they had no control over when they got visions, but that didn't excuse the risk they brought to everyone around them. CWIG management should never have assigned an Oracle to the field. Idiots.

The gizmo geeks scurried to Vidya's side. Both waited with eager smiles and twitchy fingers. Great. Scribes. Ready to jot down whatever garble and rant Vidya coughed up.

"Oh, Oracle, the here and now would be good," Bix shouted and hesitantly touched the side of the stump. When nothing happened, she rubbed at it. Dried blood came away, revealing hints of a smooth golden surface. She knocked on it. Solid, far more so than a tree stump. More like a stone. Petrified stump maybe?

"Gods damn it, Bix," Vidya blurted as though minutes hadn't passed, grabbing one gizmo from her minion and signaling the other one. "Record her every move. We need a log of everything she touches."

One of the tech minions scampered around the grid and held up a gizmo. A camera flash left spots before Bix's eyes.

"What's wrong? The director not answering your call? Not far enough up the food chain to merit an acknowledgment much less a response?" Bix's hand hovered over Mirri's remains. Warm. It'd been a day since her death, yet the remains were still warm. Autumn day. Heavy haze. Warm, but not sunbaked. Weird. She scraped the ground; char coated her fingers.

"He's probably on the phone to the angels right now, requesting they remove you from the site," Vidya snarled.

Bix high-stepped over grid markers and headed for the lab. "I hate to repeat myself, but where is the pendant?"

"What pendant?" Vidya dogged her like an aggressive basketball player. "You mean that horrible little mangle of metal that you used to wear all the time? The one Norse Ambassador Mirri took to wearing after you and I broke up?"

"Jealous much?" Bix set one pump on the ramp of the truck.

Vidya leapt up to the diamond-plated bed and body-blocked her. "It's not here. Why do you think it should be?"

Bix tipped her head back and frowned. "How exactly did you identify the remains without the pendant?"

Vidya tapped the corner of her eye. "Oracle of the Present, remember?"

Bix's heart hammered. *Please, let it be this easy.* "You saw Mirri's death?"

"Wouldn't that be incredibly convenient for all of us?" Vidya rolled her eyes. "No, I saw the political tango as the Consortium debated handing this down to the CWIG."

"Who insisted the CWIG take it?"

"None of your damn business." Vidya jumped off the truck, grabbed Bix by the elbow, and steered her away from the lab. "Every moment you're here is a moment you further compromise the investigation and the integrity of my team."

Bix dug in her heels and refused to move any farther. "I'm not sure which is more ludicrous, that you're trying to protect your team or that 'integrity' is even in your vocabulary."

"Uhm, Agent Asariri?" the minion called as his gadget chirped repeatedly. "The director says to allow her to review the site and that he wants to see her when she's done."

Vidya blinked rapidly and gawped. "Are you kidding me?"

Bix gave her a toothy smile. "Politics is grand, ain't it?"

"How did you swing this one, huh?" Vidya sighed and let go of Bix. "If you had a soul, I'd ask to whom you'd sold it."

"You should be far more concerned with your own soul, *traitor*."

A thought opened gates.

The sounds of CWIG security shouting for a search and seizure faded into the distance. Warmer air tinted with the musk of abandonment whirled around them. Streaks of struggling sunlight tumbled through the chipped shutters of the church's bell tower.

"You owe me an explanation." Bix leaned a hip against the wall.

Vidya staggered back, swearing. "Showing me your dilapidated bolt-hole may have gotten you into my pants when we were twenty-somethings, but it's not going to work now."

"I didn't bring you here to seduce you." Bix stroked the backs of her fingers over Vidya's tight black tee, checking for the pendant. "I didn't want your men to shoot you during your confession."

Vidya knocked away her hand. "What confession?"

"When a Hindu Oracle goes through CWIG orientation as an analyst, does management lock you in a basement and coerce you to sniff all sorts of things until you become an addict they completely control?" Bix crossed her arms and watched the chaos down on the hill.

"Contrary to popular belief, Oracles are not the mouthpieces of random greater powers, no matter how many psychedelics we're force-fed." Vidya backed to the far side of the bell tower. "We are Fates in training. If I pass my trials, I ascend to immortality and get threads of lives to weave. If I fail, I spend the rest of my mortal life with a corrupted brain that will render me incapable of caring for myself."

"Was the slaughter of my Dark Ops team one of your trials?" Bix sneered. "How about setting me up for exile? That something the Houses of Fate wanted too? Or was it a burn notice from the director of the CWIG? Which master did you choose to heed when you handed me the image of the *Angelic Host's armory*?"

"I didn't…" Vidya shook her head.

"Don't lie to me," Bix snapped. "I've had ten years to replay every moment. We had that op down to the direction of the wind when you called in a change of scene. If we hadn't been trying to rescue one of our own, we would have eighty-sixed the whole damn thing. But you knew that, you banked on it. You set us up."

"And where did *I* get an image of the Host's armory?" Vidya planted her hands on her hips and raised her chin. "Anyone who isn't an angel who happens across that info dies. It's an open secret."

"That's what I want to know. That's what only you can answer since *you* presented me with the photo of the new location and said the package had relo'd there." Bix mimicked Vidya's pose. Packages who were people posed a higher level of risk to the retrieval team and themselves because free will created unpredictability. For that reason, once deployed, the teams had to keep their focus forward on the mission. The guild was supposed to have their backs, but all it took was one analyst operating on contrary orders for the very worst to happen. "The angels were on us before I closed the gate. They incinerated my team. I endured all manner of interrogations from the Consortium trying to force me to confess how, oh how, I had acquired an image of the most classified and confidential secret base in all the Mids."

"The CWIG combed your trial transcripts looking for exactly

that answer." Vidya smirked. "If you wanted anyone to believe you, you should have spoken up at the trial. Now it's the word of a convicted felon against the word of a respected agent."

"I'd just lost eight team members and the package we'd been dispatched to retrieve." Bix studied the crime scene from her new vantage, noting how the trees with scraps of fabric in their boughs formed a ring outside those that had been burned. "Every Dark Ops agent knows we're shit out of luck if we get caught. The whole point of Dark Ops is the guild's plausible deniability. We don't talk, but we protect our own. We also exact our own justice."

"Using what as proof against me? The recordings of our final communication don't exist. I made sure of that." Vidya stuffed her hands in her pockets. "HQ's internal investigation put it squarely on your shoulders. As far as the CWIG is concerned, you were miffed about being passed over for a promotion. You went rogue to shame the guild. You tricked your team and got them killed in the process. There are a lot of agents who believe exile wasn't punishment enough. Then there are those who think a hundred and eighty years should've been a hundred and eighty thousand. So when you threaten me with guild justice, keep in mind they're coming for you not me."

At least the bitch admitted her involvement. Too bad it didn't come with a side of remorse and an apology chaser.

"If the CWIG investigated, then the burn order didn't come from inside. Someone else gave you the photo, a third party. The only third party to whom you are beholden is your House of Fate." Bix winced as her back twinged. "You may have destroyed the evidence that would clear my name, but it doesn't mean you're safe from your sins. I know your House's political nemesis. It will not take much to put your big bosses in a very precarious position. It shouldn't be too long before your House cleans house. Did you see that coming, Oracle?"

"My path is for the present, not the future," Vidya countered. "Besides, no House of Fate claimed responsibility for what went down, neither officially nor unofficially. You can't go after the

Houses any more than the CWIG, not without digging yourself a deeper hole."

"Nothing happens in the Mids that the Houses of Fate don't manipulate," Bix derided. "The leadership of the Houses stared at me vacuously while I was sentenced for a stunt at least one of their members set in motion. If you don't want me to ruin your House, you'd better cough up a more viable alternative."

"Why involve the Houses at all? Why not come at me directly? I can handle your wrath. I did while we dated; I doubt it's any worse now." Vidya jabbed her tongue in her cheek and raked Bix with a haughty regard. "Do you want to end me? Want to sever the Threads woven by the Fates that bind my soul to my mortal body? Are you itching to drag my essence to one of your precious gods and let them feed off me until I'm nothing more than a desiccated shell, nothing more than the basic building block of all Worlds?"

Yes, yes, actually, Bix did, but not yet.

"I will find out how you got that damn picture," Bix vowed. "I will trace it back to the shot-caller. I will delight in destroying them and their network. This grandstanding of yours isn't going to stop me. The only reason I didn't drag you out to the ether with me on the day I was convicted was because I decided your destiny would be that of bait."

"Keep fighting the battles of the past, felon." Vidya wagged her thumb at the window. "I have a job to do in the present."

"Fine. Let's focus on what's relevant to today's issue—Mirri and her mortal body." Bix flicked the corner of the photo peeking from her corset. "Dragons and angels use the native magic of the Mids to create all mortal bodies that exist here. Fish. Human. Troll. Doesn't matter. Any entity with magic that is not rooted here, the Mids actively tries to expel. Sort of like an immune system with an infection."

"Crude, but okay, I'm with you so far. The Fates get involved when there's a soul to tether to the mortal body, but gods don't have souls. They have fairly indestructible divine bodies, though, which is why my crime scene doesn't make sense."

"Rooted gods derive their power from the native magic of the Mids; therefore, the native magic accepts them in their natural deific state. They don't need contracted bodies." Bix scratched the scars in her forearm. "However, visiting gods derive their power from Other World sources, so they must contract with a dragon or an angel for a mortal body that the native magic of the Mids will welcome into its domain. Without a contracted body, a visiting god must exert considerable effort to remain here. Mirri is an Other World goddess."

"That's why the Norse ambassador was in a mortal body, and that's why there are remains for us to examine." Vidya jammed her hand in her short hair, spiking it. "That part finally fits."

"Now, here's where you might want to think like an analyst and an investigator. Something or someone forced the goddess to remain in that mortal body while great horrors were committed to her corporeal person."

Vidya finally regarded Bix without her hackles spiked. Thoughtful calculation puckered her lips and furrowed her brow. "That has to be some wicked strong magic, right? It can't be a human or any common Chwed. We're talking upper-upper-caste Chwed or one of the Consortium."

"Precisely. There are lots of implications in either of those situations. Some far worse than others." Bix stopped her mindless scratching and clutched her waist instead. "The CWIG has its thumb on the political pulse of every labor guild and every rebel faction. I need to know if this was a personal attack against the ambassador, a political volley against the Norse pantheon, or a Chwedlonol rebellion against the Consortium."

"We don't know yet." Vidya shook her head. "We don't even know if she was targeted or if she happened to be in the wrong place at the wrong time. We just started investigating. Everything is too new, and the evidence is still being collected."

"Tell me how the CWIG learned of it."

"Crap storm from on high." Vidya grimaced. "The Consortium summoned the director. He, in turn, doled out the taskers to his respective teams. The nearest CWIG field office was on site in minutes. All of Centralia was locked down within the hour. Photos were taken and sent forward to jump-start the analysis."

That explained how Hel had gotten photos of the crime scene.

"Between the time the photos were taken and I arrived, the pendant was removed from the scene." Bix huffed. "So security was lax, or someone on your team has sticky fingers."

Vidya licked her teeth and shook her head. "Take me back to the crime scene, and I can verify whether there is a photo of that disgusting gargoyle somewhere."

"Have forensics take a second look at the trees nearest the stump."

"You want me to notice that there are five nonnative and distinctly different plants growing either toward or sprouting from super stump? Yeah, we caught that. We collected samples from what we could reach along the perimeter. There's a team of forest nymphs standing by at HQ, ready to receive." Vidya paced the small space. "I'm not a probationary agent, Bix. Everyone here today is seasoned and the best in their specialty, director's orders."

"What about the limited blood spray and the absence of a void where the killer should have stood?"

"It's what forensics is working on once we can get close enough to the remains." Vidya checked her smartwatch. "We found five clerics' stoles tied to the upper boughs of trees near the inner ring. Would that have any effect on locking a goddess into her body?"

"That's what the scraps of fabric are? Cleric's stoles?" Bix pointed in the general direction of the ring of trees. "I noticed those when I arrived."

Vidya grunted confirmation.

"As far I know, stoles are just fancy scarves given out by the angels to humans and lower-caste Chweds. They definitely wouldn't have any effect on a god." Bix looked again at the crime scene. "Did you guys find anything else personal there? Clothes, jewelry,

DNA, anything that might identify how many other people were here when she was assaulted?"

"Nothing yet." Vidya sighed. "This is not a crime you can solve in an hour or a day. This is going to take time. You're going to have to learn patience."

Not an option for Bix, alas.

"Tell me what the Fates get from letting a Norse goddess become mincemeat." Bix cocked her head. The layers of the Mid World rippled, causing the walls of the church to ripple around them.

"The Houses of Fate are in the throes of their own power struggle. Even we lowly Oracles and Sages can feel the changes in the weaves." Vidya kicked a rotting baseboard, seemingly oblivious to the disturbance. "It started with your trial."

"But the Houses had nothing to do with that frame-up, right?" Bix scoffed. "Any idea which faith or church those stoles came from?"

Vidya shook her head. "It's going to take a while to piece the tatters together and run the battery of tests. If there is anything left of the insignias, it's on the CWIG to find those answers."

As much as Bix wanted to argue the point, most mainstream modern religions linked directly to the angels. The Angelic Host had created the leading faiths to ensure they had plenty of negative emotions to feed their voracious ranks.

Nasty fuckers.

The stoles could have been used by mortal zealots, Chwed youths being fractious, or by the angels themselves. Without more info, charging into the Host's inner sanctum to demand answers was a new level of stupid. Besides, if angels had anything to do with Mirri's assault, then Bix had a huge problem. Bigger than their contentious history. Angels didn't have souls and couldn't exist beyond the Mid Worlds. She couldn't drag one to Hel without completely erasing him or her, and upper-ranking gods couldn't set foot in the Mid Worlds without shattering a million different contracts.

What a disastrophy.

For now, better to let the CWIG do their research. If they could prove the angels were directly involved, then she'd get involved directly with the angels. Hel could deal with the fallout. Until then, she had other leads to hunt down. Like the missing pendant and why Mirri had come to this place.

"Bix, I do need to get back to my team." Vidya rapped on the wall. "Scientists can't be left unattended. They get themselves into—"

Gunshots ripped through the din of research. Rapid firing pops echoed.

"Those are too loud and too fast to be from standard-issue weapons." Vidya lurched at the shutters, tearing away loose planks.

The scene below stopped their breaths. White suits crumpled by the dozens. CWIG security fell in faster numbers. Bullets shredded the portable lab. Scientists belly-crawled from the eighteen-wheeler only to be mowed down on the ramp.

Three flashes. A heavy clatter. Then the truck exploded.

The church shuddered.

"Bix, get me down there." Vidya withdrew her Glock from her holster. "Now, goddamn it."

Bix scanned the tree line. "There's more than one shooter. I'm not dropping you into a death trap with no cover and no clear way out."

Vidya jabbed the nose of her gun into Bix's side. "Those are my guys providing security. I'm not losing another team."

Bix grabbed Vidya's wrist and pulled the gun across her body, easily disarming the Oracle. "Come on. Think. Bullets. Bullets are taking out every member of your security team. How many of your guys are vulnerable to *bullets*?"

"Less than half." Vidya shoved her aside and stared out the window again. "The ones who should be unaffected are down too. Heads blasted clear off. What the hell? What did you do, Bix?"

"Me? I just got here."

"Is this your revenge?" Vidya spun around. Her fist connected with Bix's face. Bix blocked the second punch but missed the elbow to her spine. Bix rammed her shoulder into Vidya and slammed the Oracle into the wall.

"Why are you dragging them into our fight? They're good men and women." Vidya snatched Bix by the hair and snapped her head back. "They did nothing to you or your girlfriend."

Bix stiffened her fingers and jabbed Vidya in the ovaries. Vidya released Bix and curled forward. Bix danced out of reach. "What would make you think I have anything to do with a slaughter?"

"One day," Vidya hissed through clenched teeth. "We've been here one whole day and not so much as a paper cut. You show up, and minutes later... Is this what you were planning while in exile? Is this your grand scheme to get back at all of us?"

"The Fates must be really disappointed in how myopic you are. Doesn't bode well for a woman offered the chance to shape thousands of futures."

"You bitch." Vidya launched at Bix. They crashed through a second window. Vidya wrapped her hands around Bix's throat and squeezed. "Why not take me on directly? Why do so many people have to die because of you?"

The weather-roughened window frame scraped Bix's spine as she bowed backward. She pushed her thumbs against Vidya's wrists, compressing the pressure points.

A thought opened one gate, but the sudden silence at the crime scene stopped her from opening the second.

"What the...?" Vidya relaxed her grip and gaped, her attention fixed on the hill. Bix arched farther back. Her heart skipped twice.

Blood swirled amid the trees. Swirled. Not sprayed. Not pooled. Not stained the ground. It swirled in silky ribbons through the air, defying every law of gravity. It skimmed over the tops of the dead and sucked out every droplet until corpses withered, leaving hazmat suits to sway in the wind. Ribbons parted, and parted again, taking on a distinct shape.

"Shit," Bix and Vidya breathed together.

Bix completed the gateway and twisted to the side. "Tell HQ. Now."

Vidya tumbled through the bell tower window onto a Kashan carpet over Carrara marble. Sirens blared. Red lights whirled. A long shadow stretched across Vidya rolling to her back.

"Agent Asariri," a surprisingly calm and familiar masculine voice greeted.

"Director," Vidya groaned, glaring up at Bix through the gate as it closed.

# CHAPTER 3

**B**ix slammed shut the gates to the CWIG director's office. Vidya would be interrogated for days and accused of all sorts of nefarious things, but she was clear of the crime scene and whatever evil drew blood ribbons into the unseen troughs of a spell sigil.

Some hundred-odd newly freed souls drifted over the smoky, desiccated remains of the crime scene in Centralia. Psychopomps should have been there before the first body fell, ready to catch the souls and transport them to the gods. On the off chance the Psychopomps had also been taken by surprise, then they should arrive any moment.

Any moment…

Swearing at the ineptitude of the Guild of Psychopomps, Bix relocated to the outer perimeter of the crime scene. The hilltop reeked of burning chemicals. The blood of the dead spooled into a pattern floating high above the super stump.

Souls of the dead CWIG teams darted amid the trees, building an undulating wall of amorphous forms. Whether towering ogre or tiny sprite, fleshy bodies had defined their perspective and relationship with the Mid Worlds. Now that relationship had been shattered, leaving only the bare soul glowing with the wealth of its experiences.

For the briefest moment, Bix wished for the power of a god, the power to read the souls, to draw in their memories, to learn everything the souls had known.

Whatever the CWIG forensics teams had found here had been destroyed by the still-burning fires. These poor scientists were about to deliver their final findings to any number of gods who would use or sell the knowledge to other gods. It would take a cooperative god far more than a week to cull that information and sift through it for useful data. That assumed a smidgeon of collaboration among the pantheons.

In other words, all that CWIG evidence was gone. Useless.

The souls flitted to and fro haphazardly. Devoid of the flesh created by the angels and dragons, the souls were no longer acknowledged by the native magic of the Mid Worlds. They no longer belonged, and they had nothing to which they could cling. Unmoored and ignored, they had only a short time before the Mids expelled them into the vast ether.

There were entities far, far worse than hungry gods skulking in the ether.

If it was too inconvenient for the Guild of Pompous Asses do their jobs, she'd do it for them. For the sake of the dead. No matter her opinion of certain individuals within the CWIG, she had a lot of respect for the vast majority of men and women in the guild.

She wouldn't let them suffer.

During her tenure in the labyrinth of the ether, she had discovered wild forces locked down and shut away, banned from the Mid Worlds. Just like her. Those primordial elementals had become her companions, easing the loneliness.

Time to phone a friend or four.

A thought unlocked one gate at the convergence in the Under Worlds. Another unlocked the sister gate in the Upper Worlds. Two more thoughts opened the gates of Outer World convergences.

The Reaping Winds came on a quiet song and an endless keen. A cold breeze built in the north. A hot wind gusted from the south. Gales rode in from all angles, combing through the layers of the Mid Worlds and touching only that which did not belong.

"Your commitment to the CWIG, to the Chwedlonol community, and most importantly to each other will not be forgotten," she said to the abandoned souls. "May your journey be swift. Pass peacefully."

Souls flared and scrambled, fleeing from the hill, fleeing from salvation, fleeing from deliverance. The Winds would not be denied. They came to cleanse anything unanchored from the Mid Worlds and would retreat only when finished, depositing the souls in the Worlds of the gods in whom those souls believed.

Bix faced the blood sigil hovering in the middle of the copse. Her heart thundered in her ears. Her skin prickled. Her pulse thrummed to the tempo of the purge.

If the Winds wiped away the spell, then a god or a Fate was behind the sacrificial slaughter. If the sigil stayed, the spell caster and their magic was bound to this World, which meant the spell caster was an angel, a dragon, or a Chwed.

The Reaping Winds abated. Not so much as a leaf had overturned, yet the souls were gone. The area was eerily still. The pop and hiss of gasses from the bellies of the mines whispered on the air. Thin coils of green and black smoke rose from the embers of the lab. Hazmat suits, camo pants, and black tees draped over the tangled web that had once been the search grid.

The sigil remained. Below it, the super stump glowed soft tones of amber through the layer of gore. The ground around it changed.

Blossomed.

A circle of verdant green rapidly spread from the stump. Weeds long ago killed by the anthracite fumes perked up, growing new leaves and sprouting new blossoms. Cracked earth settled and gave birth to more colorful plants. The non-native plants surged to lush depths and heights.

Soft springy grass and aggressive vines grew over Bix's shoes and tickled her ankles. Tiny fragrant flowers bloomed in shades of yellow, purple, and pink. The growth continued, past the perimeter of trees, down the hill into the vale, through the cemetery.

Bizarre.

It was late autumn. Chwedlonol with such magic wouldn't bother spawning an early spring. As she understood it, maintaining life against the natural cycles was an epic drain on personal resources. At the current rate of growth, someone was pouring a whole lot of personal power into Centralia. This took more juice than any upper-caste naturalist she'd ever met. The entire roster of the environmental guilds might be able to pull this off in the unlikely event they cooperated. This wasn't just a surface spread; the earth itself was being repaired.

She waded through the dawning jungle to the blood sigil levitating amid the boughs of resuscitating trees. Her back spasmed violently, drawing her up short. Muttering all kinds of questions about her sanity, she reached for the nearest curl of red.

The ring of blood shattered.

Blood crashed over her, splashing great crimson waves upon the beauty of mistimed spring. The ground gurgled. Burbled. The super stump pulsed; amber darkened to shades of cobalt. Thick blue gel, far too much like tar to be mortal blood, bubbled from the stump. Clumpy rivers of blackish blue unfurled like long fingers, oozing over her feet and the plants. It lay warm against her skin—warm bordering on hot—like stones from a massage. The new flora did not fare well. They wilted; they choked.

Suffocated. Scorched.

A bestial roar shook the ground. Brilliant lights flashed through the cloud cover. Pitch-black shadows countered the light.

Opposing ruling powers. Dragons versus angels.

Time to go…but not without the super stump and whatever remained of Mirri's body. Taking the bespelled blood and blue goop along with her? Not a good idea. Opening a gate beneath the ground would take the whole plot with her—stump, spells, and all. The risk of moving the blood magic was far too great.

Lightning struck the perimeter, and the blue goo grabbed for it, seeking the heat. Wings scaled and feathered dipped below the clouds.

If the angels caught her here, they'd blame her for the casualties and demand Hel deal with her permanently. No way, no how would she give Hel a reason to drain her of what memories she had.

Since she didn't have a mental image of the complete stump, she needed to touch it in order to move it and only it. With a whimper then a mutter, she dropped to her knees and hugged the hot gooey thing. Mirri's cooked remains pressed against her cheek.

A thought moved her and the stump through gates.

An invisible club struck Bix squarely in her chest, knocking her free of the hot stump. She bounced off shattering glass and face-planted on a cool concrete floor. The unseen forces struck her again and again, silently kicking her ass. She screamed through clenched teeth and slid her hands into her shoes, using them as makeshift gloves in a sea of crunchy and sticky as she slithered toward the source of relentless strikes.

Blue ick sucked at her clothes. It dripped from her hair and squirted between her fingers. Mirrored glass shards peeked from the viscous pools. The reflections of slivers revealed the trench where liquid lay too still amid her movement. She thrust her bare hands into the center of the illusion. Ridges carved into concrete formed a series of glyphs.

Wards.

She pressed both palms to the etched ground and opened gates to two different places in the ether. The floor directly under her palms cracked, crumbled, and vanished. Blue goo drained into the ether.

The attacks born of the infernal wards ceased, leaving only the maddening twitch in her back. Jör's antivenin should have completely cured her original plague by now. That her presence hadn't instantly slain the CWIG team meant the serpent god must have given her a new kind of sickness to spread, one that was growing in her back. Probably had a seven-day incubation period. Probably his idea of a divine timer. Naturally, there'd been no mention of it in her contract with Hel.

Gods, always ready to screw you.

Bix drew a shaky breath and shut the gates in the floor. Muttering nothing kind about the stupidity of mortals and gods, she flicked her hair from her face and froze.

A very large man held a very large sword an inch from her heart.

"Get up. Slowly." Seven feet of Viking stereotype motioned her up with the tip of his sword. He checked all the boxes—blond, blue-eyed, and built like a bear. He even had war braids in the thick beard that hung down to his heavily tatted brick-house chest. A seam below his elbow betrayed the prosthetic arm holding the sword.

"Seriously? What kind of idiot puts a window in a basement?" Bix sighed loudly and gestured at the audibly pulsating monstrosity resting behind her upon a bed of stained glass.

The stump had been big, yet still had failed to properly indicate the vastness of its entirety, which—for the record—was no tree stump. There were no squiggly roots or petrified bark, just smooth surfaces and one huge curve. It looked like a claw off a giant beast. Beasts that size had no business in the Primary Mid World. Regardless, the claw was way too big to have shredded a human-size goddess. It would just have squished her, like a gnat under a stiletto heel. For all she knew, it'd been in the ground long before Mirri's mortal body had been dumped on it. As if that wasn't weird enough, moss sprouted upon the shards nearest the claw, then went up in smoke.

"I wasn't expecting visitors, especially visitors who don't use doors." The Viking uncurled the flesh-colored rubber fingers from the hilt of his broadsword. The tip dipped to rest on her bosom.

Boys.

She rolled her eyes and planted her hands on the ground, which put her chin on top of his blade. She waited for him to move. He didn't. His sword didn't give her an inch of breathing room either. That meant she had to do the backing up. The sticky floor made sliding backward difficult. Her sodden skirt made standing impossible. It took three tries before her epic flailing let her grab on to the claw and make it to a somewhat upright pose.

The instant she touched the claw, black fire leapt into the air. She snatched her hand back and wobbled. Dreadful prickling blossomed over her palm, marched up her arm, and jabbed behind her ear. She cringed and slapped away the creepiness.

"Are you happy now?" She looked past the Viking to the mostly familiar surrounds. The walls were still a dark matte gray, but translucent sigils winked from a glazed topcoat. Actual lighting, the kind powered by electricity, had replaced the handful of scented candles. Hanging pendant lights, frosted sconces, sculptural floor lamps—all cast a soft, warm ambiance throughout a space on par with two football fields. What had once been the barren bowels of a coal plant was now an obvious home, complete with large kitchen, a robust library, a small clinic…and a full armory.

A rocket launcher lay in pieces on a stainless steel mortician's table.

"Well, isn't this a fresh brand of crazy." She carefully tested her balance. "How did you find this place?"

"Old Town Alexandria was in the throes of converting all their riverfront property into condos and shops, including this old coal plant. That means blueprints got unearthed. Some of the buildings' lesser-known secrets were exposed." He lifted one of her ruined shoes with the tip of his blade. "You know, I spent a month packing up shoes like these from every corner and crevice of this place. At first I'd thought I'd stumbled upon a fetishist's secret dungeon. Aside from the shoes, there was nothing here but a stack of mattresses, some dirty sheets, and a pile of lady's clothes circa 1950."

"My sheets weren't dirty," she objected, grasping for her shoe, missing, and yelping as her balance abandoned her.

The Viking set her saturated pump on the mortician's table, picked up her other shoe with his sword, and put it beside its mate. "Now, since I saw how you got in here, gatekeeper, how about you tell me what the hell you're doing with the Phoenix's dewclaw?"

"The Phoenix?" She leapt back from the claw, lost her footing, and landed on her ass with a splash.

The Viking had the gall to chuckle as he spun his weapon. "Most Chwedlonol would have vaporized the instant they brushed it. Matter of fact, only the uppermost castes can stand to be in close proximity to any removed body part of the Phoenix."

"Noticed you're not flopping like a fish yet," she groused, not even bothering to try to stand. A chunk off the lone dragon-angel hybrid would explain why her body didn't like being anywhere near it. The last time she'd encountered Feng up close and personal, they'd fought. He'd won. She was still bitter. Very bitter.

"True. The Fates won't let me die, no matter how nicely I ask." He laid his weapon next to her shoes and grabbed the hose bracketed to the mortician's table, turning knobs and testing streams. "So what is a gatekeeper doing with a body part belonging to the Consortium's lead investigator?"

"Feng and I have a complicated relationship." The last word ended on a screech as cold water blasted her in the face. She clamped her eyes and mouth shut as the damn man hosed her down. When the water stopped, she opened one eye.

"Still waiting on that answer." The Viking waved her aside. "Meanwhile, you're sitting on the drain, sweetheart."

Muttering nothing kind, she crawled away from the stupid claw, the stupid drain, and the stupid puddle of diluted *Phoenix* blood. Water shot her in the ass. She bit down on a squawk and glared over her shoulder at him.

"Trust me, it wasn't a look you wanted." He shrugged and continued to hose down everything near her. He passed the water over the two hand-sized holes in the mottled concrete floor and paused. His jaw popped with enough force to rattle the beads securing his beard braids, yet he said nothing about the modifications as he resumed cleaning.

The worst of the blood and glass swirled down the industrial grate, revealing two feet of etched gunmetal gray concrete running up the farthest walls and across the entire length of the basement. At first glance, the embedded ribbon formed a beautiful frame for whatever wall of glass she'd shattered upon landing.

To the trained eye, potent protection wards now lay useless due to two handprints.

If only the wards hadn't been so brutal, she would have opened gates straight to a five-star hotel room. Thanks to Captain Crazypants's paranoia and the Phoenix's claw, she no longer had the wherewithal to control the size of the gate. Collapsing the Mid Worlds in on each other in a vortex wouldn't earn her friends in any World. And, quite frankly, this was *her* home. Or it had been until her trial. The Potomac River flowed under these floors in a soothing lullaby. Decades ago, trains carrying coal to the plant had kept the time, and the plant itself had generated enough noise and stink to mask her presence from Chwedlonol out to snag her. There were no windows for anyone to spy on her. She'd welded shut the only doors and all the grates.

The big goon had probably ripped everything off the hinges when he'd invaded.

"That ought to do it." The Viking shut off the water and tossed her a towel. "There was a lot more than the Phoenix's blood in that rinse. Where exactly did your tête-à-tête with him take place?"

Technically? Their fight had started at the Angelic Host's armory during the doomed op. Feng and she had crashed through layer after layer of Mid Worlds while she'd bought her team time to secure the package. Little had she known her team was already dead.

Fucking angels.

Probably not what the Viking actually wanted to know, though.

"Pennsylvania." She buried her face in the towel and inhaled deeply. What was a dude doing with scented towels?

"Pennsyl…." He rubbed his non-fake hand over his mouth. "Of course the Consortium would want to hide that kind of news."

"Hold them in high esteem, do you?"

"The thing about any ruling group or organization is that they start with honorable intentions and within a few decades are so corrupt, they don't know who their real masters are. It's infinitely worse when the members are immortal or long-lived." He kept a wide berth as he walked a circle around the dewclaw. "Judging by the color of the fibrous tissue and weeping vessels in the root of this thing, it was recently detached. It was severed in one smooth motion. As thick as the root is, cutting it off would require multiple hacks with a blade. A bite would leave tooth marks. That leaves you and a precisely placed gate as the most obvious culprit."

"If I was going to take anything from Feng, it'd be more than a fingernail." She peered over the edge of the now filthy towel. "How can you possibly know that much about missing body parts?"

The moment the words left her mouth, she regretted them.

"Your arm…I didn't mean—"

"Roam the Mids for a few thousand years. Some things you can't avoid learning," he said, saving her from making her bumbling offense worse. He jerked his head to the side. "There's a bathroom on the other side of the library. Take a shower. Feel free to use whatever you find in there."

"The Norn. You struck a deal with the Norse Fates," she whispered. "You're an actual Viking."

When this guy had struck a deal with the Norn, he'd been a year or two away from forty. The Norn had one doozy of a deal with either the dragons or the angels to keep his body young and, well, delectably flawed. A hint of crow's feet crinkled around his eyes. Sure, he had battle scars, but he might have earned those before the contract. And to think, all those years ago, he'd probably been a family elder. Wonder what he'd wanted that had damned him to eternal life.

New arm?

"Right side of the power grid, wrong House." He scratched his beard and shook his head. "And 'Viking' was never a term they used. It loosely translates to 'go on expeditions beyond the bay.'"

Semantics aside, if the Fates of whichever House had woven this kind of lackey into her path at this juncture, then those Fates had a vested interest in her immediate future.

What were they up to this time? The Houses of Fate lived to annoy the other members of the Consortium. Fates were the forces of chaos amid peace and peace amid chaos. Regardless of House, Fates pulled the strings of balance in all Worlds.

And someone in one of those Houses of Fate—with the help of Vidya—had burned her team and sent her into exile. Whether the not-Viking was an olive branch or another dagger in the back remained to be seen.

What choice did she currently have?

"You sure you can trust me enough to lend me your bathroom?" She slowly gained her feet, wincing.

"Look, sweetheart, you can barely stand up straight, and there's no way in hell I'm touching your parcel over there. You've been here long enough to try to kill me, if that was your mission. You've done nothing worse than give me dirty looks." He poked at her shoes. "I'm gullible enough to believe this was your bolt-hole once. You clearly need it again. So go get cleaned up. Once you're not so prickly, we can figure out what happens next."

"Thanks." She gave him a thumbs-up as she hobbled toward the shelving units doing double duty as room dividers. "But my name is Bix, not sweetheart."

His lips quirked. "Tobek…and I know who you are, sweetheart."

# CHAPTER 4

Something smelled like farts. Bix buried her face in the clean towel and gagged. Boys and their bodily functions. Girls at least had the decency to leave the room before letting one rip. Usually.

Muttering and grunting traveled a path in and out of the bathroom. Shuffling accompanied rustling. Lip smacking finally compelled her to emerge from the steamy cocoon of the huge shower. She flung open the glass door and glared at the Mid Worlds' noisiest not-Viking.

"Seriously, if you want to peek, just join…"

A garbled shriek came from a pile of tumbling boxes, cutting off her rising diatribe. A cheetah-print bra dropped on a mottled brown-and-green pate.

Unless the Potomac had become a breeding ground for mutant monster toads, there was a hungry goblin on the prowl. A bulbous nose, complete with hairy wart, snuffled the gap between garter belts and corsets.

Bix pushed her hair out of her face and smirked. "Easy, easy, there, pervert. I'm not going to hurt you."

Humanity reviled roaches and rats. Chwedlonol had stronger feelings about goblins. Filthy, crafty, and lecherous to their questionable cores, goblins ate anything and everything. They were the ultimate housekeepers, assuming one liked buying new all the time.

They were kind of cute in their own revolting way.

"Gurp," the not-Viking barked from the doorway. "I said deliver the boxes, not inspect the boxes."

The goblin let out a whimper and fumbled with the upended cardboard.

"It's all right. I don't mind." Bix tucked the towel around her and picked up a pair of red satin panties from the pile of clothes the goblin was diligently refolding and putting back into the beautiful floral boxes.

"Gurp pulled your things out of storage. Pick what you need for tonight, and he'll take care of the rest." Tobek set a small wooden crate on the counter. "Miscellaneous toiletries. Use whatever, then meet us in the kitchen. Gurp, come on. Time for dinner."

Gurp drummed his fingertips together and toddled out of the not-Viking's bathroom. Tobek lingered an extra beat. "No blow dryer. Sorry."

"You're more than making up for it." Bix rifled through the boxes, pulling out things she hadn't touched in over a decade. What sort of guy put a total stranger's stuff into storage? As much as she'd liked this place, she'd been a minimalist squatter, which had to have been apparent when he took it over. So why had he taken the time, effort, and cost of caring for abandoned stuff? And it had been carefully stored. Most of it was in better condition than when she'd last seen it.

A crocheted hippie blouse tumbled to the floor. She stared at it and rubbed her lips.

Mirri had worn it the day of the doomed op. They'd had the mother of all fights over something stupid, and it'd spiraled wildly out of control. Bix had dumped Mirri's bare ass at the pantheon's condo in the District. It'd been the last time she'd seen Mirri in person.

Mirri had been sobbing.

Swearing under her breath, Bix tossed the shirt back in a box and dressed in clothes that actually belonged to her. Dark. Snug. Suited for either of her primary roles on the team—distraction or transporter. No sign of shoes, which was a little bit funny considering Mr. Bachelor Extraordinaire had catered to every one of her other needs.

Chortling, she headed for the kitchen.

Gurp hunched over the mortician's table, devouring parts of the rocket launcher. He stopped chewing long enough to give her a pointy-toothed grin. A scrap of zombie mouse fabric lay wedged between his teeth.

"Those shoes were beyond hope." Tobek slid a platter of steak, spuds, and greens at her. "Seemed like a fair trade to get him to bring your stuff here."

She shrugged and took a seat at the counter. "They were a gift from a guy I didn't like anyway. It's a fitting end to them."

"A guy, huh?" Tobek leaned on the counter and dove into his dinner. "You didn't break into his place."

"No intention of ever returning to his place except to collect handbags." She drummed her palms on the cool stone. "Thank you again, by the way, for letting me clean up here and for keeping all my things."

"You have some place you can stay?"

"I can always find other places."

"That wasn't my question." He gestured to her plate. "I know you're not a vegan. There was a pair of I Heart Bacon panties among your belongings."

"Those belong to an old girlfriend." She pushed the plate toward him.

"So you're…" He skewered a marbled hunk of steak and waved it in the air.

"An equal opportunity hedonist?" She finished for him. "Come on, you've been alive for eons, not centuries. Do you really let gender limit your pleasure?"

"I was going to say 'an emotion eater' since we've established you're upper caste and we were talking about food," he said around a mouthful. "But since you asked, yes, my door only swings one way."

"Bears everywhere are crying right now." She stood and shuffled toward the big-ass dewclaw still resting where she'd landed it. Cleaned and inert, it looked like a polished golden sculpture from some froufrou modern art gallery.

Never mind that she was the size of a hangnail compared to it.

"You sure this belongs to Feng the Phoenix? Big guy, red hair, aqua eyes, total douche-canoe?"

Tobek grunted in the affirmative. "The color of the claw is unique to the Phoenix, as is blood that burns all things native to the Mids."

"I've had the misfortune of being up close and personal with the Phoenix. This thing is like ten times his size."

"The Phoenix kept to the diplomatically acceptable humanoid form while he was the key witness at your trial." Tobek offered a half grin. "I told you I know who you are, sweetheart."

"Yeah well, goes to show that a secret tribunal can't keep a damn secret." She curled her damp hair around her fingers and glared at the dewclaw. "Safe to assume he didn't lose that by accident, right?"

"It would have been remarkably painful."

Of all the things that damn stump could have turned out to be, it had to be a body part of her accuser. She had to hide the thing, both from whoever had severed it in the first place and from anyone looking to frame her *again*.

Where in the Mid Worlds could she stash it? Definitely not in this World. Maybe with the giants? Thorns grew bigger than dewclaws in their World, but the magic inherent to a chunk of Phoenix would be a beacon to a certain group of big galoots. Magic was like truffle oil, and they were prize pigs.

Dark elves wouldn't notice the power infusion for a few days. They would, however, notice something unsculpted, raw, and plain. Someone would take a hammer and chisel to it and unwittingly summon the angels or the dragons who would connect the timeline to her return.

She really shouldn't provoke a war until she fulfilled her contract with Hel. If any of her old contacts would still meet with her, maybe one of them had a clue what do with spare parts.

"I'll come back and get my things, including that behemoth," she absently mumbled. "Thanks again for respite."

"Wait." Tobek's silverware clattered against his plate. "There's a bounty on your head."

No, she had not heard what she thought she'd heard. No. Surely not.

She spun around on her bare heel. "What was that?"

"This BOLO was broadcast to the entire Chwed community while you were in the shower." He flipped over a small computer thingy on the counter and held it out to her. The image of her at the pre-charred Centralia crime scene covered the screen. The word Wanted watermarked her bosom along with an outrageous reward offer. "You're currently wanted for acts of terrorism against the Mids. That bounty is big enough to lure even the lowest house brownie into the hunt. So, again, I'm going to ask if you have another safe place to stay."

"I can handle this." She wiggled her fingers at her sides. Oh, she really did not want to touch Feng bits again. Fresh Feng bits.

"You don't get it, do you?" Tobek crossed his arms over his chest. "There isn't a square mile on this World that isn't under some sort of observation. We live in an age where technology tracks anybody anywhere anytime. Whatever advantage you think you have by disappearing at will isn't valid anymore. One call, one text, one transmission of any kind, and you're toast. You need help. Admit it."

She matched his pose. "Why are you so eager to volunteer?"

"The Fates plopped you in my lap." He gestured to the broken wards behind the claw. "I've been their bitch long enough to get the hint."

"Doesn't mean I should trust you."

Mirth faded, leaving behind the hard planes of his anger. "Because offering you food, clothing, and shelter is the behavior of an unscrupulous man?"

"The last man to provide me with food, clothing, and shelter did so to create a dependency; he then exulted in snatching everything away while I lay homeless, naked, and starving." She sneered. "So, you'll have to do better than not ramming a blade through my heart to earn my trust."

She didn't know Tobek, his allegiance, or his agenda. Hell, she didn't even know his House. Vidya had said the Houses of Fate were at odds. Bix didn't like not knowing which Fates pulled Tobek's strings, and he'd noticeably avoided telling her. She *really* didn't like whichever House of Fate had put Mirri in the crosshairs. It could be his House for all she knew.

"Fair enough." He eyed her untouched plate, and his glower softened. "Why don't we start with a shared need, then work our way up to trust?"

She cocked her head. "What is it you need?"

He withdrew a baking sheet from the oven and set it next to her refused plate. "You lost this during the hosing."

She sidled closer to the tray. The mangled water-streaked image of Mirri's remains and the identifying pendant stared back at her. That pendant had been forged in the fires of the Yoruba pantheon by the god Ogun, a god of metalwork, politics, and sacrifices. He'd made it as a thank you gift for finding something that'd been stolen from him. She'd gifted it as a peace offering, a reminder for Mirri to be brave in the face of hostility.

"If that is what was left of the Norse ambassador, then it wasn't a political assassination," Tobek murmured, artfully dodging her question again. "That was a personal message to an untouchable, someone who couldn't be directly interrogated. Upper-caste Chwedlonol? Maybe even an archangel or one of the royal dragons?"

Or a god.

Hel had risen to Other World domination by contracting with the Angelic Host to become their embodiment of punishment, their bogeyman to the living. Every soul who believed in Hell ended up in Helheim at the goddess's feet, hers to devour, dispense with, or trade as she deemed fit. Souls were the currency of gods, and a lot of gods wanted a piece of Hel's power supply. A lot of those gods weren't in the Norse pantheon.

A lot but not all.

"I never said anything about the Norse ambassador," Bix whispered.

"Sweetheart, everyone knows the Norse ambassador met a bleak end. Rumors are rampant. The mid and lesser castes are scared shitless. My business exploded with Chwedlonol looking for protection wards." He scratched his beard and examined the ceiling. "The scars on your forearm make it obvious you have some affiliation with the Norse gods, and the wanted poster tells me you were tangling with the CWIG before you scored the dewclaw. I am capable of piecing together unusual events to form a plausible premise."

She scratched at Jör's bite marks. "Maybe you're right."

"Gurp, why don't you tell the nice lady here what her clothes tasted like?"

"Ew." She wrinkled her nose.

"Phoenix blood," the goblin answered with his mouth full. "And angel blood."

"Angel blood? I didn't see any at the crime scene, I don't think." She stared agog at the grunting goblin. "Ingesting the blood of an angel or a dragon is fatal to mortals. Why aren't you dead, shower buddy?"

Gurp fluttered his lashes.

"Their blood is like hot sauce to a goblin's palate." Tobek sucked on a tooth. "There's a reason these guys survive every apocalypse."

"So we have blood from three superpowers at the same crime scene. We only have body parts from two. We need to figure out why there aren't any angel parts and if the angels bled first, during, or after the Phoenix and the ambassador. That'll tell us if the angels were victims, conspirators, or defenders." She kneaded the knot forming between her shoulders. "I have to believe that if any angels had been defenders and had survived what happened there, my involvement wouldn't be necessary. Hel certainly wouldn't have had the political grounds to call me in from exile."

"That leaves victims or assailants as the angels' roles." Tobek gestured at the BOLO. "Why would the CWIG *want* to claim jurisdiction of a hot potato like this? How did they convince the Consortium that they were the best resource? Better than the Consortium's own investigators?"

"The CWIG didn't ask; they were tasked." Bix sighed. "Assuming the Consortium knows about Feng's potential involvement, their investigative branch is compromised. The CWIG is the next best thing, especially since they have the implicit support of the Chwedlonol guild masters and the human governments. That support gives the CWIG local resources and the micro-political knowledge it'll take to make any headway on this. As much as it pains me to admit, the CWIG is as close as the Consortium can get to an objective third party with the necessary skills."

"'Objective' is a bit of a misnomer, isn't it? The CWIG will go to great lengths to hide any evidence that even hints at the involvement of the Angelic Host in a god's assault." He looked at the BOLO again. "The last thing they want is for the Consortium members to go to war. The mid and lesser races will die in the crossfire. The upper castes will be enslaved and gutted in the game of intrigue. Blaming you for massacring CWIG employees the moment you set foot in the Mids is the fastest way to make sure your parole is revoked and to get you out of their sandbox so they can bury whatever they need."

Tobek was partially right. During her tenure with the CWIG, Bix *had* ensured all kinds of evidence had gone missing at the director's orders. However, she knew the CWIG director well enough to know the real motivation behind the warrant. The director knew *her* well enough to know she didn't use bullets to fell opponents; regardless of whatever story Vidya had fabricated this time. No, the director had issued the warrant to force his ex-agent to come in, so he could mete out the punishment the Intelligence Community believed she deserved. She had neither the time nor the desire to deal with him at the moment.

"Blaming me is one thing, proving it will take time and resources. Meanwhile, I'll keep a low profile and complete my mission." She faced the dewclaw again. "That includes figuring out why all those people had to die and if it was to hide the Phoenix's involvement in the ambassador's mauling."

Tobek cleared his throat. "When that claw bled, did the Horde and Host respond?"

"Full-on battle in the clouds." She glared at the thing as her mind rattled through the next steps in the investigation. "None of the CWIG teams could get near the claw, and you said most Chweds can't either. So, how did it get to Centralia? Pretty sure Feng doesn't shed them, and a truck hauling it down an interstate would have drawn a lot of attention."

"If the dragons and angels responded to its magic awakening, then we need to hide that claw quickly." Tobek took a worn tome from beside the stove and slid it across the counter toward her. "I checked my library for possible methods while you were cleaning up."

"Apparently not a cookbook," she muttered, returning begrudgingly to the kitchen.

"Like anyone needs directions on how to char meat with fire," Tobek scoffed.

"This is a very, very old and very, very priceless Book of Shadows." She tapped a chipped nail against a thick yellowed page filled with foreign script written in blood. A series of pictorials that were not the harsh lines of old Norse Futhark stared up at her. "I have no idea what this is."

"Dacian." Tobek cocked his head. "It's a requirement for the upper caste to be fluent in all Mid World languages. Toll keepers at the gateways only speak the languages native to the World. If you can't converse, you can't go in."

"I don't travel the established routes. Too crowded. Infinitely irritating." She might well have known all the languages at some point, but it didn't mean she remembered them. She held the book out to him. "What's it say?"

He stared at her an extra heartbeat before taking the book from her. "This is a big fucking spell. There's no guarantee it'll work. We need to be sure that hiding this thing from the Consortium is what we want."

She didn't want to be accused of maiming the love child of a dragon and an angel by anybody—much less the Consortium, who'd already booted her ass from the Mids once for a far more benign infraction.

"You want dragons or angels banging down your door? A dragon will crush this place with its foot. And angels? Psht. They do not ask questions before they incinerate everyone, trust me on that."

He gave her a flat stare. "I meant are we sure we want to keep the Phoenix's dewclaw instead of destroying it?"

"Sadly, it's evidence and, if I get desperate, leverage." She hopped up on the counter. "So, until I get the fool who shredded a goddess, I need to keep it."

"You got any girlfriends running around whom you'd trust with this?"

She wrinkled her nose. "What?"

"I said it's a fucking spell. Sex magic. Orgies. Lots of bodily fluids." He held up the book and pointed to a bunch of squiggles. "Life-creating fluids rather than life-ending ones."

Her jaw dropped. "How much spunk are we going to need?"

The lines around his eyes crinkled.

"Oh, you pig." She took a floret of broccoli off his plate and chucked it at him. "You're messing with me."

He caught the projectile in his mouth and winked. "Lil' bit."

"So? What do we really have to do?"

"Most of the things we'll use I have in the vault, but I'll need a contribution from you." He held up his hand as she glowered. "A lock of your hair, preferably from the nape with the roots intact."

She yanked a handful of damp hair from said location and handed to him. "Sorry about the wretched little pin knots."

"They'll add to the texture." He laid her offering on the page. Steam hissed, and the hair dried. He snapped the book shut with one hand. "Sweetheart, come with me. Gurp, I'll need a wing claw from an angel and a tail barb from a dragon from the vault, aged three cycles minimum, if you would?"

She took his hand and let him help her off the counter as the goblin booked it across the basement and disappeared in the labyrinth of bookshelves doubling as walls. The deeper into the maze Tobek led her, the more convinced she became that he'd hired the mother of all designers to convert the vast industrial space into a home.

"What did you mean by 'cycles'?" She felt like a kid in a museum of war and culture. Displayed on one shelf, Sumerian curved daggers, while two shelves over, sat a necklace of Egyptian blue glass beads. Amazing tapestries depicting brutal wars hung from the ceiling on clear cables so as to appear as floating walls. Some of those tapestries had aged spatter on them. It was all too easy to picture the not-Viking storming a castle and ripping those things off walls. He'd have paused for chest pounding, then on to more hacking and slashing.

Ah, she cracked herself up.

"The Phoenix burns every five hundred years, plunging the Mid Worlds into a hundred years of war. The long-lived and immortals residing in the Mids measure eras by his reincarnations, hence, 'cycles.'"

"Feng? Feng, who wouldn't sit during my trial because the rod up his ass was too stiff, *burns*? Like spontaneous combustion burns? Like poof?" She made the universal explosion hand signal.

"Whether he burns to save the Mids or to destroy them

varies by incarnation and—one can only assume—by the life that incarnation leads."

"But he always burns. That's a crappy destiny."

"There are immortals who would give anything for a fresh start." He waved her ahead of him into an octagon of vertical slabs. Each slab hosted a base element. Fountain, fire bar, fern, and fan were super easy to guess as the cardinal compass points. Base metals occupied the ordinal compass points. A round altar of bones anchored the middle of the room.

Even if she hadn't spent years popping in and out of magical fortresses, she'd know this spot was for major spell work. The room practically breathed power.

Wait.

She peered closer at the protective layers of the World surrounding them. Sure enough, they pulsed rhythmically. That was neither normal nor remotely common.

"You're not just the Fates' lackey, are you? You're a high warlock."

"Being long-lived is horrendously boring if you don't challenge yourself to constantly learn new things." He set the book on the altar, then stepped aside as Gurp entered with two large clay containers replete with engravings. "I hope you're not squeamish."

"Dude." She gestured to herself. "Bathed in Phoenix blood with a nice facial of god gore. There's really no room for squeamish after that."

He held her gaze as he detached his prosthetic arm and handed it off to Gurp. His expression took on a hint of wariness.

She wagged a finger at the rough puckers of his amputated flesh and whispered loudly, "Where are the alien worms?"

His brows drew together.

She couldn't stop the snort-giggle. "With that kind of a buildup, I expected some sort of secondary life form. At least a dozen. Maybe purple and covered in mucus? Lots of teeth, no eyes? A regular shortened arm is kind of disappointing, frankly."

The furrows in his brow deepened. "Now you're messing with me, right?"

"Lil' bit." She grinned.

Tobek visibly relaxed. Gurp laughed heartily as he left with the prosthetic.

Bix tried for a straight face. "I see why you two get along."

"The wilder aspects of magic can cause the prosthetic to short out." Tobek smirked and set about arranging things on the altar. "Sometimes technology and magic amplify each other, and sometimes they wreak all kinds of havoc."

"What's life without some havoc, eh?" She watched in rapt fascination as he smoothed her contribution of tangled hair along the center of the altar.

"If you would please hold one end of the hair?"

She did as he asked. With his lone hand, he nimbly braided the strands. He motioned for her to release her end, then tapped his hand under the lip of the altar. A bead of blood welled on his fingertip. He spoke words she didn't know. His lush rasp deepened with each melodic verse. He smeared his blood from one end of the braid to the other, coating every strand. Fine silver filaments sprouted from his blood, weaving as the weft to the warp of her hair.

Bix stared. For all that being a gatekeeper was great, magic—real manipulations of the native elements—was something she couldn't do. Not even remotely. She'd spectacularly failed the Basics of Magic class during CWIG agent training, or would have if she hadn't relocated the entire academy when they'd told her she was failing. Her inability to dabble in Mid World magic made her bestow a ton of props to those who'd mastered it. Watching magic go down was better than TV or comic books.

She really liked TV and comic books.

"You'll feel the magic push and pull at you," Tobek murmured in words she did finally understand. "There is no need to fear or fight it. I'm binding control over the dewclaw to your essence. The magic is learning what makes you unique so that it will always know you."

She gave him two thumbs-up as the air around her stroked and scratched. She braced for a playground tussle, but it was definitely more tickle fest, with particular attention paid to her back and head.

Tobek's words returned to the smooth recitation of incomprehensible things. He unlatched the clay pots. Sparks leapt as he placed a white claw at one end of the hair and a plum conical barb at the other. Their woven contributions filled with light, revealing the myriad colors within each strand. At the center, hair and filament bubbled as though melting.

"Is it supposed to do that?"

Tobek's incantations did not stop, but he did give her a reassuring wink. Purple and white tugged on the silver and teal, plucking metallic fingers out of the braid. Not fingers. Wings. Little wings the size of her palm—one feathered, one scaled. The bubbling stopped, and the lights retreated to the claw and barb. Tobek fell silent.

A flash blinded her. When the spots cleared from her eyes, an ordinary braided necklace with a silver pendant of open wings lay in the middle of the altar. The claw and barb had shrunk to become the clasp.

"For you." Tobek gestured to the necklace. "That was the easy part."

"Ooo, jewelry." She carefully picked it up. It tickled her palm, as light as bubbles without a trace of the weight of metal. "What's the hard part?"

He closed the pots and collected his book, gesturing to the hall. "Attaching that to the dewclaw."

"How do you do that?"

"Not it." He chuckled, directing her with the book. "You have to press the wings to the claw so they can take hold."

"Pfft. Easy," she scoffed.

"You say that now," he drawled. "The dewclaw is part of the Phoenix, severed or not. Attempting to bind it will be as difficult as binding the man himself."

Considering Feng had thoroughly trounced her during their skirmish, this promised to be hella hard. For whatever reason, Feng held enough hate for her that it probably imbued every last cell in his body. She would never forget how rapidly his expression had changed when she'd stood in the gateway to the Host's armory—surprise, recognition, then pure loathing. Sure, she understood defending one's turf, but the ferocity of his anger still shook her to this day. He'd fought her with the sort of wrath one would expect if she'd slaughtered his entire family and had made him watch. As far as she knew she hadn't. As far as she knew, that day at the armory had been the first time she'd ever seen him. How he'd known her, she had no clue. He hadn't spoken during their fight, and nothing during her trial had hinted at his personal problem with her. He'd been all about the facts—facts she couldn't refute even if she had been so inclined. Time in exile had given her plenty of opportunities to ponder his issues with her, yet she was as baffled by them today as she had been at the armory. Dude was one angry bird.

"I tried to bury him last time." Bix grimaced. "It never occurred to me to tie him up. Maybe he would have liked it."

"You're about to find out." Tobek paused at a shelf of cube displays and slid the Book of Shadows into a cubby. The moment he withdrew his hand, the cubby sealed itself in iron.

Clearly not a lending library.

They walked a bit farther into a room with a huge TV, long leather couch, and coffee table on which sat his prosthetic connected to a cable sprouting from the table leg. He reclaimed his artificial arm and reattached it. He wiggled his fingers a few times, then pointed to the kitchen.

She was a very good solider what with the following orders and all.

"Whenever you're ready." He grabbed a glass from a cabinet and filled it with water.

"And all I have to do is put this little pendant on that big lump of Phoenix." She eyeballed him. "This isn't some elaborate plan to tether *me* to the thing so you can collect the bounty, right?"

He chugged the water and refilled the glass. "Oh, there's going to be tethering. Stop being a chicken and get to getting."

"Fiiiine." She clutched the necklace until her nails threatened to break the skin of her palm. Three steps closer to the dewclaw and she opened her hand.

The layers of the World audibly throbbed.

"Is it supposed—" She glanced over her shoulder and halted. Tobek hunched over the counter. The glass trembled in his grip, and his body twitched.

"Tobek, what's wrong?" She moved toward him.

He held up a staying hand. His lips moved, but no words came. Blood dribbled into the unsteady water glass.

She backed away, closing the necklace in her fist and holding it to her bosom. Tobek sucked down a loud wet breath and pointed at the dewclaw. She didn't have to be told twice. One thought put her within arm's reach of the massive claw. She extended her fist to the claw. Her fingers slowly uncurled. She closed one eye and looked away.

Sort of.

The small wings surged from her palm and affixed themselves to the raw root of the claw. The claw glowed, shifting to shades of dark blue. The wings pulsed silver and gold. A sonic hum started low and built in tone. Throbbing bloomed in her jaw, squirreled around the base of her skull, and then shot down her spine. Waves of iridescence flowed outward from the claw.

Tobek collapsed. The glass shattered. Cabinet doors exploded.

Closing her hand over the wings required an obscene amount of effort. Her skin finally made contact. A boom shook the foundation of the old plant. Contracting waves rippled the layers protecting the World, sucking everything toward the claw.

Pop.

The claw shrank to the size of a silver dollar and clattered to the floor. Wholly natural silence returned to the basement. Pressures converse and inverse stabilized. Protective layers of the World settled back into proper alignment. Normalcy returned.

Bix's heartbeat became the only thundering between her ears. She let out a long breath, shook her arms, squirmed in her dress, and bowed her back.

"Tobek, are you okay?" Bix crouched over the shrunken dewclaw. The wings closed around the whole of the claw. To the idiot eye, it appeared to be a goth pendant strung on a dyed leather cord. She picked it up and tried to pry the wings apart. Not happening. No seams. The subtle warmth confirmed that Feng's claw was inside. She closed her fist around the pendant and held it to her breast once again.

Tobek stirred, groaning as he rolled to his back. "Put it on."

Bix surveyed the wreckage. "I'm thinking something that can cause an earthquake is not something I want anywhere near my heart."

"Its magic is bound to you. It cannot harm you." He levered himself upright with his artificial arm. "However, it needs to feel your pulse to maintain the protections."

Bix whimpered and wrinkled her nose as she slid the hair cord around her neck. The clasps joined themselves without her interference.

"We good?" She gestured to the pendant nestled between her breasts. "Wait, Gurp? Gurp?"

"Shower drain." Tobek dusted his hands and shook shards out of his bloodstained beard. "His escape hatch, panic room, secret labyrinth, whatever he needs it to be."

"One way to deal with hair clogs." She shuddered and trotted into the bathroom. "Gurp?"

Mottled fingers wriggled through the grate.

"Are you okay?"

A thumb poked through the grate.

"It's safe to come out now, if you want to. No pressure."

"Gurp, kitchen cleanup," Tobek called from the doorway. "Claw's gone now too. I need more concrete, Yeti dander, and imp venom to restore the wards she broke."

"Yes, yes." The grating pushed up and slid back. Somehow,

the goblin's remarkably rotund body had compacted itself—as though a boneless invertebrate—into the drain pipe. Watching him emerge from the drain was like watching a balloon inflate.

"Gurp, were you the inspiration for the Blob?" She closed one eye and peered down at him, hands on hips. He chortled and waddled out of the bathroom.

Tobek crossed his arms and blocked her retreat. "When were you going to tell me the claw was exposed to a blood spell?"

"I didn't know it mattered?" She hiked both shoulders to her ears. "I don't know how native magic works."

"The kind of blowback that nearly ripped this building from its foundations wasn't due solely to the Phoenix resisting the tethering," he growled. "There were remnants of powerful blood magic at work too."

She leaned back and sputtered. "Maybe next time you should ask if I happened to have noticed an epically huge blood sigil hanging over a tree stump that turned out to be a body part in need of magical containment, oh, high warlock."

He cocked his head and narrowed his eyes. She mimicked his pose.

"I think it's time you took me to Centralia."

She bit her lip and wrinkled her nose. "That bad, huh?"

"Gurp," he bellowed. "Field trip."

A delighted squeal came from the kitchen.

She smirked. "It's the site of two, possibly three, major crimes. I doubt we'll be the only ones there."

"Your shoes are by my jacket." He dropped the angry Hulk pose and allowed her to pass. "Two rights and a left."

In two rights and a left, she came face-to-face with three six-foot stacks of clear shoe boxes filled with the assorted pairs she never thought she'd see again. Gurp pointed to the neon camouflage pair and looked up hopefully.

"Perfect. It's nighttime; those should glow in the dark." She couldn't help smiling at the eagerness with which Gurp doted on her. It felt good, really good, to be surrounded by people again.

Especially people who wanted to help her succeed.

Tobek pulled into an oxblood leather jacket and flipped his hair over the collar. "Whenever you're ready."

She put on her shoes and envisioned the crime scene. The gate refused to open. She sighed and modified the mental image with what she recalled of the aggressive sea of blue goo. Still nothing.

"Problem?" Tobek dipped to catch her attention. "Is it the pendant?"

She waved him off. "The actual crime scene must have been drastically changed by whatever was unfolding when I bolted with the claw. I can't open a gate if I don't have a good mental picture. I can get us close, but we'll have to walk the difference."

Tobek snorted. "We're not the ones wearing high heels."

"You know they come in size Sasquatch, right?" She stuck out the tip of her tongue and pictured the old church tower.

Gates opened.

# CHAPTER 5

Gates closed, delivering Bix to the church tower with a slightly green not-Viking and a very green goblin.

"By the Fates, I'm choking on my stomach," Tobek wheezed, staggering to the window and sucking down the cool night air.

"That's your soul resisting the transport. Well, resisting me, actually." Bix peeked through the slats covering another window. The waxing gibbous moon lent a silver-blue glow to the area, but what had once been the crime scene was now a vast stretch of utter pitch. She couldn't make out a damn thing within that darkness.

Tobek braced himself on the sill. "It's worse than those carnival teacup rides."

Gurp gurgled agreement as he slid down the wall and cradled his head in his hands.

"Sorry, guys." She bit her lip and quietly laughed. "First time is the worst, I promise. Frequent flyers hardly get more than a tummy tickle. It's a trust thing."

"Something to keep in mind." Tobek shook his head sharply and slapped his cheeks. "Okay. Where are we going from here?"

"You see the black spot, Cap'n?" she said in her best pirate impression, pointing over Tobek's shoulder to the downhill location.

"Got it, Long John." He turned abruptly, knocking her backward with his bulk. His hands clamped on her hips, catching her before she hit the floor. They stared at each other wide-eyed for a few shared heartbeats before his easy grin emerged. "Did you want me to carry you down there, sweetheart?"

She patted his chest as he set her on her toes. "I bet you have swords that weigh more than I do."

"That'd be pretty stupid of me. Weapons are meant to be lightweight yet sturdy so they don't wear you out while you're swinging them." He pulled a flashlight from his jacket's inner pocket and tugged Gurp to his feet.

"I can't tell if you just called me a heifer or gave me a history lesson." Bix clomped down the brittle spiral stairway. "Both? Was it both?"

"I like my women far more forgiving than a weapon." He kept the light aimed ahead of her.

"For all that swinging, right, Mr. One-way Door?" She hopped off the bottom step then leapt aside as Gurp came hurtling down the bannister.

The goblin nailed the dismount.

They tapered their easy banter as they descended the hill through the cemetery, alert for any other signs of life. A broad hand tight against her abdomen jerked Bix backward.

"Watch it." Tobek kept his hand where it was as he sidled closer to her.

Her foot hovered over a huge pit. Moonlight brushed the walls a few feet down before the breadth of darkness swallowed even the flashlight's beam. White smoke escaped through crevices in the walls, an unnatural cauldron at full boil.

"Holy shit." She placed her hand over Tobek's sure hold and tilted forward. "Well, that explains why I couldn't open a gate."

Gurp crawled to the edge on his belly, sniffing and tasting soil from the ground and the walls of the pit. A lot of grunting and muttering accompanied his explorations as he scrabbled along the edges, into the remaining woods, and out of sight.

"He's fine," Tobek assured her, walking her back from the edge. "His palate is better than any high-tech lab."

"I could have used him earlier today," she half joked, still gawping at the earthen maw. "We're standing a half mile from where Feng's claw pierced the ground. Yes, the thing was huge, but it was nowhere near this big or deep. Is that China down there?"

Tobek crouched near the edge and grabbed a handful of dirt. He blew in his fist, then tossed the dirt into the pit. An array of green lights dotted the darkness, growing smaller and smaller… and invisible.

He glanced over his shoulder at her. "You said something about a blood sigil. Did you get a good look at it?"

"Before I broke it? Um, it was half-formed while I was up in the church." She toed off her shoe and used the heel to draw in the dirt. "That's sort of the gist. Does that help at all?"

Tobek added to the squiggles with all the finesse of an actual artist, which made her pathetic drawing look damn familiar.

"Yep, that's it. Is it a common thing?" She used his head for balance as she put her shoe back on.

He whistled as he stood. "I haven't seen that spell used since the last cyclical Great War—the last time Feng burned. Guild masters and the uppermost one percent of the upper caste used that spell to relocate and hide cultural treasures to make sure Chwed heritage survived the war. It draws on the blood of the slain to fuel itself."

"Can any member of the Consortium use that same spell?"

"No, native magic doesn't work the same for the superpowers as it does the Chweds. The magic of a superpower is derived from a pure source. Chweds' magic is a filtered blend from their creators and their World."

"You're confident that spell was not done by a dragon or an angel? Hundred percent?" She hated to belabor a point, but if the magic wielded here ruled out the angels as culprits in Mirri's death, then she could narrow the focus of her investigation to just upper-caste Chweds. There were only a million-ish of them.

Gads.

"If an angel or a dragon wants to relocate something in the Mids, they don't need the blood of Chweds to do it." He strolled around the pit, swinging the beam of the flashlight along the edge. "They're more likely to destroy the original, then build a new version where they want it."

She picked her way along behind him. "So someone gunned down over a hundred CWIG wonks to protect…?"

"You said Feng's claw was centered under the spell, right? And that no one got near it except you." He crouched again and clicked the flashlight on and off. In the deepening grays of the pit, teeny slivers shimmered.

"The remains of the Norse ambassador were on top of the claw, so she got here after Feng." Bix opened a gate under the shimmers and another in the air above her palm. Fragments of what appeared to be Hawaiian paua shell tumbled into her hand. "These are parts of a surveillance bug. I used to plant these suckers all over the place. Whatever was here merited spying."

"If a goddess's remains were atop the dewclaw, then I'm not so certain the people who did the second round of slaughtering knew about the spell. They were probably on site to retrieve the dewclaw, biding their time while the CWIG did the heavy lifting."

"Once the CWIG had it on a transport, they'd hijack the transport vehicle." She sighed. "Then I showed up—with my ability to relocate anything anywhere—forcing them to kill the techs in order to beat me to the prize."

"The blood spell probably scared them off and kept you from getting shot." He cupped her hand with his and shone the light on the broken bits. "The destination of the object moved by the spell is determined by the final thoughts of the one-percenter who sacrifices themselves closest to the epicenter."

"Since it didn't show up in your basement, it didn't heed me."

"You didn't die for it. Neither did the Norse ambassador nor the Phoenix—though his blood certainly amplified the strength of the spell. Whoever was the most powerful Chwed on the CWIG's team most likely defined the new location." He closed her hand over the bug bits. "Somewhere in the Mids, a chunk of steaming Centralia is currently defiling someone's landscaping."

"I can hear the shrieks of horror now." She snorted.

He whirled around and bolted through the trees. "That's Gurp. Those shrieks belong to Gurp."

"What?" She'd been joking, but now that he mentioned it… She kept a visual on Tobek's back, taking mental snapshots to open and close gates as she dogged his heels.

Running? No. Not something she ever did.

Tobek turned sharply and skidded sideways down a ravine. She met him safely at the bottom, no mud skiing required.

"I okay. I okay," Gurp called.

Tobek skimmed the light over the dense bed of leaves and branches until he located the goblin. Gurp crouched over a body or, more specifically, the remains of one.

Bix held her nose against the acrid smell. "Tastes like burning."

Tobek knelt across the body from Gurp, batting away the bugs. The empty back curve of a skull remained passably recognizable where a whole head should have been. Char clung to the shattered bones of the torso and arms. There were no hands. Mid-thighs down were undamaged. Half a pocket was still attached to the black cargo pants.

"Explosives took this guy apart." Tobek swept the light over the immediate area. "Looks like the grenade went off before he could release it."

"Look at his boots." Bix kicked a matte-black combat boot. "There's body blowback on the top, but no mud, no dirt, no leaves embedded in these soles."

Tobek aimed the light on the corpse's boot, then on his own dirt-caked one. "He didn't walk here, but someone did. Smaller footprints with the same type of sole left prints on the leaves. Teammate, I'd say. Came looking for him."

"Twelve nests," Gurp grunted. "Twelve of twelve around

hole. This the only body. Three other nests taste like body, but no body there."

Bix swore. "Snipers. This guy is one of the ones who took down the CWIG team. Has to be."

Tobek stood and nodded. "You remember the mortician's table in the basement?"

A very clear memory opened gates.

Bix covered her yawn and set her cheek on the cool kitchen counter as Gurp and Tobek dissected the remains of the Centralia sniper.

It'd been one hell of a first day back in the Mids, and she didn't have much to show for it, not when it came to solving who'd ended Mirri. What was the link between the Norse ambassador and the Phoenix? Why had one been mutilated and one maimed? What was their link to the relocation spell in Centralia?

The day had left her with one exceedingly distasteful next step—locating the Phoenix. He was the only survivor with a name.

She fluffed the counter under her cheek. It was so soft and smelled of warm man and sandalwood. A bit more fidgeting and her toes located a blanket. It really was such a comfortable counter.

Drilling with a chaser of masculine murmuring caused Bix to bolt upright. The smell of coffee and bacon filled her senses.

"She's awake. I'll be up in a bit." Tobek hung up his phone and tossed a bathrobe on the bed, grinning. "Good morning."

"Morning?" Bix ruffled her hair and cringed from the taste of her own morning breath. She untangled one leg from the comforter and froze.

Bed.

She was in a great big bed.

She slapped her hand over her face. "Oh, dude. I'm sorry. I didn't mean…"

"To drop into my bed? It's a good thing you're soft, or I might have minded." The not-Viking propped himself against the room divider and slid his phone in his back pocket. "Do you know you travel in your sleep? You took three trips to the kitchen counter, two to the altar in the spell room, and one to the couch in the TV room. You popped back here in between."

"If I sleep too hard, I go wherever my dreams take me." She tugged the rucked-up hem of last night's dress back down over her butt. "I don't want you to think I'm putting the moves on you."

"Next time, don't hog the covers." He pushed off the shelving unit. "Sorry about the noise. Gurp's building your room."

"My room?" She left the robe on the bed and followed him out to the kitchen.

"Your room." He poured himself a large stein of coffee. "I told you you had a place to stay, and I meant it. Gurp's giddier than I've ever seen him about the whole thing. He didn't get to use his feminine design aesthetic when he put this place together."

"Gurp? Gurp is your designer? But of course he is. Goblins are…never the first ones considered for the gig. He has *impeccable* taste." She noted the clothes hanging up by the mortician's table. "His doing?"

"Oh yeah." Tobek smirked into his mug. "All morning it's been 'pretty lady clothes,' 'pretty lady shoes,' 'pretty lady bed,' 'pretty lady sheets,' 'pretty lady—"

"I get it, I get it." She laughed. "I'm touched, really. In a positive non-mental way. Thank you, both, for everything."

"Speaking of touching, he and I completed the autopsy last night. Gurp said the residue tasted of angel."

She stopped her brain before it went too far down the vision path of how Gurp came to that tidbit, erm…yeah, whatever.

"Are you telling me the body was that of an angel?"

"No, no, we would have stumbled into a wellspring of plant growth if that had been the case." He sipped his coffee and sighed a little too happily. "The explosive residue didn't taste of gunpowder, magic dust, or any of the thousands of other combustible things. He said angel and stuck with angel."

"Does angel magic have a flavor?"

"Not that he's mentioned before."

"So we're at a dead end with the sniper." She rubbed her face until it tingled. "Okay, I'm going to change and head out to see what I can learn about Feng's connection to Mirri."

"Don't forget that bounty on your head is very much active and increasing by the hour." He slid his computer tablet thingy toward her.

She bared her teeth and growled at the reward number that had become a Powerball ticket.

"My business is upstairs on street level." He reclaimed the tablet and tucked it under his arm. "I've put feelers out for the scuttlebutt on Centralia. Shop closes at nine tonight. If you're back before then, come see me upstairs."

"About you going to all these lengths for me, you and Gurp…"

He tilted his head. "What about it?"

"You know you'll regret this, right?" she hedged. "All of this. The last group of people who had my back, they all died because of me."

Tobek moved slowly to stand beside her, so close that a breath would make them touch. His blue eyes held a wealth of understanding that only an immortal who dared to live boldly could claim. His attention dropped to her lips, then flicked up to her eyes.

"Then I'll have to be the one to get over it, sweetheart."

# CHAPTER 6

**B**ix stepped into an empty closet and closed the gates. A shouting match carried in brutal clarity from the other side of Mirri's condo. Bix nudged open the closet door and frowned. Foam and feathers littered the floor of the guest room. She moved further into the condo, noting how crystals from denuded chandeliers gleamed like tears as they lay scattered down the marble hallway. Sconces dangled from electrical wires, sputtering in sullen bursts from the great room. Entire cabinets had been wrenched from the walls in the kitchen. Piles of shattered dishes and warped cookware supported the fractured remnants of granite countertops. Exposed waterlines piffed and dripped.

Mirri had been a notable slob, but the pantheon retained all kinds of gnomes and brownies to keep up appearances of order and wealth.

Someone had been looking for something. Recently.

"Where did you hide it, klepto?" More banging. More shrieking. A lot more cursing.

"I. Don't. Have. It," gasped a decidedly childlike voice. "Never. Got. It."

A battered, bejeweled guitar case rested against the fireplace amid displaced fake logs and pebbles. A scrolled metal vent cover tapped against crumbling drywall, suspended by one screw from the air return in the second hallway.

"Liar. You're a thief. All of you. Every last one of your nasty ilk."

Bix held up a hand to block the flashing of a dangling wall sconce as she leaned against the doorway of the master bedroom… and did a double take. At first glance, a low-rent hooker reeking of back-alley bars was beating the crap out of a six-year-old girl in pink princess pajamas. The thick silver rings on every finger holding the child against the wall gleamed in the morning sunlight streaking through open balcony doors. Faint blue stains framed the child's fingernails digging into the hooker's wrist. That, combined with the total lack of moisture—tears or sweat—on the child explained a lot.

A lot that made Bix's heart skip.

"Thrúde, put her down."

The Valkyrie in the cheetah-print coat tipped her head but didn't drop the child. "Mirri's monstrous ex. If Hel released you, things are worse than we know."

"Put the draugr down, Thrúde. The only thing she feels is a tickle. The body's dead. Two days by the looks of it," Bix admonished. Mirri had spoken often of the Valkyrie platoon leader; often enough that when Thrúde had crashed a few of Bix's stakeouts to threaten her life should Bix ever break Mirri's heart, well, it hadn't taken a genius to figure out the who and why of Thrúde.

"If I beat it a little more, maybe it'll drop the meat suit. Then we can have a real talk." Thrúde slammed the child's body against the wall twice more, causing drywall to rain.

"When was the last time you were able to touch a draugr without a suit in the Mids? They're only corporeal in the Under Worlds."

"Cowards," Thrúde screeched through clenched teeth and released the child. She planted a knee-high combat boot through the wall. Twice.

Wide almond eyes far too old in the child's face blinked rapidly. The draugr sat up and smoothed her pajamas. Blue-tinted lips quivered.

Bix curled a finger over a smile threatening to emerge. "What are you doing here?"

"Yeah, thief, why are you here if you didn't have anything to steal?" Thrúde adopted a wide-legged stance, showing off every rip and run in her black nylons. A faded and loose Led Zeppelin concert tank served as a micro dress. Pants, apparently, were optional by current standards of fashion.

"I," the draugr said with great dramatic indignation, "am, was, the ambassador's courier. I thought maybe I could help the investigators find something useful."

"Bullshit," Thrúde coughed. "Hel blocked everyone remotely related to the Norse pantheon from coming near Mirri. We lose our mortal bodies and get zapped back to Helheim if we get too close."

"No, the bitch blocked *you*. I'm too low on the food chain to be included in corporate initiatives." The draugr flipped her glossy brown hair over her shoulder with all the brattiness of a precious princess. Her expression softened when she studied Bix. "The ambassador wasn't as prejudiced as the rest of our pantheon. She appreciated the value of a good disguise. I wore a new suit every time we met, so none of her Chwed goons suspected."

"Useless idiots," Thrúde muttered. "Not a single one could smell your distinct aroma of rot?"

"Hey, I recycle only the freshest corpses," the draugr huffed. "Goblins like to exist amid decay; nobody else does."

"Focus," Bix chided. "What were you two fighting about just now?"

Thrúde held her tongue but arched one pierced brow at the draugr.

"The ambassador messaged me for a pickup." The draugr folded one leg, then the other with her hands and glowered at Thrúde. "I showed to collect, as per our usual arrangement, but she wasn't here."

Bix and Thrúde exchanged uneasy looks. "How long ago?"

"A week." The draugr pushed against the wall, wriggling her way closer to standing. Grinding bones sent her sliding back to the floor. "I've been burning through suits, checking in here twice a day ever since. Except for yesterday, when this place was crawling with CWIG. That's when I knew something had gone dreadfully wrong."

"Thrúde, what brings you here? Today of all days?" Bix asked.

"The minute the girls and I got word of Mirri's death, we divvied up duties, checking all her usual haunts. I pulled the straw for here. I get here, CWIG's here. So I wait till they leave. I see this mess, then find this thing in the air vent." Thrúde flicked a hand at the draugr. "Only natural to assume it's here to steal from the dead."

Valkyries. Strike first. Ask questions…well, when they were bored, really.

"So the Sisterhood kept track of Mirri, despite Hel." Bix grinned. "Frejya's orders?"

"Our own initiative." Thrúde patted the spots on her coat. "Mirri was brought up in the Sisterhood. Just because we couldn't get close to her, didn't mean we didn't track her."

"All the time?"

Thrúde bobbed her head from side to side. "Most of the time."

"Any pattern to the times when you couldn't locate her?"

"Nope, which means she went out of her way to lose us." Thrúde sniffed. "Mirri would send us messages. Things she needed us to investigate."

"How'd you report your findings?"

"Dead drops."

"I'd collect them," the draugr interjected. "Delivered them to the ambassador."

Bix pinched the bridge of her nose. "So they could have been intercepted, read, or copied, then put back."

"Please," Thrúde scoffed. "Do I look like an amateur? All

messages were coded and enchanted. Anyone messing with the messages got runed."

Runed. Tagged by Norse god magic, which left a trail visible only to the hunters to whom the specific rune belonged. Didn't matter the body, the species, or the World; the tag stayed until the hunter removed it. Rumor had it that Odin developed the lesser-known fourth aett of runes to track the gods and creatures he'd punished, so he would always know them no matter their guise. They were the same kind of trackers Jör had used on her when he'd infected her at the behest of the Consortium.

Bix scratched her forearm. "And the things you were investigating?"

"Look." Thrúde inhaled through her clenched teeth. "I know you two were close, but—"

"Don't 'but' me," Bix snapped. "I'm here at your big boss's bidding."

Thrúde rocked back on her heels. "Hel didn't just release you, she *tasked* you? Over us?"

"Does that tell you how deep the shit is surrounding Mirri's death? I'd love your help, but I don't have time to waste playing three-card monte with the Sisterhood."

"You do know the Sisterhood isn't among your fan base, right? Nobody with ties to Asgard is."

"All in, or all gone, that's how little I'm playing." Bix opened a gate to the ether. The soft song and breeze of Worlds in motion wafted into the room. Haunting. The draugr keened through pursed lips and shut her eyes.

Thrúde glanced behind her at the gate, then back to Bix with a slight shake of her head. "What happened to you during exile?"

"This isn't about me. It's about Mirri. We have six days until Hel husks her."

"That's not a lot of time, especially for one person investigating." Thrúde looked again at the ether skimming the Mid World, then nodded. "Okay, I'll get the Sisterhood on board. We'll back you, this time. For Mirri. But when this over…"

"You'll still be Valkyries sworn to protect your pantheon's interests. I'll be free of any allegiance." Bix shut the gate.

"As long as we're clear." Thrúde jerked her head toward the draugr. "What about that thing?"

"I'll deal with her." Bix considered the broken draugr. "You said the CWIG was here. I assume this disaster is their mess?"

"No." The draugr picked at a broken baseboard. "Someone beat them to it."

"Who?" Bix pressed. This close to HQ, CWIG response teams should have been here within fifteen minutes tops, which meant whoever was here first had received the news before the Consortium had tasked CWIG.

The draugr mumbled something.

"What was that?" Bix leaned forward.

The draugr mumbled again.

"Come on, I broke your legs not your face," Thrúde carped. "Speak, thief."

"Dragons," the draugr cried, then slapped a hand over her mouth.

"A dragon was here?" Bix toyed with her pendant.

"Dragons. Plural," the draugr corrected. "Two, to be exact, and not the usual drones, but Dreigiau, as in the ruling family of all dragons."

"Damn," Thrúde whispered.

"What were they after?"

"Don't know, couldn't stick around and let them catch a whiff." The draugr gestured to her borrowed body. "But there was a doozy of a light show chasing me through the air vents."

"Did you hear anything?" Thrúde prompted.

"Over the sounds of dragon demolition?" The draugr rolled her eyes. "I got out of here and changed bodies to be on the safe side. I came back a few minutes before the CWIG showed. The Dreigiau were gone. This mess was here. Even the CWIG were shocked by the destruction."

"Did you catch the CWIG team leader's name?"

"They called him Director. Big Beelzebub-looking guy." The draugr shrugged.

The director of the CWIG. Same asshat who'd put the bounty on Bix's head. He must have just returned to HQ from this scene when she'd dumped Vidya in his office.

"I'll deal with the CWIG," Bix grumbled. "We have unfinished business anyway."

"I'll circle back with the Sisterhood." Thrúde fluffed her hair. "We'll make you a copy of our case files on Mirri, including her investigation requests and our findings. Then we'll dig deeper into those gaps in our timelines when she'd go AWOL. We never looked too closely at them because we assumed she was sneaking off to see you, honestly."

"She couldn't, not without sacrificing her mortal body." Bix bit her lip. During the first days of her exile, she'd tracked Mirri from the ether, hoping for a glimpse, hoping that there would have been some way to apologize for the disaster she'd created.

The mind-wrecking thing about the ether was being able to see without anyone being able to see you. It was less fun than it sounded, and there were things in the ether that hunted the desperate and hopeful loitering too close to the Worlds they could no longer access.

Bix hadn't been able to stay on the periphery, not here, not anywhere.

"She was pretty damn proud of that body." Thrúde sighed.

"Cup-holder height," Bix and Thrúde said in unison. "A cup, B cup, C cup."

They snickered, then sobered.

"Was her CWIG detail with her when she'd vanish?" Bix asked, bringing the conversation back.

Thrúde snorted. "She ditched them so often that I wonder what their real assignment was."

Why had Hel permitted such a lax detail? There was no way the head of the pantheon hadn't known. It more than chafed that Hel had delegated Mirri's safety to the guilds.

Every time Bix thought about it, the pain along her spine returned, apparently feeding Jör's plague timer.

Speaking of pretentious gods…

"Can the Sisterhood track down visiting gods who are in the Mids legally and illegally?" Bix could no longer ignore the infernal flashing of the sconce above the ruins of the tufted white velvet bed. She moved to turn it off, but something on the floor caught its sporadic glow. Something that flashed back. Bix waded into the mound of mess obscuring it.

"Maybe." Thrúde angled away from Bix. "Why?"

"I want to know if any of those gods has recently gone missing." Bix grabbed fistfuls of stuffing. "I need to know if Mirri was taken to spite the Norse specifically, or if she's one of many gods MIA. I need to know if it's a narrow or broad attack against the pantheons."

"Now that sounds ominous," Thrúde grunted.

Bix knocked aside strips of velvet and decorative nail heads. "If the Norse end up having to go to war over this, wouldn't the Sisterhood like to know who will rally to their cause?"

"Don't misunderstand, I'm a Valkyrie. I *like* ominous." Thrúde threw aside broken slats, pausing long enough to cut a mischievous look. "I can't promise a fast turnaround on it. We might need to be a little demonstrative in our explorations to maximize our efficiency."

"Gods help us," the draugr muttered, playing with the discarded fluff.

"Everyone is expecting Hel's wrath. The Sisterhood might as well fulfill their expectations." Bix dangled a green silk camisole from her pinky. Mirri had hated that shade of green.

"Sweet." Thrúde bobbed her head. "The girls will love inciting a riot. What are you going to do about the bounty on your head?"

"No idea." Bix wagged a finger at a bit of silver by Thrúde's boot. "That. What is that?"

Thrúde knocked the thing out from under a knot of sheets. A small, solid something spun across the floor. Thrúde stopped it with her boot and picked it up. It was a small trinket. Electricity arced, wrapping around Thrúde's hands like gloves. Swearing, the Valkyrie bounced the trinket between her palms like the proverbial hot potato.

"Incoming."

Bix caught it and waited for the charge. When nothing happened, she held it up to the sunlight. The palm-sized statue of a gunmetal lion with gold antelope horns and silver raptor wings remained inert in her palm.

"Looks like one of those knickknacks from Chinatown." The draugr wrinkled her nose. "I don't think that was the ambassador's. Never noticed it here before."

"Klepto here would know the condo's inventory," Thrúde conceded.

"Mirri wasn't a fan of these 'slavering beasts,' as she called them." Bix stroked its horns and wings. One person, exactly one, knew how much Bix secretly adored these little beasties. The Bi Xie, loyal protectors of the Chinese and dispellers of evil. Bi Xie. Bix. What was not to love?

The CWIG agent who had most likely put it here, however, might not be so in love with Bix anymore. Not if Vidya had really convinced the remaining Dark Ops agents of Bix's guilt.

"Keep it if you want. Doubt Mirri's going to mind." Thrúde gained her feet. "Speaking of, I need to circle the wagons before the girls decide you're worth the bounty the CWIG's offering. I'll ring you to set up a meeting once I get your info together."

"One problem." Bix offered a chagrined smile. "I don't have a phone yet. I haven't actually resettled since returning to the Mids."

"Stay there a sec." Thrúde wandered out of the room and returned a moment later with the beat-up guitar case covered in stickers and stones. Thrúde splayed her fingers to touch eight stones. The locks on the case popped open.

"You warded your guitar?" Bix asked. "Paranoid much?"

Thrúde ignored her and flipped up the false floor of the case. Neatly compartmented within lay two short swords, a passel of black magic bags, three semiautomatic guns, clips, ammo, and a half-dozen burner phones still in plastic.

"Gigs getting a little rough these days?" Bix only half joked.

"Pfft. The band is a great cover for making black market trades. Those get a little dicey. Fun, but dicey." Thrúde cut open a phone wrapper with a dagger, then tapped rapidly on its screen. "Phones take pictures these days."

"They took pictures ten years ago too," Bix noted drolly.

"Yeah? Well, how about videos complete with sound recording?" Thrúde tossed her the phone. "Everything is uploaded to the Web with one click, so keep that in mind when you suddenly appear and disappear. Everybody is watching everything all the time."

"Valkyries and their toys," Bix muttered. "Thanks."

"My number is in there. I'll send a pic and a time when we're ready. If you get deets, don't send them, don't text them, don't talk about them on the phone. Save it till you see me." Thrúde locked her case and held out her hand. "To Mirri's Mayhem."

Bix shook her hand. "Mirri's Mayhem."

The draugr waited until the Valkyrie's footfalls could no longer be heard, then let loose a long, loud breath. "You know you painted bull's-eyes on the Sisterhood. If someone is body-snatching gods, those girls are only one notch below divine."

"The Sisterhood can handle it. Worst case, Hel can always send them back here in new bodies." Bix lunged at the draugr and wrapped her tightly in a hug. "A courier, Drew? You used your courier legend?"

"When I go to work for one of the Consortium, I stick to the undercover persona with the deepest backstory." The draugr wrapped her spindly arms around Bix's neck. "You don't know how much I've missed you."

Bix held her dearest friend at arm's length. "Missed me? You don't blame me?"

"Blame you? For what went down in our last op? No, no, no. Honey, no." Drew put her child's hand against Bix's cheek.

"I was there. I saw everything. The Host moved the armory a heartbeat after they fried us. You *couldn't* get back to us, even if we'd survived."

"How did you escape the ambush?"

"The thing about angels is they assume everyone is wearing a suit they actually need." Drew put her other hand on Bix's face. Borrowed eyes flicked over her from head to toe. "They opted to incinerate. The smoke allowed me to take shelter in a crevice. They were too damn smug to double-check their work."

"Ah, Drew, I'm so—"

"Don't you dare tell me you're sorry," Drew interrupted, dropping her hands to her hips. "The Phoenix was on you before you cleared the gate."

"I thought I was buying the team time to acquire the package. I didn't know where we'd landed until my trial."

"Not one of us had time to realize it. We were dead before we could get bearings. If any of the team were here now, they wouldn't blame you for what went down." Drew futzed with her broken legs. "We all knew something was hinky about the last-minute change of location, but the package was that important."

"We had a chance to rescue one of our own, and we ended up losing everyone." Bix clenched her fists as old anger burned anew. "I'm going to find who was behind it. As soon as I find whoever minced Mirri, I'm going after who burned our team."

Drew squeezed Bix's hand. "You know I'm with you on both missions. Lock step."

"Thank you." Bix squeezed back. "And thank you for looking after Mirri when I couldn't."

"Oh, Bixie, babe." Drew waved the green cami at her. "You need to know the little goddess was fighting for your freedom. She spent a lot of time entertaining the other pantheons, trying to discover who set us up. Never doubt she wanted you back, badly."

"A chunk of the Phoenix was found at the scene of her attack. If Mirri was digging around our final op…" Bix kneaded the pain creeping down her spine. "There's a good chance we'll all end up like her by investigating this. Are you sure—absolutely sure—you want to get in the game with me again?"

Drew smacked Bix's leopard peep-toe pump and squawked with dismay. "If you think I'm not all up in your business even when your business is not in the Mids, you have forgotten how invasive I can be."

"Then I need your very special skills as an interrogator." Bix tweaked Drew's bare broken foot.

"Interrogation, is it?" Drew thumped her fists on her chest. "Yes, yes, yes, yes, yes. Where are we going? Who do you want me to question? What's the golden apple?"

"Vidya."

"Asabitchy?" Drew blinked. "Don't tell me you two… Oh, that's not good."

Bix grimaced. "I need you to read her soul."

"Can't I just smother it, then occupy her suit?" Drew batted her lashes. "What? She takes care of that suit. It'd be fun to wear taut and toned for a while."

"She's an Oracle," Bix cautioned. "She'll know you're in there."

"It's one thing to know; it's something else to resist me." Drew waggled her brows, then scowled. "She was one of the analysts on our account. If I learn she's the reason we were burned, Asabitchy is never going to recover from the interrogation."

"She's somehow tangled up in Mirri's attack too. I need to know whose soul I'm delivering to Hel before you kill her."

"So she was in on the burn." Drew inhaled deeply and craned her neck. "Okay. For you, I'll try to let her live through the interrogation, but I don't promise to be gentle."

"She likes it rough," Bix mumbled.

"TMI," Drew shrieked, covering her eyes. "Where are you staying, eh? You can crash with me if you want. There's an old suit whose family hasn't figured out he's gone yet. Nothing as swank as this but…"

"Thanks, but this warlock named Tobek off—"

"Tobek," Drew blurted, interrupting as her brows shot to her hairline. "Big guy? Braids? Missing a hand? As in the scrumptious-but-surly owner of Dysmorphic?"

Bix couldn't stop a smirk. "If that's the name of his shop, then yes, that one."

"He is a magnificent hunk of mystery with a fleet of muscular men at his beck and call." Drew shivered and grinned. "Dysmorphic is staffed by an endless parade of eye candy. Most of them have the brains to match the brawn too."

Bix snorted. "Frequent customer, are you?"

"Hell yes, and they don't discriminate." Drew spun her finger around her hair and puckered her lips. "Want me to do a full background on Tobek? Please? Pretty please can I have a legit excuse to take him for a ride?"

"He's warded his body with more than ink." Bix recalled how nice that body had felt surrounding her during the night. "I don't think you can get past his personal protection system without removing chunks of him."

"Warded his *body*?" Drew sucked her cheeks into hollows. "And how close were you to that body?"

"He is awfully snuggly in spite of zero body fat." Bix batted her lashes.

"Back one day and you score a top-level hottie." Drew slapped the back of her hand against her brow. "I expect all the intimate details. All. Unedited."

"No." Bix chortled. "Always some editing."

"Fine. We'll do the adulting thing and investigate the Consortium. *Then* I get the details to which every bestie is entitled." Drew flopped back on the floor. "I need a drop-off. Can't leave the corpse of a little girl in the ambassador's home, things being what they are and what not."

"Providence Hospital still your preferred boutique?"

"They do have a wonderful assortment of suits there." Drew clasped her hands over her heart. "Welcome back, Bixie. You've been gone too long."

Bix opened a gateway to the hospital's morgue beneath the draugr. Drew's giggle lingered after the gate closed.

Bix moseyed out to the great room and clutched the Bi Xie to her chest. She could still see Mirri on her knees in the middle of the room, bawling, pleading, and reaching for her.

"I'm so sorry, Mirri. I should have been here for you," Bix whispered, skimming her thumb over the engraving in the bottom of the trinket. The engraving was a code for a clandestine meeting site. A message left by a current spy for an ex-spy.

Time to find out if she had any friends left inside the CWIG.

# CHAPTER 7

The congestion of Georgetown hadn't gotten any better in Bix's absence. Cars still inched along M Street, trapped by ill-timed lights and a sea of pedestrians in the throes of shopping, lunching, and preening. A sharp right took Bix to a far less congested side street, past Blues Alley and down toward the canal.

"You should have stayed in exile, gatekeeper."

Bix drew up before a sandy-haired man dressed in autumn linen. His dappled brown eyes looked down on her in disgust. Ah, the trident of tiny hooks sprouting along the back of his left hand told her everything.

Those hooks snared disembodied souls and kept them from fleeing.

"You're a psychopomp," she sniggered, tapping the metal beastie from the condo against her lips. "Do you seriously think you look intimidating? You're dressed as Mister Mantras and Mindfulness. Are you hawking meditative coloring books too? 'Cause if they come with a pack of gel pens, I might buy what you're selling."

"No respect for the rights of the guild most adored by the gods." Another tree-hugging psychopomp appeared behind her. A woman.

"Adored?" Bix laughed "You're like the pizza delivery guys for the pantheons."

"Keep it up, gatekeeper." This from a third psychopomp, emerging from Blues Alley. From the cockeyed fedora to the Fender across his back, he at least dressed like an afterlife guide of musicians. "The bounty on your head gives us permission to wreck your ass up for what you've done."

"I've actually done a lot of things in the last thirty hours, which is more than I can say for your worthless guild. But go ahead, tell me what it is that has Team Carryout so gwumpy." She stuck her bottom lip way out as she counted the growing number of Chweds drifting closer to the side street, taking photos. Phones in an ever-widening area chirped, hummed, and played ghastly sound clips of pop culture. Pedestrians blocked the road all the way back to M Street.

Not everyone in the growing crowd was a psychopomp. Countless races of Chweds were answering the call of the stupid bounty. However, the psychopomps amassed in the fastest numbers, keeping the others from getting too close.

Greed and the need to protect the golden goose while trying to capture it.

"You messed with our guild's business." Sandy sauntered around her. "Now the guild masters are going to pay us for your capture, then they're going to pay us to make sure you never come back."

"Your business," Bix said flatly, closing one eye. "Is that the business with the jobs you failed to do when over a hundred souls were freed of their bodies in Centralia? I gave you time to report to the job site. I'd assumed events caught you—you who are granted a dash of foresight via the contracts struck between the gods and the Fates to make sure you know where and when to go—by surprise. Still, not a single pompous ass showed up."

And not one of the two dozen and growing number of psychopomps seemed remotely surprised or chagrined.

That was when it hit her.

"Oh." She chuckled softly at first, then progressively and obnoxiously louder. "Oh, the gods are going to *love* this. You guys are into extortion these days?"

A few darted guilty glances at the bolder members of the group.

"If the living don't pay your monthly 'retainer,' you let them linger, don't you?" Bix wagged her Bi Xie at those leading members. "You let them linger until you can wring something valuable from their loved ones. No payment, no journey. Not nice."

"How we manage our business is none of your concern, Other Worlder." The bluesman rolled a toothpick along his lip. "You have no right undermining the way we earn our pay."

"Me?" She flopped her hands over her chest and fluttered her lashes. "Moi? An Other Worlder? Possibly."

"Put them back," shrieked the tree hugger. "Put the Reaping Winds back."

"My four elemental friends? The ones who cleanse the Mids of things that don't belong? Those Reaping Winds?" Bix's lips formed a nice little ring, then split into a wicked grin. "No."

"We're not asking." Sandy closed the distance between them. The crowd moved in with him. Tight. Shoulder to shoulder. Heel to toe. Ass to crotch. Phone to face.

"Here's a bit of business advice." Bix raised her voice so the cheap seats could hear her. After all, when being recorded, clarity was important. "Get to the untethered souls before the Winds do."

The cries of indignation rose as a chorus, drawing those not of the Guild of Psychos into the fringes.

"Take the fresh souls to the gods like you're supposed to, and pray that none of the really hungry gods notice you've been shorting them." She turned to the bluesman and kept speaking loudly, waving her Chinese trinket. "Trust me, as one who's spent the last ten years under the yoke of godly wrath, you don't want them to find out what you're doing."

The Bi Xie trembled in her hand. Electrical volts shot down

her arm and blasted through the crowd, leaping from jewelry to phones to piercings to shoe studs. Screams broke with the exodus. Deluded warnings of angry gods cleared the side street down to the canal and up to the blinking traffic lights of M Street.

The Bi Xie settled back into her palm. Inert.

Bix pinched the smoking tip of a lock of hair and glared behind her. A security camera aimed at a weathered green door was tucked into the shadows of a narrow, long-forgotten horse passage between two row houses. The bleak tones of an access buzzer summoned her.

She hip-bumped the door, swinging it wide. Aromatics of complex spices and mystical herbs washed over her. If tranquility had a scent, this was it. A child watched her with wide eyes from the cover of a display counter. Bix offered her the Bi Xie. The child refused the beastie, taking Bix by the hand instead. They passed through a beaded curtain and a screen of wards into the tearoom next door to the shop. The child gestured to the booth at the back of the elegantly appointed yet typically Georgetown-small historic building.

Bix's heart leapt and her guts sank as she spotted the man sitting alone and staring at the steam from a copper teakettle. Supervisory Special Agent Ashtad Ba'al. This was the man who'd convinced her to join the CWIG's clandestine services. He'd pulled her from the academy into the field. He'd pushed, poked, and challenged her at every turn to make her a better agent. He'd taught her how to be a member of a team, how to value the help of others, and how to be valuable to others for more than just her relocation abilities. He'd been her boss, her mentor, and in a lot of ways her big brother.

He also epitomized loyalty to the agents within the Dark Ops units. If he believed Vidya's smear campaign, if he believed the official findings of the CWIG, or if he believed Bix had intentionally delivered her team to their deaths, this meeting was going to get really ugly really quickly.

She wasn't entirely sure she could cope with the heartbreak of losing his respect or his friendship. She rolled the Bi Xie between her hands, working up the courage to approach him.

The mirrored wall at his back reflected the warm illumination of the sconces over his glossy ebony curls. The lights danced through the bright gold streaks above his ears and shimmered across his gently sloping shoulders covered in the finest ochre silk.

A coin spun amid the steam from the kettle. Within the steam, the feed from the security camera played.

As she neared the table, the coin sparked. Not a coin, an electrode that looked like a coin. Drop one in a target's pocket, and Ashtad could use it as a tracker, a weapon, or listening device.

Electricity was a biddable bitch in his hands.

"I had the sitch with the psychopomps covered, you know." Bix slid into the booth next to its lone occupant and pried the conductor off the bottom of the Bi Xie, flicking the coin under Ashtad's loosely laced fingers.

"I hope you weren't planning on dumping that angry mob on the dinner table of some unsuspecting giants in another World." He twitched his pinky, and her coin jumped into the air to dance with his. The steam-feed showed a few of the lower-caste mob members trickling back into the side street, cautiously searching and trying all the doors.

"I did that once, and the giants *loved* it." She bumped his thigh with hers. "They enjoy surprises. Today's mob had compacted themselves into what could have been a nice centerpiece."

"That's not how you make friends, and friends are what you need now that you are no longer a shadowy operative." He poured a minty-lemony-smelling tea into one of two delicate cups waiting on the table.

Bix sighed. "And which are you now, Ashtad? Are you the friendly giants or the angry mob?"

He set the full cup in front of her and set the empty one in front of himself. "Move the tea."

"You're not my boss anymore." She huffed and scanned the room for gazes that lingered too long. No one paid them any heed.

"Move the tea, Bix. Now."

Over the years they'd known each other, Ashtad had chewed her up one side, back down the other, then round and round twice more for good measure. Usually, it'd been merited. She knew his timbre at full bellow and lethal whisper. She knew the variances in his tone when he was playing a part versus being earnest. She also knew the tension in his body when she was one stunt away from pushing him too far.

He had that tension now.

She opened two gates no bigger than the tip of her pinky. Tea drained from her cup into his. His jaw loosened up a tish. She moved the tea from his cup back to the spout of the kettle. He dropped his chin to his chest.

"Still a brat," he muttered.

Three words of his familiar teasing, and her stress level plummeted.

"Tell me you don't believe I meant for my team to die," she whispered.

"Of course I don't. Never did. But knowing it and proving it are two different things." He poured himself a proper cup of tea. "Sorry for the test, but I had to know that your time away hadn't broken you or your control."

"I had a lot of time to practice all the finer details of creating, shaping, and sealing gates. There's not much else to do in the ether. As for my mentals, I haven't been back long enough to self-check."

"That's fair." He inclined his head. "Glad you got my message. Glad you trusted me enough to come."

"You're the only one who would leave me a Bi Xie. Fortunately, I still remember the code of three hash marks on the coin you hid in the base means 'tea' for teahouse." She bounced her heel on the red-carpeted floor. "How much of my conversations at the condo did you overhear?"

He shook his head. "None. The building is warded against spying. Death metal is the filler noise, in case you're wondering.

Astral viewing is blocked by flashing images guaranteed to induce seizures. The Norse don't do anything by halves."

"Including releasing me." She grunted. "Who told you I'd been freed? The CWIG or your father?"

Ashtad's breath charged the air as his moods clashed. The positive versus the negative, the cool calm against the heated passion. His electrifying presence had a whole lot to do with being the son of the storm god, Ba'al. A lot, but not all. When Ashtad eventually completed his demigod trials and ascended to full godhood, there was a damn good chance he'd wind up more powerful than dear old Dad.

Bix desperately wanted to witness that pantheonic shake-up.

"When Agent Asariri crashed through the CWIG director's ceiling, I expected you to follow."

"In spite of what the director thinks he wants, a meeting with me will end badly for him."

"Ah, there it is, the bitterness of being disavowed." He gave her a thin-lipped smile. "If the Consortium had left him any wiggle room, the director wouldn't have let his only gatekeeper go. But the frame-up was solid, too solid. So after your botched op, I changed shops, left clandestine services, and joined CI Investigations."

"Counterintelligence Investigations?" Bix blinked rapidly. "They're like the Infernal Affairs of spy craft. Don't tell me you're burning bridges for my sake?"

He stared at the wall. A muscle spasmed in his jaw. "Have you been back to Centralia since the slaughter?"

"Maybe."

"That's a yes, then. Notice something weird? Something missing?"

The snort happened before her brain could stop it.

"It was a bunker used by the Chwed guild masters for the express purpose of plotting and scheming against the Consortium." He took a sip of tea. "The anthracite fires offer a security barrier against the higher magics."

She gawped. "That explains why none of the naturalist guilds ever repaired the area."

"A meeting was in session when everything went to hell—so to speak. A number of the guild masters were injured in the subsequent panic. One died. One more will very soon. Two are still unaccounted for."

"Plus the not insignificant assault on a Norse goddess followed by the slaughter of the CWIG team a quarter of a mile above them," she reminded him. "Were the guild masters' injuries caused by the events on the surface or because they turned on each other?"

"They say the former. I'm inclined to believe the latter. It'd be more useful if I could locate the bunker."

"Yeah, good luck with that," she snickered.

He studied her from the corner of his eye. "I'm hoping we can work together to solve this. Hel made it clear to the powers that be why you've been released. As long as I can assure the director that the situation in Centralia has been resolved and the threat neutralized, the actual detainment and punishment of the culprits is all yours."

"One problem, left hand, your right hand is already investigating."

"This is the very necessary public investigation on which many eyes are focused." He flipped his right palm up, then his left. "This hand never came out of the shadows. Catching those who betray their own requires a certain distance from the hand that feeds."

"If this investigation was personal for you, Ashtad, I'd have your back in an instant." She shook her head. "But when it comes to CWIG, they shit on Mirri from the moment she became ambassador. First with an inept protective detail and now with a low-ranking field agent leading the public investigation into her assault. So, no, I have no interest in playing well with the guild, and I have no interest in making friends with people who put a godsdamned bounty on my head."

She set the Bi Xie on the table and slid out of the booth.

"Your girlfriend selected her own security detail," he called softly. "She refused the teams we chose and demanded the pick of anyone in the guild."

That stopped Bix. She turned back.

"She was gone for a week before her remains turned up," Bix hissed, planting her palms on the table. "Her detail should have reported her MIA after ten minutes if they'd been worth a damn, even following loose-leash protocol."

"Yes. They should have. I too would like to know why they didn't, but they're dead. Husked, from what I understand." He pointed to the seat across from him.

She glared at him but took the seat.

"As for Agent Asariri, her assignment was to oversee the collection of the evidence and its secure transport back to HQ." He gave her a reproachful look. "The lead investigator into the ambassador's mauling is the director himself. You're looking in the wrong places to pick fights, Bix. You know better. I trained you better."

She slumped in her seat and sniffed. "What was the CWIG looking for at Mirri's?"

"Standard investigative procedure." He pushed his cup away from him.

"Standard procedure was to send me to plant evidence or extract it before anyone else arrived on scene." She drummed her nails on the table. "I've been to the condo. The only thing planted was your message. The CWIG team stayed for a long time. What was the director desperate to find?"

Whatever it was, the dragons had gotten to it first. No doubt about it.

Ashtad swept his hand past the conductors still spinning above the teakettle, changing the feed. Images of streets, office buildings, a few bedrooms, and a lot of nurseries flickered past as he scanned for the right station. "The ambassador's security detail filed regular reports, as is SOP; however, those reports are no longer at HQ."

"Why would they think Mirri had them?"

The images in the steam stabilized. "Be here at ten tomorrow, not a minute later. You're going to have a meeting with the director."

"The result of which had better be the end of the bounty." She memorized the image and nodded. "If he tries anything stupid, he gets an express pass and you get a promotion."

Ashtad placed the Bi Xie in front of her. "Keep it."

# CHAPTER 8

Internet street image searches with 360-degree views were the single greatest innovation ever. If only the other Worlds in the Mids would catalogue and make public every door, sewer cover, and pig trail, then Bix could verify her own missions without relying on traitorous third parties.

Not that Ashtad was anything like Vidya, and neither of them were like the director of the CWIG. The director and Bix had a consistently unpleasant history. Alas, she needed the stupid bounty off her head, because no matter how many times she could and would relocate the hunters, they weren't going to stop unless she transferred them all to the Under Worlds. The gods would be amused the first time, but not so much beyond that.

Upshot, Ashtad had read her in on the secret bunker, which might help her and a certain warlock unravel what had happened in Centralia. To that end, Bix returned to the coal plant in Old Town Alexandria, a mere five miles down the Potomac River from from her Georgetown rendezvous with Ashtad.

Tobek had asked her to meet him in his shop, upstairs from his basement home. She opted to be slightly normal and arrive via the front door. She paused in the parking lot to take in the extensive changes to the site. Gone were the rust, the grime, the soot, and the stink of the old plant. The entire twenty-five acres along the waterfront had been overhauled. The main building had been converted into a mixed-use property with shops along the ground level and residential lofts in the stories above. Cooling towers and outbuildings had been replaced by more residences built atop a parking garage. Most of the railroad tracks had been dug up and paved over. There were thoughtfully planned green spaces, picnic areas, and walking trails. From building facades to landscaping, everything had been designed with a nod to the history of the plant and to the much older port town; but there was no denying the place had been constructed to suit very modern needs.

The last of the afternoon sun lent a warm golden glow to the sea of chrome filling the parking lot outside the main building that housed Tobek's shop, Dysmorphic. High-dollar custom-built bikes rested three deep to a spot. Kit cars in pristine condition sat next to muscle cars in varying stages of salvation. Oh, and then there were the monster trucks hopped up on tires taller than a person. Light bars with skull covers, mud flaps with naked faeries, and an excess of ghost flames and barbed wire paint jobs said a lot about the owners of those trucks. Not as much as the gun racks, but still.

No wonder Tobek kept to a simple black awning for his shop. He needed it to block the glare. To the left of Dysmorphic was a front of mirrored windows and a door with a biometric lock. "BMR Labs" hung in plain cold steel over the doorway. In contrast, the shop at the other end of the building had lightly tinted windows and boldly printed shades that read, "MWA Community Classes."

If that stood for Men with Attitudes, then it totally explained the parking lot.

Of greatest interest was the wrought iron security door between Dysmorphic and the classroom. It wasn't at all clear to which shop that door belonged.

Bix slid her phone in her bra and retrieved her Bi Xie from the tooled leather seat of a beautifully restored '47 Indian motorcycle in Seafoam Blue. That wrought iron security door called to her, and the closer she got, the more it made her tingle in the delightful way a new pair of shoes did. The same sort of way a gate to another World did. Biting her lip, she curled her fingers over the etched oval knob. The pendant nestled between her breasts heated.

The door of Dysmorphic burst open.

A cyclops flew through the air and crashed into a line of motorcycles. All that pretty chrome kissed pavement. The cyclops scrambled to his great big feet. Blood flowed from his crooked nose. Tears welled in his eye.

"If you can't take a punch in the face, then there's no way you can handle a Prince Albert. We don't offer anesthetics. If you need them, go find a human to pierce your dick." Tobek propped the door open with his boot. "And pick up your mess, you godsdamned pussy."

The cyclops gingerly set each fallen bike back on its wheels. Hastily wiping his tears, he thundered to a monster truck and folded himself inside. Rubber burned as he tore out of the parking lot in a cloud of fetid fumes and speed metal.

Muttering, Tobek grabbed the battle-ax door handle and turned. His expression lit when he spotted her. His attention drifted to the Bi Xie clutched to her bosom, and his brows reached his hairline.

"Be right back," he called over his shoulder as he headed for her. "Sweetheart, you came back before dinner. Excellent."

"Do you know you carry yourself like a man who's been chewed up, spit out, and resurrected by an excess of grouchiness to do some taxidermy on his demons?"

He laughed and shook his head, extending his hand to her. "And here I am, having a good day."

Bix took his hand and leaned toward the security door. "What don't you want me to see back here?"

He reached around her and opened the door. A regular stairway with nubby rubber treads lay dead ahead. A freight elevator backed to the classroom wall. A wall of mailboxes backed to Dysmorphic.

"Leads to the apartments upstairs."

"Cagey, is it?" She ambled into the small foyer. "You're talking to a gatekeeper here. I can *feel* the gateway to another World."

"Back side of the stairs, behind a drywall illusion." He gestured to it but gently tugged on her hand in the other direction. "And for most Chweds, that gateway would take them to a random welcome center in a random World."

She closed one eye. "Yeah, but?"

"You're not most Chweds. You'd probably wind up at a heavily armed guard station."

She clasped his wrist and swayed like a six-year-old desperate to go on the ride. "Oh, come on, you can't give a teaser like that, then expect me to not look."

"It's a gateway to the six supermax prisons of the Mids."

She stopped swaying and straightened. "Well, all righty, then, maybe I will save that adventure for… Wait, I've never heard of a Chwed supermax prison. Problem Chweds are permanently removed from the Mids. I present myself as case in point."

"Yet here you are." He led her out of the foyer and back to the parking lot.

"Splitting hairs," she countered, needing three high-heeled steps to keep up with his one long stride. "The very notion of 'supermax' means the prisoners did something irredeemably awful."

"The long-lived are never irredeemable, and prisoners are kept because they are perceived to be useful sooner or later." He opened the door to Dysmorphic.

The whir of machines blended with the low hum of muted chatter as she crossed the threshold into a large and deep shop that had retained much of the old coal plant while mixing in a modern metal aesthetic. Spell sigils hid in the mortar on the mostly brick sidewalls and within the mottled brown-and-gray stain of the concrete floor. Stainless steel cabinets and counters gleamed amid stamped iron half walls that segmented eight good-sized stalls on each side of the shop. Assorted artwork and photographs were taped to the half walls and lower cabinets.

Within each stall was an occupied reclining chair or padded table. Some stalls had magnifying lights on casters. Others had stainless steel carts lugging small humming machines, surgical sets, or silicone shapes.

Every stall had a huge dude on a tiny rolling stool. Some of the men were bald. Some had buzz cuts. Some rocked the long ponytail. All of them wore latex gloves and disposable face masks as they bent over some form of teeth-grinding, padding-clenching Chwedlonol.

Not every patron was a dude, surprisingly. A few women were getting ink, and the folks flipping through idea books in the deep leather chairs at the front lounge were definitely gender fluid.

Tobek paused at one of two large display counters, futzed with a computer for half a minute, and returned to her side.

"Door to our home is in the back, just in case you ever need to take the normal route." He gestured to the archway centered in a blackened iron wall from which weapons hung. A dozen swords of various styles. Daggers. Two axes. A mace and flail. Oh, hey, what would guy décor be without a few shields ranging from extra large to codpiece small?

"Do you cut the sleeve off after you ink it?" She tipped her head at the arsenal.

Tobek barked with mirth.

Machines went silent. Stools rolled.

"Oh fine, now you all look up." She threw her hands in the air…and left them there. The linking trait among all the men working the shop became apparent. Vibrant blue eyes. Exactly like Tobek's.

"Berserkers?" She clamped the Bi Xie tightly in her fist. "So *this* is what Odin's chosen warriors do with their free time? Tattoos, piercings, scarifications, and assorted other body mods?"

"Odin's been on walkabout since Hel took over the pantheon." Tobek drew her arms back down to her sides. "Plus, he neither ruled nor chose the Berserkers. He did, however, enjoy taking credit for our accomplishments. Berserkers are chosen by the Fates. Every

House of Fate contributes retainers to the greater Mid Worlds Army. The eyes come with the lifelong military commission."

The skin tones of the Berserkers ran the gamut from pasty to pitch, and the religious symbols inked into said skins spanned a lot of different belief systems—sometimes on the same body—so sure, cross-House über-army could be plausible. But goddamn, the intensity of every pair of blue, blue eyes made her shiver.

"You did mention a contract with the Fates," she conceded. "Conveniently neglected to mention the army connection though."

"Some of our brethren make ends meet as professional brawlers." Tobek wagged an elbow at a series of dude-bro pictures on the wall nearest the front door. "These men here are damn fine artists needing an appropriate outlet."

"Customer service comes with a side of temper tantrum, though, right?" Bix teased, smiling at the guys.

"Keep up the lip, and you'll find out." Tobek grinned. "See you tomorrow, boys."

Whistles and ribald commentary followed them from the main shop as Tobek used his body to herd her under the archway into a long iron-clad corridor with strategically placed beveled mirrors.

"Left is the clinic." He gestured to a stainless steel door at the end of the hall. "If you ever need medical attention and I'm not around, head there."

"So BMR stands for Big Man Rising?"

"Berserker Medical Research." He tipped his head to the side. "To the right is the classroom, meeting hall, whatever we need it to be."

"Men with Attitudes needs a classroom? Specializing in sulking? Pouting? Ogre tossing?"

"Where do you come up with these things?" He shook his head. "Mid World Army. It's not easy being a soldier, then having to reintegrate into society. You never know when you're going to get called up, for what, or how long. Some tours can change a man, and some of those changes are quite profound. Some of those tours send the man home but keep his mind. This building, indeed the entire compound, is one of many havens."

"And sometimes the teams don't come home at all," she said, gnawing on her cheek.

"Too often." He nodded.

She shook off the creep of melancholy. "And the twelve floors above us? The neighborhing buildings? All apartments? All occupied by Berserkers?"

"Or other Chweds in need of our help." He backed her into a dinky utility room. "You are safe here. Never fear that."

A black boiler and a dented drip pan on a concrete floor occupied one side of the otherwise cramped little closet. A roaring furnace hogged the opposing wall. Pipes, hoses, and vents wound their way along the unfinished industrial ceiling.

"I was thinking more of why there would be a hidden gateway to supermax prisons right above your home, high warlock, but now that I know it's actually in the middle of a battalion of Berserkers, it makes total sense." She nodded ever so sagely, but she couldn't maintain her stoicism. Not around him and his infectious good mood.

"Exactly." He reached into the gap between the furnace and the air handler.

Hydraulic locks tumbled.

The entire wall of furnace slid aside. Amber crystals embedded in the curved ceiling illuminated a steep stairway carved into what had been the cooling pipes of the old plant. Tobek motioned her ahead.

"Thirty-one steps."

The walls were cool beneath her palms as she slowly descended stairs deep enough to accommodate someone with big feet. Like, say, the seven-foot-tall not-Viking moving noiselessly behind her. Hissing sounded, and a heartbeat later, darkness coated the stairwell. Blue-green fluorescence limned the treads and ended at a wall of black.

Tobek reached over her shoulder and pushed seven spots

of darkness. Again, the sound of hydraulics in action filled the stairwell. A huge wheel rolled aside, revealing the familiar sight of the basement home. She hopped off the last step and turned. The giant steel wheel was the canvas for a modern art installation covering a notable portion of the back wall. A series of matte-black blocks protruded amid the curve and curl of the sculpture.

"Did Gurp do that too?" She stared in awe as the wheel rolled back into place, the art installation once again complete.

"He let me do one or two things around here."

Her mouth moved without forming actual words before she managed something coherent. "You made that. Is there anything you can't do?"

"Long-lived, remember?" He steered her through the labyrinth, past the altar to a section that smelled faintly of lavender and lilies. He laid a finger across his lips and stepped aside.

Bix lingered in the hallway and bit her lip. Gurp hummed an old Romani folksong while he hung her dresses in a cleverly configured open shelving unit. Colorful cloth baskets lined one wall of white shelves. Her collection of shoes filled two more walls of shelves.

A large round bed upon a Lucite dais sat center in the space framed by shelving units. The hot pink satin sheets and a fuzzy white comforter might have been a bit over the top, but she would never nitpick such kindness.

"It's beautiful, Gurp."

The goblin shrieked and scampered up the shelves.

Not laughing nearly killed her. "I'm sorry. I didn't mean to frighten you."

Gurp peered between his fingers, then heaved a mighty sigh… and farted. Three arrangements of gorgeous blooms puffed neutralizing scent in response.

"Truly, my friend, you have outdone yourself." She headed to the display of shoes and picked up a new pair. "You added to my collection?"

Gurp slowly descended from his perch. "Pretty lady like?"

"Oh, very, very much. Everything you've done. I wish we'd known each other when I lived here the first time." She held up a second pair of new shoes. "Comic pages? Gurp, you've found my weakness."

Gurp beamed, clutching his pudgy hands to his chest. "Home, yes?"

Tears stung, and she nodded. "Yes. Yes. Thank you. Thank you, both."

"It suits you, sweetheart." Tobek leaned against a shelving wall, his expression rich with pride and indulgence. "The boys brought back some intriguing unexploded ordinance today. That sound like a meal worthy of a master of design, Gurp?"

Gurp squealed and darted from the new room.

Bix set the shoes back on the shelf. "I can't believe the lengths he went for me."

"Goblin love is a strange and wondrous thing." Tobek raised her chin with the edge of his finger and wiped her tears with his thumb. "Come tell me what you learned today while I fix dinner."

She trailed behind him as they wended their way to the kitchen. "I learned what was relocated from Centralia."

"Yeah?" He hefted two huge military green duffle bags on to the mortician's table as Gurp climbed up on his swivel stool and rubbed his hands. "That why you're clinging to a toy from Chinatown like your life depended on it?"

She set the Bi Xie on the counter and turned it to face him. "I got him to keep an eye on you."

All merriment vanished from his face. His eyes narrowed. She narrowed her eyes too.

"You're screwing with me again, aren't you?"

"You'll learn."

He smirked and relaxed, picking up the trinket. He murmured something she couldn't hear and waved his hand over the statue's face. Carved eyes closed. He grunted with satisfaction and set the Bi Xie on top of the stainless steel range hood.

The soft whisper of fluttering feathers emanated from the

statue. The Bi Xie melted into the hood. Metal grumbled and groaned. The splash guard buckled and bowed, reshaping into silver stainless steel wings unfurled over the eight-burner range. The flue blackened. Popping echoed as the smooth vertical surface warped, taking the shape of a lion's head leaning out from the vent, maw wide. Spiraled antlers pressed out farther, stretching the metal and peeling away its color until nothing was left but the golden gleam.

"That is…awesome," Bix breathed.

"It wouldn't have done it if you didn't consider this place your sanctuary," Tobek said while rifling through the fridge.

Bix hesitantly skimmed her fingers over the hood. "You don't mind this being on display so prominently?"

"What's not to like about it?" He set an armful of food on the counter. "It's a protector totem. Might come in handy if someone breaks through the wards."

"Gurp, is it okay with you?"

The goblin stuffed a six-pointed stone star in his mouth. His lips puckered and out came a grenade pin. He plucked it with a flourish. His cheeks puffed. Orange smoke shot out his nose.

"Yes," the goblin said through a tangerine cloud. His eyes crossed. His brows lifted, and he sucked in the cloud. "Better second time."

"What was in Centralia?" Tobek asked, sharpening an array of knives.

Bix hopped up on the counter. "Guild masters' secret bunker."

"Dumbasses." He grunted. "Anybody inside when it moved?"

"Two masters are MIA."

"So let's assume it wasn't a coincidence that the guild masters were there at the same time as the Phoenix and the ambassador." He cleaved a head of cabbage in one effortless whack and set half of it aside. "If the Phoenix, in his fully robust form, landed there, they would have felt it and fled."

"There were injuries, but the verdict is out on whether it was caused by friendly fire."

"Most likely bickering among themselves." He flipped the half head, added a thick layer of steak on top of it, then jabbed his knife in the steak. "Imagine the meat as the quarter mile of buffering ground. The knife is the Phoenix's dewclaw."

"It didn't penetrate the bunker."

"Since so many guild masters survived, that's my guess." He separated meat from veg and diced up the cabbage. "Plus, if you're going to go to the length of hiding from the Consortium, wouldn't you make sure you buried your secret hideaway deeply enough that a dragon couldn't accidentally break a nail on it?"

"True."

"Secondly, if the Phoenix had wanted those masters dead, he could simply have ignited the remaining anthracite stores and blown it sky-high. Fire *is* his thing." Tobek lit a burner on the stove to accent his point.

"If he'd wanted them alive, he could have dug them up like a potato." She scratched at the counter. "Either way, the ground would have been spectacularly disturbed. Instead, we have a comparatively small and singular point of impact that presumably didn't damage the bunker."

"The alarm inside the bunker was probably raised by the influx of magic happening above it."

"So again, how did a freshly severed dewclaw get there? And how did *nobody* notice? Not even the people investigating the scene." She covered her face. "Nobody except the snipers."

"Nothing about the Phoenix has hit the streets. So far, that bit of information has stayed among the three of us." He hacked up the steak. "That also means no one has seen him in forty-eight hours, because if he showed up anywhere with a piece of himself missing, the black market would be atwitter over the chance to own that piece."

"Unless he's holed up with the Host, licking his wound." She propped her chin on her palm. "Except, he didn't strike me as the Cowardly Lion, not during our skirmish and not during my trial. He'd definitely be out there, hunting a bitch down for taking a chunk out of him."

"Agreed. Everything I know of him in this incarnation says he should be making huge waves. In fact, the absence of any rumors at all about him is perplexing." He threw the raw food in a pan and set it on the burner. "So let's take a darker view of what might have gone down in Centralia."

"What if the reason no one has come looking for Feng bits is because…" She eyed the pendant between her breasts. "Feng himself is missing? Has *been* missing? That whoever took Mirri and kept her locked in her mortal body might also have enough juice to abduct the Phoenix?"

"If the Norse ambassador didn't attack him, then maybe they are or were victims together." He poured broth into the pan and stirred the pot, keeping one eye on her. "The Consortium would never admit to losing anything, much less their lead investigator. Even the *idea* that someone could hide from them—willingly or not—undermines their authority."

"That would explain why an alarm wasn't raised about Mirri's disappearance." Bix huffed with disgust. "If Feng is in the same boat, the Consortium has to be looking for him. Finding him and the perpetrator is the only way to protect their interests. They can't trust the CWIG with the sort of intel that would come from learning how Feng is being hidden from them and by whom."

"The question then becomes, who did the Consortium tap to locate him?" He pulled spices from a cabinet. "Whomever they appointed is keeping the search very quiet."

"Feng is a dragon-angel hybrid." Bix chewed her cheek. "If I'm in the Consortium, I'm tasking the race most familiar with his habits and predilections to find him."

"Dragons and angels alternate responsibility for raising, tutoring, and training the Phoenix with each of his incarnations." He threw spices into the pot. "This time around, he was the angels' ward."

"Figures that it's the race who already has a beef with me." She groaned. "They're not going to be cooperative."

"Not with you or anyone else." He thumped the spoon on

the edge of the pan and set the spoon on the counter. "Regardless of whether they were appointed by the Consortium or they volunteered to conduct the search, the angels having the lead means the dragons have to stay hands-off. Any interference by the dragons is a political disaster. They've probably already been called to task for showing up at Centralia when the dewclaw activated."

Two dragons had been at Mirri's condo shortly after her death. Had ruining Mirri's place been a hint or the carelessness of an arguably superior race? Covert op? Bait? Political jab?

"If the Phoenix is missing at the same time a goddess has been attacked and the guild masters targeted…shit." Bix dropped her head back and groaned. "I can't take on the Angelic Host with an 'if' or something that sounds like an accusation. I need to gather more solid proof before I tangle with them."

"Wise," Tobek grunted. "I'll look into what sort of magic it would take to hide the Phoenix from the Consortium and which of those choices overlap with the means of locking a goddess into a mortal body."

Bix's boob rang, the opening strain of Wagner's Ride of the Valkyries. Tobek regarded her bosom questioningly. She slid the phone from her bra and jiggled her boobs. Color stained his cheeks, and he cleared his throat.

A picture of a dilapidated room with peeling beige paint and water-stained plaster filled the phone's screen. A time stamp read ninety seconds from now. Thank the gods that Thrúde had wasted no time arranging a meet. Hopefully, the Sisterhood's records could provide a solid link between Mirri and Feng.

"Sorry to miss your dinner, but I've got to run." Bix slipped the phone back in her bra.

"Hey, you've been back for two days." Tobek put a lid on the pan and turned down the heat. "Have you fed?"

"I got accustomed to starving," she hedged. In truth, she was quickly burning through the snack Hel had given her. She did need to find another god to feed from, but she'd spent ten years being consistently rejected by them. Finding a god with enough raw energy to sustain her, a god whom she could trust not to poison or entrap her…it would take way more time than she had left to solve Mirri's case. She'd just have to make do.

"Don't discount how the native magic of the Mids affects you." Tobek looked away, but not before she caught the dawning blue glow of his eyes that spoke of a Berserker's rage. He focused on the pan and its need for a bit of hostile stirring. "Be smart, feed sooner than later, especially if you're going to confront the Host."

She bit her lip and sighed, fighting back a smile. It was nice that someone cared.

"Enjoy your dinners." She hopped off the counter and smoothed her skirt, giving Gurp a reassuring wink.

The goblin shook a finger at her.

"I'll see you tonight, right?" Tobek called over his shoulder.

"Probably."

"No probablies." He stared at the range hood. "Or those Valkyries you're about to visit are going to have a whole lot of testosterone up in their business."

Bix saluted like a proper soldier and opened gates.

# CHAPTER 9

Despair. The room reeked of despair. A rusting wheelchair sat in front of a tube TV with a shattered screen. A lone ankle boot dangled from the broken glass, suspended by a frayed brown shoelace. Sloping piles of dust and dirt sat in moats of brackish rainwater. Through the doorway, peeling periwinkle framed large rounded windows, admitting the silver stretches of moonlight.

A weathered wooden sign leaned against the fungus-covered door. *Forest Haven: District Training School for the Mentally Retarded.*

An abandoned asylum.

"For sixty-six years, locals shunted off humans and Chweds to this hellhole. In its best years, there were a whole two doctors for every thirteen hundred patients. Nearly four hundred people society deemed an inconvenience died from abuse and neglect. There were more casualties, of course. Not every Chwed leaves a recognizable corpse."

Bix turned at the thick rasp of a feminine voice deepened by battle cries, bourbon, and blunts. A hand-rolled joint balanced on burgundy lips. White rings of stuff more mystical than marijuana drifted past thickly kholed green eyes and wreathed a black mohawk. Tattoos of moons in various phases and of assorted colors covered her fingers, encircled her neck, and curled around her ears, marking the woman as an Oracle who'd ascended to full Fatehood.

"Skuld," Bix greeted with a cautious grin. During her years as a CWIG agent, she'd had run-ins with the Norse Fate. For the most part, the encounters had ended positively or with a draw. But a few had been notably not in Bix's favor. "What's a Norn doing slumming with Valkyries?"

"I heard that." Thrúde's spotted coat sleeve rolled around the lip of the doorframe, and familiar bejeweled fingers flipped her off.

"Debts are my thing, Bix." The Norse Fate fished in the chest pocket of her flannel shirt. "A lot of debts are coming due."

"The kind of debts that lead to war?"

"Possibly." Skuld tossed a small pink thing at her. "Flash drive. Everything you need to know about Mirri is on there."

The flash drive was a plastic penis and balls. Give it an erection and it spurted USB. Mirri had had a jar full of them. The tiny sigils on each testicle hosted the encryption spells. Fail to provide the right certs or castrate the drive, and it'd infect all tech within a mile with a nasty virus.

"You calling the shots for the Sisterhood these days?"

A snort from the hall answered that.

"Nah." Skuld drew on her blunt and exhaled runes of smoke through her nose. "I just hate you less than the girls do."

"Small favors, then," Bix teased, then sobered. "How much do you know about what's really going on?"

"Not enough." Skuld stuffed her hands in the back pockets of her loose jeans. "I know the Houses of Fate are circling you, trying to thread you into lives you're not meant to affect."

That sent a chill down her spine. "Do I need to worry?"

"Yeah. Yeah, you do." The Norn sniffed. "You weren't supposed to be taken off the field ten years ago. You were supposed to succeed on that rescue mission. That you failed upset a lot of futures."

"Why didn't you and the Houses fight to get me out, then?"

Skuld shrugged. "There was a chance you'd hook up with the Chimera, which could have proved useful. Didn't pan out."

"The *Chimera*?" Bix echoed aghast. "That creature is the bogeyman of the gods, the Fates, the dragons, and the angels. Possibly the only thing all four races genuinely fear. Why the hell would I want to run into it? Why would you wish that on me?"

"The creature's been missing for a while. Guess it's not ready to be found yet. Worth a shot." Skuld's grass-green eyes brightened to neon green. "And before you ask about that other creature, yes, you're on the right path searching for the Phoenix. No, I don't know who moved against Mirri. No, I have no idea if you're going to succeed. No, I'm not going to tell you about Vidya Asariri."

"One last question." Bix slid the flash drive in her bra.

"You're pushing it." Skuld closed her teeth on the crinkled paper, knocking ash to the floor. The ashes settled as green mold atop the native grime. "You want to know why we're meeting here."

Bix inclined her head. "Everything you do has a purpose."

"Glad you remember." Skuld snubbed out her smoke in the palm of her hand. "Thrúde told you Mirri would disappear now and again. This is where we'd lose her. You've got three hundred acres of possibilities teeming with old evil and new malevolence. There are traps here even the Valkyries can't get past. Happy hunting."

Skuld tromped out of the miserable room like a drunken old man, complete with swearing when she knocked over remnants of neglect. Thrúde steadied the Norn, then ducked into the TV room.

"Hey, you asked about the tally of visiting gods?" Thrúde pulled keys from her pocket. "Half dozen are rumored to be MIA."

"All visiting? None with powers rooted here in the Mids?"

The Valkyrie nodded. "Reports are still coming in as the girls...ya know. It's complicated by the pantheons recalling all their folks, even the rooted ones. Something is going on, but the blind biddy out there ain't talking."

"I'm blind, not deaf, you twat-waffle," Skuld shouted.

Thrúde grinned and clapped Bix on the shoulder. "To Mirri's Mayhem."

Bix listened to the two bicker on their way out the building. Headlights dawned through the large periwinkle window, illuminating Skuld's stumble and stagger. When one was a Fate who saw the Future, vision in the present was... How had Skuld put it? Oh right, *"Like staring up an elephant's ass, hoping to spot flowers."*

Bix hadn't been back to a zoo since Skuld had planted that image in her head. Fortunately, the old battle-ax hopped into the passenger side of Thrúde's muscle car. The telltale gurgle and growl of the Hemi engine filled the vacant hallways of the dilapidated building. Gravel kicked up against the front windows of the asylum. Heartbeats later, tires squealed on pavement. Light vanished, leaving the blanket of a moonlit night.

Not even a rustling breeze broke the remaining silence.

Vidya. Tobek. Skuld.

The Houses of Fate were heavily invested. Gods were taking the hits. The Phoenix was missing.

Bix had five days left to figure out what the fuck was going on.

To that end, she needed to get the lay of this treacherous land from a safe distance. The kind of safe distance afforded a skilled gatekeeper who possessed an intimate familiarity with the ether.

Bix stepped through gates into the World adjacent to the Primary Mid World, and opened viewing panes that allowed her to see into the asylum without actually being there. Whatever traps kept the Valkyries at bay had to be hard-core deterrents. Hel demanded top-of-the-line bodies for Frejya's chosen; they were part of the price of Frejya's fealty. If the Valkyries couldn't maneuver through the grounds, then Bix didn't want to risk her safety either.

That's where the ether came into play. The vast nothingness

existed in all the nooks and crannies separating the Mids Worlds from one another. If one happened to be within the ether, it was endless. However, if one happened to be gatekeeper who'd spent way too much time playing in, with, and around it; one would learn how to use it as a filter between viewing panes to reveal potent magic. The ether converted her view of Forest Haven into an old silent film, complete with white-outs, black streaks, and jittery cameras.

The World in which she existed was barren, devoid of flora, fauna, and even terrain. Nothing but raw, unanchored energies remained to mark the end of a World. This vestige of a once-glorious, magic-rich home to so many of the mid-caste Chweds had been annihilated by war. Stories of its demise varied widely. One constant had been the pivotal role the Consortium had played in its destruction.

She'd spent her first month of exile ricocheting along this dead World's energy lines, trying to keep tabs on Mirri, on her enemies, on life in general before she'd had to abandon her post to save her sanity.

Speaking of sanity and the lack thereof, why had a goddess of healing escaped to a shuttered asylum? An active psychiatric hospital would have been completely understandable. The souls of tormented humans and Chweds unable to reconcile current lives with past lives were like the ghost peppers of a godly diet. But an empty asylum shouldn't have been a draw. Had Mirri lured prey here to feed off their souls? Gods in any form were deadly. Mirri's meal preferences had been for those who had been tormentor and tormented in one soul; the abusers, traffickers, and pedophiles. Her favorite takeout menu had been the sex-offender register.

Bix's stomach grumbled.

When it came to food and gods, she might not be able to delay finding her own fuel source for too much longer. This was the first time she'd been this hungry while in the Mids. She could actually feel the native magic pushing at her, trying to expel her and her nonnative body. It was disconcerting to say the least.

But first, she had to locate the danger within Forest Haven.

Twenty-one treatment buildings and four dormitories yielded nothing but a bad case of the creeps. The final dormitory belonged to the children. Colorful, happy, cartoonish faces peered through brown smears and smudges in empty classrooms. Names of the abandoned kids still clung to the chipped white wall tiles.

The Chwedlonol guilds should have saved every one of those kids. They should have stepped up and stepped in. Even for the human kids. It didn't take a genius to figure out racial politics lay at the heart of the Forest Haven debacle.

She left the kids' home and picked her way toward the last building barely visible amid the woods.

The old movie scrolled by without the slightest indication, scurry, or dart of Chweds who should have been well ensconced in this thatch of parkland nestled between urban developments. No hint of sprites, pixies, dryads, or yakshis disturbed her stroll among the boughs and burrows.

Vermillion glowed ahead of her.

Color that carried through the endless ether had to be some wicked powerful magic. The closer she got, the more distinct the threads blasting the color became. Someone had clearly majored in bad-spells basket weaving. She had sweaters with looser knit.

A sliver of blue shone through the webs of traps, neatly masked amid dense red lines.

Shit.

The last time she'd encountered magical blue, it'd belonged to Feng. A sliver couldn't be the Phoenix himself. Even a remnant, however, had the potential to do horrible things.

She clutched her pendant and edged as close to the remote building as the ether permitted.

Char framed whole sections of collapsed exterior walls. Exposed brick interior walls and rusting iron cages left no doubt of the purpose of the final building. A prison. Floorboards had rotted through in some cells, allowing dense vines to grow into the bleakness with iron manacles suspended in their grasps. Deeper within, beyond the evidence of fires and vandals, the blue sliver grew brighter, then brighter still.

Her gut punched out *Danger, Will Robinson* alarms.

She couldn't make out the source due to the intensity of the blue glow. Like it or not, she had to go back to the Primary Mid World to get her answer. Swearing, she opened gates and returned to the prison and its web of traps.

Wards struck her in the chest. The Phoenix talon about her neck warmed to the point of a hot curling iron. Grinding her teeth, she shuffled through the filth, searching for the source of potent magic.

An invisible fist socked her in the gut, knocking her backward. Her heel caught in a hole. She went down in a plume of dirt.

A loud motor thundered beyond the gaping walls. A triad of headlights swept through the ruins. Bix stayed low, her heart juddering as she crept through detritus and debris, farther into the darkness and away from the punishing wards.

The headlights stilled. The motor idled.

"Sweetheart, you in there?"

Bix cocked her head.

"Sweetheart?"

She crawled toward the voice. Moonlight stretched through the break in the forest canopy. A very large man on a very large '47 Indian motorcycle waited at the back of the prison. Big arms crossed.

Bix opened gates and dropped through, landing in a crouch.

Tobek unfolded his arms and eyed her. "It's nearly three in the morning."

Couldn't say he hadn't warned her. She grinned despite the ebbing pain. While she was hardly a kid, it was nice to have someone actively miss her. It was twice as nice to have someone come searching for her when she didn't show as expected.

"Tell me you didn't hunt Valkyries." She straightened, wiping dirt from her dress.

"Valkyries aren't hard to find, so technically, no, I didn't hunt them." He heeled the kickstand into the dirt and dismounted the bike. The bike shut off on its own. No key. No push button. Just shut off. "You get in a fight with a dust bunny?"

"Maybe?" She hedged. The only other time she'd encountered wards as strong as the ones inside the prison had been at his place. Could he have been behind whatever had drawn Mirri here?

"Never play poker, sweetheart." He brushed the tip of her nose with his glove. "What'd you discover out here that you don't want me to know?"

She grimaced. He chuckled.

"I can't get close enough to find out," she admitted.

"Oh yeah?" He took off his brain-pan helmet and hung it on the handlebar. He reached into his jacket and pulled out his flashlight. "Let's go see why."

This time she walked through the ruins, dodging holes and wreckage. Tobek followed, keeping the light angled ahead of them. Prickling started at her nape and spread.

She stopped. "Here. The warding begins here."

Tobek reached over her head and plucked a ball and chain from the twisting vine. "This is old-school but still effective. Chweds and humans alike would find themselves bolted to the floor, unable to escape."

Bix swatted aside a leaf unfurling before her and took a closer look at the iron cuff. "I've seen these engravings before. Recently, even."

"Rhaetic in origin. They had a second heyday during the Spanish Inquisition." Tobek swept the light up and down the vine, revealing a dozen more dangling manacles. "This vine isn't native to the area, much less this World. This is a carnivorous guardian, circa Jack's original giant beanstalk. There's a reason there are no corpses here."

"A dozen Worlds are home to giants." She groaned. "This

thing could have come from any one of them. Any of the naturalist guilds could have traded for it on the down low."

"Or it came from an angel."

"Excuse me?"

"Ever wonder which came first, the plant or the seed?"

"Pretty sure the saying is 'chicken or the egg,' but okay, I'll bite."

"True, but not the point." He chided. "Blood of the angels and dragons seeds life in all the Mids. This plant grows from the blood of a class of Throne—the angels' hunter class."

"Angel blood can bring nonnative plants to the most unlikely or inhospitable areas?"

"One hundred and one reasons why war among the Consortium has devastating effects on the Mids." He swung his light up and down the stalk. "This has been here for a while. So however it got here, it was done years ago."

She directed his light to the fat roots fanning out beneath the floorboards and to the strange marks burned into the plant's fibers. "Branded?"

"Bespelled, likely to hide it from authorities. This thing is illegal on many Worlds for obvious reasons." He snapped the persistent leaf off the vine. Red blood wept from the broken stem. "The risk of harvesting it and transporting it would have made it cost prohibitive even for the upper-upper-caste Chweds."

"Great, so it's probably evidence of a dead angel. I think I like Feng's burning blood better."

"The manacles were introduced over time. See how the plant has grown to incorporate them at varying heights?" He tucked the ball and chain back into the vine and motioned her ahead of him. "Keep going as far as you comfortably can."

The spells and wards fluctuated in power as Bix and Tobek wended through the labyrinth of cell blocks, solitary confinement chambers, and admin offices. Bix paused each time she triggered another ward. Tobek tracked the source, leaving it as he found it on the off chance it'd been placed for a legit reason they had yet to discover. They progressed through seven increasingly gnarly barriers before the Phoenix's claw fired up.

The corridor ended at a pink-tiled great room.

Bix skirted the parts and padding of disassembled exam chairs. Shattered glass doors propped up overturned metal cabinets. Decaying file folders and paperwork peeked from the detritus of nature covering the floor. Broken bricks were scattered before the ruins of the exterior wall. If there had been windows, they were long gone. That the roof hadn't caved in from lack of support was a miracle.

"This is my stop point," she called over her shoulder, clutching the damn dewclaw. "It doesn't look like there is anything worth protecting in here, but something doesn't want us to enter…which means I really want to enter."

She waited for Tobek to saunter past.

He didn't. It took two more moments before she realized the light pointing the way was unusually steady. Matter of fact, she couldn't hear the big lug's step or the rustle of his leathers.

"You coming?" She turned. The barrel of the flashlight balanced on a dented filing cabinet. "Dude, where'd you go?"

A blast of hard air knocked her off her feet and propelled her across the room. Hard night reached out to claim her. Her spine slammed into solid brick.

The illusion wavered.

The exterior wall remained intact.

Wards kicked up their pummeling frenzy. The Phoenix's claw burned white hot. Agony ripped down her spine, splitting skin. A bitter chill oozed along her back.

She bit down on the scream.

Shadows took shape from the darkness filling the corridor. Bright white and blue lights blazed, blinding her.

"Explain your trespass," demanded a masculine voice with a thick European polyglot accent.

"Dim the lights," she keened through clenched teeth.

"You do not give orders," derided a second male voice with

the same polyglot accent. The intensity of white light increased along with the pressure of the air holding her aloft.

"I'd listen to the lady." Tobek's familiar rasp fixed his location relative to the others.

A thought moved him to her far right. The blue glow of his Berserker rage calmed her enough to open multiple doors to the ether.

A single shout ended abruptly. The white light disappeared along with the air jet. Bix hit the floorboards. Ash filled her mouth. Ash, not dirt.

"Attack me again and this whole building goes straight to the Under Worlds with you along for the ride," she gasped, skimming her hands over the floor, searching for the damn wards still assailing her.

Amber glowed softly, illuminating feathered wings and a lean man wearing Jesus sandals and tattered jeans. An angel. She closed the gates and cursed herself twice over for blundering into another angel trap that put *another* teammate at risk.

"Hel's investigator?" The angel cocked his head to the side. "Your action against my brother will be reported."

"Your unprovoked attack is the second lobbed against the Norse pantheon by a member of the Host in the span of three days. How far are you willing to push the gods' restraint?" She threw out the accusation and hoped for a reaction that would confirm the complete conjecture on which she was operating. At this point, it couldn't hurt her more than the wards were.

"The Host has no involvement in the events surrounding Hel's ambassador." The angel made no effort to approach. His black eyes flicked around her, searching. "Our orders are to keep watch over this site, to learn who comes to maintain the traps. The warlock has inspected eight of them and correctly identified their compositions. You are in his company and soliciting his consultation; therefore, you are equally guilty."

"Bullshit," she spat, knowing full well how this simplistic thinking could lead to her exile—or worse, her husking. "The

Host are the guardians of the Phoenix, and he is linked to what happened to Hel's ambassador, which means the Host is culpable twice over."

Wood shattered. The warding ceased to throw punches, but her pendant continued to burn. Tobek yanked his artificial hand out of the broken floorboard. Blood dribbled into his beard. He didn't bother to wipe it away. His blue eyes blazed with the murderous magic of his kith as his attention fixed on her.

"Sweetheart, you okay?"

"Not yet," she whispered. Her back throbbed—from the impact with the wall, the growth of Jör's cooties, or both, she couldn't tell. Spots dappled her vision. Every ripple of pain kept her mind focused on the room around them while her body wanted to relocate to Tobek's huge comfy bed. "There's a glamour on this part of the building."

"Well, angel?" Tobek barked. "Care to be useful?"

The angel backed away. "I cannot aid you."

"Are you—"

"Fine." She interjected over whatever Tobek was about to say to get him into more trouble with the angel. Diplomacy wasn't his thing any more than it was hers. They were more action oriented.

A thought deposited the angel on the floor beside her.

An unholy cry tore from the angel's throat. He thrashed. His skin smoked and his feathers smoldered. His eyes flashed between white and pitch.

Tobek's strong arms scooped her up from the floor and away from the angel. "What the hell?"

"How are glamour spells anchored?"

He turned her head away from the angel writhing and shouting. "Five points of the pentacle. The heart holds the illusion. You'll have to break three of the points to terminate the star. I suggest the ceiling first."

A thought removed the ceiling. Moonlight filled the room along with a predawn breeze. The illusion flickered.

"Think of the wall in front of us as a clock." Tobek moved

them to face the center of the back wall. "Four and eight."

Gates opened at the designated times.

The illusion of the medical room vanished.

Wing-shaped char covered the walls. Cobalt coated the scorched floors. At the heart of the room, black ether seeped into the Mid World.

Red feathers hovered in the air, trapped in the fractured seam of a broken gate. Red feathers. Cobalt blood. Only the Phoenix had red feathers and cobalt blood. Only Feng's presence could explain the burn pattern.

Her breath stopped. Chills raked across her skin.

Feng had been a prisoner here. Had to have been a prisoner, unless his volatile rage had gotten worse during her absence and he'd lost his damn mind. There *was* something to be said for a madman using an old asylum as a secret base. Could Feng have been the one who'd abducted Mirri? As a dragon-angel hybrid, he could have had the wherewithal to force Mirri to stay in her body.

He'd been the one to ensure Bix's exile, and Mirri had been actively working to undo that. It could have been enough to trigger that excessive anger of his. It was a plausible motive.

But why would he use a pentagram? Why would he need it? Chwed magic didn't work the same for the superpowers. And what about the way his dewclaw had been severed? And why use Centralia when he had this place?

"Son of a…" Tobek stepped toward the broken gate. His grip on her tightened, and he abruptly retreated. "Your pendant gets brighter the closer we get to the fissure."

A thought freed the feathers from the ill-fitted gate and delivered them to the angel convulsing in the bloodstains left by the Phoenix. Tobek swung her around to face their tortured guest.

"Listen to me well, angel," she snapped. "Take those back to your commander with a message: 'They who bring me what I truly desire will receive what they truly need.'"

The angel peered up at her through one white eye and one black. A blistered and bleeding hand clutched the Phoenix's feathers. Blood foamed at the angel's lips, yet he still managed a nod.

A thought delivered the angel to healing holy ground. For one tiny Catholic church in the mountains of northern Italy, morning mass just got a whole lot more interesting.

Tobek backed her away from the room of carnage, back to the cabinet where his flashlight still beamed. She grabbed it in her grimy hand. Tobek took off at a lope and didn't stop until they reached his bike.

Bix drew a steady breath as the heat from the Phoenix's claw abated to a dull throb. "You know you don't have to drive us home, right?"

Tobek slung his leg over his bike and perched on the edge of the seat. His sweaty brow pressed against her temple as he exhaled loudly.

"That's a good thing, sweetheart, because neither one of us is in any condition to do it."

She flicked the flashlight up to his face. Her heart skipped three beats. It wasn't sweat she'd felt. It was blood. Bright. Crimson. Blood. And it was streaming down his face from rows of raw weeping sigils.

A thought took man and machine to Dysmorphic.

# CHAPTER 10

**B**ix closed the gate the moment Tobek and his great big bike touched the concrete floor of Dysmorphic. Tobek's artificial arm pressed her torso tightly to his body, a body that went slack. His natural arm dangled at his side, no longer cradling her legs. Her heels clacked on the floor as she shoved against his full weight, trying to keep man and machine from collapsing on each other.

Lights flicked on. Three huge and well-armed men in nothing but boxer briefs sprinted under the iron archway.

"Hywl, get the bike and call the others. Xipil, grab a gurney." A man with spectacularly long black hair and an elegant beard tossed his battle-ax on a rolling tray and headed her way.

Xipil and Hywl slid their swords into scabbards that were part of the décor, then split ways. One came forward; one detoured for the clinic.

"How many of them were there?" The talker tipped Tobek's head back and angled it toward a beam of brighter light. "Angels, woman, how many angels were there?"

Bix said nothing. If she parted her lips, it'd be a scream that escaped. Jör's new plague writhed inside her. It pushed against her skin from nape to hip, scraping along her ribs, shifting muscle and nerves, seeking the tears in her flesh. Tobek's artificial palm spanned her back, trapping it.

If Jör had shortened her timer, she'd turn every World under the Norse pantheon's purview inside out.

"His bleeding is getting worse." The talker snatched a scalpel from the nearest workstation. "We have to alter the brands fast, before the angels track him here."

Bix made the scalpel vanish.

The talker stared at his hand for a heartbeat, then turned on her, his eyes aglow. "Do not start with me, woman. Chief means more to the Mids than you ever will."

"That's no way to speak to a lovely lady, eh?" The pale man with jet hair and muttonchops steadied the bike and offered a lopsided grin. "Bore da—that's Welsh for good morning—I'm Hywl, and the bossy medic here is Runjit. Those marks on Chief's face are locator spells left behind by angels. If it's any comfort, it's not the first time he's come home with these, but we do need to move quickly for everyone's safety. I'm not going to lie. It will be ugly, messy, and horrifying. Unfortunately, neutralizing angelic crap usually is."

The clatter of wheels filled the room. Xipil skidded to the front of the shop with the gurney. He seized Tobek by the shoulder and elbow of his artificial arm and swore. "He's locked on to her. We can't move his arm. We're going to have to lift them together."

"Those things cover more than his face," Runjit snapped. "We have to separate them, or we're all screwed."

Tobek's coat and gloves prevented Bix from knowing how much of that was true. Frankly, she didn't know how to help him even if what Runjit said was a lie, but these men—these fellow Berserkers—seemed to be well practiced. For whatever reasons, the Angelic Host apparently hunted Tobek with regularity. She'd walked him right into their arms.

Damn it.

Gates moved Tobek to the gurney. Without her holding him upright, he slumped into an inert ball. Without him holding her upright, her mind took off…

～～～

…and dumped her in his big fluffy comforter.

She lay prostrate in the darkness, afraid to move, afraid to breathe lest whatever moved inside her burst free.

The scent of Tobek enveloped her. The soft cotton of his bedding took her tears while she grappled with her terrors.

*Please, don't let her have released a plague on the one man who had risked his freedom to make sure she was safe. Please don't let her have infected his friends, who were so clearly loyal to him. Please, please, please don't let her be the reason another tightly knit team had to die.*

Weight shifted the mattress. A cool hand swept her hair off her neck. Careful touch peeled away the tatters of her dress and corset from the damage to her back. Gentle fingers feathered over her broken skin.

Uncallused fingers.

She jerked, but the hand splayed across her, holding her down with unnatural strength.

It didn't keep her pinned.

She locked her knees as she landed in the doorway of Tobek's bedroom. It wasn't Tobek rising from the bed.

"How did you get in here, Jör?" She held up the top of her dress with one hand against her bosom.

"Your warlock hasn't repaired his wards." Jör ambled toward her as his serpentine gaze raked her from head to toe. As a man, he was devastatingly handsome, tall and lean and impeccably attired. Yet, in a breath, he could shift to the poisonous snake of lore, monstrous in body and deed. "Your temper has always been a wondrous thing. Exposing him to his many, many enemies? No honey trap has ever been effective until you."

"What have you done?" she hissed. "Which of his enemies did you notify?"

"Me?" Jör had the gall to look affronted as he closed the distance between them. "This is all about you."

"Bullshit," she spat, retreating. "What did you leave inside me?

What sort of menace to the Mids are you and your sister creating this time?"

His smile was as breathtaking as it was frightening. "Ah, Bix, ever so rash. You're not thinking clearly. Have you fed since you've been back in the Mids? That little appetizer my sister gave you isn't enough to sustain you. You've gone hungry for so long, you've forgotten it's not normal."

"I can feel your poison writhing inside me," she whispered, backing down the hall toward the kitchen. "I felt it in the ether. I know what you've done. You cured me of one toxin, then gave me another. Hel will be furious at your game."

Jör matched her step for step, stride for stride, every move as sensuous as the serpent's slither. "You need to keep up your energy if you're going to stay rooted in the Mids. You can't solve Mirri's mauling without being in this World. My World."

"Did you cheer when you'd heard what had happened to her? Did you gloat when you drained the souls of her protectors? Did your jealousy finally feel appeased?" She backed into the kitchen counter and flinched.

"There's the temper." He placed his hands on either side of her hips, trapping her against the quartz slab. His head angled to the side. "Let me give you all that you need, my angry little one."

"No." She moved through gates to the other side of the kitchen island. "Never. Never again. We're done. I'm not coming back to you, ever."

"Do you really have the time to beg another god to feed you?" He danced his fingers along the counter, stalking her. "Can you trust another god to do it? All the pantheons sided against you, remember? I set you free."

She kept moving; to stand still was to be snared. "Hel set me free because her need for revenge is greater than her need for political favor. You did as you were told."

He moved with the preternatural speed of a god, seizing her wrists. His grip tightened. His nails dug into her skin, painfully. He twisted her arms outward, forcing her to let go of her blouse.

Stained and shredded fabric dangled from her waistband, exposing her breasts.

It wasn't the first time he'd seen them. It was far from the first time she'd been debased in his presence.

"I have endured far worse tantrums from you." Jör pinned her against the refrigerator with his body. His hair—black at first glance—gave up its greenish cast as long curls writhed and hissed, slithering over her shoulders and holding her close. "Don't you dare refuse my generosity."

Fear held her immobile. One bite from him and she'd be runed with his trackers, unable to hide from him. One bite and she'd be at his mercy again. One bite and whatever he'd left inside her would escape before her time here was done.

"Get off me, please," she pleaded. "Please, Jör. Please."

His mocking laughter filled the air as he gripped her wrists in one hand and palmed her breast with the other. His lips crushed hers, force-feeding her his raw energy. She didn't want him or his taint. She'd rather starve than succumb. She struggled.

Metal keened.

Jör flew backward.

The Bi Xie lunged off the wall above the stove and landed with a clang between Jör and Bix. Silver wings spanned twenty feet, blocking access to her. The body of the massive gunmetal lion vibrated with the vigor of its growls, louder than a jet engine. The beast's broad head bent, angling long golden horns at the serpent god scrambling to his feet.

"Impossible." Jör feinted left, then right.

The Bi Xie pawed at the ground, gouging the concrete floor. A chuff and it leapt. Jör cried out in horror and fled, vanishing in a blink.

Bix slid to the floor, shaking.

The metal beast tucked its wings and tromped back to her. A foreleg extended, and it laid its cheek upon it. Bowing. Watching her. Waiting.

Her hand trembled, reaching for it. "Thank you."

Its metal cheek warmed under her touch. A satisfied grunt rumbled up from its hollow belly. The beast backed to the far wall. It took a thundering run at the kitchen and jumped, compacting in size as it cleared the counter. It plowed headfirst into the wall. A cacophony of squealing metal echoed as the Bi Xie refit itself into the shape of the range hood. The artistic sculpture emerged, once again inanimate yet watchful.

Bix sat in the eerie silence until her breathing returned to a semblance of normalcy.

"Handbag. Handbag. Handbag," she whispered. Her jaw locked, and her lip quivered.

No. No, she would not give Jör the satisfaction of breaking her. Bad enough she'd let him see her fear. She would not let him isolate her from people. Not again. He would not manipulate her into the intimacy of feeding. There would be no return to exclusivity, no badgering her into leaving her friends just for a hint of a memory that used to be hers.

Once this investigation was over, she would have her memories back—some of them, anyway—then she would do whatever it took to learn how to husk a god. Jör would not keep the power to make her fear herself. He would not coerce her into solitude again. Never again.

Every fiber of her body objected when she pulled herself up and shuffled toward the shower. She checked the drain twice. Empty. Cold water blasted from the arrays of jets and sprays. She stepped in without adjusting the temperature, still dressed.

Hopefully, Gurp had missed Jör's visit. Having a witness to that would be more than she could bear.

# CHAPTER 11

The stainless steel drawer slammed shut with enough oomph to shake the bank of cabinets on this level and the two below. Bix tapped one heel against the ventilated grate floor and bid her grumbling stomach to quiet. Ten o'clock sharp had apparently been a suggestion as the digital clock above her head galloped toward quarter after.

No sign of Ashtad or the director.

Her erstwhile boss had set the meet in the heart of the CWIG top-security vault. Not that the eleven-story silo of tempered-glass cabinets, iron racks, and sub-vaults of stainless steel had been stamped as such. No, she knew the location by the collection of items behind the biometric locks.

Among the contents were all things she and her team had acquired for the guild. Grim shit, spooky shit, Other World shit. Oddly, the CWIG hadn't added much to their rare and deadly collection in her absence. Probably couldn't after they'd washed their hands of their best Dark Ops team.

Serve them right. Hell, when she was done serving Hel, she just might vanish the entire vault into the ether. 'Course then there'd be no legacy, no hat tip to the men and women who had acquired these things. Her team deserved to be honored for their service. Not disavowed and dusted under the rug.

Maybe she'd take a few of the items for herself, the ones that held the best memories of her team.

The air pressure in the locked vault changed. Heavy footfalls crossed the iron drawbridge with a pronounced strike of the right foot. A slight creak said new leather uppers, but the lack of a click said no heel caps, which meant rubber soles.

Jump boots. One of two dozen pairs thundering into the vault. Son of a bitch.

"Well, well, the errant gatekeeper came in from the cold." A voice smoother than freshly shaved legs spidered around the vault and burrowed into her ears, whispering fear and intimidation.

She didn't turn around. Didn't need to. She'd been derided and demeaned by the man behind that voice for years. Couldn't say she'd missed him one bit.

"Dangerous to leave me here with this much temptation, Director."

"If you weren't desperate, you wouldn't have lingered."

"Desperation is the ludicrous amount of money you attached to the bounty placed on someone who you know full well cannot be captured. A spectacular waste of resources trying to force me to come in. Had to be a blow to your budget." She turned at that point with a smirk.

The long red equine face with the curled black horns of a ram and the yellow eyes of morning pee regarded her with familiar disgust. New, however, was his choice of the black camo security uniform instead of his tailored three-piece suits. Still looked like he bench-pressed oil rigs for the hell of it, though. He had maybe six inches of clearance between his jet pompadour and the walkway above him.

"Only if I had had to pay it, which, it turns out, I don't." He hooked his meaty thumbs over his matte-black belt buckle. "I don't know why Hel freed you to do what this guild is more than capable of doing. No one here wants you, not after what you did to your team. You're a traitor to every soul in this agency. As soon as politics permits, you're gone from the Mids. Permanently."

Of course he believed she was guilty. Technically, she was. She *had* delivered eight men and women to the Host's armory, where they had met their deaths. There was no point in arguing that with the director. His guild had conducted an internal investigation and had found no evidence that she'd been set up by someone within these very walls. Nothing, absolutely nothing she could say now would convince him otherwise.

Vidya had played them all for fools.

"We both know the BOLO is about what happened ten years ago, not about what happened at Centralia." Bix couldn't blame him for being pissed. She would be too, if they switched places, but she'd already been tried, convicted, and punished. No do-overs, especially not by a lesser authority. "Since you couldn't publicly flay me back then without exposing my ties to you and this guild, you're taking the opportunity to do so now. IC justice doled out by one of their own to one of their own. You've flung me out of the shadows and into the limelight, destroying my ability to obtain legit work as an undercover agent for any employer in any World. Congratulations. Hope you can finally sleep at night."

"I did the Mid Worlds a great service by making you front-page news. Now everyone knows the sort of criminal you are."

Unspoken whispers of guilt, shame, and ineptitude scrabbled at her mind. She ignored them. They weren't her feelings or her words. They were his and his insidious brand of magic.

"You wanted me here for a reason, Director, this day, this time. Hurry up and ask me the favor."

"Favor," he coughed, choking on the word. "Favor?"

"I don't work for you." She grinned. "Never did, according to the records of those who matter. Probably even your own records. That is what happens when we're disavowed, right?"

"The CWIG isn't going to let you trot around the Mids unmonitored and unleashed." He bared his pointy canines and sneered. "You're going to be chipped, and you're going to make the effort to keep that chip, or the Consortium gets involved and out you go again. Are we clear?"

"Kiss my ass, Director." She didn't have time for this old song and dance about trackers and tethering her. "I have a job to do. Keep your people out of my way. And if that bounty isn't off my head in ten seconds, one of your kids is going to go missing from school. Every three seconds thereafter, another one will disappear."

"You will not threaten my children," he bellowed. His magic whispered choruses of doubt and paranoia meant to make her buckle to his will.

Didn't work.

She took one step toward him. "'Never take a meet if you don't know the weak spot,' your own words, Director. I know how many spawn there are, who they are, where they are, and who would pay a lot of favors to have even one of them for an hour."

The whispers multiplied the menace. She inspected her fingernails and sniffed.

"I probably ought to be grateful you exposed me to a mind fuck before I went to the ether. The entities there make your bully's magic little more than a sweet lullaby." She followed a red laser line up to the guard on the flyover and removed him from the vault. She removed two more for good measure. "You shouldn't even have this job with that abundance of precocious vulnerability."

"You so much as appear within a mile of them…" He cracked his knuckles.

"I could stand watch over their beds in the middle of the night, and those beds could be suspended over a smelting pit in the kingdom of the iron dwarves. You and your army of goons would never know." She stared way up into his brimstone fury. "Rest assured, if this bounty or any other with my name, image, or any of my associates from anywhere ever turns up in any Mid World, you will spend the rest of your days trying to piece your family back together. You have four seconds left to call off the bounty. Three. Two."

He called her bluff.

"Daddy?" A young centaur clopped around the ring below them, startling the guards. "Daddy, is *this* where you work? Cool. Oh, hi there. Is that loaded? What's in that bag?"

The director froze. Not so much as an eyelash moved. "Put her back, now."

"This is what happens when you train people to do your dirty work, then spend more time playing politics than keeping a clean house." Bix rested a foot against the cabinet behind her. "You are going to remove the bounty immediately, and I am going to take my time being a pain in your ass."

"Daddy, what are you doing up there? Daddy? Daddy?"

The director snatched his phone off his belt clip. Some taps, some clicks, a whole lot of muttered threats...

Bix caught the eye of the girl and waved. The girl waved back enthusiastically.

The vault filled with chirps and whirs. Guards checked their phones. The director presented his phone to Bix's view. Bold red letters spelled "canceled" across her wanted poster.

"The distro list, Director. Have to be sure it went wide," Bix prompted.

More muttering, more tapping on the screen. More phone chimes. He showed her his phone again.

"Your dad wanted to wish you luck on your track meet today. He's awfully grumpy about missing it," Bix hollered down to the girl. "I thought I'd cheer him up and bring you to him, just for a moment, yeah?"

"You're that gatekeeper." The girl's fingers laced over her lips, and she giggled.

"Take gold, honey. I know you can do it." The director leaned over the railing and smiled at his daughter. "Remember to tuck your legs tightly over the hurdles."

The girl lit up as if he hung the moon. Then she was gone.

"You're lucky I don't kill you right now," he seethed.

"You tried that once, right after you got the big promotion.

You still have the limp." She straightened her bangs. "Now, are we done pissing in each other's oatmeal? You and I have parallel investigations to run."

"My peers are dying in suspicious numbers since your return to the Mids," he grumbled. "One succumbed to his injuries yesterday."

The temptation to laugh in his face was high, really high. He needed her help. After all his posturing, his real reason for this meet at this time was revealed. He wasn't unlike Hel in his desperation. Fortunately for him, Bix didn't believe it was a coincidence that the secret meeting of guild masters and the assault on Mirri had happened in the same place within a day of each other. Figuring out what a bunch of labor leaders had in common with a pantheon's ambassador would bring her closer to the culprit.

If that culprit was Feng, she was going to need a ton of proof and the CWIG's help to gather it in the few days she had left.

"How many people outside the guild masters knew about the bunker in Centralia?"

He didn't bat an eyelash. That meant he'd given Ashtad the permission to read her in. Interesting.

"Members only."

"And how many of those members knew about the blood spell that moved the bunker to who knows where?"

He did a double take that time, then grunted. "The chairman, the vice chairman, and me."

"I found bugs in the crater it left behind. The kind popular with the CWIG." She pulled one piece of the Centralia paua shell from her top and set it on his forearm. "You have a leak inside the guild."

"That is what our mutual friend is researching." He examined the sliver. "Another guild master turned up dead an hour ago. Agent Asariri is at the scene as we speak."

"Another god dead nearby too?"

"It's the manner of the death that may be similar to what happened to my forensics teams." He swiped through his phone and tipped the screen her way. It was a photo of a bloody sheet in the middle of a bunch of trees and shrubs whose colors identified the location as someplace other than the Primary Mid World.

"Got it," she said, committing the image to memory.

"Whatever you discover will not atone for what you did to your team and this guild. Nothing ever will." He put the phone back on his clip.

"I'm clear on that."

"We should probably limit our interactions." He straightened and rolled his shoulders. "Neither of us can maintain this farce of civility for long."

Bix closed the gate at the new crime scene and stumbled as the gnaw of hunger asserted itself, making her light-headed. She'd look into a food source after she took a gander at the dead guild master then checked on Tobek. That she hadn't heard a peep from the guys at Dysmorphic worried her.

Trees of vibrant pinks and purples unfurled their branches, offering fragrant fruits and nutshells of drink as they brushed at her dress and hair. Grass of navy hues laced beneath her feet. She followed the sound of technicians' banter through the dense forest toward the bright white lights harshly damning the subtle beauty of one of three Worlds ruled by the dark elves.

"Are you kidding me?" Vidya marched toward her, jade eyes glittering with rage. Or maybe it was the lighting. Or both.

"Your boss sent me to look at the body." Bix made her way to the bloody sheet, skirting incident markers and forensics guys in white hazmat suits.

"What the hell happened to you in exile that makes you think using a kid is okay?" Vidya crouched over the body and flipped back the sheet. "Can't believe you'd stoop that low."

"Can't believe CWIG tech has improved so much that your phones actually work regardless of Mid World. That's a heck of a cell carrier. Not overly surprised that the guards already gossiped."

The bosom of the corpse and everything south was flawless and decidedly feminine. Blisters and blood covered the décolletage. The head wasn't attached. Arms remained intact and mostly unmarred from biceps down. Unlike the guy Gurp had found in Centralia, this woman hadn't been holding a grenade. But something combustible had hit her.

"Tapped the ley lines to transmit the communications," Vidya explained offhandedly, glaring at her. "And it wasn't a leak from inside. His daughter is talking about you on social media."

"Yeah? About what a sociopathic meanie I am?"

"Your hair," Vidya mumbled. "She likes your hair and your dress. Your style."

Bix stared at her blankly.

"Teenagers." Vidya shrugged and pointed to the scorching at the jagged stump of a neck. "This one looks like she was hit with a fireball, right?"

"Headshot with an explosive projectile. Hollow point bullet? Fireball would have done more damage to the torso." Bix scanned the immediate area. "Are those skull fragments marked behind you?"

"Team's testing to be sure. Fragments resemble charcoal more than bone."

"So her head didn't just burst, it burned at high temp." Bix picked up the corpse's left hand. A trident of hooks. "The Guild Master of Psychopomps. She should have been impervious to any known bullet type."

"Like the guys from my team," Vidya sighed. "We're looking for anything that hints at the actual projectile and haven't found anything."

"Any idea what she was doing here?"

"Looks like she was stealing some sort of treasure." Vidya stood and motioned Bix toward the lab truck. "We found it in a lead bag under a tangle of leaves where the guys are taking photos right now."

Bix took in the breadth of the crime scene. "This is dinky compared to Centralia. More like a common assassination."

"Agreed. We already checked the forest for any signs of stoles or foreign flora, nothing out of place except the victim, the bag, and her package." Vidya jumped into the truck and retrieved a soccer-ball-sized polyhedron with elvish symbols on three faces. "It didn't repel anyone. It hasn't lit up. Vibrated. Pulsed. Sung. Whispered sweet nothings. It doesn't rattle or smell. If it hadn't been for the scan-blocking bag, we would've assumed it was a piece of art."

"No." Bix snorted, reaching for it. "Elves store the most dangerous things in the most unassuming containers. That needs to be in a bomb dispo—"

A bullet ripped through the side of the lab, zinging through the space Vidya's head occupied a heartbeat before. The report came second.

"Not again," Vidya snarled, dropping to the ground. "Bix, not again. I can't...*we* can't..."

Gates opened.

Car alarms blared and air-raid sirens spun up into full whine. Trees shrieked and teetered on new hills of steel and glass. Bix staggered back as gravity forsook her brain and knees. She kissed a blend of blue grass and gray asphalt. Her ears rang, and her skin crawled.

"Roll call. Who's injured? Who's missing?" Vidya shouted, slithering out of the lab truck wedged in a gulley of fallen trees.

Answering shouts of name, rank, and status popped up around them. By the sound, Bix guessed Vidya's full forensics team had made it.

"Secure the area. This is still an active crime scene." Vidya scooped Bix's shoulders into her lap and brushed her hair out of her face. "Bix? Bix? Are you hit?"

A bead of drool tickled the corner of Bix's mouth, and there wasn't a damn thing she could do about it. Her head felt like a thousand balloons were taking it on a journey. It was all she could manage to keep her eyes open while the native magic of the Mids pushed at her, trying to expel her.

The pendant against her heart glowed, pulsing audibly. Each throb weighed her down, keeping her anchored to this World.

"Transporting the entire crime scene to the middle of HQ's executive parking lot is…one way of getting us out alive." Vidya's chuckle held the tones of panic. She slapped her wrist against Bix's brow and swore. "Come on, babe, stay with me. Where can I take you, huh? Who can help you? Who, babe?"

"Agent Asariri?" A large shadow engulfed them. "I've orders to bring her in."

Vidya shook her head. "No, it's not—she got us out of there as someone fired on us. She didn't—"

"Agent Asariri, I have my orders." A huge ogre scooped Bix up in one gloved hand. His big feet crushed whatever cars hadn't been destroyed by the relocation of the crime scene.

The ogre lumbered to an ambulance and carefully pushed Bix off his palm onto the cold metal floor of the back. A gurney would have been nice, but knowing the director, where she was headed would be infinitely more uncomfortable. The vehicle dipped toward the driver's side, and the engine roared.

Bix vacillated between lucidity and collapse as sirens wailed and potholes jostled the vehicle, sending her sliding into cabinets and jump seats. She considered opening a gate, then contemplated the vortex she'd create by being too exhausted to control sizes on either end. Then she thought about the number of places the director would have stupid nanotrackers injected into her. A wave of bile-rising panic assailed her. Images of observers formed rings around her as the director approached with a syringe of nanobots suspended in clear liquid. The syringe morphed into fangs and the director's horns writhed and wriggled into a head full of serpents, and suddenly she was in Jör's grip with his venom dripping from his teeth.

A hard hand across her cheek stung.

"Damn it, Bix. Snap out of it."

# CHAPTER 12

**B**ix jerked back to reality, panting. The power of the pendant weighed her down and kept her anchored to the Mids. The haze of hunger-fueled delusions faded, leaving her staring at Ashtad's worried face framed by the confines of a well-stocked ambulance.

"Slow your breathing, Bix. Slow it down, or you're going to faint." Ashtad pressed one hand between her shoulders, another on her abdomen. "Breathe with the pressure of my touch. In… Out… In… Out."

Flurries of electrical pinpricks drew her focus to the counting. Rhythmic, like a classical waltz. She swayed in time to the beat. The prickling moved to the small of her back and to her right hand. Her cheek rested against his silk-clad shoulder. He smelled of cinnamon and bergamot. His smooth tenor hummed a lulling tune in time with the pulsing of her pendant.

She inhaled deeply. "I missed dancing with you, Ashtad."

"You've missed too many meals," he chided. "I'm betting you haven't fed since you've been back. Luckily, I know you well enough to anticipate you taking care of everyone else before you take care of yourself."

"Look at you coming to my rescue," she teased. "The ogre in the CWIG parking lot, he one of yours?"

"I can't be seen at HQ in person for a while, but it doesn't mean you're beyond my reach." He placed his cheek atop her head. "Can you get yourself together for twenty minutes?"

"Show me the picture. I'll take us wherever you need to go."

"My guys said you cut a quarter-mile margin on the relo." He rapped on the metal ceiling. "That means you're losing control over the gates you open, which means you use a preprogrammed gateway like every other Chwed."

The doors of the ambulance swung wide. A guy and a gal in seemingly normal EMT gear helped them out of the back.

"All good?" the woman asked, looking at Bix with blatant curiosity.

Ashtad wrapped his arm around Bix's waist. "Site six in an hour. They'll be waiting for you."

The EMTs nodded, closed up the back, and rolled out. As the ambulance rumbled into the bright afternoon, the paint job shimmered and shifted to a coroner's van.

"Those were not CWIG agents." Bix wagged a finger at Ashtad. "Those were your very special friends."

"Don't ask what you don't want to know."

"Ah-ha," she giggled. "They were demis, just like you. You hooking them up with big trouble in little Chwedville?"

Demigods could never keep their noses out of trouble. No, really, they couldn't; they needed progressively harrowing feats to absorb enough magic and emotion that their bodies would morph into the final soul-sucking stage known as a full god. God of what depended on their parents and what kind of magical empathetic mixture they'd absorbed during their trials.

There'd been rumors of the CWIG outsourcing certain gruesome missions that they didn't want blowing back on the guild. It'd been a point of contention among the Dark Ops agents.

"Walk." Ashtad pulled her alongside him, ever the solicitous gentleman date to anyone watching them from the long narrow windows of gothic stone buildings framing an idyllic park.

Quad.

"The university?" She gasped. "Oh, even better, the university library? You brought me to a library? With college students? Do I still look that young to you?"

"I'm taking you to lunch, my scatterbrained spy." Ashtad threw his weight against the heavy glass door shaded by ivy-covered archways and guided her into a blast of hot air, excessive marble, white noise, and a bank of...

"Computers? Really? Shouldn't there be books in a library?"

"Paper books are so last century, you Luddite. Never fear, there are still a few to be found." He escorted her into the heart of the old library, where books of paper and sometimes leather covers filled the shelves.

"Ashtad, I think someone is trying to kill Vidya."

"Her recent assignments are cases higher-ranked agents would kill to have, I'll give you that." Ashtad led her up one spiral flight of stairs, then another.

"If I hadn't been at Centralia, she would have died with everyone else." Bix leaned into Ashtad as lucidity became harder to maintain. "Someone shot at her again today."

"You sure they're shooting at her and not you?" He accepted her weight and sent electrical pricks up and down her side, preventing her mind from wandering and her body from following. "She hasn't been in danger until you show up. I saw what happened. She bent down, you reached up."

"The camera feeds in the lab." Bix groaned. "You must love this age of technology, being able to warp electricity into whatever suits, when it suits."

"More than you might imagine." His smile was brilliant. "I had to look twice as I watched your little stunt with the director. Bold. Yet point loudly received."

"I don't know if I'm creeped out or passively placated that you're keeping such a close eye on me." She dropped her head against his shoulder.

The section of indexes and references held a light layer of dust. Artfully applied dust. Brownies performed housekeeping to accommodate any need, apparently.

"I'm glad you still trust me, twice more since my father rejected you while you were in exile." Ashtad pushed seven ostensibly random books farther back on their shelves.

A gate opened, releasing sirens' soothing songs and coils of dryads' special-blend smoke. A large lump of quills filled the gateway, and a wholly inhuman voice mumbled something unintelligible.

A toll keeper.

Ashtad answered the incoherent babble. The lump of quills dispersed in a flash of black lights.

"I'm sorry if I worsened things between you and your dad. I shouldn't have gone to Ba'al. I was just…" Bix slouched.

"Starving. You were starving and desperate. It was beyond cruel what the pantheons did to you, knowing you couldn't die from it." He hooked a finger under her chin. "When I finally make it to full god, you will never have to starve again. No matter how pissed I am at you or you at me. We've been in the trenches together. That's an unbreakable bond. Politics be damned."

She kissed his cheek. "I am absolutely going to hold you to that."

"Excellent. Now, come on, let's pretend like this is our first date, eh? This time, we'll have real music to go with our dancing." Ashtad tugged her through the gateway and into another Mid World.

Long velvet loungers and circular damask couches formed conversation niches inside a giant tree. Crystal formations provided muted multihued light. The dark stain on the wood walls could have been anything from oil to blood judging by the occupants.

Curled-horn satyrs canoodled with winsome ladies bearing the mark of the clan Sidhe. Cocky demigods squared off against cockier incubi, flinging darts made of still-living pixies at a massive pinwheel decorated with sniveling spriggans. Gambling tables hosted all sorts of upper-caste dilettantes.

Asuwang of genderless beauty wended through intimate clusters, serving libations, oblations, and all kinds of illicit goodies from across the Mid Worlds.

Below them, in the center of the hollow, an amphitheater played host to a quartet of sirens backed by a symphony of diversity. The accompanying light show almost held a candle to the performers. Almost.

"What we want is upstairs," Ashtad murmured, nuzzling her ear. "I can get you as far as the second tier of balconies. You'll need your wiles to get up to the Very Important Gods section on the third."

"I could bring the third tier down to us," she said, speaking to his collar.

"Let's not burn the barn to find the saddle soap." He trailed his fingers up and down her spine, overtly possessive yet keeping her grounded and alert as he guided her to one of three ornate staircases. "Play the right cards, and The Woolly Barrel could be your new favorite restaurant."

She cross-stepped up the stairs, watching all the people watching her. "Did I split my dress? The stares, they burn."

"You're infamous now." He palmed the small of her back and slowed his stride to match hers. He kept his chin high. His grin dared anyone who veered too close to them. "Get used to the attention."

"Because of the bounty? It's canceled now."

"The guilds, the CWIG, it's all so far beneath this clientele. These are the one percent of the one percent's one percent." He paused at the second-tier main bar and slid something to the bartender, earning a subtle nod and a sidelong glance at a shadowed table framed by carved privacy screens. "That the pantheons united against you made you interesting. That Hel went against everyone and released you to exact her wrath makes you exciting. If there is anything the bored and ageless want, it's excitement."

"That's a recipe for all kinds of bad things."

"Your days of being an unknown operative are gone. Poof. Flames. Smoke." He picked up two bubbling green drinks from the bartender. "Own it, or someone will try to own you."

Like a certain handbag.

"Well, since I know neither of those potions is for me, I will apply my wiles on the…" She did a double take. "What is that guarding the stairs?"

Something big, hairy, and tie-dyed blocked the way to the third tier.

"A Kang Admi, cousin of the Yeti." Ashtad turned his back to said cousin. "They own this place, among many other useful ones; and yes, that coloring is a personal choice, not a natural occurrence."

"All hail vibrant color," she muttered.

"Says the woman with teal hair." He winked. "Try not to husk the VIGs."

If only.

"Here's hoping for a buffet." She skimmed her nail along the edge of her bangs and headed for the explosion of color.

She was as tall as his belly button…or what she hoped was a belly button.

"Welcome, Bix the Brazen." The Kang Admi bowed. "We've been expecting you."

She curtsied as best as her tight skirt allowed. "Thank you."

Simple. When met with the unexpected, keep it simple. Obvious questions, like "who's we?" or "why are you expecting me?" would have been prudent, but her stomach had long ago passed the point of caring. Hunger didn't afford the luxury of spy craft or caution.

She despised being hungry. She despised that teensy bit of nourishment from Hel that now forced her to restart the cycle of starvation unless she fed regularly. Next time, a new clause in her contract. A food clause.

Thank the powers that be for the unexpected benefit of

keeping Feng bits in her pendant. How it knew she'd needed its help was beyond her, but without its intervention, she'd be floating in the ether again.

The Kang Admi stepped aside and gestured up dark-carpeted stairs. Her heels made no sound as she emerged on a narrow balcony decorated with nothing more than a single black leather bench running the entire curve of the tier. The faintest light brushed the railing but didn't brave the recesses. Didn't need to.

Gods glowed with raw energy.

A half-dozen dinners sat far apart, outwardly uninterested in each other's company. The sirens' performance kept their attention riveted to the amphitheater. She aimed for the brightest light. Three-piece dark suit, burgundy silk shirt, paisley pocket square, shaggy black hair with zippo hair goo, and ostrich ankle boots—buckled not gored.

"The pocket fob is a nice touch, Phobos."

The Greek god of fear smiled a deliciously sinister smile, exposing sharp canines. It wasn't a timepiece he kept on the gold chain dangling from his vest pocket, but it sure pulsed like one.

"Time has never been my concern, Bix, but I hear it's yours this week. Four days left. When the sun sets on the seventh…" He blew into his fist, then opened his hand. A desiccated sprite tried to take wing and crumbled into dust. "You're looking hungry. Where's Jörmungandr? Lost what it takes to keep you satiated?"

The moment she heard the handbag's name, it was too late. Fear rose before she could quash it.

Phobos sat forward and inhaled, drawing in her scent with a wave of his hand. Amber irises framed dilating red pupils. "Trouble in paradise?"

"It was never like that." She countered too quickly; his low satisfied chuckle said so.

"Ah, so you've come to offer up a bit of 'that,' is it?" He grimaced. "I don't want a serpent's sloppy seconds, even if they have been on a shelf for a decade."

Before Jör, she'd loved this part of the meal, the appetizer of bait, the entree of hook, the entremets of heavy petting, and a plate of raw divine energy. It'd all been a grand, glorious, gender-indifferent game.

Now she felt dirty and ashamed.

Phobos watched her beneath hooded eyes, his sneer adopting the twist of revulsion.

Own it or be owned, Ashtad had warned. She couldn't keep allowing Jör this much power over her.

A quick scan confirmed the other gods watching her, watching Phobos. No time like the present to grow a pair. Right now, she had the undivided attention of a god with a need he didn't yet know he had.

She'd had ten years in exile to plan for moments like this.

Her most recent stay in the ether had provided one key advantage amid the plethora of disadvantages. She'd made new acquaintances. Beyond the elementals of the Reaping Winds, she'd encountered husked gods regaining sentience. They were far more dangerous than their fully cognizant counterparts. Ravenous and confused, these reawakened gods had no concept of who they were, why they existed, or how to control their magic. She'd empathized with them. Deeply. Thirty years ago, she had been in their exact position. She was indebted to the entities who had helped her out of the ether and twice so to the god who had taught her how to feed, clothe, and care for herself.

The least she could do was to ensure her new acquaintances were similarly indebted to her. Call it meal planning.

If she played tonight's game right, she just might get an early return on her investment by snaring one of their fully fueled family members, one who'd fought to keep his fractious family together. One who'd lost that fight and one of his beloved brothers.

Oh, the Greeks and their tragedies.

"A pity, Phobos, there were all manner of interesting things up on that shelf with me." She shrugged. "Some of them had questions, ever so many questions about life and *requited love*."

"My brother is the god of requited love." Phobos slid to the edge of his seat. "Are you saying you found him? Anteros?"

Anteros, the green-eyed son of Ares and Aphrodite, possessed twice the heart-stopping beauty of his mother and none of her vanity. As the story went, his mother had indulged in a particularly spiteful fit of jealousy that had put all of her children and grandchildren in the crosshairs of a rival pantheon. While Phobos and his twin had rallied their siblings to fight, Anteros had gone behind their backs and negotiated a peace accord—the price of which had been Anteros's very essence.

He'd been adrift for hundreds of years when Bix had stumbled upon him in the ether. Unaware of his past, barely aware of his present, Anteros had exuded precious, innocent love with his entire being. He'd reminded Bix of Mirri in her unguarded moments, so much so just being near him had made Bix's bleak heart ache. Eventually, it'd become too painful to stay with him. Leaving him alone to face the terrors stalking the ether had been as far out of the question as returning him to his family, so she'd made an investment in their shared futures.

"Even feral, Anteros is still quite charming." She planted her hands on Phobos's knees and touched her nose against his. "We had long chats about the hollow existence versus the fulfilling sort as he relearned how to speak and process emotions."

Phobos sniffed and sat back, arms wide across the back of the couch. "Tell me where my brother is, and you can sup your fill, creature."

If she was too eager, he'd use it against her. No, she had to make him understand only she could give him what he wanted.

"What, do you think the ether has been mapped? Type some coordinates and expect your GPS to get you there? 'Turn left at the black hole. In three point two miles, take a right onto vast expanse of nothingness.'" She tsked and straightened. "No, what you want to know is how much longer you have to wait before Anteros makes his way to the Under Worlds searching for souls to steal. How much longer you have to wait to find him, draw him back into the fold, and help him become a real god again."

Phobos jabbed his tongue in his cheek. "How do I know you're not putting me on?"

"This from the man wearing the heart of the last woman to screw him over?" She snorted. "How do I know you've got enough juice to make this worth my while?"

"In this narcissistic age of false introspection and oversharing?" Phobos laughed and patted his lap. "Every day a doctor, an academic, a new woo leader, a social media celebrity, and Bob's goat next door is identifying a new phobia. As long as those idiots believe in their fear more than their faith, I will have a surplus of souls and raw energy."

She hiked up her skirt and straddled his thighs. Her hands skimmed over his bristled cheeks. Her thumbs locked under his chin. "I returned Anteros to the Under World convergence two months ago. I imagine he's still fighting for survival in the warrens. You should probably ask Hades if you can borrow one of his dogs. It ought to be quite the hunt."

Phobos blinked rapidly. Her lips touched his brow, and she drank his energy. His strong hands gripped her hips and pushed her away.

"If you're lying, Bix, I will take my revenge on your loved ones."

She grabbed his shirt and yanked him closer. "Someone's already beaten you to it."

She fell upon him like the ravenous beast she was. Ten years of starvation, and she finally had a real meal. Nerve by nerve, vessel and artery, muscle and organ, everything came back online, everything thrummed. Raw energy burned, it cooled, it was liquid, and it was light. It was the most satisfying dish and the most intoxicating drug.

The tips of her hair sensed the minute movements in the air. Her pores exulted in the texture of her clothes, of his clothes rubbing against her. She breathed in the richness of aromas saturating the club. Her eyes took in the layers of Worlds pulsing at the edges of ether surrounding this World. It was all so vibrant, so real.

So alive.

What she would have given for these moments to last eternities, but all too soon, she drained the god's tank.

She slapped her palms against Phobos's chest and eased off his lap. The big lug tipped over, unconscious. She tugged down her skirt, then patted his cheek. "Thanks for the fill-up."

Somehow, early in their relationship, Jör had twisted her feeding sessions into sexual encounters. She'd lacked the strength to refuse him, physically and emotionally. It felt good—no, glorious—to be reminded that she could sustain herself without whoring herself.

Her renewed personal energies pierced the invisible forces trying to expel her from this World. With less effort than a blink, she moored herself firmly amid the swirling, complex native magic of the Mids.

A gatekeeper from an Other World? Yes. One who would not be forcibly removed. Again.

There was an extra bounce to Bix's stride as she strutted toward the stairs, making sure to meet the gaze of every god who dared to look at her.

Bix the Brazen.

She could work with that.

# CHAPTER 13

**D**ysmorphic was dark and eerily quiet in the wee morning hours. Bix slipped off her shoes and padded around the shop, a shoe in each hand. She'd been here before, but it felt so different now. Now she could feel the potent magics imbuing the building and flowing from its residents. They batted at her like gentle ocean waves. For each cresting tide, the magic contained within her pendant pushed back.

A song. A dance. A simple joy of existence.

She inhaled the musk of the men living here. It blended with the oils of the leather and antiseptics of the tools. The cool concrete floor held tiny patterns that tickled her toes, patterns she hadn't noticed before. Spells, knowing the owner.

And there was a certain something with the air. The large industrial air vents whirred and hummed, so it wasn't a stillness so much as a...

"He is indisposed now, if Chief is the one for whom you are looking."

Xipil stood as still as a statue at the end of the long iron corridor. Battle-ax in one hand, wrists crossed in front of him. His hair had been pulled up into a high ponytail, exposing the shaved sides. That she could see that much in the darkness made her giggle.

"Indisposed and at home, or indisposed and elsewhere?"

"Thank you for trusting us to care for him."

That made her pause.

"It was obviously difficult for you," Xipil said solemnly. "Therefore, your choice was noted and appreciated by all of us."

She fully faced the Berserker, who had yet to relax his vigilant posture. "Even Runjit?"

"Especially Runjit, for whom Chief is like a father."

"Not a father figure to you, though. You have too much respect and not enough resentment." She ambled toward him. "Why do you call him Chief?"

"He has many names, but Chief is a culturally common honorific suitable for the diversity of our ranks." Xipil adjusted his grip on the ax but didn't heft or hold it in a threatening manner.

"Xipil," she said, drawing out his name. "Where *are* Hywl and Runjit?"

The Berserker didn't look away. His expression didn't change at all. Damn it.

"Did the angels come for Tobek?" She bit her lip, dreading the confirmation. "Did they find him? Are Hywl and Runjit okay?"

Still no reaction.

"No, you're too calm to be the last man standing, and your eyes aren't floodlights. You're guarding something." She listed to the side, peering around him. There was nothing but a wall. And a teensy draft. "That used to be the door to the clinic, Xipil. Why does it look like a wall now?"

Still no answer. Face still impassive.

"Xipil," she cajoled, grinning as she clacked her heels—still in her hands—together. "I can make the wall disappear, but I'd rather be the nosy neighbor instead of the destructive one."

His lips pursed, but he didn't try to block her.

"Let her in, Xipil. She may have insights."

The hard rasp caused her to spin with a squeak.

"Tobek, how did you sneak…" She batted at the big lug wearing a vest with a super-deep hoodie that obscured his face. Her hand passed through his image. "Oh cool, a hologram."

Locks snicked. The end of the hall opened to an overbright clinic with all sorts of hospital things: beepy things, flashy things, tubey and needley things. Three gurneys were parked in front of a stainless steel wall of square doors. Two operating tables anchored opposite sides of the rear quadrants. Two padded surgical chairs held the nearer quadrants. Lights, monitors, and gizmos hung from the ceiling by robotic arms. Squarely in the center of the room, a massive double pentagram slowly spun.

An angel had been nailed spread eagle to either side. One blond with ivory feathered wings slumped forward. Blood stained his torn shirt. The other angel, brunet with darker ecru feathers, had a gash from wide temple to narrow jaw. Elaborate markings peeked from the collars and cuffs of their button-downs.

The prisoners had bled out into a perfectly round puddle at the base of the pentagram, a puddle growing vines with thorns and fragrant blossoms. A leaf unfurled, reaching beyond the edge of the ring and recoiling. The expansion and retreat repeated over and over.

Runjit and Hywl stood wide legged and somber faced outside the nascent thicket. Runjit's glorious mane had been tamed under a turban. Both men had dried blood and dawning bruises smattered over their bulky bodies. Disks of scored wood and etched stone lay at their feet. Each Berserker held fistfuls of engraved iron shackles.

The third set of disks spread before a large blossom of rough crystal projecting Tobek's impossibly realistic image. Considering the last time he'd come close to angels, she wasn't surprised by his absence.

Bix put on her shoes and took a spot by the door, waiting for someone to speak. Tobek's hologram turned slightly, but not enough to allow her to see within the shadows of his hood.

"You've fed."

"Yay me?" Bix waved her hands in front of her chest.

He grunted. "I've been researching the traps we found at Forest Haven."

"Shouldn't you be in bed?" She glowered at Runjit, even though her commentary was directed at the hologram. "Doped up on painkillers and green gelatin?"

Marble was more animated than the formerly scalpel-wielding Berserker.

"Something about the final room we entered bothered me." Tobek gestured to the disks on the floor and the manacles in his men's hands. "You and I were interrupted before we could complete our inspection."

"We can go back there now if you want." She jerked her thumb over her shoulder. "I can take one of your guys with me."

Tobek pointed his gloved artificial hand at one of the large monitors. It burped to life.

A raging forest fire filled the screen. Thick black smoke swallowed trucks and first responders. Hoses sprayed water to no avail. The news chyron at the bottom of the screen explained it all: *Firefighters battle blaze at Forest Haven. Three hundred acres destroyed. Arson suspected.*

"Are you kidding me? The Host would rather burn the evidence that could lead us to Fe-eends, fiends," she stammered, catching herself before letting the scorched bird out of the bag.

"Apparently, your offer of a trade was declined," Tobek drawled.

"Dumbasses." She stomped and huffed. "Pompous. Arrogant. Holier than thou. Dumbasses. Do they think I'm not going to find out which of their rank set me up? As soon as this contract is over… life is not going to be fun for them."

"Their arrogance does make them easier to trap," Tobek said, drawing her back to show-and-tell.

She flicked a limp wrist at the two angels attached to the pentagrams. "Are these the two the Host sent to hunt you?"

"The others are in the chiller drawers." He tipped his head toward the wall of square stainless steel doors.

"Clinic implies a place of repair, not dissection, you know that, right?"

Hywl snorfled, then sobered.

"So what can I do to help?" She wrinkled her nose. "Get rid of the dead angels?"

"They're not dead." Runjit flipped up the wooden disk nearest his foot like a Hacky Sack and caught it.

Both angels' heads snapped up. Hate, bright and feral, blazed from black eyes. Words she did not recognize flowed from their split lips. Runjit dropped the disk on the ground. The angels seized, then slumped.

"While we have successfully weakened them, we haven't been able to contain them without using actual restraints." Tobek crossed his arms. "Ideas?"

"But you have contained their blood, right? Constraining the weeds there is your doing?"

"Hywl's doing."

"I was a cleric before I was invited to serve the Mid World Army," Hywl explained.

"A cleric?" Bix rubbed her hands and stepped farther into the room. "A cleric with stoles?"

Hywl cocked his head, brow furrowing. "One stole. You never wanted to accrue those accursed things."

"Accursed," she echoed.

"My time in secular service predates 1-800-GOT-FAITH," Hywl hedged. "In my day, a cleric's stole was a bill from an angel, something I had to wear every day until I repaid the miracle performed by the angel."

"And the payment took the form of…?"

"How ever many deeds the angel demanded." Hywl laughed miserably. "An original stole is woven from an angel's hair. It allows the angel a direct connection with the bearer, even if the bearer is in a body that angel didn't create."

"Slavery," Runjit groused. "A cleric's stole is a band of slavery."

Hywl hung his head and thrust his jaw forward. It took

a moment for him to speak. "Made to be ever so beautiful, enchanting, and impossible to be rid of. Leave it on a battlefield, find it folded with your armor. Discard it in a raging fire, find it in the lining of your coat. Give away the coat, find it part of the bandages holding your insides inside."

"Ew." She patted her waist. "What happens to the stole once the debt is repaid?"

"The debt is never paid," Runjit said, his accent thickening with the intensity of his hate. "Even after the debtor's death. The debt is passed to whomever the debtor had the greatest negative emotional relationship."

"Because angels feed on negative emotions." Hywl shot Runjit a chiding look. "Best reason of all to not be an asshole to anyone ever. Extreme karma."

Her mind boggled. "And if the angel dies?"

Hywl grimaced. "Then it passes to the angel's superior, who decides to keep, forgive, or promote the debt."

"I'm sorry to sound like a child with a bad case of the whys," she said sheepishly. "I had no idea miracles resulted in indentured servitude."

"If the debt is promoted or reaches the top of the Host hierarchy, then it goes into the Host's treasury to be used in negotiations with gods, Fates, guilds, and the Dreigiau. Power over others is far from priceless." Tobek massaged his natural hand with his prosthetic. "Why the keen interest in stoles? There were none at Forest Haven."

"That we saw, but we also saw evidence of a fire." She reassessed the size of the clinic. "The angels in the chillers, how many are there?"

"Five." Tobek motioned her to the death drawers. "Thrones of the Host always hunt in teams of seven."

She pulled out the five trays holding the dead angels. Even in finality, they truly were beautiful, and like everything beautiful, they used it to their malicious advantage.

"Mind if I, uh…?"

"As you will, but try not to enter the trap in the center."

It took a few minutes, a mess of props, and a lot of help from Xipil to set the stage, but when she was done, the gist was right, even if the scale was off.

Every detail from the photos Hel had shared with her, reproduced in some fashion.

Five angels hung from the ventilation at the five points of a pentacle drawn in duct tape on the floor. Iodine dotted the floor around the center. A rolling stool and paper cap stood in for Feng's claw and Mirri's remains near the center.

"There." She patted Xipil on the back.

Runjit's face twitched violently, likely from an onset of apoplexy. Hywl had blanched from pale to pasty to ghostly throughout the setup. Tobek…she couldn't tell. He still hid under his hood.

"At what are we looking, sweetheart?" Tobek asked with an odd echo to his voice. Maybe the crystal was running out of juice.

"I think Forest Haven was a testing ground that culminated in a grand experiment in the burn room. There was a pentagram. Right? Plus the blood of angels. There was also a fissure that allowed traces of ether into the room. And in the center of everything were feathers that seemingly floated in midair."

"The room repelled the angels; they refused to cross the threshold." Tobek nodded.

"This, this is what the people behind Forest Haven were working toward." She opened her arms to encompass the room. "This is Centralia before the bunker's relocation spell."

Four Berserkers swore in unison.

"A portal that passes through ether," Tobek growled. "The framework of a functional portal has long been rumored to be possible, but never has one been successful. Different from a gate because gates bypass the ether."

"There was no evidence of ether in Centralia, which makes me think they've mastered the process. There was char on the trees in Centralia, but that was easily dismissed as a byproduct of the fires plaguing the area." She gestured to the unfurled rolls of toilet paper swaying from the electrical conduits overhead, running down the walls, and stretching toward the center circle of meat-eating weeds. "However, the weed growth made no sense whatsoever. The plants were far from indigenous to that part of Pennsylvania. Worse, they were thriving amid an area rife with anthracite fumes and contaminated soil. But if weird weeds spring from angels' blood, then all this TP is blood spray."

"Which corresponds to the open wingspan of a suspended angel," Runjit conceded. "And the scrubs currently covering the angels' faces? Blindfolds?"

"Stoles," Hywl croaked, then cleared his throat. "Stoles used to summon the angels, but how did they force them to appear? Stoles control the bearer. The bearer doesn't control the angel."

"All magic operates on a path of exchange," Tobek corrected. "The trick is to be more powerful than the guy at the other end."

"Then the angels who died there had to be lower rank." Hywl harrumphed.

"Not if the Phoenix was at the other end," Bix ventured, unsure of how much Tobek had told his men.

Another round of swearing said he hadn't told them. The man truly had kept it among their downstairs triad. Bless him. However, seeing as how she was the reason angels had shown up on their doorstep, it was best if his men understood the scope of the crap storm that had sucked them into its vortex.

"The char on the trees at Centralia. The char in the room at Forest Haven. Feng spatter or Feng temper? I don't know. I don't know enough about him." She shrugged, toying with her pendant.

"We'd have the answer if we'd had a chance to reexamine the burn room." Tobek sighed loudly. "Or if Centralia hadn't triggered the relocation spell."

"I bet if you wake up one of your friends there, they'll have an opinion on my theory." Bix bit her lip and leaned toward the pentagram. "I'm pretty sure this is how the bad guys got the dewclaw to the hill, which means they could have sent the remains of the Norse ambassador along the same path."

"Having killed her elsewhere." Tobek widened his stance.

"Ether rips apart anything made to exist in the Mids." Bix clawed at the air, demonstrating the movements. "It's possible ether minced the ambassador's contracted body after it passed through the origin portal, freeing the goddess from her fleshy prison. The destination portal would already have been opened by Feng's claw, so we could assume the ambassador's remains simply completed the trajectory he started. Maybe the dewclaw is all that remains of Feng."

"We'd be in the throes of war initiated by the dragons against the angels if he was dead." Tobek countered. "I'll buy that he's injured, possibly grievously, but not dead."

"Now we're talking about angels being slaughtered at two different points at the same time, the Phoenix being injured, and no one, *nobody*, noticed?" Hywl jostled the chains in his hands. "Ten angels minimum. The Host has to know. Centralia was out in the open, a public space, albeit remote. It wasn't warded against the Host like this place is. Right?"

Tobek nodded.

"So let's ask the pair you have here." Bix gestured at the two angels.

Runjit rolled his eyes. "Cooperative is the last thing angels are known to be."

"Yeah, well, you'll get no argument from me on that," Bix muttered.

Hywl looked between Runjit and Tobek three times before he picked up the disk at his feet. "I'm sorry, but I have to know. If someone is sacrificing angels, I…I have to know."

The living angels jolted back to alertness and immediately began babbling.

Bix sashayed to the edge of the thicket. "Hi. You can keep praying to whomever, but while you do, take a look around the room and let it sink in. I need you to tell me if this is how someone could rip open a portal in the layers of a Mid World."

One of the captives wasn't a total idiot.

"Allow me to return to the Host, and I will gather the answers you seek."

"Awesome." Bix clasped her hands together and scurried around to the other side of the pentacle. "And you?"

This angel, not so helpful. He spat things, not all of them words.

"Well." Bix flopped her hand over her bosom and wiped off the loogie. "You clearly are unaware of my history with your race, and how much I really hate all of you. So, since you choose to be useless…"

"Bix, wai—"

Tobek didn't get to finish before Useless Wonder dropped into the ether. The scream lingered in the clinic after she closed the gate.

The clearer it became that the Host was tied to Mirri's death—even if they were victims—the more disinclined Bix was to have any margin of forgiveness for their race. If they had foreknowledge of Feng's situation, it meant they had foreknowledge of Mirri's abduction. That meant they could have stopped what had happened and *chose* not to.

Hel's wrath would be notable. Bix's would be unforgettable.

Useful Angel watched her return to his side of the pentagram with white eyes instead of black.

"Someone just joined our party remotely," Hywl cautioned, jerking his chin toward the remaining live angel. "Only the shot callers can coinhabit a lesser angel's senses. The white eyes give them away."

"Hello, archangel, welcome," she greeted sickeningly sweetly, directing his attention up to the hoisted brethren. "For a limited time only, we're actually on the same side, seeking the same very specific thing, something the minion from Forest Haven probably forgot to mention when I delivered him to *healing* ground. Good-faith gesture and whatnot."

The archangel said nothing as the pentagram made its slow

revolution. The Berserkers turned their backs to him. Tobek didn't move. When the angel was once again facing Bix, his white eyes locked on her.

"Gatekeeper, we will meet in the bar known as Hella Fella in one hour. The meeting is with you alone." He blinked and one eye flipped to black. "The price, however, is the death of this vessel."

Heartless bastard, but hey, what did she really care?

"Bix, don't do it," Hywl begged.

"You have one hour, archangel. If you're late, I'll end another pack of Thrones." She opened two gates. One for the angel. One for her. She paused for a moment and faced the crestfallen Berserker. "Sorry, Hywl, really I am. But there are questions I have to answer, and I'm running out of time."

# CHAPTER 14

**B**ix landed in the kitchen of the basement and ogled the butt encased in worn black work pants swaying over a ribbon of freshly etched concrete. "When you work too hard, your voice changes in the hologram. FYI."

"It wasn't physical labor that caused it. It was the spellwork to secure our home." Tobek sat back on his heels. Oh, he truly wore the super-deep hoodie, but the pink rubber gloves were different from the hologram. "I must apologize."

She toed off her shoes and padded over to his work. "For what?"

"I was lax in repairing the wards." He snapped off the gloves and stood. "That endangered you. I apologize."

"Me?" She cast a sidelong look at the gouges in the floor of the kitchen. "Oh. That. I'm good. I'm sorry I broke your protections, but hey, the Bi Xie worked."

He took her hand in his natural hand and squeezed. "I found your phone and a party favor in my bed. They're there on the counter."

Party favor?

She spotted the pink penis flash drive and grinned. "I don't suppose you have a computer I could borrow?"

"A tablet is in the top drawer by the fridge." He locked glass lids on amber jars and added them to a shelf in the armory.

Clearly not herbs and spices.

"Let me know when you're done with the angel bodies, and I'll dispose of them. Or you can clear your guys from the room and I'll get rid of the room, whichever."

"We store the corpses until we've catalogued their scarifications, which tell us things like sphere, choir, and rank. That tells us their job, their boss, and whether they have stoles outstanding…among other things." He stumbled and caught himself on the stainless steel table.

"Ah, damn, the ones you were keeping alive." She hurried to his side and draped his arm over her shoulders. "I promoted someone's debts, didn't I?"

"There are those among our brethren for whom freeing debtors is a personal cause." He leaned on her and motioned to the couch.

"Like Hywl."

"For a time. Hywl had hunted the Choir of Miracle Workers for so long, he'd lost himself, so I invited him to the shop to help him break the cycle." He sank into the depths of the leather couch and sighed. "Obsessions, addictions, all those repetitive thoughts and behaviors have claimed more Berserker lives than any battlefield."

"Runjit too?" She dashed back to the kitchen for her gadgets.

"Think of Runjit as Hywl's battle buddy, his sponsor, if you will." He stretched his legs on the couch. "Both men have had difficult histories with the Host."

"Get the impression that's a requirement for someone to be invited into the ranks of Berserker." She set her things on the coffee table and nudged him with her thigh. "When was the first time you were runed by Thrones?"

"Runed?" He detached his artificial arm, setting it on the coffee table. "I suppose there are similarities in the branding by different types of hunters. It was before I signed on with the Fates."

"They did that to a mortal? Why?" She rolled back the edges of his hood, careful not to touch his face.

He caught her wrist. "Don't do this."

"Do what?" She tried to shake off his hold.

"I don't want your pity or your guilt." His grip remained solid but never tightened, never triggered pain.

"Guilt?" She flicked him in the back of the head. "You are a grown-ass man who has outlived civilizations. You've known from the minute I showed up here that I was tangling with the Consortium. You still came looking for me. You still hunted wards with me. If you weren't prepared for angels to show up, then you're an idiot, which is not my fault."

They stayed on the brink of awkwardness for several heartbeats.

He finally chuckled and released her. "Quite true, not your fault. Glad we agree."

"Is your face going to rupture every time you're in close quarters with an angel now?" She gently set his hood along his shoulders and bit her lip.

All his beautiful long hair had been clipped short. His long beard was gone. The entire layer of epidermis had been removed from his face. A clear plastic mask had been molded around the raw angry dermis. Neoprene straps crisscrossed the back of his head to hold the mask in place.

His chest ceased to rise or fall.

"I'm totally calling you Herr Schmidt from now on," she whispered in his ear, grabbing the tablet and the penis drive. "The raw, inflamed skin really sells it."

"The Red Skull worked for Hydra," he drawled, kneading the scars around his amputation. "I work for the Fates."

"I would not be surprised if Marvel fashioned Hydra after a House of Fate." She saluted, taking a seat on the floor by his hip. "You didn't answer my question about a safe perimeter."

"Doesn't happen with every angel. Those who use the brands only make them skin-deep." He adjusted the pillows. "It's why I get to keep most of my face."

"How long until the restoration clause of your contract with the Fates kicks in?" She searched the tablet for a power button, top, side, back.

"Soon, just long enough for the Fates to feel sure that I am sufficiently humbled and hampered." He reached over her shoulder and pressed his forefinger against the screen. The tablet hummed and lit up.

The port she could find without his help. The boy drive slid into the girl port. She kept her thumb across the flash drive as the encryption runes scanned her thumbprint. The screen filled with file folders.

"How much longer do you have?" he asked quietly.

"With this thing?" She pulled a face. "There are at least forty file folders on here. I have no idea how many subfolders or files. Could take me…"

"Not the data," he clarified. "You told Hywl you were running out of time. How much time do you have left?"

She swiped her finger on the screen repeatedly, looking for any indication that Mirri had known Feng. Drew had mentioned Mirri's investigation into the infamous armory incident. Odds were good she would have tried for a meeting with the prosecution's key witness. The Sisterhood would have been her first outreach in the hunt for leverage. Fortunately, the Sisterhood was a big fan of indexes and cross-references. Bless them, they'd even tagged the files with keywords. Of course, Missing Phoenix wasn't one of them, but Wanker Detail was.

"Sweetheart, how long do you have?"

"Four days," she answered with distraction. "I have four days and three nights before I am expected to deliver the soul of whoever mutilated the Norse ambassador to Hel."

"What happens if you need more time?"

"Then I'm in breach of contract and I will not be the only one to pay the consequences. Hel likes to maximize collateral damage."

"Let me do the sit-still work." He held out his natural hand.

"Tell me for what I should be looking while you meet with the archangel."

She stared at the screen. There were so many moving pieces to the puzzle. This drive and its contents were just…shit, she didn't know what was on here, so she wouldn't know what he shouldn't see or what he'd remove if he didn't want her to see. The man worked for the Houses of Fate. This was intel from the pantheons possibly exposing the dirty secrets of the Consortium. This was all a political clusterfuck.

But she was running out of time, and she couldn't hope to succeed without help. More help, that is. Tobek had repeatedly proven to be a fount of reliability and usefulness. And Skuld had technically delivered the intel, so why not trust in Fate for a bit longer?

She always had worked best with a team.

"Okay." She squeezed his hand. "Let me figure out what I need."

"Fair enough." He pulled his hand back. "You certain you are looking for a perpetrator with a soul?"

"I'm feeling ninety percent sure. The notion that spells are involved in this says it has to be a Chwed. An upper-caste and highly educated Chwed. I'm leaving ten percent because I'm not sure what role Feng is playing." She found the folder containing the dossiers of Mirri's protective detail. Ten years ago, Mirri had churned through twenty agents before settling on a team that stayed with her for five years. Then, over the course of four weeks, Mirri had replaced her entire team, even the B shift. It happened again six months later. Then again at sixteen. She'd kept that team until three months ago. "She changed needs."

"What was that?" Tobek rolled toward her, then swore as the side of his mask scraped against the armrest. He resumed his position of staring at the ceiling.

She flicked through the names, looking for anyone familiar. Anyone with whom she'd worked. Anyone with whom…

Vidya.

Gods damn it all. Vidya had been a member of Mirri's protective detail. She hadn't lasted long, but Vidya had never mentioned it. Every perfect opportunity to do so, and she hadn't mentioned it. One ex working for the other? Yeah, no way was that coincidence. On either woman's part.

She needed an objective third party.

"So, Chief." She twisted around and laid her elbow on Tobek's thigh. "You've put together tactical teams at some point in your unending life, right?"

He didn't need skin to show his opinion of her question. "Once or twice."

"If I give you dossiers, can you follow the changing team combinations and skills to figure out how or—better yet—where they were being used?"

"Xipil has the knack for identifying those types of things quickly, but I can keep the information private if you prefer and do it myself."

Hell, in for one, in for all.

"Your boys helped me stage a reenactment of an angel slaughter. If they didn't know they'd been recruited to my cause, I think they know now."

He barked merrily once, then groaned, gently laying his hand upon his chest. "They like being able to exercise their other skills, especially in front of a woman who brings them nothing but excitement."

"Poor guys." She snorted and wagged the tablet. "This thing has encryption on it that's keyed to me. I don't know how to copy it for you."

"Black cord under the table's lip. Not the blue one, the black one. The blue one charges my prosthetic."

"What? Don't want me controlling your hands?" She fluttered her lashes, feeling under the table's lip for the cords.

He stared at the ceiling and kneaded the air with his natural hand. "That is an entirely different conversation for an entirely different day."

She blushed and busied herself with hooking up the tablet to the table. "There are photos on here too. I'm looking for a clue into what changed in Mirri's life five years ago. It could be people, it could be politics, it could be anything, but it resulted in her changing her protective details, a lot."

"We'll look into who was watching the Norse ambassador other than her CWIG detail and the Sisterhood," he said. "Surveillance is Xipil's bailiwick. Hywl and Runjit can catalogue the angels before Gurp cleans the clinic."

"And you're going to stay here and rest, right?"

"Take your phone with you. I'll call as soon as we have intel."

She grabbed her phone and left the tablet on the table with the drive plugged in. She stood over him and put her hand on his. "I don't think I've said it, but I definitely mean it: thank you. Thank you for helping and for caring."

"You may have three days left with Hel, but your time here with me has no limit."

She smiled and opened gates. "Glutton for punishment."

# CHAPTER 15

Leather probably would have been a better choice of attire for a trip to Hella Fella, but then Bix would have blended in with the upholstery. Judging the regard of the grizzlies bent over their lunches in these off-peak hours, no one in this church-cum-fetish bar considered her anything more than a beard.

Excellent.

Aged bronze tiled the ceiling of the nave. Mirror-lined alcoves contained thick chains, glossy and matte metal boxes, and candles. Pedestals that once hosted statues of saints now presented sculptures of definite sinners in collars and leashes. Calligraphy scrolled across price tags tucked into corners of paintings depicting beautiful men being very tame to highly restrained. The stained glass windows original to the church remained. The splendor of angels in parted billowing robes offered up a whole new interpretation in their current setting.

At the back of the church, lofted above the iron-and-wood doors, rose the blackened choir loft. The five-panel art piece backing the loft would have fit nicely in Tobek's home.

He'd probably kill her over the theme.

At the other end of the church, an electrician sporting winged ears shimmied under a DJ booth centered in the chancel. Cables unspooled from industrial spindles that doubled as bar tables in the transepts. Black hatches in the dance floor in front of the chancel stood wide open.

"Can I help you, ma'am?"

She turned toward the friendly voice. A young man in a duty black, long-sleeve T-shirt with Hella Fella's name and logo emblazoned down the left side polished glasses behind a diamond-plate bar. His dark ginger shag hung in his eyes. He had angular features and plump lips that must have earned him plenty of tips from scads of regulars.

She hopped up on a swiveling stool and walked her fingers over the thick resin protecting a collage of black-and-white photos that formed the bar top. "I'm waiting on a lunch date."

The bartender grinned. "Here? And you agreed?"

"I'm partial to the name."

"Ah, so you're a lookie loo." He lined up the clean glasses on a shelf next to the ice well. "Your kind usually comes on Thursday nights for the floor show."

"I bet that is something spectacular. Any other nights you'd recommend?" She spun around on the seat, making idle chitchat as the timer on her phone counted down the seconds until she went hunting for Thrones. Not that she could afford the distraction, but she couldn't afford the Host dicking with her either.

"Weekends we have a line, but Tuesdays…" The young man stopped his polishing. His joy faded, and he took a step back.

"Two ales, the darker the better," a gravelly voice demanded. "Then take your polishing to the other end of the bar."

"Yes, sir." The bartender pulled two pints with full heads, then made himself scarce.

Big, bald, and broad chested perched on the stool beside her. A deep olive complexion had been heavily marked with swirling scarifications. Black eyes that brooked no shit bored into her. "Everything you know, now."

"Uhm," she drew out the word and counted the bottles on the top shelf. "No."

He seized her by the hair and smashed her face into the bar top. "I don't play games, gatekeeper."

Bullies really pissed her off.

Chairs slid, and customers tromped closer, threatening the archangel. Their protection warmed the cockles of her heart, but she hardly needed it. She opened the floor beneath the archangel. His black biker boots tipped into the gate, but not the rest of the angel.

"You think your parlor tricks will work on me, you pathetic creature?" He yanked her head back, fully levitating over the open gate.

"It was a warning, asshole."

The next gate separated his hand from his wrist. He hissed and jerked his arm away. His snarl…softened into a sneer.

"I see you haven't completely forgotten how to defend yourself." He perched on his seat again and pointed to his severed hand still in her hair. "You don't remember me, though. That much is obvious."

"Get the feeling we weren't friends." She untangled his meaty fist and wagged it at the slack-jawed men who had sort of come to her aid. They shuffled back to their lunches, casting sidelong glowers and whispering about horror fetishes. She dropped the angel's bleeding hand on the bar top.

"I'm Samael," he supplied, handing her a wad of napkins. "For my blood in your hair. And as for whether we were friendly, that depended on the Phoenix's cycle and the side you took."

Now there was a rabbit hole she really wanted to jump down, but time…limited time was a bitch.

"I have a hot date with a bottle of bleach and a hedge trimmer when we finish here." She waved off the napkins. "Why demand the death of the lesser angel?"

"To protect your warlock and his friends."

Not the answer she was expecting. "Why care?"

"They're soldiers in the Mid World Army." He inhaled deeply and refitted his wrist to his arm. With the sound of wet noodles being violently stirred, his body repaired itself. "When the times to defend the Mids have arisen, we all have set aside the petty crap that's built in the off years, and we do our duty. Those are the kind of men who matter in battle. Those are the kind of men for whom there is always a need."

"A minority opinion among the Host, but one I respect." She inclined her head. "What do you know about portals?"

"Less than you do, clearly." He mopped up the blood pool blossoming into red algae with tiny teeth. "Four years ago, a team of angels began investigating punctures in the protective layers of certain Mid Worlds. The leadership of the Host believed you were behind them."

"Me? You all fixed me up with a one-way ticket to exile."

"We both know that just because you're not on World doesn't mean you can't open a gateway." He chugged the first beer and belched. "However, the punctures are sloppy, unstable, and fracturing like candy glass. As much of a pain in my ass as you've been over the eons, you've never been sloppy."

Gurp might have disagreed, but she took the angel's compliment. Truthfully, she *had* opened gates from exile. Sometimes to help those like Anteros get closer to home, and sometimes to remind certain powerful entities that she was still out there in the ether, thinking of them not so fondly.

"The leaders of the affected Mids have reported fluctuations and anomalies in the atmosphere and magic." Samael wiped his mouth with the back of his hand and slid the empty pint glass down the counter to the bartender. "The Host tracked those back to the punctures."

"Like the rip at Forest Haven?"

"The one you reported at the looney bin?" He grimaced and nodded. "That was the first time the Host had a link between the environmental reports and those of missing miracle workers."

"The goons you had stationed there to keep watch didn't detect it?"

He shook his head. "That room had been warded against us.

We knew there was something off about the entire site, but we couldn't tell what it was."

"Is that why you burned down Forest Haven? Because you finally knew what was in the room?"

"We didn't raze it." He alternated his attention between the door and the mirror behind the bar. "We too wanted to study it further to learn the weakness in our race that had allowed it to exist in the first place. You did something to break the wards, which exposed the breadth of magic stewing there. The fire, that was the dragons."

"Dragons? How are they involved in all this?"

He eyed her pendant, and his scowl deepened.

"Feng," she guessed. "They know he's MIA. That was the skirmish in the sky above Centralia. They felt his magic, and they answered. Your guys also answered."

"You won the draw," he noted. "We thought Feng had moved with the bunker, and yes, we knew about the bunker."

Ashtad's leak in the CWIG, most likely. Not her primary concern, not while she had the attention of a semi-cooperative archangel.

"How long has Feng been gone?"

"Five years."

She choked. "What?"

"He's been gone five years." Samael chuckled without mirth. "At first, the Consortium insisted he'd gone dark to investigate some case he'd been chasing. A year passes, still no word—we're all long-lived, so a year is inconsequential in our timeline—but after three years without so much as a sighting, his coworkers finally get worried. The Consortium taps the Host to check in on our missing ward—discreetly, so we don't blow his cover if he really is deep under."

"Naturally," she said drolly.

"Now it's been five years, and we still don't know where he is. It takes effort and a lot of magic to hide from the entire Consortium. They're wondering why he's hiding…and *what* he's hiding."

"He was beyond reproach at my trial. What changed?"

"The case he was supposedly working when he vanished stemmed from your trial, and you know what a political nightmare that was." He finished the second beer and signaled for two more. "My guess? He went undercover and got too deep. He had to pass too many tests of loyalty for whomever he was collecting evidence against, and it all messed with his head."

"Are you seriously telling me he's been someone's *prisoner* for five years?" she shouted through a whisper.

"I'm telling you I think he was tested. I don't know if he passed or failed. I don't know if he's spent five years as a prisoner or an accomplice." He caught the full pint sliding back down the bar. "Figured you'd be happy about his predicament, what with your recent history and all."

Angels, really starting to make the gods' lack of empathy downright cloying.

"Feng's been gone five years, and four years ago, someone figured out how to open portals. Two of those portals left pieces of Feng behind." Bix rubbed her souring stomach. "Is he the only one who knew how to rip a hole in the layers?"

"He wouldn't know, doesn't need to. No one in the Host did. Until your little show-and-tell today, we couldn't figure how the punctures were being created." He glanced behind him at the speakers firing up in the chancel. "Dragons and angels move freely among Mid Worlds by the very nature of what we are and our relationship with the native magic. What we don't do is get anywhere near the ether that these crappy fissures are letting in to the Mids. Only Fates and gods can survive an encounter with that stuff."

"So if whoever is doing this didn't need Feng for his knowledge, then they must need him for spell ingredients. Specifically, *pieces of his body* for the ingredients." She groaned with disgust. Feng was an angry, dickish jackass, but to be kept prisoner for five years and used for parts? No one deserved that.

"Whoever is doing it might get off on slaughtering angels. Nobody likes the race in charge." Samael leaned on his elbow and angled toward her. "However, transporting something through the ether means they're using two sets of pentacles powered by two opposing races. Angels aren't their only victims. They need the Other World magic to corrupt the flow of the native to define a destination."

"The missing visiting gods," she sighed. "That's why they've chosen visiting gods instead of rooted ones. Rooted gods would only enhance the native magic. If they're using visiting gods at one end and summoned angels at the other, then they're planning something bigger. Something far more potent than…"

Than an attack on the guild masters? Could the labor leaders have been the target? Ashtad had said they had all been together in the confined space of the bunker, which was perfect for a hit, especially if a portal leaking ether was the weapon. But something must have gone wrong because the portal didn't break the ground. Or something had protected the bunker, much like the relocation spell had protected it. Too many unknowns still.

She needed copies of the crime scene photos from Vidya.

"If those idiots are using punctures to transport Mid World items through the ether, it means something in the ether is helping them do it." Samael hopped off his seat and rolled his shoulders. "I shouldn't have to tell you that the things in the ether aren't benevolent. Whoever is using portals has no concept of the dangers to which they're exposing all of us, even themselves."

There had been entities in the ether patrolling the borders of the Mids. She'd assumed they were hunting for lesser beings like her to torment, but what if they'd really been guarding the fracture points? A shiver shot down her spine.

Bix's phone vibrated along the bar top, startling her. Herr Schmidt showed up on the screen. She tapped Ignore. It didn't work. The phone kept whirring.

"Better get that." Samael slapped cash down on the counter. "We're done here anyway."

"Wait," she called after him as she answered the phone. "What?"

"Grab the archangel and get out of there, now." Tobek bellowed on the other end.

The air inside the bar charged, tickling the tips of her hair.

"Samael," she shouted, bolting after the archangel.

He turned.

The protective layer of the Mid World rippled. Tore.

Rage contorted Samael's features. Jet feathered wings unfurled. He tipped back toward the puncture, reaching out to her.

Bix leapt.

Bix rode Samael like a cowboy on a pissed-off bull. Her thighs clenched his hips. Her ankles hooked in the small of his back. His mighty wings beat furiously as he fought the invisible pull. She buried her face in his neck lest the claws beneath his feathers rip her to shreds. His body jackknifed, and he roared.

They hit a pool with a splash, then a slurp. Heat suffused her body. Fried angel stink filled her nose as thick goo jerked them down. Samael's muffled roar took on an agonized timbre. A second distorted agonized howl answered.

The claw nestled at her bosom scorched her skin.

She didn't dare open her eyes.

Gates dropped them out of the trap.

# CHAPTER 16

**B**ix pushed Samael through a gate into the only neutral zone she knew—Mirri's condo. Down absorbed their landing. Goose, not angel.

"Stop, Samael, stop with the wings, I can't see past them," Bix sputtered at his throat, flinging gunk from her face and eyes.

"It's still got me," the archangel growled, thrashing. "Can't break loose."

"Pause the wings, or they're going to get nipped by a gate." She opened a gate and slid it around the walls, spinning to ceiling then floor and back to the wall like some horrible amusement park ride. "I've got you. If they do it again, I'll move you again."

He did as she asked, but his heart beat so strongly, it ricocheted around in her head.

"There. Multiple holes," he grunted, scraping blue goop off his boiling skin. "The idiots at the other end are still punching holes in the protective layer."

"Your stole," she hissed. "Promote your stole."

"My what?" He struggled to sit up, wiping his massive wings on the comforter, the carpet, and any other bit of fabric.

"Your stole. That's how they've leashed you. If you don't want to get incinerated by a swimming pool of Feng blood, promote every godsdamned stole you have into the Host's treasury."

"Are you mad?"

"No, but I am itchy and covered in hot goo. Fortunately, the goo isn't eating through my flesh, unlike some other people here."

"I am a goddamn archangel," he shouted, clawing at his skin. "I will break free of their inferior magic and sow ruin upon them, their family, their race, and generations to follow until they are extinct."

She snatched him by his ears and shook him. "They have Feng. Are you stronger than the Phoenix? We just took a bath in his blood. This is bigger than Forest Haven and wholly different from Centralia. If you want to save your ass and the Phoenix, then promote your godsdamned debts now."

His black eyes flipped white, flipped black, white, black, white, black, white.

She slapped him. "Stop it. Focus on the now, or so help me, I will let go and let your enemies have you."

"You don't understand the value of those debts," Samael snarled.

"I don't, you're right." She pointed to the bed smoldering around them from Feng's blood. "I give you to the count of five before I stop fighting to save you. Then your debts end up in the treasury anyway because you'll be dead. Five. Four. Three."

She unlocked her ankles and stilled the gate.

The holes sucked him away from her, pulling his wings into a void. He clutched on to her with both arms.

"Fine," he shouted, gnashing his teeth. "It takes time to promote them."

"Hurry up," she groused, casting the gate into ricocheting motions again. "Before they figure out how to cleave you from your wings."

His head dropped back, and he convulsed. The scarifications on his skin smoothed beneath the blisters raised by Feng's blood. She held him as he shook.

His wings drooped to the floor, freed from the punctures in the air. His arms went slack around her. His heartbeat faded.

"Samael?" She grabbed his chin. "Samael?"

Nothing.

She thumbed open an eyelid and snapped her fingers before his black eye. "Hello? Dialing an archangel. Anyone else in there? Hello?"

Damn, they'd abandoned each other toot sweet and in a hurry.

"You need a hand in there, Bixie babe?"

Bix twisted on the bed and wept with relief. A no-neck middle-aged man in a tweed jacket and mustard-stained shirt hovered in the doorway, pushing his square glasses up his crooked nose.

"Drew? Oh gods, Drew."

"I've heard of sex so hot it could melt, but dayum, girl, did you have to get literal about it?"

"Funny, ha-ha." She groaned, taking a better look at the bedroom in which they'd landed. Old damage had been erased. Crystal chandeliers had been rewired and reaffixed. Walls had been patched and painted in pastels. "I need to wash this stuff off him. Did they repair Mirri's bathroom to the way it used to look?"

"Nope, that got upgraded along with the kitchen and foyer." Drew set a scuffed loafer into a puddle of Feng's blood, and the shoe sizzled.

If Bix didn't know what the destination looked like, she couldn't open a gate there. She'd have to move Samael the traditional way.

"Stay where you are, Drew." She grappled with Samael's weight, trying to move the angel despite his inordinately heavy wings. "This stuff will burn through your suit."

"This one's about to expire anyway." Drew waded through the goo and took one of Samael's beefy arms over his shoulder, assuming the bulk of the archangel's weight. "His wings will get beat up by the doorframe, but he ought to fit in the shower."

Getting Samael into the master bath proved incredibly difficult. The disastrous comedy of awkward gracelessness eventually ended with Samael propped up against the shower wall with all showerheads, jets, and doohickeys aimed at his huge body. His nose pressed against the corner as if he'd been a naughty, naughty boy.

Bix stood back next to Drew, their heads tipped at matching angles.

"If that crap is in his clothes, we really should strip him." Drew took off his glasses and dried them on his lapel. Both his glasses and his clothes had been heavily damaged by the blue goop.

"I don't suppose there are shears somewhere around here?"

"Vanity drawer, second down on the left."

Bix looked at Drew's reflection in the mirror. He shrugged. "Hey, it's a free place to live. The brownies fixed this place up right nice after the dragons' visit, and Hel hasn't come knocking yet. I like to live above my means."

She fetched the scissors from exactly where Drew had said they would be. "If there are any clothes around here, I need to change too."

"Go use the guest bathroom. I'll snip Mr. Pretty out of his clothes." Drew waggled his brows and took the shears from her. "Help yourself to the closet in there. Based on the selection, Hel planned on you staying here instead of the warlock's."

"Don't kill him, Drew," she warned. "I need him alive and passably cooperative."

"Yeah, I guessed that from your arrival." He picked up a blade of red algae tangled in her hair. "Go on, I'll meet you in the great room in a few minutes."

She checked the shower drain before stepping into the guest bath and smirked. She'd never be able to look at a shower drain again without thinking of Gurp. At least she knew Tobek was in good hands with the goblin. Though whatever Tobek had found that had merited the call…

Shit. Her phone was at the bar. Shower first. Fetch phone later.

As good as getting clean felt, time was a wasting. She

reluctantly left the oasis of sanitation and headed for the guest closet. One look at the choices and her stomach turned.

Jör.

He had a particular preference of undergarments in which he liked to dress her. Dark green silk and satin embossed or embroidered with serpents. From the sheer stockings with detailed black back seams, garter belts with serpent's heads for the clips, bra cups lined to resembled coiled serpents. Fangs, everywhere on everything, long venomous fangs ready to bite, to poison, to force her into submission.

Even when he wasn't here, he made it hard to breathe. What should be simple fashion choices had devolved into another form of his intimate oppression. He ensured that anyone she dared invite into her bed saw him, his claim, his…

She scratched the scars in her forearm until they burned, using the pain to break the spiraling thoughts. These were just clothes. Just until she got home. Getting dressed was no big deal.

It *couldn't* be a big deal.

The sound of a buzzer brought her out of the room, hopping on one foot as she put on her shoes.

Drew exited from the master suite, dripping wet, wearing tatters and a broiled suit. He held the shears in slasher-star style.

"I'll get it," she called, waving him back.

She peered through the peephole and got an eyeful of an olive knit beanie and frayed flannel. Bemused, she flipped the locks and opened the door.

The lopsided dimples she recognized.

"Hi, ma'am, you left this at the club." The ginger barback extended her phone to her. "It's been blowin' up, so I figured you needed it kind of bad."

"Wow, thanks." She took the vibrating phone and cocked her head. "How did you know to find me here?"

He pulled his fist into his sleeve and rubbed his neck. "I, uh, checked its activation data. GPS put it in this building."

She sort of understood what he'd said. "You hacked my phone?"

"No good deed," he muttered under his breath and held up his hand. "Whatever. You're welcome. Have a good night."

"No, no, dude, I'm impressed, not pissed," she hollered after him. "Thank you? Really, thanks."

The door to the stairwell slammed against the wall, and his racing footsteps echoed back down the corridor.

"Sorry, didn't mean to be an asshole," she sighed, closing the door.

"If you know where he works, you can always go back and tip him." Drew leaned against the doorway to the master suite.

"Gods, cash." She clicked through the phone. Nothing from Thrúde. Herr Schmidt, however, kept vibrating in her palm. "I haven't stopped long enough to reintegrate to that point of blending in."

"There, take it." Drew tossed his battered wallet on the kitchen counter. "Now, come see what I found."

She followed him back to the master bath. Samael was still out cold. Still in the shower. Only now he was nude. Mostly nude. Red manga bikini briefs hugged his round ass cheeks.

"That…" She fought a grin. Lost.

"Right?" Drew cackled. "I kind of have a teensy bit of respect for him. I'd have a whole lot more if he wasn't an angel."

"Archangel," she sighed. "With whom I have no idea what to do."

"Dump him in a church? That's been our go-to in the past. Let his choir deal with him."

"He's vulnerable right now, a little too vulnerable." She didn't know what promoting the stoles had done to him, but that none of his peers had come to his rescue at any point during the summoning said his greatest allies right now might be his old enemies.

No way, no how could she take him to Tobek's.

"Leave him here, then." Drew sniffed. "I have to get a new body, and you need to sync up with Herr Schmidt there. It'll give the brownies time to come out and fix up the place again. Worst they'll do to him is comb his feathers and polish his head."

They both snickered at that last image.

"Don't suppose you've had any luck interrogating Vidya?"

"I can't even get close to her." Drew followed her to the master bedroom, hanging back as she opened gates to the ether to clear away the remnants of Feng's blood. She didn't want the house brownies burned by it. She cut thin lines, taking the room back to the studs and subfloor.

The next gate dropped soggy Samael into the guest bed. Creaks from the bed frame confirmed his landing.

"Asabitchy's being tailed," Drew shouted, turning off the shower in the adjacent master bathroom. "By Thrúde's crew. Some other group is shadowing the Sisterhood. It's a sick game of piggyback, and I can't tell if Asabitchy even knows she has an entourage."

"They're probably CWIG. Vidya's been shot at twice now, both times at crime scenes." Bix clicked Answer on the phone.

"Gods damn it all," Tobek swore at the other end. "Sweetheart, are you okay? You get the archangel to safety?"

"A pool, Tobek." She curled her damp bangs around one finger and closed her eyes. "We went through a *pool* of Feng's blood, and I don't mean a wading pool."

More swearing. "Did you get a lock on the location?"

"No, my eyes were closed," she admitted. "How'd you know they were targeting the archangel?"

"The last team the Norse ambassador assembled, they were Miracle Worker hunters."

"Like Hywl." She made a moue of pity. "Did he know any of them?"

"We all did," he said sadly. "Come home. We found things on the drive, things you need to know."

"I need to bring a friend along. Is that okay?"

"Meet us in the classroom next door to the shop."

"We have one stop to make, then we'll meet you there. Ten minutes, tops." She shut off the phone.

Drew raised his brows. "Sweetheart? Sweetheart? You have *that* man calling you sweetheart?"

Bix batted her lashes. "I don't mind it."

"Oh, Bixie, babe, it's not the term, it's the man saying it." Drew puckered his lips and fluttered his hands over his chest, tittering. "I'm going to need a new suit before we meet with all that meat."

"Why do you think I took ten?"

# CHAPTER 17

The classroom for the MWA bore a strong resemblance to a beer hall. Long wooden tables. Benches. The curved stage boasted a huge movie screen; three projectors rested in iron cages bracketed to the ceiling. Along the outer wall stretched a length of stainless steel countertop punctuated by deep sinks supported by matching lower cabinets. A subtle hum from a few of the cabinets hinted at refrigerators.

Four Berserkers perched on the tables nearest the stage, grumbling amongst themselves. One still wore the deep hood.

Apparently, Tobek's Fates didn't think he'd been sufficiently chastised yet.

The click-clack of two pairs of high heels echoed on the concrete floor, drawing the Berserkers' attention. Drew giggled and licked her lips, tossing her raven tresses over her shoulder, every bit the celebrity impersonator whose suit she wore.

"Nose clean?" Drew faced Bix and wriggled said nose.

Bix tapped her own left nostril. "Damp tidy."

With a tiny noise of frustration, Drew turned away and addressed the last details of acquisition. "Society today really needs to focus on the larger issues of morality rather than small-peen-ality. A hospital bathroom should not have been a pickup locale for a suit like this."

"You have to admit, the look on the guys who made that suit available was priceless." Bix twitched as lightning flashed and thunder boomed. Heavy rains pounded against the building.

"Not as good as it should have been once they realized you dumped them in Bang Kwang Prison half a World away."

"Thailand has a special treatment program for foreign detainees." Bix snickered. Drew slapped her arm and laughed too.

"Ladies," Hywl greeted with a broad smile and open arms.

"No way that's a lady," Runjit muttered, crossing his arms.

"Friends call me Drew." Drew thrust out her perfectly French-manicured hand to Tobek. "You must be *Chief*."

Tobek extended his prosthetic hand and bent over Drew's knuckles, murmuring, "Welcome, Anudrengr. I've been expecting you."

"Oh, they don't make 'em like they used to." Drew's dead eyes sparkled as she reclaimed her hand and fanned herself. "The Hood is a great look for you."

Bix cocked her head. Drew had admitted to being a frequent patron of Dysmorphic. Sure, the new suit would throw most people, but not a high warlock. Plus, Drew hated being called by the name the Norse pantheon had slapped on her ages ago... unless, apparently, it came from the lips of the not-Viking who somehow knew her ancient name. There was definitely a shared history here.

One they didn't want her to know based on this ridiculous act of first introductions. She opened her mouth to ask, but Tobek spoke before she could.

"Xipil, it's all yours." Tobek handed a remote to the Berserker standing quietly to the side with his hands behind his back.

"I am honored you allowed me to review these most interesting reports." Xipil bowed and clicked a few buttons. The room darkened. The windows blacked out.

Tobek gestured for Drew to sit across from him at the centermost long table. Drew sat atop the table instead. Bix hopped up on the table behind the hooded wonder, her knees against his broad back. Tobek reached behind him with his natural hand and patted her ankle.

"Since expediency is of greatest import, I have selected five points that I believe encapsulate what happened to the Norse ambassador." Xipil pointed the remote at the projector. "This is the meeting she took one day before confirming her initial selection of CWIG agents to protect her."

Pink trees. Navy grass. The same World of the dark elves in which the Master of Psychopomps had been recently murdered.

Mirri, in white cotton and crochet, all ash-blonde wavy hair and come-hither hazel eyes.

Bix's heart lurched, twisted, and caved in on itself. A cool hand covered hers and squeezed. Sympathy rolled off Drew. She squeezed back and focused on the other person dwarfing poor sweet Mirri.

He stood as tall as Tobek but with a swimmer's lean body that made his shoulders appear extra wide. The exquisitely tailored blue-black suit and the aquamarine dress shirt with three buttons undone underscored the apple-red hair feathering down his back. The red goatee with blond streaks had been perfectly trimmed to a fine point reminiscent of Sir Francis Drake.

Yep, in his almost life-sized glory up on the big screen loomed the lead investigator for the Consortium, key witness in Bix's trial, and apparent supplier of swimming pool goo.

"Feng the Phoenix," Bix said to the room. "When was this?"

"One month to the day after your trial." Xipil bowed again. "This is their first meeting, according to the records provided."

Bix glanced at Drew.

"I was still waiting on a body to hijack to get out of the old armory." Drew shrugged. "I didn't connect with Mirri until much later."

Tobek's chin went up, but he said nothing.

"I'm sorry I left you there." Bix squeezed Drew's hand, then asked the room, "What do you guys know about the polyhedron Feng's holding?"

"Diplomatic pouch," Runjit of all people answered. "The exterior proportions are no reflection of the contents. It could be as large as a dining room in there or as small as an ampoule."

"You know what they say about size mattering." Drew leered at Runjit. "But he's right. Mirri had five much smaller ones she kept in rotation for official business. She used them mostly for packages that had to cross gateways into other Mid Worlds. I could fit all of them in a regular messenger bag."

"Gateways often scan for more than they ought. This style of diplomatic pouch ensures the contents remain secured against prying." Runjit regarded Drew with disdain. "The use of elvish symbols instead of the pantheon's native language is another layer of security. The three inscriptions identify that as a Norse pouch."

"Exactly those inscriptions? They're not universal or anything? Can't belong to anyone else?" Bix tugged her phone from her bra.

"Norse pantheon only. Since the Phoenix has it, we can infer that he is couriering it for the ambassador. If he opens it, he breaks eons of contracts and agreements," Tobek confirmed.

"It's the job of an investigator to snoop, so let's assume he knows damn well what's in it. Similarly, we can assume that by giving him the pouch, Mirri wanted him to know. She's sweet, not stupid," Bix leaned over to Drew. "What are the odds you know Vidya's phone number?"

"Asabitchy?" Drew snorted and took Bix's phone, rapidly typing numbers into it.

"The Guild Master of Psychopomps was killed yesterday with that pouch in her possession. The CWIG took it into evidence. Not coincidentally, someone shot at the lead agent as she was handing that pouch to me." Bix sent a message to the Oracle. Odds were high Vidya would have a conniption upon reading it.

"Like they shot the CWIG forensics teams after you arrived at Centralia," Tobek reminded.

"Yeah, the connection isn't lost on me," Bix sighed. "Great work, Xipil. I'm sorry for interrupting. What's next?"

"These meetings between the Phoenix and the ambassador

continued with some regularity for the next five years," Xipil continued. "The pouch was exchanged at each meeting. Each meeting lasted no more than thirteen minutes."

"She had a thing about that, Mirri did." Drew piped up. "Didn't matter with whom she was meeting, it was never longer than thirteen minutes. Two minutes for the exchange of pleasantries. Nine minutes to get to the point of the meeting. One minute to confirm next steps. One minute to politely depart. She would get up and leave at twelve minutes and thirty seconds. You could time it with a stopwatch. Some of us might have done it on more than one occasion."

"I bet that went over well with certain blowhards from the other pantheons." Hywl sniggered. "Oh, or the dragons, who take filibustering to a whole new level."

The magic thirteen minutes. Mirri had tried to keep the download of her day limited to thirteen minutes, and Bix had tried to think up thirteen minutes of details she could share about her day. That had been the spark that had ignited the epic blowout their last day together.

Bix's last words to Mirri had been, *"I don't have thirteen minutes to share with you."*

Irredeemable asshattery there.

"You said they stopped meeting after five years." Bix smacked the phone against her thigh. "Did you narrow down a date?"

"I did, but I believe the date is less important than the new— albeit infrequent—meetings she began taking six months after her last meeting with the Phoenix. After each meeting with this man, she changed her CWIG detail." Xipil clicked to another image.

Drew bounced in her seat. "Oh, oh, I know this one. That's one of the Dreigiau at Mirri's condo."

The pronounced sharp cheekbones of the royal dragon in humanoid form could cut glass. His rich ebony skin shimmered in the sunlight. Dark jewel tones in a scrolling pattern reached back to frame a hairline of thick springy curls in deep shades of claret. Plum serpentine eyes looked right into the camera.

They'd looked at her with the exact same stoicism at her trial. Third row, standing behind his twin sister, who had sat behind the reigning queen of the Dreigiau.

"Rummir Dreigiau," Tobek offered up the name. "Note the absence of the diplomatic pouch. The distance she keeps from him and…"

Xipil flipped to another picture. Rummir had regressed from stoic to pissed. Arms crossed, full glower, and this time he was armed. Mirri appeared wan. Bags under her eyes. Most interesting were the scratches on her face and arms.

"When was this taken? Other than at dawn." Bix wagged her phone at the rosy sky.

"Eight days before her remains were discovered."

"The day before she vanished," Drew shouted over the clap and boom of the storm outside. "She looks like hell. I guarantee you she didn't look like that the last time I saw her. She did not look like she went three rounds with a machete."

"Thorns," Bix and Tobek said at the same time.

"The Sisterhood kept losing track of her at Forest Haven," Bix explained. "I'm willing to bet this morning—the morning this photo was snapped—was right after she found the heavily warded prison building where angels had been slaughtered and Feng's blood spilled."

"A god could have made it as far as we did, if not farther," Tobek conceded.

"Ah, shit," Drew sighed. "Now we know why Mirri specifically was taken."

"The Chweds behind all this needed visiting gods to open one end of a portal. Mirri was a visiting god, plus she found their secret test site." Bix thumped her head against her phone. "If she told Rummir Dreigiau about Forest Haven, and he did nothing to protect her…"

"…then shows up at her place the day she was attacked…" Drew pursed her high-gloss lips and shook her head. "This makes the Dreigiau look culpable in a goddess's assault. This is not good."

Bix's phone vibrated, leaping from her hand as "Ride of Valkyries" played. She hit Ignore.

"Anyone here have an in with the Dreigiau?"

Again the phone sang out. Again she hit Ignore. Three more times she played the game, until a deafening roar of souped-up engines and squealing tires drowned out the storm. High beams pierced the night brighter than the lightning. Horns blared.

The Berserkers stood and drew weapons from under the tables. Tobek held up his hand, staying his men. Green flares burst beyond the shades.

"We have company." He adjusted his grip on his short sword. "The wards are keeping them at bay."

Her phone rang again. This time she answered it.

"Get your pert little ass out here right now, gatekeeper."

Bix hung up and headed for the door. "It's okay, guys. They're here for me."

Drew scurried behind her and grabbed her arm. "They sound ready to drag you out for a lynching."

"It would end badly for them. They know it." Bix patted Drew's hand. "I'll be fine. Meantime, if anyone knows how to set up a meet with a dragon…"

"I'll arrange it," Tobek assured her. "First, see to your friends before they antagonize my men beyond their restraint."

A thought moved Bix under the awning of Dysmorphic. Winds howled and rain blended with fat balls of hail. Muscle cars and pickup trucks idled in the parking lot. Women of every type of muscular stature perched in open car windows and stood in truck beds, inured to the weather. Headlights illuminated illegal weapons both modern and ancient in the ready clutches of the Sisterhood.

"This is a shitty place to hole up."

Bix held her hand up to the glare, making out Thrúde perched on the hood of a purple '70 Road Runner. Bix braved the deluge, meeting the Valkyrie halfway.

"What's got you guys so pissed you brought this on?" Bix gestured to the storm.

"Skuld," Thrúde shouted, spewing rainwater.

"She cheat at poker again?"

"Someone took her. Left this behind." Thrúde stuffed into Bix's hand a photo of a wrought iron gate in front of a cemetery. In fat black marker, someone had written:

*5 x 5 x 5*

Bix's gut sank, and she swore.

"Yeah, I thought you'd know." Thrúde snatched back the sodden message. "What the Hel does it mean? Who has our Norn?"

"Five angels. Five gods. Five Fates." Bix raised her face to the storm. "The people who minced Mirri have Skuld."

Bix rolled her shoulders and smoothed her dress. Clean. Dry. Most importantly everything underneath was devoid of serpents. In the few minutes it had taken Tobek to arrange a meet with someone from the Dreigiau, she'd scuttled off to change. Hywl had volunteered to keep Drew entertained, while Runjit and Xipil calmed the battalion of Berserkers ready for a showdown with the Valkyries. Whether that showdown was destined for the streets, the sheets, or both was not her business.

Except for Thrúde. That particular Valkyrie had homework, namely the completed list of missing gods. Something linked those gods, something that had put them in the orbit of the rotten Chweds. If Bix could find the link, she could track that to the Chweds holding Skuld.

Taking stock of the missing Fates, that was a different matter. She'd given Tobek and Vidya a heads-up, but since the Houses were in the throes of infighting, she didn't hold any hope of extracting useful intel from them. This whole debacle was probably a grand game to them anyway.

She checked her phone for an answer from Vidya about the diplomatic pouch. Nothing. Not terribly surprising, but decidedly unfortunate for the Oracle. It was almost as if the woman wanted Bix to end her.

"They will smell nervousness on you. I suggest you focus on the issue if you wish to negotiate successfully." Tobek took her hand and laid it on the crook of his arm as they picked their way up the leafy slope.

Between the full autumn moon and the spectacular lightshow at the top of the hill, the path to the pit at Centralia was as clear as a cloudy day.

"It's not nerves; it's restlessness." She put her phone away and clung to his arm, more for the surety of his presence than the stability over the terrain. "I've been baited, and the hook worked. Why leave a message at Skuld's abduction? Am I taking too long for them? Are they getting bored waiting for me to haul all their asses to Hel?"

"Did you consider that the message was from Skuld herself?"

"I…" She glared up at him. "I…had not."

"She would have seen it coming." He stepped long over a steaming crack in the ground, easily lifting her in his stride. "She might be playing out the hand, putting her faith in you to get her out before the Chweds get their way."

"Gah," Bix groaned and changed subjects before her head exploded. "So what's your deal with the dragons anyway?"

"Long-lived, so are they."

"Nice evasion," she sighed. "But thanks for arranging this."

"I'll wait for you here." He set her on the ground. "If you need me, you've only to look my way."

She squeezed his hand, then strode through the dead trees… and jerked to a full stop. What had been a bottomless pit was now a field of wildflowers. Where Mirri's remains had rested upon Feng's claw, there grew three small trees whose trunks had braided together. Branches swayed low, heavy with crimson-tipped roses of yellows, whites, and pinks.

A single yellow petal fell from the nearest blossom and drifted on the breeze, coming to rest on her breast.

"It is a Widow's Tree. When the Norse ambassador fled from this World, she did so with a heart filled with love and sorrow. See how the petals are attracted to you? She weeps for you still."

Bix pressed the petal to her aching heart and faced the gruff grumble thick with a Danish accent. Plum serpentine eyes watched her without blinking. A ball of raw dark energy crackled in a hand covered in deep jewel-toned scrollwork.

"You do not recognize me," he rumbled.

"You were at my trial along with your sister," she countered. "You are Rummir Dreigiau."

"Spoken as though a stranger. This should be interesting." Rummir sighed with great annoyance and closed his fingers over the energy ball. It vanished. He pivoted on his heel and sauntered across the field. His black leather pants creaked with each long-legged stride. His claret Henley stretched over bulging muscles when he hailed the lone figure at the edge of the forest line.

A stunning woman of equally dark ebony skin yet contrasting pale jewel-toned facial scrolls turned ever so slightly toward them. Rummir's twin. Her long fingers splayed over the seam of old and new ground. Pastel electric rainbows arced and sizzled, raising buds and seedlings. Rummir joined his sister and mimicked her pose. Darker rainbows crackled from his fingertips and raked the ground. Plants wilted in typical autumnal repose.

"Sister, the goddess did not lie." Rummir flicked a glance at Bix. "What we witnessed at the trial proves true. They stole her aspects when they seized her memories. She is little more than a foundling now."

"Aspects? Foundling?" Bix blurted, then cursed herself. *Great opening gambit, dummy.*

"Then we will begin again with a proper introduction," Rummir's sister said with a mere trace of her brother's accent. Vibrant amethyst eyes, bolder in hue and consideration than Rummir's, fixed on Bix. Pity softened the female dragon's elegant yet undeniably fearsome features. "I am Raspoine Dreigiau, and this is my brother Rummir."

"The Dreigiau Queen-Ascendant and her enforcer." Bix inclined her head. "Thank you for meeting with me."

"We have been awaiting your call." Raspoine's gaze dropped to the pendant around Bix's neck. "It pleases me that you are the one who recovered Feng's claw."

Bix closed her hand over the pendant. "Care to explain to me why the Dreigiau involved the Norse ambassador in hunting the missing Phoenix?"

"Quite the other way around." Raspoine's smile was fleeting. "We are forbidden from interfering in Feng's tenure with the Host, no matter what form it takes, until he specifically invites us."

"Why did Mirri come to you two?"

"Due to the extended absence of the Phoenix, our queen had asked us to place some discreet inquiries into his whereabouts. The Norse ambassador's well-known advocacy for your freedom provided the link."

"The guise, you mean." Bix snorted. "What did Mirri get from you for her troubles?"

"Advice. Passive support is the best we could offer her. She understood." Raspoine folded her hands in front of her, ever regal. "There are formalities between the Horde and the Host that must be acknowledged and demonstrated. It is…frustrating to be sidelined at such a time as this."

"So when she told your brother about Forest Haven, politics prevented you from protecting *her* from the people behind this?"

Raspoine looked to her brother.

"I offered; she refused," Rummir groused. "Said it would draw too much attention from the Consortium that would be misconstrued. The next day, she was gone. A week later, she was mutilated."

Yep, sounded like something Mirri would do, especially if she knew the Sisterhood was only a bat signal away.

"Why were you at her condo?" Bix eyed the brother. Something was off about him. He'd barely breathed during her trial, but tonight he couldn't stop fidgeting. "What were you looking for?"

Rummir pursed his lips and looked to his sister.

Raspoine took her time answering. "Feng had been investigating certain security breaches."

"Among the dragons?"

"The scope is," Raspoine tipped her head from side to side and steepled her fingers, "not insignificant in its breadth."

"By all reports, his behavior changed after my trial. Is it safe to assume these security breaches are the cause?" She wasn't going to name the archangel Samael as her source, not in front of dragons. That'd be bad politics to say the least. One gaff per night. New policy.

"Your trial exposed a truth no one wanted to admit." Raspoine nodded. "Hence the reason he was receptive to the Norse ambassador's overtures regarding your situation. Their collaborations had borne fruit."

"The diplomatic pouch. Feng was keeping it for her?"

"Contains the evidence they had gathered," Rummir answered this time. "That was what we were seeking at her home. If it is opened by the wrong people, the resulting damage will be extraordinary."

"Blackmail," Bix posited.

"Among other things." Raspoine stared past Bix and frowned, presumably at Tobek.

At some point, Feng had entrusted the pouch to the dark elves. The Master of Psychopomps could have been claiming it on behalf of the investigation into Mirri's death or could have been stealing it from the dark elves' vault. The place was guarded with men and magic, but it wasn't impenetrable. Not for someone who could bypass doors and walls. If the Master of Psychos had been authorized to collect dark elf souls, then she would have had the ability to bypass all the protections.

Sometimes souls had to be captured, and they could be wily little suckers.

"Feng didn't think the evidence was safe with the Host or the Horde. That's interesting." Bix toyed with that idea for a bit. "To whom were they going to present their findings?"

"I can only assume they would have assembled another Consortium tribunal." Raspoine brought her attention back to Bix, her expression perplexed. "If the breaches expose corruption among the highest levels of the reigning powers, Feng's recourse is extremely limited."

"The reigning powers being the Consortium, not just the Horde and the Host?"

Rummir grunted an affirmative.

"That explains why Feng was taken, and that Mirri's mauling is about more than ripping open portals using Feng bits." Bix pinched the bridge of her nose. "If they're after the evidence, then the portals make sense. But what do they need with Fates? How does that change the spell?"

"Time," Raspoine murmured. "Dragons' and angels' natural opposition creates a two-dimensional balance that binds the Mids together. When the opposing powers of gods and Fates are added, it creates a four-dimensional balance. The heart of that four-dimensional balance is what anchors time in a linear manner. If whoever is behind this knows the right spell, then with three of the life forces of the four original powers, they can destabilize the balance. They can alter time."

# CHAPTER 18

"**W**here is it, Vidya?" Bix shouted into her phone, standing amid the upended contents of the CWIG's precious high-security vault. Files continued to rain down from the upper levels as Drew left no stone unturned.

She'd exchanged Tobek for Drew after the meeting with the dragons, needing the high warlock to research the spell to which Raspoine had alluded. He'd offered his men to help her search for the diplomatic pouch, but she didn't want to start a war between the CWIG and the Berserkers should things go sideways. For Drew and her, this was old home week.

"After your stunt with the director's daughter in the vault, did you really think I'd log anything into that no-longer-secure place?" the voice on the other end of the phone derided. "You're there now. Don't deny it. I've seen it, which means you've seen my present."

A smaller replica of the diplomatic pouch sat on a tempered glass shelf with the right evidence-log identifier of the right case number, but the wrong piece of evidence.

"Vidya, the evidence—the real evidence—from the Psychopomp assassination contains the item for which Mirri was killed." Bix ratcheted down her temper, grasping at a mote of calm. "Think about what you say next very carefully."

"I'll log it in with the director in the morning," Vidya said with too much cheer. "Oh wait, mandatory team-building exercise lasting all day. Maybe we'll get early release? Probably not. Those things always run long."

"Vidya…" Bix cautioned.

"You know, I'm not entirely sure when I'm going to be able to retrieve it, much like I wasn't entirely sure what the hell happened to you after an ogre made you disappear. All those favors I called in trying to locate you. Guess you're going to have to—"

Bix hung up the phone and punched the only icon on her screen.

"Speak," barked the voice at the other end.

"Grab the Oracle now. Lose the tail." She hung up, sent a photo, then stuffed the phone in her bra. "Come on, interrogator, you're up."

The balmy autumn night summoned tourists and residents alike to the streets of historic Old Town Alexandria. Buskers, vendors, and artists peppered the boardwalk outside the Torpedo Factory. Restaurants along the waterfront propped their doors open, luring customers with the scents of seafood, brews, and pastries.

Bix clutched Drew's hand tightly as the crowd pressed in on them. He'd opted to wear a lanky gender-fluid DJ, rocking large headphones around his neck, an undone bow tie, and a trilby. The rolled-up sleeves of a wildly printed sport coat kept it all casual. The tinted sunglasses hid the bloodshot eyes caused by suffocation. The thick leather bracelets covered up the bruises left by restraints.

"Ten o'clock, back to the marina, gray anorak," Drew said casually as he waved to total strangers.

"One of Tobek's men." Bix rested her head on his shoulder, playing her part of doe-eyed tourist. "I need the balance in case the Sisterhood forgets the bigger picture."

"Sprawled on the river wall at your eleven. Fountain outside the food court at your four." He doffed his hat at a pair of little old ladies ogling him as they passed. "Friendlies?"

Dark T-shirts, loose slacks, and flip-flops could have been the go-to uniform of dozens of fraternities from any of the surrounding colleges, but the red patchwork newsboy caps belonged to a specific fraternity of Chweds.

"Nixen," she murmured, catching the Berserker's eye but not veering toward him. "Water mercs who can shift sizes to be as small as a penny or as big as a prize heifer. Skills include drowning you with a touch, and you don't even have to be standing in water."

"My suit's already been asphyxiated once tonight. Twice would be redundant." Drew steered her away from the boardwalk into the crush of pedestrians heading up King Street for the bars, boutiques, and restaurants.

"Their presence tonight could have nothing to do with us." She lingered among the small gathering surrounding the busker playing heavy metal on water glasses. "This is prime hunting ground for them. Collegians congregate around here before hitting the clubs in the District. Nixen have a weakness for the young, drunk, and daring."

"Yeah? Well then, why do I feel like we're being followed?"

"Because you are," whispered a husky feminine voice. "Body thief."

"Always a misfortune to see you, Thrúde." Drew offered an arm to the Valkyrie. "Stroll with us?"

Thrúde aimed the narrow end of her guitar case at Drew's crotch. "Can't believe you took home the trash, Bix. If the Berserkers can't help you with your ten-year itch, let me introduce you to a few couples who'll be more than happy to welcome you into their games. How about a couple of couples? A little orgy action to get you back into the totally tactile grind?"

Bix looped her arm through the Valkyrie's and walked her away from eager ears, down the less crowded Union Street. "Where is the Oracle?"

"Where's my Norn?"

"Waiting on me to find her," Bix drawled. "Vidya is one long step in that direction."

"In that case, the paranoid bitch was already here when you sent me to fetch her." Thrúde ambled with a swagger, knocking hips with Bix. "The girls tailed her into a parking garage off Queen."

Bix turned at the next block, doubling back to King. Queen was two blocks north of it. "Why is the Sisterhood tailing Vidya?"

"You check the drive? You notice how many people in the CWIG Mirri burned through?"

Bix nodded. "She was using her protective detail as researchers and hunters."

"What? Why?" Thrúde shook her chalk-striped and teased mane. "She already had us."

"The agents had easy access to things you didn't," Drew taunted.

"Maybe." Thrúde paused and threw a couple of dollars into the bowler of a busker playing folk ballads outside the ice cream parlor. "Why have we been stalking Agent Asariri? Because she's the last of Mirri's CWIG goons still alive."

Drew swore under his breath.

"How recently was the board wiped?" Bix hardened her heart again. Vidya's ability to survive apocalypses bore too similar a resemblance to cockroaches.

"All but Mirri's active detail were picked off in the weeks leading up to our girl's disappearance."

"Tortured first?"

"Those whose bodies were found, yes. Others simply vanished." Thrúde reached inside her bra and pulled out a lipstick-stained napkin. "Our recent rabble rousing turned up leads, rumors, and whispers about more than just the missing gods."

Bix took the list and cast a swift eye over the names, recognizing a few. "Someone pieced together what Mirri was doing and how close she'd gotten. They wanted to know what she knew without alerting her."

"We're trying to figure out why Asariri is so special. What's kept her alive when the others died?" Thrúde stopped in front of a brick-front row house wrapped in scaffolding and tarp. Across the street, a big green P denoted a parking garage poorly disguised as a historical building. "Usually the last man standing is the one who betrayed them all."

Bix opted not to tread that path, considering her team might say the same about her, if they'd lived. "You guys know you've been followed this whole time?"

"By other than the body thief?" Thrúde bared teeth at Drew. "It's been a fun game of cat and mouse. They're good, whoever they are."

"Not CWIG?"

"See, that's the interesting part." Thrúde set the bottom of her case on the curb and crossed her wrists over the top. "We expected to spot the spooks. They haven't come anywhere near. It's like they're deliberately leaving her to fend for herself."

"Shit out of luck." Drew sniffed and smirked. "Karma is about to bite that bitch in the ass."

Bix eyed him. "You didn't. Tell me you didn't whisper to certain agents what Vidya did to our team."

"No, no." Drew held up his hands. "I probably would have once I read her soul and had the whole story from her, but not before."

"How do you want to play this?" Thrúde thumped her case on the ground. A whistle answered from the second floor of the garage. "Box her in? Or are you going to take her on a trip?"

"That garage has six exits. She can bolt for any one of them, creating a lot of noise to draw well-meaning innocents into this." Bix swept the area with a calculating gaze. "Drew and I are going to head back to King Street. You guys flush her toward us. Let her think we're the least of the evils. Safety in the crowd and whatnot."

"Mouse, mouse, time to come out of your house." Thrúde withdrew her phone and winked. "To Mirri's Mayhem."

Drew led Bix back toward the throngs of tourists on King Street, crossing the street twice to avoid the dogs curling lips in his direction.

"We should go on dates more often. I like the attention we draw," he mused, checking his reflection in every possible surface. He laced their fingers together, swung their hands, dropped his trilby on her head—all the typical actions of a dude on a date. He capped it when he hailed the roving flower vendor and bought Bix a rose, kissing her on the cheek.

He inhaled sharply. "Gun."

"Walk toward Market Square, keeping to the crowd, and my finger might not spasm on the trigger."

Bix glanced at the gun pressed into Drew's back. White hoodie, torn jeans, and filthy sneaks could have been anybody. Too bad Bix knew that body intimately.

"Vidya, you're making a mistake."

"Then you'd better make introductions." The Oracle didn't look at Bix. Her eyes were too busy scanning the surrounds. "Because I've had it with strangers hunting my ass, and you just had a nice long chat with one of them."

Drew released Bix's hand. He reached between them and seized Vidya's wrist, spinning around behind her and forcing her arm behind her back.

"Asabitchy," he hissed in Vidya's ear. "I am officially insulted."

Vidya paled. "Drew?"

"Miss me, little traitor?" He jerked up on Vidya's arm and pushed her ahead, compelling her to resume walking.

Bix moved closer to both of them, taking hold of Vidya's upper arm as Drew slid the gun into his waistband and tugged his jacket over it. He braced Vidya's other side, draping his arm along her shoulders.

"But I heard you die." Vidya blinked rapidly, staring up at Drew, slack-jawed. "Your screeching. I heard you. Saw you."

"Heard? Saw?" Bix's grip tightened on Vidya's arm. "You had a godsdamned vision of what was happening? And still you're smug?"

The things in Bix's back twitched, spasmed.

"Angel fire is fucking hot, even in a borrowed body." Drew

jostled Vidya, smiling with unbridled hate. "Don't worry, I'll figure out a way for you to experience it firsthand."

"Not as long as I have info your bestie needs," Vidya said haughtily. "We all know the value of info in our business."

"You're going to show him everything, Vidya, every secret, every joy, every memory," Bix said without pity. "You're going to let him in to read your soul."

"Like hell." Vidya struggled, but Bix and Drew held her fast.

"I have given you nothing but opportunities to be cooperative, to show that you had the slightest remorse for the disasters you instigated. I'm giving you one last chance. Tonight. Right now." Bix tracked a red cap changing water bowls outside the pet shop and another pouring customers' water in a restaurant window.

"We're going to start with the location of the diplomatic pouch and work our way back to the burn you enacted on our team," Drew purred. "Now, we can take a table at a nice little bistro and get reacquainted like civilized people, or Bix will drop us somewhere no one will hear you scream. I'm hoping for the latter."

"You can't read me without my cooperation, draugr," Vidya spat.

Drew pressed his nose against hers. "Not only can I, but I promise to make it the most painful experience you've ever had, Oracle."

"Fine, you want intel?" Vidya twisted toward Bix. "I worked for your ex for a few months. She seemed to know about our history, but we didn't talk about it. It was professional on both sides. Her only interest in me was my access to Dark Ops rosters."

Bix stopped, catching a glimpse of the Sisterhood trailing them. "Why? Why did Mirri want a listing of Dark Ops agents?"

"She said it had to do with springing you from exile." Vidya huffed. "She wouldn't say any more than that. Once I busted my butt getting that list out of the vault, then out of the guild, I found myself reassigned to babysitting forensics teams. No gratitude from her. No formal censure from the guild. Demoted without explanation, blamed on reorganization."

"Current or former?" Bix asked with distraction, noting one team of Valkyries tracking the Nixen as the guys shimmied up drain pipes. A Berserker tracked both of them. "Current or former operatives, Vidya? Now."

"As far back as I could get." Vidya tried to shake off their hold. Failed.

Something was wrong, off. Why were the Nixen going up? No rain in the forecast. Why were they moving away from water? They had to sense a predator in the area, one who flew below the radars of the warriors trailing them. Where was the new threat?

"You know what all Dark Ops agents have in common?" Drew sighed. "We're all upper-upper-caste, well-educated specialists who can get in and out of any Mid World undetected."

"Not to mention amoral with great aim," Vidya popped off.

That snapped Bix's attention back. "Is that why you're being recalcitrant? Because you think I'm in league with dirty agents?"

"We should kee—" Drew slumped over Vidya as warm wet sprayed Bix. Vidya hit the pavement with a cry. The flower in Bix's hand burst apart. The window behind her shattered. The sound of slicing air chased destruction.

Fire blossomed inside Bix's lung.

Panic erupted on the streets.

Drew's headless body shielded Vidya from people scrambling to escape. A stampede of alarm rolled like tides. Pedestrians tripped over each other. Those on the street tried to enter the buildings. Those in the buildings tried to escape into the streets.

Bix tried to breathe, tried to speak. She tried to focus on a hospital emergency room, but white-hot agony anchored her to the moment. Jör's plague slithered under her skin from hip to nape, scraping along her bones and inflaming the damage in her lung. The taste of mist and midnight filled her airways. Shifting shadows knocked out streetlights and traffic lights. More glass splintered. Bricks crumbled.

Sirens streamed through the night but made no progress into

the chaos. More people slammed into her, sending her staggering into the street. Her heel caught in a grate, tumbling her over the hood of a trapped car. The agony intensified. She pushed off the car as the driver shouted obscenities at her.

Sounds swirled around faces as she strove to breathe. The things in her back writhed. A cool breeze fanned across her spine.

They were escaping. The things Jör had left inside her. New poisons. New deaths. She had to get away. She had to abandon her team. Again. She had to do it to save them. She had to get away from everyone before the things, before they…

Strong hands closed around her hips and swung her out of the street. The balls of her feet dusted the ground as the confident hold carried her through the morass of insanity, dancing the grand waltz of madmen.

Wherever they went, darkness and destruction followed.

She tried to warn her rescuer, to say beware, to tell him to run away. Nausea conspired with dizziness. She was hot, far too hot, and there was keening. Lack of air muddled her mind. Her hold on consciousness faltered.

A gloved hand cupped her jaw and forced her head up. "Stay with me, sweetheart, stay with me."

"Couldn't save the boy, Chief, but we got the girl."

"You got us both in one suit, but the threads of Fate in this one are fraying. She needs a hospital now. Trauma unit. The bullet tagged this body, then Bix. Bix was hit twice after that. Double shot to her lungs. She can't open a gate." Vidya's voice but Drew's words. The draugr must have taken over Vidya's body.

Bix tried again to speak, to focus, but lucidity waned.

"Can't get a car in or out of here," groused a Berserker. Hywl perhaps. "Too many people for the bike. Your call, Chief."

"Then we do this old-school and pray the Oracle survives."

The arms holding her upright enveloped her, holding her safe even as they exposed themselves to the plague Jör had embedded within her. She couldn't fight it anymore. A tear trickled over her cheek as darkness claimed her.

# CHAPTER 19

**B**ix scrabbled back to awareness. Prostrate. Not in a bed. Whatever she was on was cold and hard, not like zero-body fat hard, but hard like a…

Steel surgical table.

The polished floor gave it away. And the stainless steel U-shaped headrest against which her cheeks pressed as she stared at the ground way below. And the great big boots bracing a rolling stool. And incessant beeping. And the muttering. Lots of muttering.

A cold damp towel draped over her neck and head. Similar relief covered her from hips to toe. Oh, but her back was a wasteland of white-hot writhing pain.

"She's coming around." Boots and the stool rolled to her left.

"Easy, easy, sweetheart." Tobek's familiar rasp soothed with distraction. "Two bullets out, one more to go. I need you to stay still and present. Runjit, how's her pressure?"

"Elevating too rapidly." Stool rolled to her right. "She's at risk of going dark again."

"Sweetheart, listen to me. Listen to the sound of my voice. You're going to be fine. Just a little bit longer."

He was digging around in her back.

Her back.

Where the things Jör left lived.

She had to get away from everyone. Now.

She lurched. The cloths held her down. Stupid rags. How weak was she that she couldn't throw off some damn rags? She reached for the one on her head.

Her wrists were bound. Surely not. Surely no one would...

"Hold her down," Tobek barked.

Lights exploded, then fizzled into darkness. Monitors quickened their beeps. Screeching shredding steel drowned out the shouts of men, many men.

Still she fought to be free.

The more she fought, the more she gagged on mist. Air still refused to enter her lungs. The infection took its harvest from her body. Ruin gathered in heaps crashing to the floor.

She had to get loose. She had to get away from everyone. She had to save them from Jör's misanthropy.

A spiraling fog of navy and mulberry gathered light and form, building substance amid the dark destruction. Ostrich ankle boots and dark cuffs solidified amid the whirling clouds.

The cloth was whipped from her head. A broad hand stroked her hair, then seized it in a tight hold, jerking her head up. Amber irises glowed around pinpoint red pupils.

"Enough, creature," Phobos commanded. "Your fear is potent yet unfounded."

She gagged and gasped. Pain ran the length of her body. What disease had she set loose? What disease had the power to summon the Greek god of fear?

"Phobos, you should not be here," Tobek shouted over the din of destruction.

"Do not dare to command me." The god of fear tapped the restraints on her wrists, and they fell away into the ebbing fog. "Your fear tethered you to mortality, old one. Now you scrape and hoard to regain a semblance of all that you once were. It is not enough to do what needs to be done. It will never be enough for her."

"Phobos, she will at—"

"Your men should go while they still can." Phobos flicked his hand, and the damp blanket weighing down her lower half slithered to the ground. He drew her naked body off the surgery table and forced her to stand on her feet. "You are welcome to stay and be a victim of the devastation you fostered."

Tobek bellowed the order for retreat.

"Poor creature, how mighty you once were. How horribly love has rent you asunder. How sad you cannot remember." Phobos gently held her head against his shoulder. He pressed his lips to her temple.

His fingers speared her ribs. No mercy. No hesitation. They dug inside her, prying bones apart and gouging organs.

Destruction redoubled. The ceiling collapsed. Exposed wires sparked. Pipes burst. Darkness thickened.

Bix convulsed, panicking for sweet simple breath in a sea of agony and confusion.

Phobos hummed softly as his fingers sifted through tissue and vein. "Ah, but here we have it."

Wet sucking echoed between her ears as his hand exited her chest. The nauseating heat left with it. Her collapsed lung finally filled, not with air but with the raw energy pouring off his body.

"There, there, the worst is over now." He tucked whatever he'd taken from her into his vest pocket, then cradled her head in both hands. His long fingers swept her wet hair from her tear-sodden face. "Drink from me and quiet your fears."

His lips were gentle. Chaste even. The raw energy he poured into her was far from it. The energy tipping into her mouth met the energy oozing into her lungs. Cool healing spread first. Nausea and dizziness dissipated. Her breath came and went without pain or labor. Before too long, she was whole once more.

Best of all, she could open a gate again.

She moved to the remnants of the wall behind Phobos and let out an exultant cry. His rich chuckle filled the room.

What was left of the room.

All that was left in one piece was Tobek. Stance wide. Arms crossed. Hood up. A bright blue glow emanated from his cowl.

Her guts sank. She covered her mouth with trembling hands and looked from warlock to god. "Did we stop it? The plague?"

Tobek unfolded his arms and cocked his head. "Plague?"

"There is no plague, Bix. Jörmungandr cured you as promised." Phobos removed his suit jacket and handed it to her.

"But the things in my back?" She pulled on the coat, covering up her nakedness. The silken lining delighted her oversensitized skin. "I felt them escaping. I couldn't stop them. I tried. Oh gods, I tried. All those people, those terrified people."

She stared at the mounds of debris littering the floor, at the wide open space where walls, cabinets, and coolers had once stood. A bomb might as well have ripped apart the clinic. Even the tinted-glass-front windows and doors had suffered, spilling their shards into the empty parking lot.

Perhaps Jör hadn't left her with a viral plague but a plague of some huge insect-like horrors. Defeat pressed down on her. How was she ever going to be free of him?

Phobos lifted her chin. Pity softened his expression. "So old, yet so much like a child. The novelty terrifies you. The unknowing. We should never have allowed you to become a husk."

"You…you *husked* me?" She blinked up at Phobos. "Are you one of the seven with my memories?"

A tortured groan escaped Tobek.

Phobos tapped her chin with his thumb, his gaze searching hers. "Do not fear the mist or the midnight, Bix, for they are but shadows. Shadows are yours to shape and command. They are subservient to one of your aspects, the aspect of a Shadow Caster."

"Aspects?" She struggled to think. "The things in my back? Shadows?"

Phobos puckered his lips and tipped his head from side to side. "The darkness is what you need it to be when you need it to be, but it *is* a part of you. Think of when you've noticed it.

When you were in distress? When someone you cared for was in distress?"

Her knees buckled. She dropped to the floor as her world crashed down. "Me? All this time? Me? Not Jör? Not…"

"I'm no great fan of the serpent," Phobos drawled. "But for this irrational fear you've harbored, he is not to blame."

She waved a helpless hand at the mess surrounding them. "And the destruction? What of the destruction? Here and at the waterfront?"

"The darkness lashed out on your behalf without clear guidance or intention." Phobos brushed drywall chips off his collar. "This damage is trifling on the scale of what you can do."

"I am the danger. It is rooted in me, originated by me."

"Yes," he cried joyously. "You are a great danger to those around you. But you can learn to command the darkness just as you learned to command the gates."

"Will you teach me?" Her voice cracked as she fought a new onslaught of tears. "Once I'm done with Hel's contract, would you teach me to command the darkness?"

"What you need is beyond my ken." He slid his hands into his pockets and cut a reproachful glare at Tobek. "But when this is over, join me for dinner, and I will help you find the right teacher."

She nodded. "Thank you."

"There is a lot at stake," he cautioned as fog formed around his feet once again. "The rising dawn leaves you with three days. By dusk on the seventh your time runs out. You must succeed in this. It is imperative to far more than the Norse pantheon or the Phoenix."

"Phobos—"

"I have a hunt to which I must return, but I look forward to our next date." The god of fear faded into the fog.

In a breath, Bix was alone with Tobek.

"I cannot begin to apologize for ev—"

Tobek held up a hand.

She bit her tongue and tugged on the hem of the borrowed suit jacket.

"Runjit and Hywl are waiting in the shop, what may or may not be left of it." His voice was rough, far rougher than his usual rasp. "There are discussions we must have. All of us."

"Tobek, at least let me th—"

Again with the hand. He swept that hand in the direction of the doorway that had once been. She padded obediently through the maze of the rubble and live wires, down the gouged corridor into the mostly unmarred shop proper. The pictures had fallen off the walls and some of the upper cabinets had been dislodged, but compared to the clinic…

Two Berserkers shut up and stood up. Between them, a gaseous goblin rubbed his hands frantically.

Never had she been more acutely aware of being a woman. An apparently detrimental-to-everyone's-welfare woman. Wearing a jacket four sizes too big for her.

She pinched the lapels together.

Tobek didn't look at her. Instead, he took from Runjit a small clay box inlaid with elaborate scrolls and knot work.

"We have a new threat." He removed the lid and tipped the box so she could see inside it. "This is what we dug out of you."

Two mangled cones of blue-and-white marble shimmered and sparkled under the intermittent lights.

"I've never seen bullets like these." She held one up, noting the pattern of micro fractures in the blunted tip and a divot in the other end. When she closed it in her fist, it warmed but did not burn as it had while inside her.

"I haven't either." Tobek rolled the other bullet around the box but didn't touch it. "They melted my instruments and a dozen containers before Gurp identified their source material."

"Angel bones." Gurp ground one foot atop the other and hung his head. "Made from angel bones."

Rage built inside Bix. Had that last fateful op been all about these damn things? Had someone else on her team been compromised by the same people who'd turned Vidya? Had Vidya sent Bix's team to the Host's armory so her co-conspirator could steal *bullets of angel bones*? Of the eight members of Bix's team, half of them could have survived carrying the bones.

There was one person who knew for sure.

"Vidya," she whispered, putting the cursed bullet back in the enchanted box. "What happened to Vidya?"

"Medevacked to Fairfax Hospital." Runjit's lips thinned. "Still in surgery. It's not looking good."

"And Drew?" Bix's heart dropped to her toes. "He'd taken up residence in her body. If he didn't jump before the doctors started surgery, his presence will skew all the machines' readings. The anesthesiologist will mistake his pulse as her pulse. They can't put him under, but they can kill her with an overdose. And if they have to shock her to compensate, they'll hurt him."

"Anudrengr made it to a new body in time," Runjit assured her. "The draugr is fine."

If Drew had made it in and out of Vidya, then there was a chance he'd read Vidya's soul. Should the worst happen and Vidya not survive, Drew would know where Vidya had hidden the diplomatic pouch. Mirri's work would not be lost.

Yes, it was a callous thing to focus on the work instead of the victims, but Bix wasn't a doctor or a therapist. She couldn't patch up Vidya or Mirri and set them back to rights. The only thing she could do for them was to catch and punish the person or persons who'd hurt them. Based on the damage she'd done to the clinic, she had more than one method of exacting punishment. If only she knew how the hell she'd done it.

"Xipil and a few of our brethren are looking after your friends." Hywl scratched his sideburns, revealing long gashes down his arm. "They have the hospital staked out. Anudrengr is staying close to the Oracle. They'll call the moment she's out of surgery."

"The Oracle is lucky the draugr was there. It kept her alive long enough for us to get her help." Runjit shook his head. "The bullet grazed her yet still inflicted significant damage. If it had lodged inside her instead of you…"

"It would have decimated her body," Bix said, recalling how

intensely the bullets had burned within her. "Angel bone ammo has to be what was used on the teams in Centralia and on the Master of Psychopomps, because those bodies were supposed to be impervious to most projectiles. Plus, since these bullets also pierced my skin, I'm willing to bet they were used on the gods who've gone missing too. Race, species, magic, none of it matters. These things guarantee a kill. Probably what they plan to use on the Fates too."

The Berserkers swore. Gurp whined.

"The bones of angels are weapons of mass destruction." Hywl rocked up on the balls of his feet and puffed out his cheeks. "How did these jerks get their hands on this many bullets?"

"Pretty sure they're the leftovers of the angels used to open the portals." She grimaced. "What else do you do with a corpse you don't want anyone to find?"

"Hack it up into such tiny pieces that it floats below the radar of the choir tasked with retrieving the Host's dead." Runjit laced his hands at his nape. "But carving angel bones, that's no easy feat. Aside from a dragon's maw, there are maybe a handful of artifacts capable of such a thing."

Tobek huffed. "That's why the Horde and the Host have those artifacts locked away in their respective strongholds."

"Unless one of those strongholds had been penetrated by a third party." She smacked her forehead. "The Phoenix was investigating security breaches. Maybe they started with my botched op. Maybe someone else was successful."

If Vidya was right and other Dark Ops teams were involved, then Bix didn't like where the evidence was leading her.

"Our guys found the sniper's nest, but the sniper was long gone. There were scorch marks and traces of blood, but no brass or anything comparable left behind." Hywl wiped rubble off his chest. "Snipers mean rifles and scopes, but what sort of guns can fire angel bone ammo? They melted surgical steel, so normal guns can't be the answer."

Everyone looked to Tobek.

"I know of no substance that can support the mechanics required."

She squared her shoulders. "I know someone who probably does and more than likely wishes I didn't know to ask."

"You'll want to dress first," Tobek suggested. "And I recommend rest for all of us. It's been a long night with the promise of a hard day ahead."

Runjit nodded. "I want to check how well everyone is healing when you get up. Even you, Bix."

She didn't bother with an answer as the two Berserkers shuffled off toward the stairs to the apartments.

Gurp patted his belly. "Gurp eat. Sleep later."

"Pace yourself." Tobek clapped the goblin on the back. "We made quite a mess."

Gurp took Bix's hand and held it between his. "Glad you okay now. I bring you new shoes. Make you happy again."

She stooped and kissed his mottled head.

The goblin grunted twice, then waddled towards the remnants of the clinic.

"You know you just gave him an eye full of assets," Tobek drawled.

"Least I could do."

"Come home." He took her hand and headed for the boiler room. "You haven't slept in two days, and you're emotionally wrecked."

She didn't move.

He stopped. "What is it?"

"Thank you, as always, for coming to my rescue, and the rescue of my friends."

"It's been mutual rescues so far." He indicated his hidden face.

"And thank you for letting Phobos past your wards," she hedged. "Clearly you two have a lot of contentious history."

"I can't take credit for his appearance." He exhaled loudly. "Phobos couldn't ignore your summons any more than the wards could withstand your distress."

"Summons?" Bix shook her head. "I didn't summon him."

"That you weren't aware of doing it doesn't mean it didn't happen." Tobek gestured to the surrounding damage. "I need to research stronger building substances while you rediscover this new side of you."

"You were surprised I didn't know." She pursed her lips, tamping down a fresh wave of tears. "When we met—for the first time I can remember—you said you knew who I was. I assumed you were referring to my infamy with the Host and Hel. You weren't, were you?"

He let go of her hand and adopted a wide stance. What he didn't do was answer.

"I see, so our history—yours and mine—is something we're not going to discuss."

Still no answer, but the fringes of his cowl glowed with a dawning blue light.

"Fine. I need the box of angel bullets, please." She held out her hand but didn't move toward him.

"Phobos kept one of them. He knows the damage it did to you." He put the clay box in her hand. No argument. No hesitation.

"If that's the price he wanted for preventing me from losing my mind, then he's welcome to it." She clasped the box in both hands and bit her tongue, pushing back the wall of fear and confusion hovering at the edges of her every thought.

They stood in the quiet of Dysmorphic for a long time, neither speaking. She wasn't sure what the negative emotion was, the one hiding behind the fear and confusion. She reached for it, though. It had to be better than the others. Was it anger? If so, it wasn't a familiar anger. Should she be mad, mad at Tobek's omissions, mad at herself for not asking the high warlock about the non-bugs in her back? No, she wasn't mad. It wasn't anger burgeoning within her. Something bleaker.

Sinister.

"I cannot imagine what it's like to lose everything, even the most basic concepts of self." Tobek spoke quietly; his tone held a wealth of misery. "Then to be exiled again, but this time aware of the nascent connections denied you."

"We're opposites in that, right? The Fates will not let you forget what they take from you, and the gods will not let me remember." She drew a fortifying breath and tried to smile. "It's better that I don't know whatever it is you're reluctant to tell me. I am, according to quite a few people now, incapable of coping with my own memories. I shouldn't presume to take on yours as well."

"Sweetheart, I…"

"It's okay. As long as you don't sabotage me, I'm not going to pry into your life like some asset I'm trying to turn. You've earned that level of respect from me for this go-round."

"So come home." He motioned her toward the boiler room again. "We'll tilt at windmills together after we get some sleep."

Again she didn't move. "No."

"If this is about you being a Shadow Caster, you don't need to fear hurting me. The Fates will not let me die, and I've tried every possible way."

"Yeah, your eagerness to feel pain hasn't escaped my notice." She jostled the box. "But like Phobos said, I have three days left. Vidya gave me a lead on the flunkies, but I don't know the shot caller behind them. That's whom I need to fulfill my contract."

Once she fulfilled her contract, she could tell Mirri it was safe to live again. Once she fulfilled her contract, she could finally evict Jör from her life and regain her dignity. Once she fulfilled her contract, she'd be one step closer to shucking the ignorance that made her so vulnerable and dangerous.

She refused to be husked or exiled. Again.

# CHAPTER 20

Glass clicked and clattered in the fridge at Mirri's condo. The tiny drumbeats contrasted with the booming baritone so committed to the raunchy club anthem that Bix had ample opportunity to observe the scarifications covering Samael's back. Perfectly linear, like beautiful Asian script.

Couldn't read a word of it. Alas.

Samael turned with a beer bottle microphone to his lips and his fist in the air. Froze. Glowered.

"Did you know I'm a Shadow Caster?"

He barked and took a sip. "Told you you were a pain in my ass. You've destroyed Worlds with the combined might of your aspects. Saved a few along the way too."

There was the thing about *aspects* again. Note the plurality of the term.

"And we've fought, you and I?"

"We've led armies against each other and beside each other." He leaned on the counter, scratching the last remaining scarification on his pectoral. "You haven't changed your style of clothes yet, so you haven't relearned how to be a Shadow Caster."

She patted the front of her snug sailor dress. "My clothes?"

He winked and popped open a beer using the edge of the

concrete counter. "Thanks for the new duds, by the way."

"Hel's hospitality." She gestured to the condo, then to the only bit of clothing he wore. "Gaiman's *Prelude* in briefs is a bold statement for an archangel, but you do wear them well. I assume the brownies left you a choice of pants and shirts?"

"Did you see what they did to my head?" He bent forward and scuffed his gleaming pate. "Softer than a faerie's teat. And my wings? De-matted and trimmed up as if the encounter with Feng's blood never happened."

The breath of levity dissipated.

She set the clay box on the counter and pushed it toward him. He eyeballed it, then her, then it again.

"You've been to visit your warlock." He pushed the box back toward her using the beer bottle. "That's warded against angels."

"Oh, sorry." She unlocked the lid and dumped the contents into her hand. She held the bullets up to the kitchen light.

Samael took one from her. He sniffed it. Tasted it. Rolled it between his hands and held it against his brow. "One of Uriel's chosen. Esthira, captain of the troop assigned to guard the Phoenix's residence. This bone belongs to her."

"These were fired into a crowded street last night."

"These the only two?" He handed her back Esthira's bullet and took the other one. "Gemmarin. One of Michael's lieutenants. A hunter sent to locate Feng a month ago."

"Uriel and Michael." She dropped the bullets back into the box. "The last time we talked about Feng, you spoke of 'a team,' not 'my team.' These fallen soldiers aren't yours either."

"Science isn't my gig. Neither is nursemaid."

"No, it's more than that. When you were attacked, no angel came to your aid. But when you promoted your stoles—an action that usually happens upon death—your eyes flipped between black and white, which means another archangel checked on you during what could have been misconstrued as you dying." She eyed him.

He eyed her.

"You're the executioner." She slapped the counter. "You're

not helping me because you want to rescue Feng. You've been tasked by the Host to erase him. They were checking to see if he erased you first. Does the Consortium know the Host no longer wants Feng rescued?"

"Killing Feng out of cycle is bad for *everyone*." He took two long swigs from his bottle. "We're talking hundreds of years of wars that will rip apart the Mids, annhilate entire Worlds, and starve every member of the Consortium until they either die or are reduced to husks. None of the lower races survive."

"Godsdamn," she gasped. "Are you kidding me?"

"Not even a little. He's that integral to native magic. The cycle of his life and regeneration mirrors that of the magic itself. Besides, one doesn't actually kill the Phoenix; he can only be forced to burn." He peeled the label off his beer. "There are two ways to make that happen: expose him to ether or bring in his nemesis, the Chimera."

Skuld had mentioned the Chimera when she'd given Bix the files on Mirri. Skuld had hoped Bix had found the thing while she was in exile. Was this whole mess with Mirri and Feng why the Norse Fate had wanted the Chimera found?

"So the bogeyman of the gods and Fates is also the only thing that can take down a dragon-angel hybrid?" Bix massaged her forehead. "I'd heard the Chimera has been missing. Do you think the people holding Feng have it too?"

"No. I'm pretty sure the Chimera is precisely where it wants to be." He finished his drink and stuffed the label inside. "But if it did decide to show up, it might be convinced to help me lock up Feng for the safety of the Mids."

"Lock up Feng," she echoed flatly. "So the Host is more afraid of the holes in the protective layers of the Mids being created with Feng's body parts than they are of the retribution of the dragons or the Consortium for making Feng your prisoner."

"Better our prisoner than whoever he's with now." He thumped his chest and belched. "The bodies of those sent to find him keep coming back in pieces. Then gods went missing, and pantheons started asking questions. When Hel freed you, all bets were off."

"We took a bath in his blood." She lowered her hands and shook her head. "You have to know he's a victim, not a mastermind."

"I don't know that." He got two more bottles from the fridge. "I've removed some pretty twisted individuals who would maim themselves to succeed in the greater game."

"No matter what his role, you trying to take him is why the Chweds behind this chose your stole. That's why they've come after *you*. You're a threat to their prize power source." She steepled her hands and pressed them to her lips as scenarios played in her head. "What if Feng had discovered damning evidence of treason and corruption the likes of which have never been seen before? What if you're being ordered to lock him up as a means of burying the evidence and the investigator?"

Samael stared at her for many heartbeats. His black eyes reflected her image but gave no hint to his thoughts.

"To me, possessing evidence like that moves him up from accomplice to the new head of the criminal organization. That stuff is bound to be used as leverage, either for his own gain or for the organization's." Samael opened his second bottle, and his expression softened. "You've seen how volatile he is. Now imagine if his time undercover broke him, broke what little control he had over his temper. Feng can do some pretty gruesome things to a body created to exist in the Mids, even without losing a nail."

"You're talking about Mirri." She closed her eyes, but it only made the image of Mirri falling victim to her trust in Feng all the more vivid. It was possible, what Samael said. It was totally and completely possible. Mirri had been looking for a co-investigator; she had enlisted the help of the dragons. Mirri had found Forest Haven. And if Feng didn't want to be found and if he'd wanted to keep the evidence for himself…

But if he'd wanted to keep the evidence for himself, why had he left it with the dark elves? Why would he have attacked Mirri, then left her remains where they'd be linked to his dewclaw?

No. No, the evidence didn't fit with Feng being a villain.

Bix sucked down a ragged breath and opened her eyes.

"You still think he's a victim." Samael tapped the dewclaw hanging around her neck with the tip of his bottle. "Okay then, how do *you* explain how your goddess was trapped in her mortal body?"

"Angel bone fragments," Bix countered, placing a hand over the spot where she'd been shot. "Those things are probably being used on Feng too, to make him bleed into that swimming pool you and I visited. Remember that pool? The one that fried your fricassee?"

"Nothing made from either the Horde or the Host is going to harm the Phoenix." He waved his bottle in negation. "Feng's duality—his being half angel and half dragon—enables quite the opposite effect. His body will absorb those foreign bits and absorb their power."

"So if someone were to shoot these at him, he'd get stronger." She picked up a bullet. "What kind of rifle can fire these little bullets of mass destruction?"

"Not rifles." He shook his head. "Not bullets."

"I heard the gun reports when they were used at Centralia. I witnessed the marksmanship last night."

She refrained from mentioning being riddled by said not-bullets. If she and he were frenemies, he didn't need to have that kind of intel on her.

"Bolt shafts detonating, not gunfire," he corrected. "Those are arrowheads. Pay attention to the divots in the bases. It's where the shafts attach, shafts that explode during flight to enhance speed. Those were fired from custom crossbows made by the Host when Feng burned the last time."

"Made by you?"

"Used by me and a specific choir, yes. Made by me? Nope. I am the beneficiary of innovators and inventors." He motioned to her face. "Don't look so shocked. Just because angels are the same race doesn't mean we're always on the same side of an issue. Brother sometimes has to kill brother, and sometimes one brother must be sacrificed to fell a greater enemy."

"But the accuracy and the range…" she argued.

"Crossbows made by angels, from angels." He took a drink and hitched a shoulder. "We're awesome, even in death. No other race comes close to the cruelty of which we're capable, especially that which we inflict upon ourselves."

"So how would Chweds have gotten hold of these angel crossbows?" She glared at him. "And don't say 'Feng did it.'"

He puckered his lips and kissed his bottle. It took a while before he answered. "Scavengers from the last cyclical Great War? Newer weapons are locked down tight in the armory."

"And the Host's armory, it's never been breached?"

He stared at her with reproach. "You should know better than anyone about that."

"Yeah, yeah." She sighed. "But you're sure you're sure? No one before? No one since?"

"Between your botched attempt and Feng's sudden departure, inventory is taken regularly, frequently, and obsessively. The armory itself is relocated at random intervals to keep someone like you from happening upon it again."

"What about the tools used to make the crossbows and the arrowheads? Those in the armory too?"

He held up one finger and closed his eyes. His finger twitched as though turning pages. He smirked a few times, then grunted, opening his eyes. His smirk devolved to a scowl. "Mislaid around the time of your exile."

She cradled her face in her hands. "You've got to be kidding me."

"Feng said the same thing about six months after you'd been booted." Samael drained his third bottle of beer. "The cover-up was covered up. My peers are displeased that I know to ask the question."

"I'm not sure who sucks more, the Chweds behind this or the Host."

"At this moment, the better question is how have we not reclaimed the missing items?" He constructed a tower with his empty bottles. "The Chweds get so full of themselves because they think we're not watching, that we're too self-involved to pay attention. They forget they occupy bodies we've provided. We always know. *Always*."

"Except when one of them runs off with the Phoenix and tools capable of making arrowheads from your bones." She hopped off the kitchen stool and smoothed her skirt. "Of course, you could have a traitor in your midst, which would explain a lot. After all, brother sometimes has to kill brother."

"Or whoever is behind this isn't in a body we've provided." He knocked over his bottles. "That makes the culprit a dragon, a rooted god, or the Phoenix himself. You know which way I'm leaning."

She considered that for a moment. The spell work ruled out all three of those options. But Mirri's request for the Dark Ops rosters narrowed down the list of culprits drastically. Oh, she really wanted to be wrong about where this was headed. Really. Really. Wrong.

"Enjoy the digs. You've roughly fifty-six hours until the lease expires." She turned away, then turned back again and pointed at the broken bottles. "Those sloppy portals allow ether to seep into the World, and ether screws up your ability to track, right?"

Samael straightened. "Most of the ones investigated have been reported to us, not found by us."

"The disturbance in magic is too negligible to hit your collective radar?"

"It's a contact lens in a sea of jellyfish." He fluttered his fingers, imitating said globs. "Keep in mind too much ether would be deadly to any mortal and the Phoenix, and it would be a means of escape for the gods they took."

"True." She grabbed the box of angel arrowheads. "Any ideas

how his captors and or crew are moving in and out of his prison-slash-headquarters without you guys knowing it?"

"You're the only gatekeeper." He cracked his knuckles, and the shattered bottles reformed into an amber Pegasus with bull's horns. "Psychopomps can only move souls along negotiated chutes to the other Worlds, and they were the first folks the Consortium went after."

"So that's a no, then?" She opened two tiny gates and delivered the box of angel arrowheads to Tobek's nightstand. "Come to think of it, even the Phoenix has to feed. How do you think they're managing that without drawing attention? Victim or not, that much blood loss requires some sort of nosh to keep the blood flowing."

"He can't die of starvation." Samael worked his jaw until it popped. "He'll be powerless, weak, possibly even delirious, but he isn't lucky enough to die from it."

"Yeah well, been there, done that, still bitter about it," she muttered. "Let me know if you learn anything about why the Host stopped looking for the tools that hack you guys into tiny combustible pieces. My number is on the counter."

# CHAPTER 21

A naiad burlesque show provided the entertainment on the center stage at the Woolly Barrel. It'd certainly drawn a different kind of clientele to the main floor, but the second-floor bar still held all the ambiance of backroom deals and smoky subterfuge.

Particularly at one table shielded by an ornately carved screen.

"Bix the Brazen, we welcome you back." The Kang Admi blocked the view of players behind the screen with his abundance of tie-dyed hair. "The third floor is available to you whenever you desire."

"It is so lovely to have my needs met without even asking." She beamed. "However—"

"I've got this." Ashtad clapped the Kang Admi on the arm and leaned against the screen. "Didn't expect to see you today."

"Walk with me?"

Ashtad's brow furrowed. "Give me a moment to wrap up here, yeah?"

She nodded and pivoted on her heel, heading for the railing overlooking the raucous floor show.

"You reek of Greek," hissed a too familiar and unwelcome voice.

Her stomach lodged in her throat. "Go away, Jör."

"You're under contract with my pantheon." He trailed a finger up and down her arm. "I want to know why there's an archangel in our embassy."

"First, my contract is with your sister. You're just a witness." She slanted away from him and drew her shoulder up to her ear. "Second, it's a condo, not an embassy. Third, fuck off."

He spread his arms to either side of her, pinning her against the railing. "Hel wants an update on your progress."

The darkness rippled along her spine. This time, she didn't fight it as it tore out the back of her dress.

Jör's eyes widened. He tipped her over the railing until her feet no longer touched the ground, one hand heavy on her nape, the other firm on her hip. She bucked against his grip, but he held her fast.

Fear, thick and heavy weighed her down as every eye in the bar fixed on her. Shame stilled her thrashing and burned her cheeks. The darkness retracted.

"Finally," Jör whispered.

Light sizzled and burst.

Jör skidded across the floor in a trail of smoke.

Ashtad grabbed Bix's feet and pulled her back to the surety of solid ground. He wrapped his arm firmly around her waist and hauled her up against his side. An orb of raw electricity crackled in his palm.

She tried to stop quaking. Couldn't.

Jör regained his feet and smirked. His tongue lashed out and extinguished the smoldering of his chest pocket. He causally doffed his nonexistent hat to Ashtad, even as his gaze shifted to her. His lips moved. She didn't need to hear his voice to know his words.

"Tick, tock."

Two Kang Admi bodily separated him from her. In a blink, Jör vanished.

"You okay?" Ashtad murmured into her hair, closing his fist and snuffing his innate weapon.

It took a few more heartbeats before her stomach settled and her breathing calmed. "Thank you. So much for Bix the Brazen, eh?"

"There is always somebody bigger, somebody stronger, somebody smarter. It's not your failure or your fault. It's life. Don't be ashamed of it." He squeezed her, then let go. "Besides, among my people, fried snake is a delicacy."

"Your *people?*"

"Defined as anyone who has ever met Jörmungandr."

She closed her eyes and snickered.

"Come on, let's find a sufficiently private booth where we can watch the people instead of being the people who are watched." He settled his palm in the small of her bare back and steered her to a series of draped nooks and tufted benches.

She slid to the center of a small curved booth and gasped as her skin touched the decadent Other Worldly velvet.

A Kang Admi arrived with a tray of frothy drinks and a small pile of silver and gold bangles. "A gift with sincere apologies for the discomfort you experienced."

Bix nodded with gratitude. The Kang Admi closed the dark lace curtains framing their nook, affording the illusion of privacy.

"I heard Agent Asariri is in the hospital, outlook grim." Ashtad stretched his arm along the back of the booth.

"That's why I'm here." She toyed with a braided bracelet. "How many demis have been Dark Ops?"

He paused with his drink in midair. "Lots."

"So they weren't always contractors." She nodded as her gut sank. "You aren't just a liaison who switched sides."

"There was a time when demis comprised the whole of Dark Ops—the era of Director Stheno, Ligeia Stheno, the Gorgon." He whistled low and grinned. "It was a good time to be running the god gauntlet under her leadership. There were at least three dozen of us. Glory days, my friend. Glory days."

"You're a fan, clearly." She side-eyed him.

"Director Stheno was the one who promoted me to team

leader." He took a sip of his drink and kept on grinning. "She's also the one who made me take you on as a probationary agent. I fought her so hard on that."

"Dick." She bumped his leg with hers.

"No, no, you know I'm glad she insisted, though in hindsight, I suspect she'd hoped I'd run you out of the guild." He patted her head. "Stheno had a good eye for talent no matter how raw."

"And when she left?"

That sucked the joy off his face. "It wasn't her departure that was ugly, it was the months leading up to it, when she'd clearly gone off her rocker."

"The former director lost her marbles? It wasn't a spell or something? Political attack?"

"Thoroughly investigated. It's why she held her seat for so long after her behavior changed." He shrugged. "Some think it was the stress of the job. Some say it was personal issues."

"You worked for her directly. What do you think it was?"

"Truthfully, I don't know. I had one extremely odd meeting with her, and after that, I kept our team as far from the flagpole as possible." He set his drink on the table and withdrew his arm from the back of the booth. "She'd become a dictator and micromanager, hypercritical, with a need to control everything."

Bix snorted. "That kind of management doesn't work in our line of business."

"It turns good people resentful and makes them hostile." He cupped his drink with both hands and got lost in the foam. "It makes them prime for poaching by other guilds and antiestablishment cabals."

Bix rested her chin on his shoulder. "That include the demis?"

He nodded. "The first to go. Director Stheno had taken to punishing us by withholding the dangerous ops, sticking us on protection details, or location security. We can't get to full-god status with shit assignments."

"So why did you stay?"

"It was a train wreck from which I had to protect my team." He tipped his head to touch hers.

"I don't remember any of the hullabaloo about Stheno," she whispered. "Sure, it was way above my pay grade, but the rumors... I should have heard them."

"Then I did my job." He finished his drink and tapped the glass against her arm. "You see, middle management's purpose is to weed out the weak lower ranks and to provide top cover from the crap rolling downhill. Once you have a good team of direct reports, half your job is done. All that's left to do is build a big umbrella."

"So why'd you let the new director split us up?" Bix pouted.

"There was only so far you were going to grow under my leadership. You were already chafing. I'd put you in to head the new team, but..." He picked up the stack of remaining bangles, sliding them over her wrist.

"Management never liked not being able to confine me, track me, or punish me." She shook her new adornments, smiling at the glinting metals. "But they did love to use me as long as no one from the Consortium called them on it. I was almost embarrassed for management at how quickly they threw me under the bus."

"I am sorry I didn't push to learn who gave you the image of the armory." He spun her bracelets, sharing just enough energy to make them glow. "Someone inside the guild getting their hands on that level of classified intel should have made us hungrier to trace the source instead of cowering in fear of the answer."

Bix patted his hand. "That was never on you. You weren't in my chain of command at that point."

"Covering our ass from external pressures is one thing—unavoidable. But a CYA on the inside..." Ashtad took another drink and winced. "It's why I moved to CI."

"You know I'm going after whoever burned my team. I'm not turning the mastermind over to the guild. Not even to you."

"I'm not entirely sure I'll fight you over it," he muttered into his glass. "That's not why you sought me out tonight, though, is it?"

She withdrew a lipstick-stained napkin from her bra and handed it to him. "Any of those names look familiar?"

"These are all visiting gods."

"Missing visiting gods," she clarified. "Gods I suspect have met or will soon meet the same end as Mirri. They just lacked a pantheon leader with balls as big as Hel's to raise a ruckus."

He cursed and took a closer look at the list. "All but three were demis around the same time as Stheno. Two were demis she attempted to recruit into the CWIG but who shut her down in no uncertain terms."

"Back up a second." Bix's heart sputtered and leapt. "You said she was a gorgon. Now you're saying she was a demi like you?"

"Gorgons are born demis; they're daughters of gods." He held her hand. "These women ran the gauntlet to full godhood like the rest of us. Only they failed, either because they chased the wrong thing or took on an adversary they couldn't beat. Rather than let them die, their pantheons made examples of them. Cautionary tales to the rest of us."

"And failed demis become mortal Chweds," she mused as more pieces of the puzzle tumbled into place. Samael had said whoever was behind this didn't occupy a body created by a dragon or an angel. Demis—failed or still in the game—had an undeveloped body of a god.

"Instead of devouring souls, they grow one." He took another sip. "But they fight to stay anchored in the Mids because the Fates want nothing to do with them."

"If they lose their grip on their mortal shells, then they're food." She managed a tiny flicker of sympathy for the cult of failure. "Demis become what they absorb, so what do gorgons typically absorb?"

"Entitlement, envy, jealousy, cruelty, all the negative emotions." He shuddered dramatically.

"Sounds like the kind of divine STD you'd pick up from hanging out with angels for too long," she mused.

"Precisely, and gorgons are a sorority of bitter, brilliant

bitches." He finished off his second drink and thumped her still-clasped hand on the table. "The only group they hate more than the Host who tainted them are the gods who made them hideous by any standard whenever they're overcome by negative emotion."

So. Many. Things. Fit. A former leader of Dark Ops. A body the Consortium couldn't track. Intimate knowledge of the Host, and an ax to grind against the guild masters who'd removed her from her job.

"And the guild masters voted in a gorgon as the director of the CWIG." She rolled her eyes.

"The guild masters weren't looking for a wife with that nomination. They were looking for someone to protect them from the rapacious needs of the Consortium," he chided. "Stheno excelled at that for a hundred years."

"Until she mysteriously cracked up." Bix tapped their clasped hands on the table. "I don't suppose you know where Stheno is these days?"

He shook his head. "Host prison, maybe? Dreigiau dungeon? She survived being terminated from her job, of that I have no doubt."

"What about hiding out with the gorgon sorority?"

"Doubt it. They were instrumental in her takedown." He thrust his jaw forward, pulling a monster face. "Think about it for a minute, a society of women predisposed to cutting everyone off at the knees? Can you imagine the infighting?"

She wrinkled her nose. "Never mind. How about names of any demis loyal to Stheno? Particularly ones with Dark Ops training or comparable experience. Images are better."

Ashtad tugged his rubber-encased phone from his pocket. "How much of this is about who burned your team?"

"This is about something way bigger that might link back to that." Bix watched his photos flit past, challenging herself to memorize each. "A gorgon who spent too much time with angels would have known how to get a specialized team of demis in and out of the Host's territory without triggering the Host's security."

"We demis don't inhabit bodies created by the Horde or the Host, so the Host would have had no warning of intruders." He swore under his breath. "It's completely possible. It's completely possible someone from that op used the intel to send you into the crosshairs as their distraction."

"I'd long assumed the setup was personal, but I could have been way off base. We could have been convenient."

"There's a finite number of demis who would have taken that heist job." He swiped through images on his phone. "It's a bad political move in the long-term, bearing in mind the dependencies gods have on the angels. However, short-sightedness fosters stupidity. Depending on where the demis stood in the race to godhood, some of them might have even gotten a bump in ranking around the time of your exile. Help me narrow it down— what else can you tell me about the demis involved?"

"Last night, the Nixen ran *away* from water. I assumed it was due to a water-centric predator, someone skillful enough to avoid attracting the attention of Valkyries and Berserkers." Bix scratched her back against the bench cushion. "I also assume that same predator sent Vidya to the hospital last night using a weapon made from tools stolen from the Host's workshop. I suspect that weapon was used to kill the Master of Psychopomps too."

"Water, eh?" He grunted, selecting a different photo album on his phone. "There *are* demis who have an affinity with water, no doubt. Assassinating a guild master could be an interesting assignment to a newer demi, but Agent Asariri would be of no interest. Unless you were with her again. You would definietely be of interest to a demi, mostly because of your tie to Hel."

"I think you're selling the Oracle short. Vidya dodged their two previous attempts." Bix tried not to think of Vidya sprawled on the sidewalk, bleeding. "I'm downright certain a team of demis was behind the massacre at Centralia. Same weapons used at all three sites."

Ashtad stilled. "One flaw—picking off fish in a barrel doesn't get a demi much."

She brushed her lips against his ear. "It does if they're using bullets they carved from the angels they slaughtered in an effort to start a cross-World war."

Electricity lit up the bar, bursting glasses and bottles alike. Ashtad dropped his phone in her hand.

A picture of a graffitied entryway centered in a dilapidated brick and plaster apartment building filled the screen.

"Take us there. Now."

# CHAPTER 22

The rank stench of booze, body odor, and pee punched Bix in the face as she closed the gate to a flophouse. Sirens screeched outside boarded-up windows, muted by dueling, blaring bass beats and wailing infants. Free papers, used diapers, and plastic shopping bags added to the trash piled on worn stairs. Thick paint pulled clumps of drywall away from water-stained walls.

Bix's heels clacked loudly on the torn vinyl steps as she followed Ashtad up four flights and down a dismally lit corridor of tagged doors and vomit-stained runners. A gateway somewhere in the building beckoned to her gatekeeper magic.

Ashtad put his hand on the doorknob of a central unit. Sparks flared. The lock clicked. The door swung wide, groaning.

Fresh air and gray light welcomed them into another World. Mosaic floors depicted crests and seals from assorted pantheons. Cold lava formed textured curving walls in deepening shades of black. They held no art, no lighting, no visible interruption in their continuous flow.

Until the third bend in the walls.

Photographs. Drawings. Notes. Sheets upon sheets of papers and scrolls plastered the walls surrounding simple stone furniture that offered the barest semblance of comfort. Long benches sat askew to a table covered in CWIG armory contraband. Steam coiled up from cups and bowls set amid modified weapons and black magic bags.

"Looks like they were just called away." Ashtad didn't veer from his path. "Someone is still here, though. I can feel their energy."

Bix picked up a long dowel shimmering amid food and tools. The rod warmed in her hand. Angel bone. Smoothed. Honed.

Son of a winged bitch.

A thought moved the table, the tools, and the stores of angel bones. No way, no how was she leaving that kind of danger to herself lying around. She kept one rod of bone in her hand, just in case.

"You got balls coming here, Son of Ba'al."

A young woman sporting a black tank top and black cargo pants emerged from an unlit corridor. Blisters and raw red blotches marred the woman's face and arms. Green ointment seeped through bandages covering her hands. The mystic's symbol for the third eye wept from the center of her brow.

"This place has been home to transitioning demis for longer than you've been alive, Imara." Ashtad stuffed his hands in his pockets. "You look like you've gone a round with a fire fairy."

"Wings, yes, fairy, no." Bix opened gates behind the demi. A jab of the raw angel bone against Imara's skin sent the woman caterwauling forward.

"Cunt," Imara spat, spinning around. The demi thrust out her arms, grabbed the air, and yanked it toward her.

Water gushed down the hall in frothing waves. Bix moved to safety atop a bench. Ashtad pulled one hand from his pocket and flipped his palm up. Electricity crackled and leapt into the foam.

Imara juddered and screamed through clenched teeth.

"Really need to think through the attack before you commit to it." Ashtad closed his hand and ceased electrocuting his fellow demi. "You'll never make it past the half mark with that kind of impulsiveness."

"I suggest a bit more time in unusual weapons training too." Bix brandished the angel bone. "Looks like someone got burned firing a crossbow composed of angel parts. No one warned her that the bolt shafts explode."

"That would be funny if she was still being hazed." Ashtad laughed, then sobered. "Otherwise it's an outright betrayal by her own team."

"I'm the best sniper they have." Imara bared her teeth and snapped like a beast. "I even shot your girlfriend, here. Three times."

Ashtad flinched but didn't look away from Imara.

"Yeah, but here I am and all kinds of healthy now." Bix pranced in a circle atop the bench, offering up a view of her bare back. "Can you say that about the other snipers? 'Cause it sure looks like you all are using the same kind of weapons."

"Can you say that about the Oracle?" Imara hocked a loogie into the swirling water.

Bix ceased all pretense of conviviality. "Did you take down the Norse ambassador too?"

Imara's gaze jerked up, then bounced between Ashtad and Bix. "I told Stheno she'd gone too far with that one. An ambassador is someone people notice when they go missing, not like the other gods. But once the ambassador found Forest Haven, I had to wing her."

The darkness scrabbled along Bix's back. Wing her. That meant Mirri's shooter did not equate to Mirri's final assailant. Bix forced her mind away from the image of Mirri's pendant resting in entrails, away from the memory of Drew's headless suit over Vidya's exsanguinating body.

There was a time to be a dervish and a time to be deliberate. It was not yet time for the dervish. Not yet. Soon.

The darkness stilled, and Bix breathed.

"Did Stheno torture the ambassador, or did she outsource that to you too?"

"Do you know what absorbing the crap that comes from

torture does to a demi?" Imara shook her head vehemently. "And a tortured *god* to boot? I clipped the ambassador. I never touched her. I sure as shit didn't stick around once Stheno took over."

Bix laced her hands over the end of the angel bone and pressed her forehead to her thumbs. She had the name. The motive. The means. The opportunity.

Now she knew for certain Mirri's assailant had a soul.

She could fulfill the contract. All she had to do was find the gorgon. Minions made awesome leads. All she needed was one, and it didn't have to be this one.

"Eight cups." Bix swept the angel bone through the open space. "There were only eight cups on the table that was here. There should have been eleven. Right? There were twelve snipers in Centralia. We found the body of the one who didn't make it."

"You're the one who stole the dewclaw." Imara sneered and eyed Bix. "Stupid thing screwed up the attack. It diverted the portal opening to the airspace instead of underground. The plan had been to introduce ether into the guild masters' bunker and kill all those simpering, whimpering, backstabbing bastards. Stheno wants that chunk of him back, badly. At least she knows how to bring you low now."

"And how badly does she want the Norse diplomatic pouch?"

Imara puffed her prideful chest. "You think those Berserkers are going to stop us from getting what we want from the Oracle? They're just thugs with long lives. We're demis with untold magics in our arsenal. We'll have the pouch before nightfall."

"What happened to the three unaccounted-for demis, Imara?" Ashtad asked quietly. "Did you abandon them? Did you leave your teammates behind to save your own ass?"

"Bite me," the demi hissed.

Ashtad held out his hand again, palm down. Three quick bursts of light hit the water and raced for Imara. The demi spasmed.

"You haven't garnered enough magic to make the water recede yet, which really speaks to how poorly you thought this out." Ashtad discharged two more lines. "I, however, can keep this up for years, centuries, even."

"One d-died at Centralia," Imara stammered. "The others d-during acquisitions."

"Acquisitions of weapons or of stoles?" Ashtad pressed.

Bix let him lead the rest of the interrogation. There was a code among demis, and she didn't need to be in the middle of a reckoning. She had what she most needed, so she moved her bench closer to the wall of intriguing sketches. Now, she was no engineer, nor had she ever played one on TV, but certain symbols within the sketches looked awfully familiar. She tucked the angel bone under her arm, then snatched every sheet that seemed in theme. They looked somewhat like schematics, but for what? Something big, assuming the measurements were in feet and not centimeters.

Oh, but the papers stank. Oh boy, did they reek of something bitter. Bix blinked rapidly as her eyes burned. She held the sheets as far from her nose as she could manage while still holding on to the clues.

"Gorgons had the stoles," Imara derided. "Huge collection they kept on hand to summon fuck buddies from the Host. We raided that stash years ago."

Had to be lower ranking angels they'd summoned if failed demis possessed the requisite power to turn the stoles against the angels. However, that explained why the gorgons had turned on Stheno. Turning your lover to stone in the throes of making the beast with two backs had to be physically painful. Gorgons needed someone inured to their curse, and angels scratched that particular itch. The stoles didn't allow the angels to reject the women they'd once found beautiful.

"So what killed them? What killed your teammates, Imara?" Ashtad demanded. "You could have traded stoles for the weapons or weapons for stoles, so it's neither weapon nor stole."

Imara didn't answer fast enough. Ashtad lit her up again.

"F-Fates," Imara keened. "The Fates knew we were coming. They fought back."

"Stheno is mad," Ashtad cried. "Fates? She's going after Fates now? What did they do to her?"

Stheno had three out of the four prime powers of magic. Everything she needed to effect an imbalance. And with Feng, she had the power source to fuel the mother of all spells.

"Time," Bix said as realization dawned. "Stheno wants to change time, back to before she became a gorgon."

"The Houses of Fate ruined her. They set her on a collision path with the Chimera." Imara sniggered. "If she hadn't lost that final battle, she would be a goddess on par with Hel herself."

Again with the Chimera. As often as that creature came up during the course of this investigation, it was odd the Consortium hadn't made a concerted effort to find it. Of course, they hadn't made a concerted effort to find Feng either, and his demise meant the end of the Mids. There was something very suspicious going on with the Consortium.

How much of that had Mirri and Feng stumbled into during their investigations?

"Surely all of you know this is a test you will not pass." Ashtad sighed. "You will die demis. You aren't even going to be considered for a gorgon."

"We have the Phoenix. We cannot fail," Imara crowed.

The layers of the World rippled.

"Bait, Ashtad. Imara is bait. They're opening a portal." Bix hollered. Her heart raced as she tracked the fissures uncoiling far too neatly. If Stheno pulled Ashtad through, he'd be horribly burned by the swimming pool of Feng blood at the other end. The same pool Bix and Samael had landed in. But this time, Bix knew what was coming. This time, she'd move Ashtad before they landed. This time she'd stay in the pool.

If Stheno opened that dawning portal, Bix would be taken straight to the gorgon and to Feng.

"Stheno knew you'd find us eventually, Son of Ba'al, even before your precious gatekeeper got sprung." Imara cackled and thrust her hands at the water, revealing herself as a maestro conducting the tides to flee. "Stheno knew you'd assume anyone still here was an idiot. You played right into her plan, Seneschal of the Demis."

"Not a portal, Bix, an illusion of one." Ashtad spun toward Bix. "Get down."

An arrow ripped through the cavern. The shaft detonated, lighting the pages coating the walls. Flames roared. Bix jumped off the bench and landed in a crouch by Ashtad.

"Stand your ground, Bix. We can't let them leave." Ashtad rolled his wrists as brilliant blue orbs built within his grasp.

"I got this." Bix opened a gate in front of Ashtad's brow. An arrow zipped through it. Imara's head exploded instead. "For Drew, you varletess."

Two men and a woman wielding crossbows materialized fully amid great plumes of black smoke. The dark rubber coating their fatigues wouldn't help them any more than the Kevlar vests or gas masks. They might have if Ashtad had been alone.

But he wasn't. The unfamiliar darkness within Bix grew, ever so slightly. Three gates started small, no bigger than a fingernail. The woman noticed it first.

"Retrea—"

The demi didn't get a chance to finish. The gates expanded inside the demis, tearing them apart mercilessly. Disconnected body parts sizzled as they fed the dying fire. Crossbows clattered to the floor.

"That never stops being unnerving." Ashtad coughed as he extinguished one orb and rolled Imara's headless corpse to her back.

"How did you know it was an illusion? That there was no portal?" Bix wiggled her shoulders as the darkness scrabbled beneath her skin, eager for release.

"When Imara removed the water, it disturbed the illusion she'd subtly crafted while we interrogated her. Water gods, even those training to be one, are skilled at tricking the eye." He searched Imara's pockets and scowled. "I should have noticed that someone was preying on demis long before now. I've been too focused on the problems inside the CWIG. I'm letting down my own kind."

"There were eight bowls and cups on the table when we arrived. There are four corpses here. That means Stheno only has four demi minions left." Bix stuffed the pages into his waistband. "Don't burn those, we need them."

"That means we bought the Fates a little time, but only a little." He waded through the thick haze, the lone orb casting light over the gore-painted weapons. "We need Imara's body. She's radiating an unfamiliar energy that's making *my* hair stand on end."

"Even now?" Bix gathered the fallen weapons and disarmed them.

"Worse now." He grabbed two of the crossbows and hissed as his skin burned. "Third contact on my phone is a doctor we can trust to keep things quiet."

Bix hung the crossbows over her forearms like handbags, using her new bracelets as buffers while she collected the unused bolts and remaining angel bone. "If Stheno is after you now too, then there is only one place we're heading."

# CHAPTER 23

Stacks of green-board drywall sheets sat like builders' sphinxes to either side of the BMR clinic's door. Tiny people in hazmat suits climbed each other's shoulders to wield hoses shooting purple spray foam in between warded wall studs. Reptilian gremlins ran electrical wires along the ceiling. Familiar red-capped Nixen repaired drain lines in trenches along the floor.

One pushed back his welding mask and thumbed off his torch. A double elbow twitch drew the attention of the plumber next to him. Both stared agape at a limp, bandaged hand dangling from a surgical table.

Their twinned high-pitched whistles brought all construction to a stop.

A square steel door popped open. A stainless steel tray rolled out from the wall of corpse containers. A scowling goblin set aside a roll of blueprints.

"No stopping," Gurp barked.

"But, sir." The Nix pointed to the body.

Gurp stared at the body. Everybody stared at the body.

"Sorry," Bix called from the doorway. "I forgot I'd made a mess."

As one, the workers faced her. Ashtad, with all his years of leadership and political maneuvering, managed to keep a straight face. The long-drawn-out snigger was not as repressed as he probably hoped.

"Work, work," Gurp commanded of his contractors as he jumped off the tray. "Now, now. No more late. Pretty lady need room done now."

A chorus of hoses spat back to life. Construction resumed.

Gurp waddled over and eyed the crossbows. His bulbous nose bobbed. He smacked his lips and hummed happily. He ducked under her baggage and headed down the hallway. "Come, come. Use next room."

She dutifully followed Gurp past Dysmorphic—which overflowed with lower- and mid-caste Chweds queued for the stalls—into the classroom.

"Bixie, babe, what the hell happened to you?"

A wizened Korean nurse sporting floral scrubs and white clogs ceased pacing between rows of long tables and scurried forward.

Until Ashtad cleared the doorway.

Ashtad swung a crossbow and knocked the old woman across the room. With the prowess of a demigod unchecked, he leapt atop a table and raced to his prey before she could stand. His boot pressed to her wrinkled throat. "Anudrengr, you body-thieving bastard. You survived the angels' ambush, and you've been in hiding all these years?"

Drew wheezed. "Aw, Sparky, I haven't missed you either."

"Let her up, Ashtad." Bix sighed, shielding Gurp from the overdue reunion. "She's part of my team, then and now."

"How did you escape?" Ashtad ignored Bix, aiming one of the unloaded crossbows at Drew. "Not the body, the location."

Drew jabbed her finger in the toe of Ashtad's loafer. Ashtad relaxed, minimally.

"Ho-ho…" Drew cleared her throat and glared at Ashtad until the demi ceased stepping on her altogether. Drew wiped her throat and cleared it again. "Host moved the armory so Bix couldn't come back for us. They relocated the contents, but they didn't move the actual cavern in which they'd anchored the armory. I'd hid in a fissure. Once the angels and their cleaners abandoned the spot, I started the long crawl home. Ever try going somewhere without a body? Takes a while."

Ashtad scowled at Drew. "Why didn't you reach out to me?"

"We'd been burned from the inside." Drew sat up and smoothed her silver bob. "Besides, you, dear godlet, harbor all the prejudices of your ilk. I bet you haven't even acknowledged the goblin in the room, have you?"

Ashtad glanced over his shoulder at Gurp. His lips thinned, and he hopped off the table, muttering, "Goblin."

Drew made a face behind Ashtad's back and winked at Gurp. Gurp turned away from the demi to face Bix, gesturing to the bay of sinks set in the long stainless steel counter along the back of the room.

"Work for body, yes?"

"Perfect." Bix smiled contritely as gates relocated Imara's corpse to the counter. "Again, I am so sorry, Gurp. I didn't mean to expose your team to my issues."

"Make good stories." Gurp chuckled and sidestepped a big blond not-Viking with long hair and longer beard complete with war braids.

"Wha…?" Bix's jaw dropped.

"Sweetheart, we really need to discuss the baubles you're collecting." Tobek sauntered into the workroom with Runjit and Hywl at his heels. The former pushed a small cart of surgical tools. The latter rolled in a man-sized crate on a dolly. All three pulled on thick red gloves. Tobek relieved her of her burdens, never breaking eye contact with her. Rampant mirth made him youthful.

Maybe that was the result of extreme dermabrasion.

"What happened to Herr Schmidt?" she whispered.

Tobek leaned down so his furry lips brushed her ear, causing her breath to hitch. "Humbled and hampered, remember?"

"I get the feeling you're never actually hampered." She nuzzled his neck.

"Only if she asks nicely." He grinned and tempered his humor as his attention shifted to Ashtad. "Ashtad Ba'al, it's been a while."

"Chief," Ashtad greeted, drawing out the word as Hywl and Runjit unrolled a heavy plum mat along the nearest table.

"Et tu, Ashtad?" Bix whispered loudly. First, Tobek had called Drew by her ancient name, revealing a shared past neither of them wanted to share with Bix; now Ashtad was all "Chief" with the high warlock, exposing their shared past.

Tobek looked at her, but didn't explain. Naturally.

Ashtad's attention lingered on Tobek before it shifted to Bix. His brow wrinkled. "Chief helped me find my feet here in the Mids after Dad kicked me out of the pantheon to start my trials."

"This personal or professional for you, Ba'al?" Tobek handed over the arrows to Hywl.

"Careful, those explode," Bix blurted. Hywl lifted his pinkies as he gingerly lined up the bolts with their angel bone arrowheads atop the purple mat.

Boys.

"Both, as it turns out." Ashtad set his crossbows on the mat.

"Good. It means you're properly motivated." Tobek motioned Ashtad toward the corpse. "I assume this is here at your request. She's quick to dispose of the dead."

"When they're headless, they're useless," Drew cooed, coming to Bix's side.

Ashtad ignored the draugr. "I noticed an unusual charge coming from Imara. It's persisted even into death."

"Imara of the Slavs?" Tobek stroked his beard. "Perun's granddaughter?"

Ashtad rubbed his neck. "One and the same."

Tobek winced. "That's one way to end a betrothal."

Bix gasped. "Be-who-what now?"

"Arranged marriage to bolster relations between storm gods." Ashtad waved it off. "It was never going to happen. Imara despised me, and I couldn't find an aspect of her to respect. Offering her the chance to kill me is probably what Stheno used to recruit her into this…whatever we're calling this mess."

"Stheno the gorgon?" Drew squeaked. "That crazy bitch is alive even after the Consortium said she had to be removed as director? That's supposed to be a death sentence."

"The director of the CWIG is technically a guild master, so the Consortium charged Ligeia Stheno's peers with removing her permanently as a reminder of the dangers of hubris. Unfortunately for everyone, she knew where the bodies were buried." Tobek traded his red gloves for common latex.

"The guilds' ineptitude and corruption are biting them in the ass now." Runjit cut away Imara's clothing and tossed the scraps in the nearest sink.

"Stheno must be taking out the guild masters who could narc on her as she enacts her plan." Ashtad slid his hands in his pockets and grimaced.

Tobek inspected two fist-sized implants protruding from Imara's torso. Bix looked away as he angled a scalpel over the implant between the corpse's breasts.

"What are the odds the guild masters actually know—or at least suspect—Stheno is behind this recent spate of ills?" Bix asked.

"I bet they suspected within moments of the bunker being hit. When she was director of the CWIG, Stheno used to provide the security for their meetings there." Ashtad shuffled aside as Runjit rolled a magnifying lamp over to the autopsy. "They have no one to whom they can run. The Consortium will most likely execute all the guild masters for their failure to remove Stheno the first time."

"To get leverage over the Consortium that ordered her death, Stheno needs the diplomatic pouch." Bix plucked the drawings from Ashtad's waistband. "She probably learned of it from Feng while she was torturing him."

"Stheno could have pressured the Master of Psychopomps to steal the pouch without telling her what was in it." Ashtad looked over Bix's shoulder. "The demis working for Stheno botched the retrieval."

"Like they botched Centralia." Bix spread the pages out on a nearby table. "Everyone is hoping to exploit the contents of the pouch for their use. There must be serious shit on some high-ranking members of the Consortium in there."

"That could explain why Hel took the risk and freed you. If *she* knows about the pouch, then she's got the Consortium by the balls. By all ruling conventions, it belongs to Hel." Drew set her cheek on Bix's arm and reviewed the drawings along with her.

"Yeah well, the pouch is not in my contract with Hel, and I have less than thirty-six hours to drag Stheno's soul to her. I'm hoping these sketches will give us a clue to the gorgon's location." She slid the papers around the table, trying to fit the pieces together to form a greater picture, a useful picture. "The markings on some of these pages are the same sort engraved on the manacles used by the CWIG for upper-caste confinements. The same kind of markings we found at Forest Haven."

"Similar but not the same." Ashtad picked up a page for closer inspection. "These look like Aramaic but aren't."

"Rhaetic?" Tobek asked, setting the second implant beside the first on a stainless steel plate on the rolling tray.

"That one is." Ashtad to a page by Bix's hip. "Symbol for time."

"Which is what she's trying to change." Bix compared the marking Ashtad indicated to those on the other pages. "She has Skuld, so we have to assume she already has the other four Fates she needs."

"Even if she has the Phoenix, the angels, the gods, and the Fates for the three necessary pentagrams, she still is missing one critical ingredient—the life essence of the Chimera. Without it, she cannot cause a collapse in the space-time continuum. Without it, she cannot move time." Tobek rolled the magnifying lamp over to the tray and cut into one of the implants.

An iridescent tile of reds and oranges shimmered under the light.

Tobek's artificial hand smoked. He tossed the tile on the tray and shoved the whole thing away as his knees buckled. The other Berserkers gasped and sank to the floor. Ashtad clutched his throat and stumbled for the nearest chair.

"Guys?" Bix and Drew eyed each other.

"T-take it," Tobek wheezed.

Bix lunged for the tile.

Another hand beat her to it. A dark hand covered in scrolling jewel tones.

"A curious summons, foundling."

# CHAPTER 24

"**I** didn't summon you, Rummir." Bix stared directly into plum serpentine eyes full of questions. "But if you screw over my friends right now, I'll do the same to Feng."

The dragon swept a considering glance around the room. "I am honored to be a part of the team you have assembled. The sidelines are…"

"Frustrating, I believe is the term your sister used," Bix finished for him, holding out her hand for the tile.

"Yes, she did." He closed his fingers over the thing.

Everyone drew a loud, clear breath. Rummir ambled to the table of angel weapons and tipped his head. Hywl scrambled to his feet and lurched toward the cache.

"At ease, angel hunter," Rummir drawled, examining the bolts, arrowheads, and crossbows. "We are the ones who gave your commander this muting fabric on which the body parts of the Host are resting."

Hywl stilled and arched a brow at Tobek. Tobek nodded, wincing as he flexed the hand of his prosthetic. Metal plates and circuitry gleamed through the large hole in the flesh-toned rubber. Hywl backed away from the dragon, opting to help Ashtad to his feet. Runjit reclaimed the rolling tray and pushed it to the mat.

"I took these implants from three dismembered demi bodies moments ago." Rummir tossed five silicone-covered implants on the mat. "I understand now how they met their end."

"Y-you were tracking us?" Bix sputtered.

"I believed these were the breadcrumbs you wished me to follow." Rummir took Imara's second implant from the tray and kneaded it. "You have left many since our meeting, all enlightening. I admire your use of destruction to hide the message. It is a new approach for you."

"Bix has always been adept at obfuscations," Ashtad ventured. "We are honored that the Dreigiau have sent an emissary to assist the pantheons in their quest for justice."

"Yes, yes, you are one who understands politics." Rummir chuckled. "It was once her greatest attribute, yet as a foundling, she has not learned its value."

Ashtad inclined his head. His body shouted, *Roll with it*.

Bix wasn't against entertaining Rummir's delusions, as long as the dragon didn't try to take Stheno for his own justice.

"These rectangular implants contain Feng's scales. These round ones his claws." Rummir withdrew a severed golden claw from his jean's pocket, sending everyone back a few steps. Smirking, he blew into both fists. When he unfolded his fingers, flawless silicone encased the claw and Imara's tile. He tossed those next to the others.

"Too small to be dewclaws," Ashtad noted.

"Wing claws," Tobek said, joining the gathering around the mat. "The silicone has been bespelled to hamper the natural effects of the Phoenix's stolen parts. They would otherwise have burned through the demis."

"And made them very easy to find." Rummir crossed his arms over his chest. "Once the casing is damaged, the spell is broken and the parts are traceable."

"Why the hell would anyone agree to those implants?" Runjit tsked.

Bix patted her pendant. When she'd first arrived in Tobek's

basement with the dewclaw, he'd warned her that Phoenix parts burned anyone dumb enough to touch them. That'd proven true again with the vat of Feng blood in which she and Samael had been dunked.

Feng blood burned.

"The third eye," Bix blurted. "The mystic's symbol for the third eye had been newly burned into Imara's brow."

"Right." Ashtad nodded, then shook his head. "That particular symbol is not commonly used by the Slavic pantheon."

Tobek wadded up a clean glove and closed his eyes. When he opened his hand, the glove tangled and twisted until it formed a small latex version of the third-eye symbol. He lined up the repaired implants—claw, scale, third eye. "Sacral, Heart, Third Eye, these were in the corresponding placements on the body. It doesn't change the demis' physiology. It doesn't lend them any of the Phoenix's attributes or aspects."

"Smart little bastards." Rummir tugged four metal vials—each the length of a finger, etched with more spell work—from beneath his collar. "Burned into her brow, right? Burned using Feng's blood. That is what these vials I removed from the dismembered demis contain."

Bix flinched, recalling the damage a field of Feng's blood had caused. "Why? Why do this to themselves?"

"Gateways." Tobek harrumphed. "This is how they've been moving around without detection."

"Tricking the preprogrammed gateways into thinking they are Feng." Rummir tucked the vials back under his shirt. "The wing claw of an angel—or in this case, the Phoenix—and the scale of the dragon—also from the Phoenix—verifies authorization. The blood on the third eye communicates destination. The hack is brilliant."

"We can use these." Tobek inspected the implants. "With your help, Prince Rummir, we can use these to locate the Phoenix. Sweetheart, you'll have to open the first gate."

"I'll be doing more than that," she huffed.

"Master Hywl, pick up an implant, if you will," Ashtad prompted. "No gloves, bare skin."

Hywl scratched his sideburn but did as Ashtad asked…and immediately dropped it with a yelp. "Damn, that feels like a molten mace burrowing."

"Stheno would never take the risk of these winding up in the wrong hands." Ashtad picked up the same implant and held it without effect. "The one thing the previous hosts had in common—"

"Other than being ex-CWIG operatives," Drew muttered.

"Was that they were demis," Ashtad finished as though Drew hadn't spoken.

Tobek swore softly. "It'll take time to modify the spells so the rest of us can wear them."

"Time is what I'm running out of." Bix sighed. "Besides, I can't risk taking anyone with me."

The men regarded her with varying degrees of skepticism and surprise.

"Look who's developed an unhealthy hero complex," Drew chided.

"Nothing like that. I know better." She waved off the rebuke. "However, there are three big problems with entering the Phoenix's prison. The first is the matter of the gorgon herself. She will use the magic with which the gods cursed her to turn anyone not of the four big races into stone."

"Mirrored sunglasses." Ashtad rocked up on his toes, then down to his heels. "Invented by Chweds who had to dance attendance upon the gorgons. Stheno will avoid looking into our eyes for her own protection."

"We sell those in the shop." Runjit jerked his thumb in the direction of said shop. "Those aren't a problem."

"Seriously, sunglasses thwart a gorgon?" Bix asked.

Everyone else nodded. Apparently common knowledge.

"Okay, then." Bix waved a hand at the pages spread out on the nearby table. "Second, if I did my math right, the measurements on these schematics are for a huge tank. I've been in that tank. It is filled with Feng's blood. That's how they trap the angels summoned via stole."

"Phoenix blood that burns even demis," Ashtad griped. "Can you use those drawings to get us near the tank without actually being in it?"

"No." She stepped aside as the rest of the group shifted their focus from the implants to the pages. "None of these are drawings of the actual tank, just the components, measurements, and assembly instructions. There are no 'final product' images."

"That would have been too easy, eh?" Drew grumped.

"Fire suits," Hywl said. "They're cumbersome, but they'll take the brunt of the blood. And they're easily shucked once we're clear of the tank. We're well stocked in those too."

"Two problems solved." Tobek smirked. "What else do you have?"

"There are fractures in the layers of the World surrounding Feng." She wrinkled her nose. "Those fractures allow ether to seep in like a haze. That's how Stheno has been hiding the Phoenix from the Horde and the Host. That's also how she built a prison that will kill Feng should he attempt to escape or should a dragon or angel attempt a rescue."

"Ether is not something you can vent to make it dissipate. Once it's in…" Rummir exhaled loudly through his nose, releasing a wisp of purple smoke. His markings blazed, then ebbed. "Feng's been gone five years. That ether has to be reaching critical mass."

Bix scratched the scars in her forearm. "Which means the Fates don't have long before she guts them along with the other gods and angels."

"Respirators?" Runjit offered. "Oxygen tanks? Will either work long enough to buy you time?"

Rummir shook his head. "Ether will dissolve anything made to exist in the Mids. Flesh, metal, stone, doesn't matter. It is more insidious and fast acting than any corrosive agent found in any World."

"As a demi, I can survive ether, so that means I'm in on the rescue," Ashtad announced. "You can't do this alone, Bix. The rest of Stheno's demis are likely guarding the Phoenix and whoever else she's collected."

"Me too, I'm in," Drew chimed in. "What? Suits are disposable. If I'm lucky, I'll get to wear a demi home. If I get spaced, then I'll see some of you in a few hundred years."

"You may not die in the ether, but you will pray to anyone listening to let you." She looked away from the pity painting everyone's features. "This isn't about me. You two need to understand that you will be lost *in* the ether and *to* the ether. Neither of you is a full god, so you will be unable to leave until you find someone—or something—you can ride to a World."

"That makes this rescue exactly the type of high-risk, higher-reward I need to earn my way closer to godhood." Ashtad jabbed a finger in the pages on the table. "Which means there is no way you're talking me out of going with you."

"There are a lot of entities in the ether that will do horrible things to you to alleviate their endless boredom," she warned. "There are reasons they cannot access an inhabited World."

"Those are just undomesticated vehicles. I'm an excellent trainer. I'll use them to get home." Drew adjusted her suit's rack. "We're a team, you and me. Have been, are now, will be. You're not leaving me behind either."

"There are only three complete sets." Runjit put on the red gloves and sorted the repaired implants from the bespelled.

"The third set is mine." Tobek, with one look, dared Bix to challenge him.

He'd enjoy the pain of the implants and of being spaced until the Fates reset his timer. She knew it and he knew she did. His fetish wasn't something the others needed to know.

"Grown-ass man." She shrugged. "You all know the risks. I welcome the help, but you cannot depend on me for your safety. You know what happened to my last team."

"I was your last team, and I'm still with you." Drew rolled

her eyes and leered at the Berserkers. "Now, which of you cutie patooties is going to stuff me?"

Hywl elbowed Runjit, grinning. "I'll get more sterile tools. Pick a table, you intrepid few, and don't get too comfy."

Ashtad and Tobek stripped off their shirts and unzipped their pants, hopping up on tables at opposite ends of the row. Each man bore many scars—Tobek's covered in a wealth of ink, Ashtad's bright against his otherwise flawless skin. Drew squealed with lascivious delight as Runjit rolled his surgical tray beside her table.

"A moment, if you will, foundling," Rummir murmured, reclaiming the unusable parts of Feng.

"You keep calling me 'foundling' like I was abandoned by my parents," she said with a halfhearted censure. He'd said that they used to know each other. Maybe he did know something about her family.

"When you dragged yourself out of the ether, you were *found* by the god Hades in the convergence of the Under Worlds, were you not? Childlike in your ignorance? Without protector, guardian, or friend? Is that not the definition of a foundling?"

"How do you…Who told you that?" She stared at the dragon's broad back as she trailed him to a corner farthest from the others. "Did Mirri tell you that when you two were trying to find Feng?"

"The dragons have many contracts with many pantheons. Learning more about you was merely a matter of asking the right questions of the right deities."

Hades didn't discuss his rescues, so it had to have been one of his flunkies, his super-nosy brothers…or a titan. Titans were the worst gossips.

"You must destroy the World in which Feng is hiding," Rummir murmured, casting a wistful look at the comedy unfolding between the draugr and the Berserker. "On the return journey, the pendant you wear will lead you to a sanctuary for him. All you have to do is open a gate, then allow yourself to be drawn by the power of the dragon royal family. But whatever happens, you cannot let go of Feng."

His insistence prickled her nape.

"Why? What aren't you telling me?"

"The fragments of the Phoenix you left for me to find? My sister and I were able to use them to reach out to him, to touch his mind." Rummir cupped the bangles from the Woolly Barrel. Streams of richly colored light seeped through his fingers. The metals twisted and curved, tickling her arms. "Feng is broken. Mentally. Physically. I saw his tortured thoughts. I felt his emotional riot. He will fight you with more vehemence than your initial encounter at the armory. You must be prepared. He will not make this easy for you, but you cannot let him die."

Considering she didn't do hand-to-hand combat very well, and that he'd thoroughly thrashed her that last time, she was not looking forward to leveling up the skirmish with a man who'd gone from angry to flat-out lost his mind.

If only she'd found the Chimera as Skuld had hoped, maybe she and it would have stood a chance of actually rescuing Feng without her having her ass handed to her. Samael had made it abundantly clear what would happen if Feng burned out of cycle, so rescuing the Phoenix was her only option to save everyone in this room and the whole of the Mids. In short, she was signing up to be beaten up.

Whee?

"Well, shit," she breathed. "I guess it's too late to go back to being just the chick in charge of transportation."

"Take these." Rummir released the modified bracelets, one silver and one gold, each with a long prong shaped like a talon that rested on her middle fingers. "My sister and I offer what help we can while remaining at a distance safe for all of us."

"Given how quickly his prison will implode if you guys try to tag along, I appreciate your restraint." She inhaled deeply and smiled with all the courage she could muster as the enormity of what she was about to do took hold. "You cannot hand him over to the Consortium after this, and he can't go back to the angels under any circumstance. They believe he is a criminal mastermind and want to make him their prisoner. You can't let a man who's been tortured for five years languish in some cell until it's time for him to burn. It's beyond cruel."

"Feng's future and his hopeful rehabilitation are what my sister and the queen are negotiating with the Consortium while I am here with you." Rummir's expression darkened. "You may trust that once you bring him to us, he will not be departing our care."

"Someone is bound to demand the evidence he and Mirri were collecting. Whoever it is, is the last person who should get it."

"Leave the games of politics to those who are skilled in the art." He turned back to the minor surgeries in process, crossing his arms over his chest.

"Make no mistake," she added, standing head to shoulder with the dragon prince. "Ligeia Stheno is Hel's, not the Horde's or the Host's. Do not get between me and the gorgon. Politics be damned."

"We will not be able to keep the Host at bay for long. Every archangel sensed these stolen bits as they were exposed, as did every royal dragon."

Which meant Samael couldn't be far behind. She liked the guy, but he had a job to do and a deep conviction of Feng's guilt.

"Raspoine has assumed responsibility for your actions in this rescue endeavor. It is the best she could do to delay the Horde from hunting those who took him, but it is only a delay. Your time to succeed is more finite than you realize."

"Joy."

"You two ready?" Tobek called, taping gauze over his incision sites. "We need to do this in Centralia. At the spot you pulled the dewclaw."

Bix counted up Berserkers. "You leaving Xipil in charge of the shop?"

"He's still at the hospital." Drew exhaled loudly and tugged her scrubs back into place. "He insisted on keeping watch over Asabitchy."

Bix cursed herself for not asking sooner. "How is she?"

"Medically induced coma. The rest I'll tell you after." Drew took her hand and laced their fingers. "Focus on the mission. No distractions, just like old times."

Bix double-clenched Drew's cold hand and nodded. "Okay, what and who am I moving with us?"

It took less than five minutes before Bix's mix of miscreants and a squad of Berserkers stood in the middle of the Centralia slaughter site, staring at the braided rose tree still in bittersweet bloom. Turned out, the Berserkers all kept go-bags with weapons at the ready for full-on war. Tobek kept two go-bags—one for brute-force war *and* one for magic war. Bix didn't ask about the bottles, the pots, the poultices, the anything that came out of that second bag…and there were a lot of odd things that made an appearance. Many of which ended up in five urns, each engraved to reflect one of the five core elements of magic on one side and the symbols from the demis' den drawings on the other.

At least that was how Ashtad had explained it while Tobek prepared the urns and his men did a quick scout of the site. Runjit and a handful of men had remained at the shop to convert the classroom into a triage station while Gurp and his crew rushed to restore the clinic.

Berserkers, apparently, preferred to be ready for the worst.

"Anytime we want to get on with this?" Drew zipped up her fire suit. "I can smell me burning. Starting to feel it too."

Tobek and Rummir joined Drew and Ashtad. Rummir dragged his thumbnail down the center of his dragon's brow. Blood welled, thick and shimmering.

"This might leave a permanent mark," Rummir warned.

"Time to grow bangs, then." The demi held his hair back. "With what are you branding me?"

"Keter, a potent symbol of the crown to open your minds to the native magic of the Mids." Rummir painted the brows of

Ashtad, Drew, and Tobek. "Since you will not be using a standard gateway to make the journey, the third eye is moot."

"Sweetheart, would you place my men where you best recall the angels' final positions?" Tobek gave Hywl red gloves and a familiar length of smoothed angel bone. "Hywl, stay here at the center with me. Once she shuts the gate, use this rod to break the lines. All of them."

Hywl nodded. "Break all five lines. Got it."

"This puissant spell will attract unwanted attention. We can't leave traces of the magic for someone else to tap. Your role is critical. Be swift. Do not hesitate." Tobek clapped his second on the back, then put on his mirrored sunglasses. "The rest of you fall back thirteen paces from the bracing points. Anything comes through that gate, kill it. Anything approaches this site from any direction, kill it. I don't care if it's Horde, Host, or hooligan. Clear?"

A boom of grunts confirmed.

"That's a bit harsh," Bix muttered as she led five Berserkers— each carrying an engraved urn—to their respective places around the field of wildflowers. The rest of the squad blossomed out behind them, weapons of great variety at the ready.

"Prince Rummir—"

"They used Feng's blood to paint the pentagram's lines," Rummir spoke over Tobek. "So you need me to supply the blood lines this time."

"Only an archangel or a royal dragon can compare to the Phoenix," Tobek conceded, putting on his fire suit.

"Once my blood hits the urns, the timer starts." Rummir stared at Bix. "You have eight minutes before the lines that bind us draw you back to me. That is the maximum time I can grant you."

"Wait," she blurted. "How sure are we that this isn't going to fuel the spell Stheno is planning to use with the Fates?"

Rummir, Drew, and Tobek exchanged an odd look.

"There's a huge chance we will do just that, Bixie," Drew said. "Do you want to call off the mission? Abort the rescue? Now's the time."

Bix's heart hammered. The final go call. Ten years ago, she'd made the call to proceed with a rescue. Ten years ago, her team died moments later due to her decision. It was easy to say "go" when there was a long history of success, but it only took one disaster to make her question everything to point of indecision.

"This rescue can't succeed without you, Bix. You're the only one who can move the Phoenix and any other prisoners Stheno has despite the ether. Our jobs are to protect you so you can save the greater Mids," Ashtad assured. "We all know and accept the risks."

"We all knew back then too, babe." Drew patted Bix's back with the huge mitt of the fire suit, knowing as only best-friend could the root of Bix's hesitation. "Don't let one epic fail overshadow all the wins we had, okay? High risks, frequent dangers, and the constant promise of near-death, are but some of the reasons we chose—choose—to protect the Mids from the field rather than from behind a desk, right?"

"Right." Bix nodded dutifully. "Embracing the unknown comes with the gig. Okay then. Let's make it happen."

"You are the force that opens the gate in this World, sweetheart," Tobek explained, tucking his suit's hood under his arm. "That's why we don't need to kill a bunch of angels. The prince's blood lines give us the means to travel—akin to a magical bungee cord. The implants will draw us toward their owner— toward the Phoenix. The prince's blood on our brows will allow him to pull us back."

"Assuming the ether does not sever our connection," Rummir amended.

"I'm implant-less. How do I end up where you all do?" Not that she wanted Phoenix parts inside her, not after experiencing embedded angel bits.

Tobek pulled on the hood of his fire suit and held out a gloved hand to her. She took it without hesitation. He looped his arm around her and snuggled her spine to his padded chest. The clear face shield of his suit bumped against her head.

"Simple," he shouted through the fire suit. "I don't let you go."

"Bix, set your phone's timer." Ashtad put on his sunglasses, his game face, and the hood to his fire suit. "We don't know what we're walking into, but I'm fairly certain it's not an easy in and out."

"Right. Don't want to lose the team in the throes of battle. I'll set a two-minute warning, then the final out." Bix reached into her bra with her free hand and set two timers on the phone—one at six minutes and one at eight. She'd already taken two baths in Feng goo, so she'd passed on the fire suit and the claustrophobia it'd caused her. "We'll start when I open the gate."

"Anudrengr, keep an ear open for the alarm." Ashtad waved. "On your go, Prince of the Dreigiau."

"Take your places around the tree. Angel hunter, brace yourself. Good luck, all. You'll need it." Rummir yanked a dagger from his waistband and gashed both arms. His scrolls glowed, and his mighty scaled wings unfurled, blacking out the sun with their jeweled beauty. His blood flowed in ribbons through the air, never touching the ground.

Bix shivered at the memory of the last time she witnessed blood defy gravity. So much had happened since then. This whole adventure had started out as an assassin's charge and had escalated into a mission to save the Mids. Thank the powers that be for a team who had her back; otherwise, she'd still be floundering instead of trying to muster up the courage to face a portal-ripping, Phoenix-torturing, angel-slaughtering, goddess-maiming gorgon. Oh, and hey, let's not forget that impending ass-whooping she was scheduled to take if everything went *well*.

As long as she got Ligeia Stheno's soul to Hel, it would all be worth it. As long as she finally got to tell Mirri—

"Get ready," Tobek bellowed as the ribbons stretched for the urns. Upon contact, the urns swelled with blinding light and soaring song.

"Now," Bix shouted over the din, starting the countdown.

"Now," Ashtad and Drew answered in unison.

She slid the phone in her bra and opened a gate. Tobek jerked back violently. His hold on her remained fixed, drawing her along with him safely nestled against his body. With a gasp and a prayer, she closed the lone gate.

Worlds zoomed past in firework flashes.

# CHAPTER 25

They landed. Not in an aquarium of blue blood, but on an industrial grate above it.

Small blessings.

The industrial grate ended at the edge of the glass tank. Splintered sunlight illuminated a great hall of rose quartz. White marble floors extended to a large balcony overlooking an endless field of lavender surrounding a lake so clear, flecks of orange and white could be seen.

A wondrous pastoral beauty…destroyed by the wisps of ether cutting through stone and scenery.

What appeared at first glance to be unlit passages off the massive room pulsed, expanding in micro-measurements. Dark clouds of ether wound along the ceiling, slunk down the walls, and swallowed whole segments of windows and lofts. Fragments of stained glass peppered the floor. Crystal droplets from decimated chandeliers gleamed amid deep gouges chiseled into the floor. Wilting weeds grew from scorched and stained carpets carelessly tossed over heaps of broken furnishings inlaid with tarnished silver and weathered gold.

Something inside Bix recoiled. A tear dribbled down her cheek. She wiped it away only to note the thickness and hue. Blue.

Goo. She looked over her shoulder and up, way up.

Behind her—suspended by iron manacles engraved with arcane spells, from thick trunks of aged carnivorous plants—hung the Phoenix in his humanoid size and form.

What was left of him.

Wings—once plush with feathers of graduating hues of red, orange, and yellow—had been plucked, exposing the raw vermillion membrane. Golden wing claws had been cut out below the roots. Whole patches of scales were missing from his barbed tail. No stubble had regrown to hint at his once lush red hair. Skin once bronze and firm over rippling muscles now lay like crepe paper of a dull taupe hue over nothing more than bones. Bright blue blood dripped from the gouges and tears riddling his body, trickling through the grate into the pool.

The prisoner Phoenix bore no resemblance to the wrathful guard of the Host's armory or to the bitterly arrogant key witness in her trial. Sure, she'd known from the moment Samael had confirmed his disappearance that he wasn't going to be in good shape, but…

Damn.

"Well, well, look who deigned to show," hissed a voluptuous woman of limestone skin and serpent hair. She held an angel's crossbow leveled at Bix's chest. The four demis flanking her aimed their bows at Ashtad, Drew, and Tobek. "What? You didn't really think you could use our gateway and not alert us to your arrival?"

"Ligeia Stheno." Bix stepped from Tobek's hold as her small team fanned out along the grate. She took in the rest of the captives, each nailed to a singular pentagram up on a platform of torture.

Five angels, five gods, and five Fates.

No two Fates hung next to each other, nor two gods, nor two angels. Each race had been positioned as an end point of their own pentagram mapped out in deep gouges on the floor.

Skuld hung directly across from Feng, her mohawk now a flat knotted mat. Traces of black eyeliner streaked down her face, rendering her a morbid clown. Blood welled in red from the five points of impalement, yet dripped in ever-changing colors to a containment pool below.

The angel to Skuld's left appeared more of a dryad tangled in a tree. The roots scrabbled along one of the troughs dug into the floor, intersecting with four other angelic contributions at the center of the pentagram, giving rise to the monstrosity imprisoning Feng. The eyes of the angel had been gouged out—no dialing an archangel for aid.

Stheno and her band were not screwing around.

"Aborted goddess, rejected angel groupie, and terminated guild master," Bix drawled with a disinterested sniff. "What a disappointment to be in the company of an abject and repeated failure such as yourself."

"You're a bit early, Bix, or is it late? I suppose that depends on which lover you wanted to save." Stheno swung the crossbow and fired at Tobek.

Lightning struck the bolt before it cleared the bow. The double explosion blew back over Stheno. Harmlessly over Stheno and her stone skin. The demi beside her was not as fortunate. Half his face blistered. To his credit, he only yelped. His aim on Drew didn't falter.

"Ashtad Ba'al, I should have known you'd take the mission with your favorite probationary agent." The gorgon laughed, and her serpents hissed. "Do you think she's figured out how much you're in love with her yet?"

"I've loved her like an annoying little sister from the moment you inflicted her on me, but then how could you recognize any form of love, Ligeia?" Ashtad descended the steps of the platform casually, removing the hood of his fire suit as one of his peers tracked him with a loaded bow. "The Greek pantheon never showed you any. The Host showed you lust, which you quickly confused for love. The sorority of gorgons finds any sort of intimate respect anathema. No, the closest you ever came to love was from your fellow demis, until you became an outsider and just another means to an end. Even those who stand with you now, they don't care if you live or die. They care only that they survive this mess and take one large step closer to godhood."

Drew used the distraction to quickly descend from the other side of the platform, ripping off her fire suit with all the fervor of a madwoman. Cackled like one too as she ascended the nearest platform to a barely lucid god in a body Bix didn't recognize.

"Who is… Anudrengr? Stop that body thief, now," Stheno shouted.

A bolt flew faster than Ashtad could respond. Drew's borrowed body incinerated as she lunged at her target.

"Too late, bitch." The head of the tethered god snapped up and cackled. He wriggled his hand against the nail pinning him to the pentacle. He grunted and writhed. "Why can't I move?"

"Angel bone nails." Stheno ambled to the small pool into which the god's blood drained. "How *does* one kill a draugr? Rumor says trapping it in a living body whose original inhabitant is more powerful, so powerful that it will crush you into oblivion. You've an affinity for rushing headlong, Anudrengr. Every team leader you ever had complained of your recklessness. Guess it's finally caught up to you."

Drew's struggle increased, this time in earnest. "You've weakened him, Stheno. You gave me a fighting chance to own a god's body. Do you have any idea what we will do to you?"

Bix opened a gate at Drew's hand. Layers of the World shattered. A puff of ether blossomed in Drew's palm and swallowed it. Drew screamed in pain and panic.

"No? Not working out the way you planned, gatekeeper?" Stheno spun around and draped one arm along the lip of the pool. "Every one of these beautiful contraptions is surrounded by a little something I've spent years perfecting."

"Turning the protective layers of the Mid Worlds into little more than sugar glass." Bix scrutinized the air around the pentacles, searching out the tears Stheno had used to draw Samael and the other angels into the pool.

They weren't hard to spot.

Grotesque punctures formed a second ring behind each of the abductees. Fractures connected one puncture to the next, then spidered out, coating the entire protective layer of the World. Everything as far as she could see had been deliberately cracked.

Shit.

"This is far more advanced than Forest Haven," Bix admitted reluctantly. "This entire room is a spell awaiting its final component."

"A spell of opposites that will pull apart existence as we know it until it collapses in on itself, folding time to a point established by the location of each of our vaunted guests." Stheno relaxed her stance and waved the bow at the sacrifices surrounding them. "It will take us back to the last time the Mids began to burn. Back to the day I swore my allegiance to the Host and to the Phoenix."

This incarnation of the Phoenix twitched in his shackles and groaned.

"I needed one last great feat to ascend to full godhood, and in his *infinite wisdom*," Stheno shouted and spat the last words as she withdrew a bolt from the full quiver at her hip, "the Phoenix gave me the surest challenge: to kill his nemesis, the Chimera."

"Clearly, you failed. You're a gorgon, not a god." Bix inspected Feng's prison. She only had one shot at moving him and couldn't risk being thwarted by the myriad spells Stheno had in play.

"I did. I failed," Stheno admitted with surprising candor. "The Chimera refused to kill me and sent me back to my pantheon defeated. For my arrogance, for my hubris, and for their amusement, my pantheon chose the punishment of gorgon. Hades locked me away as my once flawless body rebelled against me, growing this smothering crust of stone."

"The serpents are an improvement," Ashtad taunted.

"The moment Hades released me from my cell, I went in search of the Chimera." Stheno turned with arms wide, waving bolt and bow. "Behold, the hidden Mid World of the Chimera. It took time to find—hundreds of years—before I discovered this tiny pocket, this pathetic mockery of an Upper World, this piece of existence built by none other than the Host who set me up to *fail*."

The gorgon nocked the bolt and fired at the pool beneath a god's feet. The four demis followed suit with the remaining gods' pools. Glass shattered and divine blood flowed into the second set of troughs of a second pentagram, also leading to the focal point of the Phoenix.

"But did you know? The Chimera wasn't home." Stheno rested her elbow atop the tank of a Fate Bix didn't recognize and nocked another arrow.

"The Chimera vanished after the last Great War. No one has seen or—"

"Lie," Stheno shrieked over Ashtad and fired across the pentagram, splintering another Fate's tank. "The Chimera didn't *vanish*. The gods husked the damned thing and kept it secret. I had to wait three hundred years for my revenge. That's how long it took the coward Chimera to drag itself out of the ether."

The demis broke the other Fates' tanks with their bolts. Iridescent blood flowed into a third pentagram. Where the lines intersected with the other pentagrams, tiny portals opened, casting out a web of fractures.

Tobek shouted through his face shield, "Sweetheart, we're running out of time. Save who you will, but you need to move them now."

"I can't." Bix spoke up so Stheno could hear her. "I move one person, one thing, and this whole World collapses. This is a trap, one she started the day she abducted Feng."

"Every day since being burdened with this liability of a soul, I have studied, planned, and plotted my revenge—the mutual ruin of the Phoenix and the Chimera." Stheno rapidly fired five bolts at the wards embedded in the glass of Feng's pool. Spells ruptured in peals of musical notes. Glass melted. Tides of blue blood swept across the pentagrams and cupped the vortexes spinning at the convergences.

Tobek muttered something unintelligible behind his face

shield. Ashtad ran for the platform steps as Feng's blood burned the cuffs of his fire suit and melted his bunker boots.

"Lo, one day, the Fates were kind." Stheno wagged a bolt at Skuld. "I strolled into the CWIG new-recruit orientation, and there in the middle of the class was the missing piece."

Curses from Ashtad and Drew rang in perfect clarity.

"Me? You mean to use me as your means to strike at the Chimera?" Bix scoffed. "Why not do it when I was one of your Dark Ops agents? When you actually had a modicum of control over me?"

"You stupid cow," Stheno castigated, rearming. "Even now you are deliberately blind. Every mission you undertook for me was meant to jog your memory. Yet you still stared back at the World without a glimmer of recognition. That's when I knew what had happened to you. That's when I learned the truth of what the gods had done to you."

Bix took one step back. "You are mad."

"You, Bix, *you* are the Chimera," Stheno crowed, taking aim. "And with you here, I can finally complete this spell and attain my godhood."

Bix recoiled and looked to Tobek. He refused to look at her. His determined avoidance confirmed it more than if he'd said the words. Her guts cramped and her heart stopped. She looked to Ashtad and met a wealth of confusion and shock. No, he hadn't known. He was too young, perhaps. But Drew…

Drew, her dearest friend, watched her with nothing less than tragic apology.

Oh gods, oh gods, it was true. Skuld, Samael, Rummir… all of them…all of the immortals, all of the long-lived…Hel, Jör, Phobos, Hades…all of them. All of them knew. All of them had known all along. Even when they'd exiled her, they'd known.

The monster who could destroy gods, Fates, dragons, angels, and entire Worlds…she was the monster. She was the bogeyman. She was the freak who'd given away her memories because…because she was a horrible thing…because she'd done horrible things. Was that…was…

She spun around and stared at Feng. She was his end. She made him burn, over and over and over. Every cycle, his destiny was to be destroyed by her.

No wonder he'd despised her on sight.

"If you turn back time to your final battle with the Chimera…" Bix choked on the word but couldn't afford to focus on what it meant, what any of this meant. Her focus had to remain on the mission and nothing else. Time was running out, and she had to figure out the escape plan Stheno had built into this World. No way, no how did the former director of the CWIG leave herself with only one out. She turned to face Stheno. "You'll fight the Chimera in all her glory, fully aware, fully armed, and fully capable of killing you again. You are doomed to repeat your failure."

"No, because I now know your weakness." Stheno fired a bolt at Bix. The demis followed suit.

Bix twisted aside. The bolts sailed past her, fletchings tickling her cheek and neck. Feng grunted loudly as the angel bone arrowheads pierced his abdomen. His papery skin closed over the holes. The hybrid dragon-angel drew a less feeble breath as the bits of his fallen brethren gave their power to his body.

A few more direct hits and Feng might be able to lift his head.

"Don't hit the Phoenix, you idiots," Stheno screeched, rearming, "Empty your quivers into the Chimera and only the Chimera."

"Ba'al, the Phoenix's blood," Tobek boomed. "Burn it."

"Gleefully." Ashtad pushed the small orbs he held in each hand together until they formed one large pulsing ball that audibly throbbed.

Demis fired out of sequence. Ashtad let loose. Lightning flashed and forked. Multiple explosions and cries filled the air. Fire raced across the floor, devouring the vines of angels and the blood of gods.

A wall of flames blinded Bix.

Heat blossomed in her breast. Her breathing seized.

Tobek tipped Bix across his body and cradled her in his artificial arm. "I got you, sweetheart. I got you. Try to contain the shadows. Don't let them near the pentagrams."

She would have done as he asked if she'd known how, but it took everything to cling to a semblance of calm as mist and midnight filled her mouth.

"Stay with me, sweetheart. Stay in the moment." Tobek raised his natural hand. Green currents tore through his suit from shoulder to glove and rushed from his palm, peaking in silver spears that drove through the flames and into the hearts of the demis.

"A little help with the floor, Chief," Ashtad shouted. "I can't break the lines on my own."

Tobek held Bix firmly and directed his attack at the floor. The men's disparate magics struck marble repeatedly, blasting shards and gore through the thick smoke.

The ribbons of the Fates glimmered through the haze.

"The fire isn't affecting the vortexes," Ashtad called. "How do we stop a spell in action?"

"You don't," Stheno cackled. "None of you have the power to stop what has begun without ripping this World apart. I see the shadows. The Chimera is bleeding. Our timeline is over."

Bix punched her fingers into the weeping hole in her breast, keening to keep herself from blacking out as she extracted the arrowhead. Fighting back the wave of nausea, she stared at the hateful little bit of marbled blue and white pulsing in her trembling hand.

If she let the shadows into the vortex, she could go back in time and stop herself from giving up her memories. She could warn herself of the danger of angel bone bullets, of the burning of her Dark Ops team, of the attack on Mirri and Vidya...

And if she went back in time and stopped her present from happening, then she'd never have had the relationship with Mirri and Vidya, or Ashtad and Drew. Who could say if the Tobek of her past would treat her with the same kindness as the Tobek of her present.

According to Stheno, the Chimera had languished in the ether for three hundred years.

Three hundred.

Not long in the time of gods, yet gods were—on the whole—heartless. Hel had said she, Bix, could no longer withstand the pain of owning her memories, so she had asked to be husked. If she—if the Chimera—had felt that kind of pain, then she wasn't heartless. Perhaps, she'd given up everything to stop herself from devolving into a worse kind of monster. Perhaps, she'd given up everything to prevent herself from becoming apathetic. Perhaps she'd given up everything to preserve something more important.

Or someone.

If she went back in time, she'd undo the sacrifice. She must have had good reasons to have done what she did. Surely. Otherwise, the gods wouldn't have agreed to help her. Right?

Whom did she trust more: the fully aware version of past herself, or this half-cocked bumbling screw-up version?

A thought opened gates.

"No," caterwauled Stheno. "No, damn you, no."

"Bix is spacing the vortexes." Ashtad stopped wrecking the floor. "We're running out of time before the ether claims us all."

"The fire hasn't killed enough of the tree holding the Phoenix." Tobek turned with Bix still in his hold and directed his magic behind him. "You finish off the plant. I'll take on the manacles."

Bix gripped Tobek's fire suit and pulled herself upright as Ashtad's magic lit up the carnivorous plant like a massive Tesla coil.

An unholy, anguished cry ended with a damp thud.

"Enough," Tobek barked.

The men stopped their destruction. The haze parted, leaving only the embers of a smoldering stump to cough up feeble coils of white smoke. Feng curled into a fetal position amid jagged marble and the embers of his own blood. Broken manacles littered the floor around him.

"Ligeia Stheno, you are defeated, again." Ashtad marched across the ruins—sidestepping the coils of ether seeping into the World.

The gorgon lay alone amid the remains of her grand plan, gripping the bleeding stump of leg amputated by an ill-placed quiver and one well-placed lightning bolt. She took in the wreckage, sobbing as Ashtad hauled her to her remaining foot without care or mercy. The juddering of her serpents spoke of the voltage he served her as he hauled the gorgon away from a rupturing fracture.

"You were never worthy of being a god." Ashtad dragged Stheno toward the platform on which Bix and Tobek still stood. "You're not even worth killing."

Stheno's sobs lightened and built into a malicious cackle. "Didn't you ever wonder why the Consortium sentenced you to a hundred and eighty years for your crimes, Bix? Such a random number, that, don't you think? Did you ever do the math? Three hundred years as a husk in the ether and twenty years flitting about the Mids as a CWIG agent. Now add to that a hundred and eighty years in exile, and what do you get?"

Bix held up the shimmering arrowhead and tried to regulate her breathing as dizziness threatened her ability to stay in this ruined World. "Five hundred years. The time between the cyclical Great Wars."

"That's right. The Consortium needs you, they need the Chimera to kill the Phoenix, but on their schedule. Are you really going to do them that favor after everything they've done to you? Look at Feng. He'll never be sane again. If you let him out of here, he and his broken mind will become a danger to the Mids. If you kill him now you do him a favor and save the Mids, all while screwing over the mighty Consortium. If you kill him now, you show him mercy." Stheno's eyes glowed with certain madness. "Doesn't he deserve your mercy?"

Of course he did, but deserving it and getting it weren't the same thing. And the sudden change in Stheno's strategy didn't encourage Bix's cooperation either.

"I'm not starting a war prematurely so you can drag us all down with you, Stheno. I'm taking you to Hel to where she will judge your actions." Bix scanned the pentagrams still holding the Fates, gods, and angels aloft. Frustration clawed at her skin even as her wound toyed with her lucidity. "However, I could be convinced to request she kill you quickly, if you'll tell me how I can free your victims without causing them further harm."

"Ether is the only way," Stheno sniggered. "Everyone in this room ends up in the ether. This era of peace among the Consortium is over no ma—"

Stheno vanished. Ashtad along with her.

"No." Bix stumbled and turned around. No sign of Tobek. "No, no, no, no. The timer didn't go off."

Bix reached for her phone and came away with ashes. The arrow had struck her phone before her breast.

"Shit, shit, shit."

"Ether is the only way to free us, Bixie," an unfamiliar voice whispered across the eerie silence. "Take the Phoenix and go, now."

Bix turned toward the voice. Her heart lodged in her throat. Ether had seeped through the hole she'd opened in Drew's hand and now wound around him, dissolving the mortal body of the god he inhabited as it ate through the World.

"No, Drew, jump to me. I will host you. Happily. Please, please, Drew, jump."

Deep brown eyes in a round face watered, letting one tear trickle over plump cheeks. "No regrets, Bixie. No blame. The mission is all that matters. I *will* find my way back to you. You are the beacon I cannot resist. I hope you will forgive me."

Tears flowed unchecked as the ether consumed the last of Drew and his god.

"No," Bix cried softly. "No."

"You must end this World, Chimera," a weakened rasp groaned. A Fate, one she didn't know. He seemed an ordinary man of ordinary features somewhere in his middle age. A nail of angel bone pierced his thigh, right above his thick amputation scars.

"The Mids cannot afford for the things in the ether to find a safe haven in these remnants." A second Fate gasped. This one was a woman with pointed ears and vulpine features. Thick scars, like those on acid burn victims, covered half her face and neck. "Take the Phoenix, destroy this World."

"Tell me how I can save the rest of you." Bix furiously wiped her tears. "Tell me how to do it before the ether takes you too."

"The ether isn't going to kill most of us. Sure, we'll get roughed up, but we're as resilient as the gods." Skuld's green eyes glowed lime. "Only the angels will end, and that will be a blessing for them. You know their futures will be worse if they make it back to the Host."

Those angels had failed to protect the Phoenix. They'd exposed the Mids to danger, had made their kin vulnerable, and had lacked the wherewithal to off themselves. Yes, the Host would make them suffer quite a bit before they turned these poor guys into next-gen weaponry.

"Hurry, Chimera, before the ether reaches the Phoenix. Take him to the Dreigiau. Trust no one but the twins. Hurry, there is still a chance for balance to be restored."

"Fates," Bix sighed, pressing a hand over her weeping wound. "You better not be dicking me over again."

One thought spawned twenty gates and cast them around the premises. Dervishes of destruction shattered the fractured layers of the World. Hateful props of torture vaporized with the faintest brush of ether. Fates tumbled freely into the vastness. Angels combusted; their ashes sparkled like glitter.

Bix refused to look away as the ether flayed the contracted bodies of the gods, needing to witness the mauling Mirri had endured, to understand the prison that still trapped Mirri's beautiful mind. Within Bix, the sinister rage throbbed and scrabbled, clawing its way toward greater sentience.

Once the last god sprang free of its corporeal bond, Bix opened gates at the four convergences and issued an invitation to old friends. The Reaping Winds arrived with a keen of outrage, stirring up the ether and chasing it down corridors and walkways, into gardens and lakes. What was once idyllic beauty was transmuted to nothingness, to the absence of being.

When she was certain the destruction would persist without her, she jumped off the platform and crouched beside Feng. Tobek and Ashtad had successfully freed him from his shackles. He now lay as a tangled lump of emaciated skin and bones. She laid a hesitant hand on his bare and bruised shoulder.

The native power of the Mids radiated up her arm and throbbed in her jaw, threatening to blow her skull wide open. She pursed her lips and screamed.

Feng jerked his head up and inhaled sharply. Wild eyes looked at her and through her, unseeing. Broken wings twitched in the rubble, wrenching his back. He cried out. She stretched out on the ground in front of him and closed her other hand over his frail bicep peeking from under his scraggly wing. He thrashed and struggled.

"We're going to dance again, Raging Red. This time, I'm going to lead, okay? Okay. It's going to be okay. I got you." She tucked herself closer to him as he tried to pry her loose.

A gate opened.

Native magic surged over them. The bracelets around her wrists glowed. The talons grew into great scaled hands, one scrolled in darkness and one in light. They closed gently around Feng's shoulders.

The pendant about her neck spun into a whirlwind of song.

Feng shoved at her violently, baring teeth and snarling. The dragons' hands held him fast. Bix clung to him for dear life as they tumbled out of the dying World into a cocoon of native magic and were swept away.

# CHAPTER 26

Dirt, rich brown loam—freshly tilled and pungent with welcome—made for a soft, graceless landing in the middle of a dark silo. The grit adhered to Bix, extinguishing the smoldering Feng goo that he'd gotten on her. But hey, she and her fragile package had arrived safely-ish.

Even if said fragile package still tried to fling her off him.

"Easy there, I'm going, I'm going." Carefully, she untangled her limbs from his, wincing as her wound objected. "Just need my arm back and my leg. You can have the shoe wedged under your butt. Promise I don't need it back…whatever is left of it."

Strong hands around her waist hefted her off the Phoenix and carried her outside a ring of singing stones. Music played softly like one of those New Age moaning whale collections while large stones subtly rotated through earthen tones in time to the rise and ebb of the songs.

Bix wiped dirt from her eyes and blinked rapidly.

The helping hands belonged to the reigning queen of the dragons. There was no way Bix could ever forget this frigid face of utter beauty. From the golden scrolls limning her dark body to the golden flecks in her purple gaze, the queen hadn't looked away from Bix throughout her trial.

"You succeeded," the reigning queen said with more than a hint of surprise. "You chose to save the Phoenix."

Bix gestured with both hands at the skeleton trembling in the dirt pit. "Ta-da?"

"We will take it from here." The reigning queen eyed Bix. "You may go."

Bix gauged the round, earthen chamber. It was windowless and unadorned. Six women of different builds, different coloring, yet sharing intricate scrollwork circled the room. To their right flanks, stood a somber man of complementary build yet contrasting scrollwork.

The Dreigiau Seven Queens and their enforcers.

Top of the top of the food chain, and Bix only cared about two of them. Raspoine and Rummir stood behind her, expressionless. Their attentions ostensibly fixed on the queen.

"Feng is not to be imprisoned, shackled, or handed over to the Host for any reason. His recovery and continued welfare are the responsibilities of these two." Bix motioned at Raspoine and her brother.

A twitch here, a lash flutter there. Probably the closest dragons got to chaos in a confined space.

The reigning queen drew herself up, doubling in height. "You dare?"

"The Phoenix is now under the protection of the Horde—all of you." Bix removed her remaining shoe, standing barefoot in the dirt. "If at any time I learn that he is in the company of the Host unattended by these two, I will take him. If I learn that his care has been shifted to any member of the Horde other than these two, I will take him. If I learn that ill has befallen these two, I will take the Phoenix, and I will keep him."

She might not have been able to remember the long, sordid history of the Phoenix and the Chimera, but she knew the immediate history, and she knew people were afraid the Phoenix would burn out of cycle, which she *could* cause by dragging him to the ether since she didn't have a clue how to directly force to him burn. She wasn't above using the dragons' fears to get what the Fates wanted.

Whatever the Fates were up to, five of them from different Houses had placed the burden of a peaceful-ish future on Feng being with the twins. So, burdening the twins was going to happen.

"You've no idea what you ask," the reigning queen hissed.

"I get that a lot. And you're right, I don't know." Bix sidled closer to the queen. "But you should not mistake these conditions of his release as a request."

"I accept." Raspoine spoke with alacrity. "My brother and I accept the honor of being the sole caretakers of the Phoenix for the duration of this cycle."

Gasps and whispers slithered around the silo.

"Raspoine, do not allow this nemesis of our race to dictate your future." The reigning queen returned to the more common size maintained by the others in the chamber. "You are training to ascend. The Chimera plants this distraction to undermine your rule and the trust of our people."

"Your advice is sage and valued." Raspoine bowed. "However, there will be no peaceful ascension without the Phoenix to oversee the passing of rule. That is our tradition and a tradition respected by the majority of our people. Without him hale, hearty, and in possession of his complete faculties, there will be those who proclaim the change of rule invalid. They will exploit that fault into a rallying cry to instigate a war that will last well beyond the burning of the Phoenix. Therefore, I accept the Chimera's conditions. May I raise the Phoenix to his full glory, and in so doing raise myself to be a queen ready for the challenges the dragons will face in the new era."

The reigning queen glowered and exhaled loudly. "Your choice. I have made my objections clear. From this moment until he burns, the Phoenix is your responsibility. So let it be known."

"So let it be known," echoed the other dragons. Pair by pair, they winked out of the chamber until Bix was alone with Raspoine and Rummir…and Skeletor.

"You're still going to be able to ascend, right?" Bix pushed her filthy hair from her face.

"Even if we have to pick up arms to ensure it," Rummir muttered.

"Thank you for your insistence, Bix." Raspoine inclined her head. "I am glad that despite no longer knowing us, you chose to trust us."

"Well, you two helped spring him." Bix winced, watching Feng attempt to make sense of his new location. "You're not going to bury him in here, are you?"

The twins smirked in exactly the same way, but Raspoine answered, "This is a rookery, a place of healing for newborn dragons who had difficult hatchings. Even though he is a creature of light and fire, these muted surroundings are intended to soothe the riot in his mind while the soil aids in the repair of his body. Like you, we will begin at the beginning and build anew."

"For what it's worth, pink quartz, anything lavender, and koi fish are probably going to be triggers, just so you know." Bix pressed a hand to the wound in her chest and blew out a long, stabilizing breath. "Both of you knew I was the Chimera, neglected to tell me, yet still encouraged me—Feng's historical nemesis—to save him. Why?"

"We were unsure if you would believe our words about such a personal topic at this nascent stage of our reacquaintance." Raspoine crossed her wrists over her heart. "If we were mistaken, forgive us. The circumstance is new to us."

"Yeah, it's new to me too, but thanks for taking a chance on this version of me." Bix removed the bracelets that had helped her hold on to the Phoenix. "Here. I like you two, but I don't want your hands grabbing me unexpectedly."

She kept the pendant with Feng's dewclaw. It'd been helpful a time or two. Plus, she and he had a hot date in the future at which point the claw might come in handy. If he ever got well enough to ask for it back before then, she'd deal with the negotiation at that time.

Rummir snorted and accepted the bracelets. "Your friends await you in Centralia. They have secured the gorgon. May Hel make her suffer for her sins."

"Thanks to you and the guys, Stheno's efforts to change time have been thwarted." Bix puffed out her cheeks and looked one more time at the broken Phoenix. "Let's hope what we all accomplished today staves off the war she so desperately wanted."

Something was wrong. Bix smelled charred flesh before she cleared the gate. One step across the threshold and her guts sank. Blue floodlights cut through hard night. Berserkers raged and roared. Metals clashed.

Angels swarmed the sky. Their unholy fire immolated one brave warrior after the next, razing the once tranquil memorial in Centralia. Another team was felled in flames.

That was it.

The one push too far.

The Host thought they could assail with impunity. That none but the corrupt Consortium could hold them accountable for impulsive slaughter. That politics shielded their unjust attacks from public exposure. That their wealth of magic entitled and excused them.

They were mistaken.

The Chimera could destroy immortals; angels were merely long-lived.

Bix seized hold of the sinister seed within herself and screamed. All the pain and anger she'd suppressed from the moment she'd seen Mirri's pendant in a pile of gore could no longer be contained. Shadows exploded from her, turning the night against her prey. Corporeal claws of darkness snatched angels from the air and tore them asunder.

"Hit the deck," boomed Tobek's familiar bellow. "Get down! Get down!"

Still Bix screamed. The primal release raked along her bones and expelled itself with the force of a hurricane until the sky roiled with her intentions. Round and round the storm spun as she fed her heartache to the wild magic. She screamed until she was hoarse. Her body swayed, caught in the release.

A single rose petal tumbled in the wind and settled over her heart. White. Pure. Untainted. Unmarred.

Bix broke. Her knees gave way. Her cheek pressed against soft loam. Keens devolved into sobs as she curled into a fetal position under the fragile boughs of the Widow's Tree and wept. Time meant nothing to her as she grieved.

The ops team she'd lost to a traitor. The two ex-girlfriends mangled physically and emotionally. Her best friend sucked into the vast ether.

Those who'd trusted and believed in Bix the Gatekeeper had suffered so much for her. There was nothing she could do to take away their torments. No solace. No succor. She couldn't even show her gratitude for their sacrifices. The souls of her ops team had been drained by voracious gods. Her exes languished in their respective comas. And Drew, at this very moment, was enduring a terror unlike any he could possibly have known before.

Then there was the monster buried within her and the conspiracy of silence by those who knew her truth…her vulnerability.

Hands—one warm and real, the other exposed, sparking hardware—scooped her against a solid chest and furry beard. Gently, Tobek rocked her, never saying it would be okay, never telling her to stop, never uttering false placations. He just held her while she cried, stroking her hair and holding her close.

It felt so good to be held that she cried even more.

Eventually, her tears abated, leaving her with a throbbing head and a chill wind on her bare back. She lifted her head from Tobek's chest and groaned.

"I've snotted all over you."

He wiped her tears with his thumb. "Of the fluids we've encountered today, snot is not that bad."

"Pretty sure the Feng goo is burning through your shirt right now." She snuffled and looked at the wreckage around them, illuminated by early streaks of dawn. "Your poor guys. You've suffered losses. What happened?"

"The Archangel Samael," he said, his features hardening. "He and his choir appeared the instant Prince Rummir left."

"Samael?" She put a hand in the middle of his chest and leaned way back. "But I got to Feng first. What could he possibly... No, don't tell me..."

"He took Stheno." Tobek pursed his lips. "Ba'al is badly injured, even for a demi. He did his best to—"

She held up one hand, quieting him. She opened gates and moved everyone on Team Bix back to the classroom next door to Dysmorphic. Living or dead, whatever she recognized as a Berserker, she moved to sanctuary. The souls of the dead fanned out to the perimeter, ever the protectors even in death.

Their chief, she kept with her in Centralia.

"Samael didn't mention where he was taking her, did he?"

Tobek shook his head.

"I should have seen that betrayal coming. He's an angel. It's what they do." She rolled to her knees, then staggered to her feet. Someone had definitely thrown her under the bus, a whole parade of them judging by the aches and objections of her body. "It appears I have some final arrangements to make before I meet with Hel."

Tobek braced his bleeding arms on his knees and frowned. "Sweetheart, we still have time to find them."

"No, actually we don't." She raised a hand at the dawn breaking over the tree line. "It's the morning of the seventh day. I have until the sun sets tonight to ensure the safety of those I've failed. I am beyond grateful to you and your men for all that you've done for me. You'll never know just how grateful."

Tobek surged to his feet. "You can't give up."

"I'm not." She coiled her filthy hair at her nape. "I'm going to be in breach of contract, which is going to have long-term consequences for me. The fine print forbids me from starting a war among the Consortium, but to get Stheno, I'm going to do just that."

"Before you go on a rampage…" Using his boot, Tobek rolled over a set of wings attached to a torso and nothing more. He placed his foot on the pectoral beside a gnarly scarification of one glyph outside an intricate knot.

"Samael has something similar on his chest."

He nodded. "This brand denotes an angel cast out of the Host, disavowed. If Samael has one, then the Host proper isn't your target."

Her shoulders slumped as the weight of complete failure pressed down on her. She hung her head and closed her eyes. "So we have no idea where the bastard went."

"Whatever Samael's plan, we can figure it out before nightfall. Together."

She opened her eyes and met his still-glowing gaze. "Are you saying that to the gatekeeper who crash-landed in your basement a week ago or to the Chimera?"

He pursed his lips and gave a slight shake of his head.

"Oh, I forgot, you're not going to tell me," she mocked bitterly. "Not even when it has enormous impact and relevance to a mission that could have ended in all our deaths. How many of the Berserkers who came here today—who died here today—knew that they were in cahoots with a monster?"

His brow furrowed. "You shouldn't be so hasty to categorize yourself."

"Did you befriend me because of some greater Mid World Army strategy? Did you clothe and shelter the Chimera while it was still docile so that you can manipulate it when it grows increasingly hostile? Am I your baby elephant? Is your charity the string you hope I won't know I can break?"

"We should get you to the clinic. Your wound is still weeping." He ignored her questions and gestured to the hole in her dress from which dark mist flowed.

She curled her fist over her mouth and fought back the wave of despair. Men. She had shitty, shitty taste in men. Jör had shown her similar kindness when they'd begun, and all too soon, her dependencies had made her his prisoner. How long would it take Tobek the high warlock and military commander to pull the same stunt? How many times would she let herself be a victim?

Never again.

"Thank you for your concern, but no," she said coldly. "You've done enough and lost men because of me. I've jeopardized all of you far, far more than I ever had the right to do. Go home, bury your dead. Give my best to Gurp."

"Swee—"

A thought returned Tobek to his men at Dysmorphic.

She took a few moments to wander the battlefield, examining the range of damage the shadows had effected at her command. Phobos had said she was capable of great destruction, and she'd managed this without knowing what she was doing. It would have been magnificent to harness the shadows again.

Would have.

Disavowed or not, Samael was safe from her. The places an archangel could hide with a gorgon were limitless. He'd been after Feng, so why had he taken Stheno? What did the gorgon have that he wanted? Maybe they were bonding over their hate of the Host? Of the Chimera?

If she had had another week, she could've hunted his manga-covered ass down. If she'd had Drew, she could've found him in half that time.

She suffered no delusion that Hel would be merciful in light of Bix's failure to bring her Stheno's soul and the proof contained within it. While Bix wouldn't tolerate being infected with Jör's venom again, Hel still had the power to turn the pantheons against her. Bix would once again be evicted from all the Worlds and starved. Her only sanctuary would be ether. One hundred and seventy years of starvation.

At least this time, she would enter the vast nothingness

knowing she could become a monster more horrible than the things already out there.

Bix closed her eyes and sighed. Maybe she and Drew would find each other. Maybe this was a Fate's way of getting them back together.

One could hope.

Samael's angels—or what remained of them—she dumped in the chancel of the Basilica in Rome. If the Host was confused about that message, well, they could fetch her back from exile to ask her to explain.

# CHAPTER 27

**B**ix swung by Mirri's condo and the leather bar on the off chance—the extremely off chance—that Samael had left her a message. A ransom. A nanny-nanny-boo-boo, even.

Nothing.

She asked after the ginger barback, but he had a family thing and wouldn't be in for a few days. That left her with one more to-do in this World.

Maneuvering the labyrinth of Fairfax Hospital required magical string and a Minotaur. Instead, Bix sought out certain men with a specific shade of blue eyes. She passed at least twenty blending in as orderlies, visitors, and even a vending machine stocker. Not one of them posed as hospital security. Not one loitered outside nurses' stations. Not one dared to be conspicuous.

As long-lived as Berserkers were—assuming they stayed on the safe end of a weapon—had covert behavior become second nature? Or was hunting a part of their nature that had made the men attractive to those who recruited Berserkers?

Either way, she was grateful they were here. Grateful they had kept Vidya safe against the demis and Stheno...despite their chief and his suspicious silences.

A janitor rolled past, whistling a recognizable song. He caught the elevator and held the door. Bright blue eyes looked directly at her. She scurried aboard with a perfunctory nod, maintaining her silence as they rode. The doors opened on the critical care wing. The whistler seamlessly passed her off to a teddy bear of a man with a patient advocate lanyard. His nice soft voice blended with the white noise pumping through speakers placed every ten feet. If he spoke words she was intended to hear, she didn't.

Her thoughts were of Mirri.

Mirri was going to be assaulted once again in the name of revenge. Hel was going to rip the last filaments of sanity from Mirri in an effort to gain the proof Hel needed to demand the Consortium execute Samael and Stheno.

Bix had failed, not only Hel but also Mirri. Hel had given Bix a chance to save Mirri from further pain and distress, and Bix had failed. She'd had Stheno, right there, right in front of her, and Bix had chosen to save Feng first. Mirri would have wanted her to save Feng, Bix had to content herself with that. And she could…if she used her final hours wisely.

No matter what, Bix was destined to return to the ether and the torments therein, but there was a possibility she could arrange for someone else to protect Mirri from Hel. To do it, she'd have to make the arrangements through a third party so she didn't tip off Hel to her intentions.

If only she knew how to consciously summon Phobos again…

Her Berserker guide paused at a wide wooden door with a narrow glass panel above the push plate. He nodded, smiled, then disappeared down an adjacent corridor.

She forced her brain back to the moment and paused with her hand on the door. *Deep breaths.* Whatever condition Vidya was in, she could handle it. She'd seen worse, done worse.

One more breath and Bix shouldered open the weighted door. The wound in her breast twinged, and she winced.

"She's here." Xipil unfolded from his seat at the end of the narrow corridor and tucked his phone in his pocket. "You are about to enter a clean room, Bix. If you would please…?"

She followed his gesture toward the adjoining bathroom. A pair of pristine pumps sat atop a floral box. She clutched her fist over her grimy dirt, blood, and feather-encrusted chest.

"Gurp?"

Xipil bowed.

Of the many ways she'd planned on killing Vidya, infection from battle spatter was unworthy of their history. Truth be told, she didn't really want to kill Vidya. What she'd wanted was an explanation and at least a hint of remorse. She might not be in love with the Oracle and hadn't been for a while, but she had good memories of that time.

Good memories were important. She'd need as many as she could hoard to survive the next hundred and seventy years in the ether.

Ten minutes later, bathed, wearing fresh clothes, and having tossed her old attire in the hazmat can, Bix faced Xipil again.

Only Xipil was taller and blond.

"Still have to use the hand sanitizer." Tobek indicated a pump bolted to the wall. "Then you can go in."

"You had to have burned rubber to get out here from the clinic." She made quick work with the horrible alcohol gel.

"I'm a high warlock with a gateway above his secret lair." Tobek stepped aside, pressing a green button on a sliding glass door. "And I knew you wouldn't leave this World without seeing her first, no matter how antagonistic your history."

She stopped in front of him and searched his face. "What about your men and your dead? I am not more important than they are."

"Let me worry about my priorities." He tucked her hair behind her ear with his damaged prosthetic hand. "I'll stay out here. Give you two time alone. Just come see me before you go, please?"

"I don't think that's a good idea." Her mind said to lean away from him and his touch, but her body did the opposite. "I said I wouldn't pressure you to tell me about your past, as long as you didn't sabotage me. Not telling me I'm the Chimera feels a lot like sabotage."

"You gave up your memories for reasons to which I am not privy." He searched her face with his pained gaze. "Telling you what I know of you will come from a place of bias that will have consequences neither of us can foresee. It is better for you to get to know yourself through your own experiences, without me tainting your evolution with a history from which you fled."

"And the enemies to which my ignorance exposes me? My vulnerability is somehow okay with you?"

"No," he said sharply. "But I am trying to protect you the best I can without hemming you in or tying you down. You are no elephant. There is no string. I am just a man trying to be your friend."

She wanted to believe that. She did. Trust came down to *choosing* to believe. In a hundred and seventy years, when she'd completed her sentence and returned to the Mids to kill the Phoenix, the choice might not be so hard for her. Of course by then, she'd be an ether-trained monster he wouldn't want to befriend. So, why not cling to the good memories of the week they had together and leave it at that?

"You want another snot shirt, don't you?" She sniffed.

He kissed the top of her head. "I want a lot of things."

"Before you visit her, you should know Miss Asariri is in a medically induced coma." Xipil explained from the corner. "She has forfeited all control over her lower body. The specialists are concerned they will have to amputate both legs due to the spread of necrotizing cells."

Bix's heart ached. "She's an Oracle of the Present. She had to have seen the snipers set up the nest. Why didn't she take cover?"

"The alternatives if she had?" Tobek motioned her into the sealed room. "She placed her faith in her House. What happens next is up to them."

Considering Vidya had hoodwinked them by burning Bix, trusting her House was a bold move.

Bix entered the clean room, and her breath caught. Vidya lay prostrate in a bed set at an angle inside a large hamster wheel. Her once rich mocha skin had a green cast. Machines breathed for her, circulated her blood for her, and lived for her.

"Surviving being hit by an angel arrowhead is no small feat, even with the help of a draugr." Bix straightened the blankets, getting an eyeful of mummy bandages running under Vidya's breasts down to her ankles. The moons of her oracular trials covered her arms and nape. "Makes me wonder why you're fighting so hard to stay in this World."

A machine beeped, startling her. She laughed at her own paranoia.

"You'll be pleased to know that Drew beat me to the ether." She ran her fingers through Vidya's short hair, spiking it in the way the Oracle preferred. "Once I leave here, I will be leaving the Mids to complete my full sentence. You will never have to see me again. Whatever compelled you to betray me, whatever caused you to sell out my team…I have to forgive you so that I don't go mad trying to understand why. Don't get me wrong, what you did still sucks. Balls. Big hairy sweaty man balls. But I know the woman beneath the bold 'n' cold façade you wear for work. I know that you actually do care, and that somewhere deep inside, you do regret what happened. So I forgive you…even if I still want to know why you did it."

"You fear for her future and your own."

She jerked around with her heart pounding. Phobos reclined in the window, watching the activity below.

"How did you know I needed you?"

"I am intrigued by the manifestations of your summoning." He tipped his head from side to side. "It is novel."

"Novelty is priceless to gods." She clasped her pendant, not entirely certain of how she was summoning him. "I need an intermediary between me and Hades."

"No."

She straightened. "You're not even going to hear me out?"

"With whom do you think you're dealing? Mortals?" He stood and smoothed his suit jacket. "Hades heard your prayer and agrees to your request. He says to deliver Mirri to your old room."

Bix blinked rapidly. It'd been a thought, not a prayer, but then she and Hades had shared an odd bond when he'd helped her out of the warrens of the Under Worlds thirty years ago. Plus, he was a god, and an extremely powerful one to boot.

"And the cost of his help?"

"Hel's outrage is payment enough." Phobos sauntered to her and skimmed two fingers over her wounded breast. Her body absorbed his raw energy, closing the wound. He cupped her chin and inhaled deeply. "All spurned lovers share a secret: the pain and the pettiness comes from caring. They cannot stop caring, no matter how much they try. The nonsensical things they do are complex expressions of their love, however twisted it all seems to others."

Bix raised her brows, then furrowed them.

Phobos released her as the fog of navy and mulberry swirled up his legs. "Dinner, Bix the Brazen. I need to know more about this summoning and its effects."

The sucking sound of the seal parting on the glass door turned her around. Tobek entered, his face a mask of concern. On the other side of the glass stood the last person she expected to see.

"What's he doing here?"

Tobek glanced over his shoulder. "Cian? He's the Oracle's son."

Bix snorted and eyed the ginger barback eyeing her. "You're what, twenty-one? Barely?"

"Says so on my work application." The kid pushed his olive beanie off and stuffed it in his pocket before cleaning his hands with the sanitizer. "Seventeen, though, if you check my adoption papers or my college admissions. Thirty-four for the RPGs. Twenty-six for the gateway passes; those adult-only Worlds are hella lame."

"Adoption?" Bix body blocked the boy from reaching Vidya. "What's your game, little hacker?"

He scowled at her. "No game. She's my mother."

"Bullshit." Bix crossed her arms under her bosom. "I'm not

one of the guys. I actually know Vidya, and I know she doesn't do nurturing, much less kids."

"That's what she said when Social Services dumped me on her doorstep ten years ago." He thrust his jaw to the side. "That's what she said when I snuck out the fire escape that same night. That's what she says every time we fight. But you know what else she says? 'Stick with me. I'm trying to figure it out. Repentance isn't a smooth road. It's just a necessary one.'"

"Ten years ago?"

"In two weeks." He peered around her. "We were going to celebrate our anniversary with a trip to Bali. We'd been saving up to go to the temples at Ubud."

Bix choked on a snort. Two weeks shy of a full ten years was not long after Vidya had betrayed the team. Had Vidya believed that raising an orphan was atonement for her sins? Had her House of Fate demanded the safekeeping of this kid to repay the loss?

Only if the kid was important.

"What makes you so special to the Houses of Fate?" she demanded.

"Pull up your sleeve, kid," Tobek muttered.

"Man, I just cleaned my hands," Cian moaned.

Tobek yanked Cian's right sleeve up past his elbow. A tiny stalk with a tiny dingy green leaf curled in the boy's elbow.

A Sage. The boy was a Sage. The masculine equivalent of an Oracle. That explained enough that Bix didn't worry he was going to stake Vidya through the heart. The Houses of Fate were far more conniving.

The mom thing, eh, she still had her doubts.

"Phone." She gestured to his distinctly square hoodie pocket. "Give me your phone. Unlock it first."

He rolled his eyes and huffed, but he handed it over. She thumbed through his apps, then his photos. There were plenty of shots of him and Vidya over a span of years and scads of science stuff. Space Camp. Mad White Hatters. Take Your Tyke to Work Day.

"Satisfied? Can I see her now, or are you going to be the frosty she warned me about?"

"Hey, manners," Tobek growled, bumping the kid with his elbow.

"The night you returned my phone to me, did she set you up to it?"

"No?" He rubbed one foot along the back of his calf. "She has this picture of you two that she hides in the top drawer of her dresser. She looks really happy in it. Happy like I've never seen her. I was hoping we could've… I just wanted…"

"You wanted to talk to her about your mother so you could understand the woman who'd raised you," Tobek rumbled.

"I know the photo. It's the only one I let be taken of me back then. Vidya was a little older than you are. She hadn't joined the CWIG yet. She hadn't learned the breadth of the dirty secrets the guild masters keep hidden from the public." Bix tapped through to the actual phone feature and rang the only number she knew.

A disgruntled grunt answered.

"Thrúde?"

"Gods damn it all, gatekeeper. I've worn a rut in the stage waiting for my Norn."

Bix pinched the bridge of her nose. "I had to space her to save her."

"I'll let the other Norse Fates know. They love a good game of Marco Polo." Thrúde shouted the news to whoever was in the background. A rousing cheer blasted through the phone that made even the sullen teen smirk. Apparently, the Valkyrie was hanging with more than the local chapter of the Sisterhood. "You and me, babe, drinks until we're both shitfaced. I want all the deets."

"I'm…I'm going to need a rain check on that."

Sudden silence at the other end. "We'll get them. We'll pick up where you left off. Mirri's Mayhem doesn't end until our sister is avenged. Tell the testosterone to expect us for the full debrief."

Tobek harrumphed.

"Speaking of Mirri…" Bix closed one eye. "I need an image

of her, of where she is right now. Where specifically in Asgard."

Rustling at the other end, then a muffled, "You're going to steal from Hel?"

The men gawped.

"I can't let her husk Mirri." She shrugged.

"That might be the biggest favor anyone could do for Mirri, wipe that nightmare from her mind," Thrúde argued.

"Worse nightmares come in their place." Bix sighed miserably. "Being husked isn't the bad part. It's becoming sentient again. It starts with awakening to a crushing of your chest and not knowing what breathing is or that it will abate the agony and the terror. Fear escalates from there. Every common function of your body becomes a series of causes and effects you have to relearn. How to eat, what to eat, where to find it. The pain of hunger can subside, but it's different from the pain of exhaustion, and that's different from the pain of sustaining a blow. Every little thing, every tiny detail, gone from your mind. The people around you still know the old you, the you that was brought into existence as an infant and raised in a family or community. They cannot fathom that the adult they see before them is more unformed than a fetus. Trust me. I have experience in this."

A long stretch of silence. A click. Dead air.

Bix closed both eyes and swore. The phone chirped in her palm. On the screen, a frost-covered lily bloomed on a singular naked branch jabbed into a cluster of white rocks over which a dusting of snow glistened.

"Hel will know what you've done," Tobek cautioned. "There is no path back to her good graces after this."

"The nonsensical things we do are complex expressions of our love." Bix repeated Phobos's words. One thought moved Mirri to a simple room with a simple bed in the heart of Hades's domain. Yes, Hades had a reputation with, for, and despite women, but a damsel so shattered she couldn't exist outside the prison of her own mind, that woman was nigh on sacred to him. Mirri would be in good hands with Hades.

"Don't look at me like that, any of you." Bix glared at the men. "My actions have consequences. I accept them. I'm going into this knowing what awaits me, knowing that no one else deserves it."

"That makes it worse," Cian whispered, drawing his hand over his mouth. "Is that what happened to you after Mom swapped out the pictures?"

Bix did a double take. "What did you say?"

"She said you knew." Cian looked at Vidya and grimaced. "The picture of the Host's armory? She replaced the original picture with one of the Host's armory so you would end up there."

"I did know, but she never admitted it. Never showed remorse for it." She handed the kid back his phone. "She's been nothing but a bitch since I returned."

"Because she's being watched, all the time." He sidled around Bix and went to Vidya's side. "She doesn't know who they are. Just that the first time she told them she wouldn't betray a team of agents, a hurricane tore through four communities in Maryland. The only deaths were Sages and Oracles. Middle school kids."

Tobek and Xipil stood straighter.

"She should have told me about the coercion before she betrayed us. No matter our past, she should've known I—and every member of my team—would've helped her." Bix scowled at Vidya's comatose body. "The CWIG has protocols in place to deal with extortion, blackmail, strong-arming, and all that crap, because it comes with the territory."

"I don't know why she didn't. That's why I…I'd hoped you did," the kid confessed. "I'd hoped you could help her now, help both of us."

"Aw, Cian, I wish I could help, I really do." Bix gave him an apologetic smile. "I would be on that case like a tongue on a flag pole in the middle of a blizzard. Sadly, my time in the Mids is up. I have to go admit to a pissed-off goddess that an angel stole my serpent-haired agent of doom."

"Tall guy? Green snakes? Mom saw him." He swiped over his phone repeatedly. "In a vision at dinner the other night."

Bix's stomach flipped twice, then plummeted while her heart leapt into her throat. "Did you say a *guy* with green snakes?"

"Yeah, snake guy and the big boss at the CWIG were having some sort of fight. She doesn't trust her boss, so she stole this from evidence and said we had to keep it away from everybody. There's like some big conspiracy around it." He turned his phone to her.

The Norse diplomatic pouch.

"Son of an actual bitch," Bix wailed as all the pieces slid into place, all the dastardly desperate pieces. "I know where Stheno is. That is what Samael is hoping to get for her."

Tobek grabbed the boy's phone and whistled.

"I have a chance. One very slim chance, but I'm going for it." Bix wagged her finger at Cian. "Protect him, Tobek. This one knows where Vidya hid the diplomatic pouch. Don't go after it, not yet. Not while eyes are on her or on me. If I don't make it back…"

Tobek nodded. "I understand."

"No one is ever going to find it," Cian scoffed.

"They will if they find you, kid." Tobek took the boy by the nape and gently shook him. "There are magics aplenty out there to make you confess without you ever realizing you spilled the beans."

"But…"

"No buts." Tobek lifted his chin. "Where are we going, sweetheart?"

"This one is all me." She clenched her fists and shook her head.

"You're going to be outnumbered again. Let us help."

"Yeah, I can help," Cian offered. "I want to."

"Thanks, and if I make it back, you'll have plenty of opportunities to join my special cray. But this part is personal. I'm going to finally stand up to my worst nightmare." She opened gates. "It's all about the handbags."

# CHAPTER 28

Half the house was underwater. Deliberately done, not a remnant of wrath, at least not anyone else's wrath. Jörmungandr had constructed his home within a massive water cave tucked into an icy cliff. The fjord lapped at glass walls and floors while exotic woods formed grand barrel ceilings. The furnishings were large yet minimalist, with rooms set far apart and no interior walls to define them.

Perfect for a serpent god who needed the extra space for slithering while he hunted his prey.

Bix's body twitched violently.

She'd spent enough time here curled up in the shadows filled with self-loathing after a feeding while Jör tossed her a snippet of a memory for being a good pet.

The air turned thick and cloying. Her heart rate sped to a wild asynchronistic beat. Her skin cooled and crawled. Her stomach constricted, and a whine developed between her ears. She pleaded with her mind to knock it off. To stop the panic attack. To give her a chance to be as strong as she really, really needed to be right now.

The moment she'd moved Mirri out of Asgard, she'd entered the very gray and highly disputable terms of her contract. Her memories that Jör held as warden might well end up staying with

Jör, but then again, they might not. Not if the serpent was half the shyster she suspected.

In the heart of Jör's home, Stheno as a buxom brunette lounged on a chaise in diaphanous skirts that spilled over two shapely and flawless legs. The gorgon was obviously familiar with her surrounds. A glass of red wine sloshed in one hand while the other plucked ripe berries from a small fountain embedded in the floor.

Two men seated in mid-century modern chairs flanked opposing sides of the chaise.

"You get to keep the gorgon once I have the evidence your little busybody gathered. All of it, originals, no copies." Samael perched on the edge of his seat, big arms braced on his black-denim-covered thighs. The obligatory beer bottle dangled from two fingers.

"Jör, my love," Stheno sighed, "Without Samael's help, I would be dead right now. It's a small price to pay for our future."

"Ten years, Ligeia." Jör crossed his legs and flung one arm over the back of his chair. "Ten years I waited for you to arrange the Chimera's freedom as you assured me you could. Ten inexplicably long years I waited while you made the situation worse and worse until you went so far as to allow things from the ether to gain footholds in the Mids. *My* Mids. Your ineptitude forced my hand."

"So you punish me by abandoning me when I needed you most?" Stheno cried. "You ruined my plans for revenge when you hacked up her girlfriend and shoved her through the portal. If you hadn't ruined that spell, then the guild masters would be dead, the Phoenix would have been blamed, and the Chimera—"

"The Chimera would still be exiled." Samael shook his head. "The snake is right. The Host would never have relented on her punishment if the Phoenix hadn't been implicated in the Norse ambassador's gruesome mauling."

Jörmungandr. Jörmungandr had attacked Mirri.

Bix's heart shriveled. Her back split from a thousand tiny gashes.

Shadows grew.

"Whose side are you on?" Stheno shrieked.

"My own," Samael snarled. "You were supposed to bring me the evidence Feng had collected in exchange for a curse-free body. I didn't question your methods until you started baiting the Chimera."

"You should have let the ether claim the Phoenix the moment the Chimera was free." Jör toyed with something hanging around his neck. "He is a distraction we cannot afford for her to have."

"You bastard." The gorgon threw a berry at Jör. Juice splattered over his crisp white shirt. "You never planned on letting me kill the Chimera, did you? You promised me you'd help me end her permanently."

"And you promised to change time." Jör flicked the offensive pulp from his chest, which caused his collar to shift, exposing his pendant.

A gargoyle with raised claws and curled horns.

The last trace of fear slid from Bix. Fury, crystalline in purpose and honed with intent, expanded into every pore.

"Jör doesn't have the Norse diplomatic pouch, Samael." Bix stepped forward, drawing the darkness with her.

The archangel bolted up from his seat, mighty wings unfurling. "Chimera, I've got no beef with you. It was always about the Phoenix. I told you that."

"I found the Phoenix. Did you really think I hadn't found what he and Mirri had been working on?" Bix tipped her head to the right, and a wave of darkness blanketed that side of the home. "This could have gone so many other ways for us, because—despite all your angelic qualities—I like you. Instead, you chose to become my enemy by attacking my allies."

"You delivered Feng to the dragons. You made your choice of allies pretty damn clear." Samael launched a ball of angel fire at her.

The darkness swallowed it.

"Stheno using your stole, that was all for show, wasn't it? A little trust catalyst between you and me. Clever. Damaging your beautiful wings? Very convincing." Bix sneered more than smiled and opened two gates. "I really do like those wings."

"No." Samael's eyes widened. So did the gates. He howled in anguish. His wings thumped to the floor, severed. Blood rushed everywhere, turning into a field of razor-edged red algae. The archangel staggered forward, then back, deprived of the counterbalancing weight he'd always known. He dropped to his knees and stretched a trembling hand for his wings. "Wha—what have you done?"

The wings vanished.

"No." He stared at her in horror.

"The hand, you should have learned from the hand." Bix shrugged. "Your comrades from Centralia ended their time in the Mids with a trip to the Vatican. You, I think, will have more fun chatting it up with the Russian Orthodoxy."

Before the denial finished forming on his lips, she dispatched him and his blood plants to Moscow.

A slow clap filled the new silence.

"There's that beautiful temper," Jör cooed, rising. "But you really should have killed him. Samael is the wrathful sort."

"Turns out, so am I." She considered Stheno scrambling up from her seat. Bix didn't have sunglasses to shield her from the gorgon's magic. She was the Chimera. A gorgon's magic meant nothing to a monster of Bix's caliber. "Was it you who coerced the Oracle into betraying my Ops team?"

"Are you kidding me?" The gorgon jerked her head around, hissing. Soft, milky skin crackled and firmed as a pale crust of limestone spread over the surface. Brown braids writhed and hissed, opening eyes and mouths. "I wanted you to complete the original mission. The package—the agent you were supposed to rescue—had intel on the Houses of Fate that would have made the last ten years unnecessary. That agent could have convinced the Phoenix to enact the time-changing spell willingly, and you would still have been too green to be anything more than another sacrifice."

"The people trailing Vidya? Who are they?"

"Mercs?" Stheno put the chaise between them and gripped the curved back. "Unaligned for certain. They weren't there to protect the Oracle and they didn't stop Imara from harming her. I could find out more for you if you let me go. I could find their leader. Be your mole inside their operations."

"Hmm." Bix closed one eye as the darkness continued to flow from her, skimming the floor and rising up the walls. "No."

"But—"

"She can't let you live, Ligeia. She has to deliver someone to my sister, someone to be held accountable for the egregious affront to the Norse pantheon. Someone with a soul." Jör sauntered up to Bix, ever sinuous in his movements, ever confident in his possession of prey.

Give a god a flinch and they'd own you.

No more. No more flinching. No more cowering. No more fearing his bite. No more being an addict desperate for his drug of memories.

No, this time, this time Bix held her ground and his gaze.

"I didn't assault Mirri," Stheno objected. "Not to the extent you did. Not so badly she couldn't recover physically. I only needed to break her mind a little bit, just enough to discredit her. I never needed to shatter her completely. That was your revenge for every time the Chimera chose Mirri's bed over yours."

Jör stroked Bix's cheek with the backs of his fingers. "We are eternal, you and I. You will always be mine, my precious Chimera."

His lips descended on Bix's, hard and cruel. She didn't run. She didn't balk. She didn't need to. He stiffened. His lashes fluttered. He gurgled, unable to gasp.

Mist and midnight pierced his body, impaling him on long shadowy claws.

Bix ripped the pendant from around his neck.

"Handbag."

# CHAPTER 29

Bix watched without a flicker of feeling as Stheno screamed and writhed in agony, fighting to keep her soul within her body. The native magic of Helheim burrowed beneath the gorgon's skin, separating sustenance from the wrapper of a failed god. It should have been horrible to behold, the way the flesh and stone warped without regard for physical limitations.

*Should* have been.

Jör didn't fight his situation. He floated as if weightless in the clutches of the darkness. A smirk played at his lips as he closed his eyes and crossed his hands over his chest in peaceful repose.

Ever the serpent ready to strike.

"You're late." Hel strode into the conference room, signing papers and handing them off to a hapless minion. A large hound trotted at her heels. The goddess paused beside her napping brother and tipped her head. With a grunt and a shrug, she turned to Bix. "What did you do with Mirri?"

Bix lifted her chin. "I gave her a fighting chance at sanity."

Hel went toe to toe with Bix. "Did you think her own pantheon incapable?"

"Yes." Bix looked all the way up to the goddess's pale irises contrasting her deep red pupils. "In intention and action."

"Spoken with the confidence of proof, which is what I hired you to find." Hel pursed her lips but nodded. "What did you bring me?"

"A story in three parts." Bix pointed to Stheno. "The first arc, if you will."

"No, no, no," Stheno keened. "He did it. He mauled a goddess from his own pantheon. All this was his—"

Hel flicked her hand, and Stheno's body fractured into tiny bits. No more mouth, no more lungs, no more ability to speak. Nothing but crumbs and a glaringly bright soul, rich with experience. Hel jabbed her hand into the miasma and drew it to her mouth. The goddess closed her eyes and purred deep in her throat. Her hands slid back and forth over each other as her brows danced. She pinched a bit of miasma and fed it to her hound.

The hound tasted the soul, then trotted over to the remains of the body and gobbled them up.

"Jörmungandr?" Hel said slowly, her eyes still closed. Ice crackled along the floor, skittering beneath the darkness.

"Yes, sister?" he answered with equal languor.

Glacial spikes lanced the darkness and drove into him. He seized, and his eyes opened. His mouth formed a perfect ring of silent surprise.

"You did this." Hel made it a statement not a question and certainly not a question her brother was in any condition to answer. "You caused me to look a fool. You risked war among the Consortium. All for what? It's not jealousy as the gorgon believed. Why, then? Why this game with the Chimera?"

Jör tried to speak, but a spear of ice in his throat prevented it. Hel slashed a finger through the air, and the spear retracted.

"Your reputation will recover. It always does." Jör coughed and patted his throat, clearing it a few times. "Besides, my patience for the long game is not as enduring as yours."

"But?" Hel prompted.

"But the Chimera crawled from the ether thirty years ago with stories of denizens therein, stories that brought to mind our old enemies. So I investigated and confirmed her tales. What was fashioned ages ago to be a security barrier is being used as staging ground by our foes. We cannot afford for the Chimera to continue to hide from her responsibilities as this vacuous shell of who she really is."

Hel regarded Bix thoughtfully. "So you made her suffer."

"Suffering makes her desire greatness." Jör had the gall to gloat. "Suffering makes her reach for the aspects she suppressed when she doled out her memories. Look at her now. The Shadow Caster is reborn because of this recent misery."

"You son of a bitch," Bix seethed, and the darkness responded, coiling around him as a thorny thicket.

"Even now, still so weak and yet…" He stared at the ceiling once again, refusing to try to escape.

"And yet she doesn't know how to take her memories back from you." Hel hooked her thumbs in her pockets. "Even now."

Bix scowled. "He has to give them to me."

"No. You gave them. You take them. If you want them, figure it out," Hel commanded with a cruel twist of her lips.

Bix stumbled back, bumping into the hound, which snarled.

"Figure it out, Chimera," Hel baited, stalking her. "Take what is yours."

"I-I want to," Bix stammered. "I want my memories back, I do. I want Jör to be punished for what he did to Mirri and to me. I don't know how."

"Husk him," Hel bellowed.

The walls of the room quaked and whined. The hound barked.

"You've already taken the first step, Bix," Jör assured with that wretched patronizing tone he always used after feeding her. "You've reached out with the shadows, trapping your prey. Next is about what you can't see, but what your essence recognizes."

"I don't understand," she snapped. "Stop with the riddles and just say what you mean for once."

"Your darkness, my little Chimera," he moaned. "I can feel it seeping into me, suffusing every part of me. Body, mind, and magics. It is the elixir I crave, the balm for the addiction feeding you created within me. Let the darkness draw me in to you. Draw all that I am, all that I know, all that I was, and all that I will no longer be. Let the darkness fill you, fuel you, and enlighten you."

Bix swayed in the throes of ire, horror, and fascination as the darkness within her extracted textures lush and indulgent from a god thousands of years old. Primordial forces sprinkled within him were deeper, richer, more satisfying than what she'd derived from his raw energy.

And it was too much. Far too much.

Her skin swelled. Veins turned leaden. Organs inflamed. Her brain pounded against her skull. Senses overloaded. Mist seeped from her eyes, nose, and ears.

She crumpled to the floor, unable to move. Hel's hound backed away, whining.

A cool hand brushed her hair from her face. Hel's expression filled with concern. "Until you unlock the fullness of all your aspects, you will not be able to husk either a god or the true evils entering the ether."

Bix heard the words as garbled bursts behind the drone of excess.

"For his crimes against the Consortium, he must be husked. As head of the pantheon, it is my duty to dole out that justice." Hel thrust one hand behind her. More icy spears punctured her brother. Frost spread over him, sliding through the darkness. "Per our contract, creature, I restore your memories to you, full and unedited."

Images burst behind Bix's eyes. A barrage of sights and sound clips flooded her mind.

"Permitting my brother to pursue his unrelenting obsession with you was necessary to the greater plan. You play a very large part in that plan. To that end, you have allies within the pantheons, few but certain. These allies will help you find your way back to being the High Executioner for All Worlds. But make no mistake, to become what you must, you will face greater challenges than what my brother inflicted upon you and yours."

Bix drew an unsteady breath as the mental and physical onslaught abated. It was all she could do to nod as her gaze cut across the room.

Jörmungandr the once mighty serpent god faded into a gossamer shadow, neither man nor deity, but a hollow shell.

A husk.

Hel stood and waved her hand. The glass of the conference room walls parted. What was left of Jör drifted into the vastness of Helheim.

"Our contract is fulfilled, Chimera. You are free."

# CHAPTER 30

One arm, sure and strong, clutched Bix close to a bare chest covered in tattoos. A partial arm's rounded bicep cushioned her head. Her hands kneaded Tobek's long wiry beard. Her lungs filled with his clean scent of soap and sandalwood.

The not-Viking hadn't said a word since she'd landed in his bed at whatever ungodly hour she'd finally pulled herself together enough to bolt from Helheim. Tobek held her as she trembled, babbling fractured thoughts while she chased down some semblance of logic behind the restored memories.

"No wonder Jör was always so cryptic. These memories, they're not linear. They're not topical. They're not remotely connected. They're just fragments. Random pixels in a greater picture, a picture that is part of a video that's probably Hobbit-movie length."

"We'll figure it out together," Tobek murmured, ever the rock. "Now that you're here to stay, you and I will figure everything out together."

"That would violate your 'no telling me about the past' rule." She burrowed closer to him. She chose to believe in him, in his stated truth that he was trying to be her friend. Maybe with his help, she could avoid becoming the monster of legend. Maybe this version of the Chimera wouldn't be the bogeyman. Maybe she could be a champion instead. Of who and for what, she didn't know yet. She wasn't a clandestine agent or an exiled felon anymore.

For now, she was going to focus her energy on finding Drew and whoever had convinced Vidya to burn her team. Oh, and on learning the finer details of being a Shadow Caster. Plus, retrieving the Norse diplomatic pouch and possibly picking up where Mirri and Feng had left off. Yep, all that should keep her busy for a bit. Always good to have a purpose.

"I'm going to crimp your sex life, you know that, right? Like, imagine if you had a girl here and I drop in like this, all unexpected and unannounced."

"I conduct my assignations offsite," he drawled. "As for what else I might be doing in here when you drop in, well, it should hardly be a surprise."

She poked his shoulder. "You're not a sock guy, and there's no bottle of lotion in your side table."

"I meant sleeping." He chuckled. "But I notice how quickly your mind tumbles right into the gutter at the slightest provocation."

She smoothed his beard over her chest. "Hel said I had to learn the fullness of all my aspects, plural, if I want to return to being the High Executioner for All Worlds. Apparently, the Chimera is more than a gatekeeper and a Shadow Caster."

"That must be a lot of information to process on top of these broken memories."

"She and her brother also said there's an ancient evil building an army in the ether. I encountered them during my exile and didn't know it. Jör believed some of them might already have snuck into the Mids." She traced the scars on his hand. "Makes me wonder if the Fates let themselves be captured by Stheno as cover for getting spaced, to gather firsthand intel."

"Wouldn't surprise me, knowing the Fates as I do," he conceded. "As for what crept into the Mids, scouts most likely. This is good information to have. I'll alert the other branches of the MWA. We'll expand the focus of our patrols."

"I'm not sure I want to alert the CWIG. They'd probably try to align with the enemy to gain more power. 'Nobody likes the race in charge,' to quote a disavowed archangel." She wrinkled her nose. "Probably better if Ashtad decides if his guild can be trusted with the intel at this point. How is he, by the way?"

"He has some unexpected friends with rather unusual interests in helping him heal. He'll be pleased to know you're sticking around. You'll need to keep getting him into trouble if he's going to make it to full godhood." Tobek flipped the ends of his beard up and tickled her nose. "As for the young Sage, Xipil has taken him under his wing while the boy's mother remains in the hospital. The kid is staying with him for now."

"Xipil is a good man," she said, rubbing the end of her nose. "And, you, high warlock, are an excellent friend to have."

"Speaking of friends and disavowed angels," he paused and arched a reproachful brow, "Gurp is framing the wings you dumped in your room. I've warded them."

"Not going to let me wear them for Halloween?"

He puckered his lips and shook his head. "I advise against it, unless you want to be an even bigger target than you already are. One feather from those wings could buy you a lifetime of indulgences on the Chwed black market."

"I don't plan on selling them, but I do enjoy collecting them." She fluttered her lashes.

"Then I should increase the strength of the spells and wards around the compound," he noted drolly. "I predict living together is going to be quite an adventure."

She laughed and tugged his beard. "Well, you *are* a glutton for punishment."

# OTHER BOOKS BY K.A. KRANTZ

Can't wait for the next book? Subscribe to K. A. Krantz's email
newsletter at
kakrantz.com


**If you enjoyed this book, please spread the word and
leave a review with the retailer of your choice.**

# ACKNOWLEDGMENTS

To my family, for their continued love and support. Only 299,955 to go, Dad. To Jenn Stark, for inspiring me to write this series and for enduring my adolescent sense of humor. To Linda Ingmanson, my development editor, for making me better at party introductions. To Toni Lee, my copy editor and fact-checker, for making sure my effects were not affected by transient intransitive verbs. To the amazing team at Gene Mollica Studios: Gene, Cristin, Deborah, Sasha, Katie, Christine, and Cyrus; thanks for making Bix look so good in pictures and print.

# ABOUT THE AUTHOR

KAK splits her time between Cincinnati and the DC 'burbs with her faithful hairy beast. When not writing, she indulges in a shoe obsession, conducts a love/hate affair with paintbrushes, and pretends she has enough upper body strength to wield power tools.

Visit her website at kakrantz.com for free flash-fiction, blog posts about her latest fancies, and more. If you're on Twitter, she'd love to hear from you. Tweet @KAKrantz.